"An ingenious story… The author impressively conjures a complex tale brimming with unpredictable twists and turns, and her double narrative is pulled off with artful delicacy."

— Kirkus Reviews

"Loubna Hassanieh's romance *Where Will My Heart Beat?* brings good and evil into stark contrast in an epic tale of young lovers torn apart… The main characters are sympathetic as they embody the struggle between human, ethical, and spiritual values and a worldview in which money and power are all that matter. Descriptions of people and places are perceptive, involving multiple senses to evoke images of beauty, ugliness of form or spirit, and danger. Feelings and states of being are described with insights that dive beneath the surface, as when fatigue is defined as being made up of "desolation, boredom, and hopelessness." Philosophical and spiritual musings add depth."

— Foreword Clarion Review

"…Creative, visionary novel… Hassanieh's fluid, lyrical writing style captures this journey of self-discovery in five parts, effectively transitioning between present and past by incorporating a mixture of omniscient narrative, first-person storytelling, and poetic-styled reflections… From sibling rivalry and family rebellion, to love, loss, and secret betrayal, the story explores universal themes. Laced with poignant and surprising unveils—from character connections and unexpected deaths to long hidden betrayals—the narrative keeps readers invested as the drama comes full circle. Overall, *Where Will My Heart Beat?* blends well-crafted exposé with the mysteries of the human experience, lending the book a magical lingering charm."

— BlueInk Review

# Where Will My Heart Beat?

Loubna Hassanieh, PhD

Archway Publishing books may be ordered through booksellers or by contacting:

Archway Publishing
1663 Liberty Drive
Bloomington, IN 47403
www.archwaypublishing.com
1 (888) 242-5904

ISBN: 978-1-4808-7002-4 (sc)
ISBN: 978-1-4808-7003-1 (hc)
ISBN: 978-1-4808-7001-7 (e)

Library of Congress Control Number: 2018964138

Print information available on the last page.

Archway Publishing rev. date: 03/14/2019

To all the freethinkers and those who are willing to change and evolve—past, present, and future

Dear Emily

My family & I are blessed to have known you

Let love fill your life

Roshra

# Contents

## Part 4

## Part 5

# *Acknowledgments*

**This book** never would have been written had it not been for the collective effort of all that ever existed and took part in my life.

My deepest gratitude goes to Khaled, my husband, whose shoulder I cry and dream on.

I am forever grateful to my son, Jason, for reading and rereading this manuscript, imbuing it with his youthful and indomitable spirit. To my daughter, Grace, who always fills me with hope and brings me closure on the fairness of life.

I am greatly indebted to my parents for managing to raise me in Beirut during the grueling years of war and for opening my eyes to unconditional love and boundless giving. To my sister, Hala, whose positive outlook on life makes me turn my face to the sun. To my aunts and my grandmothers, the women I watched growing up, and the life lessons they etched in me.

Special thanks go to Dr. Catherine and Dr. Matt MacLean for their genuine support and helpful feedback. To the special women in my life—Wendy Brauer, Karen D'Atri, Catherine MacLean, Theresa Miller, Donna Reiffen, Vicki Skelton, and Sharon Wise—who reintroduced me to the wonderful world of novels and whose educated and sensible outlook on life carried me through.

Many thanks to Chris Day, editor at Archway, for his fresh perspective and aesthetic touch.

Finally, I am forever grateful to all the teachers and professors who carried me through my education and to all the teachers of the world for their sincere and hard work.

I maintain that the human mystery is incredibly demeaned by scientific reductionism, with its claim in promissory materialism to account eventually for all of the spiritual world in terms of patterns of neuronal activity. This belief must be classed as a superstition ... We have to recognize that we are spiritual beings with souls existing in a spiritual world as well as material beings with bodies and brains existing in a material world.

—Sir John C. Eccles

# Part 1

We meet ourselves time and time again in a thousand disguises on the path of life.

—Carl Jung

# Chapter 1

Serene hit the snooze button for the third time. The sun had already risen, but her mind was not yet ready to welcome its glorious rays. "Sleep is a universally gratifying sensation for the body and a rejuvenating break from the conscious mind," she remembered her professor's words. What if sleep was what she needed a break from? What if it was sleep that was exhausting her body?

She tossed and turned, stretching her arms and legs, trying to get her body to obey. Through her window, she could hear the morning buzz. Thankfully, she no longer woke to the cacophony of cars and machines. Instead, her mornings were blessed with the sounds of nature: roosters crowing, birds tweeting, and donkeys braying in the distance. The morning breeze settled on her face, a cool aromatic mist seeping deep into her pores and tickling her torpid senses, but she still felt tired. Even though she had been in Mar Elias for a month, her sleep patterns had not yet stabilized. *Was Sonia mistaken all along?*

At the thought of Sonia, her eyes popped wide open. It was Wednesday, and Sonia was expecting to meet for lunch in the main cafeteria of Mar Elias General Hospital. Although their lunches were always short, they were enough to anchor her, rekindle her interests, and empower her with great élan to push forward. Sonia's keen eyes always saw right through her. Her friend's power over her was truly amazing in that way. Her "you're looking good today" was good enough to brighten Serene's day with optimism. On the other hand, her skeptical look helped widen the mysterious chasm that drew Serene into the abyss of depression.

She gazed at the ceiling fan as it wobbled, spinning on high. She rubbed at her exposed arms. She couldn't sleep through the night without those blades blowing oxygen onto her face. She hopped out of bed, turned off the fan, and walked to the bathroom, hoping to wash off the film of salt deposited on her skin as a mocking witness to her nightly sweat attacks. She looked at her pale face in the mirror and softly massaged the skin over her throat. Did she really scream in the night—or was it only in her dreams? Her neck and back ached, and her arms were sore. For the past two days, her work schedule had been intense. She still felt the strain in her upper body. Dealing with kids at her previous job was effortless, and most days were uneventful. At the current physical therapy center, however, things were different. Her job as a physical therapist was becoming increasingly onerous, yet thankfully distracting.

She stepped out of the shower and wrapped herself in a towel. A thump shook her apartment door.

*Seven o'clock!*

She sighed in dismay. She usually opened her front door a couple of minutes before seven and waited for the newspaper boy, who would smile shyly, mumble a good morning, and with downcast eyes and ink-black fingers, hand-deliver the paper. She charged to the door, her heart galloping faster than her legs, but he had already walked away. She picked up the newspaper and took it straight to the trash bin. She never read the paper. On the contrary, she was so happy to be away from any publishable daily politics and city business news, but something in that young boy's smile, his sun-darkened face, his dispirited eyes, and the ragged clothes that hung on his small, slim figure made her stomach knot. A desire to help him saturated her heart and mind, but she did not know how. He had repeatedly refused to accept her gratuity.

She went to the kitchen and opened the window. She unlatched the exterior wood shutters and pushed them out into the morning sunshine, unraveling the picturesque tableau that had delighted her senses ever since she arrived in Mar Elias. She could see the backdrop of vivid green mountains surrounding the town in a continuous range, like a protective wall. This town had a strikingly healing effect on her. Its many lakes, wildflower fields, and hiking trails detached her from the sticky matrix she had been embedded in all her life. She toasted some bread, spread it with honey and goat cheese, and slid it into a paper bag. She would eat it on her way to the clinic.

As she passed by the living room, she stopped to kiss the photo displayed on the coffee table. She could not believe a whole month had passed. It seemed like she moved into town yesterday. She slouched her shoulders at the thought and sighed. A day down the calendar was a day closer to going home, reuniting with the two people Serene cared most about. She would give anything to hold Noura's chubby face in her hands and kiss it, to hug her and smell her potpourri skin. Waking up to mornings cradled in Kameel's arms used to connect her with her earthly life, ordinary life, making her feel safe and loved. However, that safe feeling had disappeared lately with the birth of Noura and the increasing responsibilities of life.

But she knew that going home was still far-fetched. She still had a lot of work to do on herself. Back in her bathroom, she stopped again to look at her face in the mirror. It looked drained and in need of rescue. Exhaustion had deeply rooted itself in her eyes and complexion, where it had become a permanent dweller. She applied some lightweight makeup to conceal the circles under her eyes and brighten her look. She put her hair up in a negligee bun and then went to her closet and chose a sage green shirt to go with her denim. Bright shades would leave a good impression on Sonia, who was always critical of her wearing somber colors. "Show me what you wear, and I tell you who you are," she remembered her friend's words.

She smiled.

She clutched her purse, picked up the sandwich bag, and stepped outside. She was renting the top flat in a three-story apartment building, right on Hamra Street. She skipped down the stairwell and strode into the morning sun. Mar Elias was a small town, and Hamra Street was its commercial center, where shops for all possible needs were lined up on both sides. Naturally, mornings were the busiest time of the day. Streets were humming with people running errands, and the sidewalk tables at the coffee shop were fully occupied with people reading their newspapers over their morning coffee.

Locals walked or rode their bicycles around town. Cars were rare and usually only used by non-locals on a visit to the hospital. She always walked by the main bakery on her way to work. Nothing made her mouth water like the smell of freshly baked bread and pastry. She reached for her sandwich and took a bite. Shop owners raced to greet her as she passed them by. Their voices were welcoming. They briefly updated her on their daily news.

"The meat is fresh today. It hasn't even made it to the fridge yet," the owner of the corner shop shouted.

"We milked this morning, and the heirloom tomatoes are fresh out of the garden," his wife added, proudly stacking the tomatoes on display.

Their friendliness warmed her heart. Everybody knew her by name. They also knew what her purpose in their town was. The physical therapy center where she worked was two blocks west of her apartment. The heat of the sun shining on her back drove her forward, warming her body.

She was appreciative of the job opportunity given to her in this remote and charming town. It came to save her from the suffocating monotony that had threatened her sanity and the wearisome volatility of her mood. Two life-changing events—the death of her brother followed by her pregnancy—had rekindled her past dreams and nightmares, intensifying her anxiety. Time could not completely obliterate her fears, but they had gone dormant for a while.

"Shed your fears," her doctor had said. "It's completely normal to have some form of anxiety during pregnancy. It's the fear of the unknown—and the overwhelming power of anticipation!"

Serene wanted so desperately to believe her.

Serene's childhood was tarred with nightmares and cold sweats that often ended with her screaming and kicking. Some nights, she would fall back asleep, cradled in her mother's arms. Most nights, however, when nothing could curb her fear and gasping for air became difficult, her parents would take her out on a stroll through the neighborhood.

"Time to go chase some fairies," her mother would say.

Cold or hot, they went out. Her father would pretend to whisper to fairies hidden behind a tree or a bush, coaxing them to bring her presents in the night, and leave them by her bed for when she woke up.

Her parents learned to stray away from a list of habits or objects that used to frighten her. Particularly, Serene was afraid of water, especially when it covered her face. It wasn't the normal kicking and screaming of a baby, and later a child, that accompanied every bath. It was screaming to the point of asphyxiation, to the point of turning blue. For as long as she could remember, she showered with her head tilted back, wiping away any drops of water that trickled down her forehead. She never swam in a pool. She always refused to get in the water when she accompanied her friends to the beach. Drowning was always the climax of her nightmares.

Serene was not a person who could look fear in the eye and confront it. She would be twenty-seven years old in two weeks, but on the inside, she was still a child, apprehensive about issues that others dismissed insouciantly. Was age supposed to make her stronger and wiser—or was it supposed to awaken her insight into the endlessness of life's mystery and the insignificance of her struggles in this vast, indifferent universe?

"You have to conquer your inner demons," Kameel whispered as he hugged her goodbye. "And you have to learn how to do it on your own. I can't help you. No one can."

As Serene entered the physical therapy center that morning, she made a promise to herself. She would no longer postpone her patients' hydrotherapy sessions. It would be therapy for her as well. Was it not the sole reason she had set foot in this town, to work on healing herself? She understood that the sooner she took action, the sooner her mission would come to an end, allowing her to resume her normal life. None of her colleagues at the physical therapy center knew about her fears, and they were not going to judge her. As for her patients, they were battling their own physical demons. She would just have to keep to the shallow end of the pool and stay close to the edge. She did not have to submerge herself beyond her waist.

Her scalp tingled at the thought of standing in water. She did not realize she had been picking ferociously at the cuticle of her right thumb until her skin stung and started bleeding. She stopped by the schedule board behind the front desk to take note of the sessions scheduled for the day. *I can always start hydrotherapy next week*, she thought.

She sighed in relief at the idea. She sucked at the scar on her finger as images of herself floating in the pool streamed through her mind. She would have to ask someone to take a picture of her standing in the pool since none of her friends or family members would ever believe she actually had done it. And maybe one day she could put an end to her anxiety and accompany Noura to the beach.

Just maybe.

She had been working at Mar Elias's physical therapy center only for two weeks when she accumulated enough referrals for both morning and afternoon shifts. The majority of her patients came from the hospital. She knew it would only be a matter of time before she was asked to run some of the sessions out of the hospital's rehabilitation facility. The idea excited her because the center for the hospital had the latest equipment and technology.

Serene took her job very seriously, and she was completely focused on her patients. Therapy sessions were mostly short, and all were conducted with a sense of urgency. Since her patients showed up mainly for postoperative rehab, they were usually transients. She didn't feel compelled to converse outside her profession or feel obligated to try to build long-term relationships with them. Her professional competence and honest nature carried her a long way, causing her referrals to stack up in the short time she had been on the job.

"Someone's becoming popular here," Shatha said as Serene examined the schedule board. Shatha had been on the job for close to four years, since the advent of the hospital in Mar Elias. She had watched the town blossom into a big rehabilitation and convalescence center. "Let me know if it's too much. I don't mind helping you," she added.

"Thank you, Shatha. I'm fine, really."

Serene did not really care for Shatha. She found her fickle and disingenuous the minute she met her. She tried not to rely solely on her snap judgment, but the more she got to know Shatha, the more alienating she found her.

"By the way, I need to brief you on this patient when you're ready" Shatha said, tapping the schedule board with her fingers. She inched her way closer to Serene, a strange focus in her eyes. "I worked on him for a while. He's difficult to please."

"Thank you. I'll definitely read his report ahead of time and prepare myself. I'll make sure to come to you if I have any questions."

Serene walked away, dismissing Shatha's offer in her mind. She wouldn't need Shatha to update her on her patients. She knew her stay in Mar Elias was only temporary, and she was fully aware that Kameel would never consider moving away from the city. Besides, she had always treated her profession as just that. A profession. She had always left her job at the clinic, and she never brought it home with her. All the kids she had worked on in the past were amiable patients, mainly with fixable sports-related injuries. Kids didn't harbor ill thoughts; they were physically and emotionally resilient, and best of all, they had the will to recover, making her job less challenging.

It was a rather uneventful Wednesday morning. By the time she finished with her third patient, her stomach had begun to churn. Feeling excited to meet her friend for lunch, she grabbed her purse and headed out. The hospital was two blocks west of Serene's work. The town was small and simple to navigate, and all four corners were within walking distance.

Before the hospital was built, locals used to rely mainly on the fruit of the land and small local farms for their meat and other animal products. However, with the construction of the hospital five years ago, things started to change. Two- or three-story apartment buildings mushroomed everywhere to accommodate hospital visitors and workers. Convenience stores started to expand in size, their shelves filling up with canned food, products locals had managed to live without all their lives. Thankfully, the town did not lose its peacefulness and tranquility, which manifested itself in the tempo of its daily life.

The hospital and its buildings were monumental. The project stretched over three blocks, and still had ongoing construction in several sites. Nevertheless, the buildings were aesthetically unobtrusive. They were built from natural stone, had green tile roofs, and were surrounded by gardens of tall pine and cedar trees. Serene thought it to be a masterpiece, for it was a state-of-the-art hospital in a peaceful, organic, and friendly environment.

Serene usually met her friend at the cafeteria, on the ground floor of the West Building. At lunchtime, the cafeteria was always filled with white coats. Self-conscious and intimidated, Serene straightened her posture and quickly scanned the room, trying to spot her friend. She saw Sonia standing at the other end of the cafeteria, surrounded by three of her colleagues and deeply engaged in what seemed like a fun conversation. Serene was so happy for her and was sure Sonia would thrive during her residency at the hospital. She grabbed a table for two and waited for her friend.

Sonia was always the beauty queen in high school. Pleasant and full of joy, she always found a reason to laugh, and she kept a positive outlook on life. Every boy and girl wanted to befriend her. Serene dropped her guard around her friend and found herself, though only temporarily, filled with mirth and hope. And now, in her white coats, Sonia somehow looked even more pleasant and attractive. Even Serene, her longtime friend, often found herself dazzled by her beauty and inspired by her charm.

Although the two had been classmates since first grade, Serene had never tried to break into Sonia's circle. Full of diffidence, Serene was never considered a threat to the egotism of other girls, and there wasn't a social group she couldn't belong to. However, she preferred to be a peripheral observer, nomadic between ephemeral friendship ties. She did not socialize at all with her schoolmates during elementary or middle school, and she never had a best friend, regardless of her mother's desperate efforts to find her one. As a result, Serene never had playdates or sleepovers, and she never joined any sports teams.

Until one day, Sonia, vivacious as always, approached her at the end of recess.

"Do you want to go watch cartoons at the movies this weekend?"

Serene did not know what to say. She, for one, had never cared for cartoons, thinking they were silly.

"You should join us Friday afternoon at the theaters," Sonia pressed on, smiling expansively. She then walked away, as if she had seen the tension sweep over Serene's face.

Several girls hovered around the seat next to Sonia that Friday evening at the movies, but she had already saved it for Serene.

As Serene sat at the cafeteria table, waiting for her friend to finish her conversation, she started reflecting on their relationship and how it had intensified during high school. She remembered how the two of them had made a pact to stick together through college. It was Sonia who tore open the cocoon for Serene to see the light. It was her proven friendship that eased Serene's way into social intermingling. It was her unwavering support that allowed Serene to gradually accept her nightmares as inconsequential disturbances and eventually forget about her fears and anxiety. Naturally, Serene grew to value her friend's opinion and trust her judgment.

Serene also remembered how, ever since Sonia had made the decision to go to medical school, their times together had precipitated into brief phone calls and rare weekend visits. Sonia couldn't help her through her mourning when her brother passed away, and she wasn't around during her pregnancy. It was during this testy period of Serene's life when the nightmares revisited her in full swing. And since Sonia left the city altogether and came to Mar Elias General Hospital for her residency, the two of them barely saw each other.

"You need to take a break from your routine," Sonia suggested over dinner last Christmas. "You'll like Mar Elias. The town is basically a big rehab center, and the people are nice and welcoming. You'll definitely have time to reflect and readjust. I can help you find a job in your field. It doesn't have to be at the hospital if that's too much for you."

Once again, Sonia came to the rescue. Serene was desperate to get away. She remembered mentioning the offer to Kameel and how he initially dismissed the proposal as a disruption to their jobs and household routine. He eventually came to concede, but Serene's situation was only getting worse.

Finally, Sonia caught sight of her friend waving to her from the table and went to join her.

"What was all that babbling about?" Serene asked as she hugged her friend.

"Everybody's so excited about this Saturday."

Every year, the town celebrated the return of summer with a festival that would kick off at sundown and proceed until the early hours of the morning. The tradition went back several generations, and it had become more elaborate through the years, especially since the advent of the hospital. It had been the highlight of discussions around town lately. Serene did not care to go, but she could not spoil her friend's excitement.

"I'm hoping there's a white dress sitting somewhere in your closet," Sonia said, raising her eyebrows quizzically. "Otherwise, my friend, prepare to go shopping."

Serene relaxed her body against the back of the chair, wilting at the idea.

"It's the dress code for this event, you know. We can't mess up the dress code!"

"I don't have any dresses with me—let alone anything white." Serene was hoping it would be a good excuse to skip.

"I'll pick you up Friday afternoon, and we'll go check the stores in Uptown," Sonia persisted, winking at her friend. "Last year's summer festival was a lot of fun. You'll basically meet all the locals and all the doctors at the hospital, except for the ones working that night, of course. People also come from surrounding towns. Excellent opportunity to mix and mingle."

"I really prefer to skip."

"I'm not going without you. You don't want me to miss out on such a fun event, do you?"

Serene did not answer.

"Let's get some food before I'm called back."

While they filled their plates from the salad bar, Serene tried to come up with an excuse that would convince her friend.

"I like your top. It lights up your face!" Sonia interjected.

Serene had been enjoying the distractions of the day. The last thing she needed was to succumb to her own perturbations, but she couldn't see herself going to the festival and wished Sonia would stop trying to convince her. As they got back to the table and started eating, she realized Sonia was looking at her worriedly. "I'm fine. It's just that I'd rather rest this weekend. I've been working long shifts."

Her friend did not respond.

"It's the same house, over and over," Serene added, suddenly regretting it, hoping the pandemonium of conversations around them would siphon off her words.

"It's just a dream," Sonia blurted as she stood up and hurriedly grabbed the folders she had with her, realizing she was being called back to duty. "Come on now. We've been down this road countless times before. I'm sorry I have to head back. I promise to catch up on Friday." Sonia disappeared into the crowd, and Serene sat munching on her salad, staring at the white background.

*It's just a dream!*

The same words she had been hearing her whole life, but these recurring dreams had unwaveringly disturbed her. To this day, she didn't know why. As for the people in them, some left her with a good feeling, while others upset her—or even terrified her. Their faces were always blurry and shapeless. Although she knew they were all in her mind, she could not simply dismiss them. How could her mind make up such complex stories, complete with their intricate elements of design? And if it wasn't the work of her mind, then what was speaking to her? And what did it mean? Why her?

# Chapter 2

"Whose house was it that we used to visit?" Serene asked her mother one morning. "The one sitting on a beautiful hilltop in the countryside, all built of white stone, red tile roof, and windows of stained glass?"

"I don't know what you're talking about, honey. We never visited a house like that."

"It seems so real. I can see its smallest details. It's a beautiful house. I loved it. I love it."

"Was it in a book you read, or a TV show, or maybe a movie?"

Serene was never satisfied with her mother's answers. It always seemed like she was brushing her off. Shouldn't her mother have answers to her nagging questions? Her dreams were too distressing to not be real.

"Does anyone we know own a ranch with horses? I love horses. They're fun to ride," she said on several occasions.

"No, honey. You've never seen a real horse. I've never even seen a real horse in my life."

"I used to ride a horse. A big beautiful horse. I rode it to the river. How come you don't remember that?"

"Just because it's in your dreams does not mean it actually happened," her mother said, taking her in her arms and hugging her tightly. "Put your dreams behind you and don't let them take over your life."

At one point during her childhood, Serene's obsession with horses consumed every minute of her waking hours. She couldn't get them out of her mind, and she begged to see one every time she had the chance.

She was to turn thirteen in a week, and her brother was less than eight. Her family had just finished eating dinner and was watching television in the living room. She sat leafing through her horse book. Her brother, in love with cars and trucks, had his collectables spread out on the living room floor. He was bent over the coffee table, assembling a classic toy car.

"Do you like balloons?" her mother asked her out of nowhere.

"Yes, I love balloons. Why do you ask?"

"What do you say we fill this room with tons of balloons, dim the lights, play your favorite music, serve your favorite food, and maybe hire a clown or a magician?"

"Why would we want to do that?"

"Well, to celebrate both your birthday and your graduation from middle school," her mother replied jovially.

"No way," Serene bellowed. "I won't have a party at my house. No one will come anyway."

"Of course they will," her father assured her. "Sonia for sure will come. We can invite the whole class if you want—or you can just pick a few friends. You'll get a lot of gifts, and your friends will be very happy. We'll make sure of that."

"I have no friends. And, no, Sonia won't come because none of the other girls will be interested." She dashed out of the room, tears streaming down her cheeks. She did not leave her bedroom until it was time for school the next morning.

"You know very well what I want for my birthday, so why not just get me that?"

The following week, Serene got a birthday surprise. Throughout middle school, her mother and brother used to walk the four-block distance to pick her up at the end of the day. They always waited for her behind the school gate, under the big eucalyptus tree. Serene loved the sight of her mother and brother since it meant going home. She eagerly searched for them in the crowd as soon as she stepped out of the classroom. However, that day, she could not spot them. Anxious, she ran to the eucalyptus tree, but she couldn't see them anywhere. For those couple of minutes, she felt lost and abandoned. And then she saw them. They were sitting in the car, and her father was in the driver's seat. They were waving at her and calling out her name.

"I thought you forgot about me. Why are you all here?"

"It's Friday," her father responded. "I left work a little early so we can take you on a drive through the countryside."

"We're going to hike and pick wildflowers," her brother said grudgingly.

Serene looked at him inquisitively, but he shrugged. Serene was skeptical and surprised with her parents' unusual spontaneity. Besides, her father never came home early from work, especially not to go hiking, which he didn't care for at all.

They had been driving for at least an hour when her father veered off the highway. They followed a narrow mountain road through gentle rolling hills and green meadows. The landscape was unadulterated and mesmerizing.

"Roll down your windows and inhale the fresh air," her mother said, entranced by the opulent scenery. "It's not the same air we're breathing in the city."

The road ended at a clearing with a few scattered parked cars. They all stepped out of the car and stretched their legs. A big wood sign read: "Welcome to The Ranch." There was a picture of a horse on it.

Serene was swept with excitement.

"Happy birthday!" her parents shouted in unison.

She tugged on her father's shirt. "Will I be able to ride one? Please?"

"That's why we're here, silly," her mother said.

Serene ran to the stable, her brother stumbling after her. She stopped suddenly to find a few horses grazing behind a fence. "Oh my God! I cannot believe how beautiful they are," she shouted.

A man approached her parents. "Good afternoon, everybody. Welcome to the ranch. Are you here to ride?"

"Just our daughter, Serene," replied her father.

"How exciting! Hi, Serene. I'll be your instructor today." He shook her hand. "Have you ridden a horse before?"

"Yes, I know how to ride a horse."

Her father, standing behind her, shook his head and gestured no to the instructor.

"And how about you, young man?" the instructor asked.

"I'd rather drive a car."

"All right then, let's get you a horse, Serene."

Serene followed him to the stalls.

"These are your choices, right here." He pointed to a group of horses.

"How about the red one?"

"Sure. You picked Aseela. She's old—and very gentle." He walked up to Aseela and scratched her long neck. "Let me show you how to mount her."

"I know exactly how to do it," Serene asserted.

What Serene did not know is that what happened next would bring her parents to tears.

Without hesitation, she lifted her hand to Aseela's face.

The horse cocked her head, her ears happily pointed, and leaned in to smell Serene's hand.

"You're so beautiful." Serene gently stroked Aseela's neck.

Serene walked to Aseela's left side and gripped the reins. She slid her foot into the stirrup, pulled her body up, and swung effortlessly into the saddle. She gave Aseela a pat on the neck before turning to face her parents, a victorious smile on her face. They did not smile.

Serene took off with her horse and started riding around the ranch. The experience was simply magical. She was no longer connected to earth. She was soaring in the big blue sky. She felt liberated. She reached an inner tranquility she had never experienced before, but that would revisit her every weekend thereafter, when the whole family accompanied her back to the ranch.

"Did you guys hear the tramping of Aseela's hoofs? It's the same sound that has been ringing in my ears for as long as I can remember."

Ever since she rode Aseela for the first time, Serene stopped seeing horses in her dreams. However, the other dream—the one that woke her in a jolt, made her heart jump out of her chest, and caused her throat to ache for hours—would not subside.

She's not in a familiar place.
She's standing in a big and airless room.
It's a hot day.
The air is stale and chlorinated.
The pool is huge.
Somebody in the room is shouting angrily.
She's scared.
She wants to leave.
She wishes she could disappear.
But she can't move.
Something is weighing her down.
A young man and an old woman are arguing.
Why are they arguing?
She feels confused.
She screams.
Stop.
She yells.
Please.
She cries.
She begs.
They don't seem to hear her.
Why?
She screams louder.

They still don't hear her.
She can't hear her own voice.
No one is looking her way.
She's confused.
A deafening sound.
A sudden, vigorous blow to her body.
She staggers under the force of the blow.
A sharp pain in the head.
Blood everywhere.
She falls in the pool.
She's submerged in water.
The water is not clear.
It feels like mercury.
She can't breathe.
Why?
Voices disintegrate.
Darkness.

Serene's eyes popped wide open. She was panting, unable to move. It was dark. She could hear the pounding of her heart. She felt the throbbing at her temples, but she couldn't lift her arms to rub at them. Her body was as stiff as a log. She could feel her nails digging through her palms like sharp blades. She tried to steady her breath. She heard the rhythmic sound of the ceiling fan and realized she wasn't submerged in water. She wasn't drowning. It was just a dream. She was safe. She closed her eyes and took a deep breath.

*It's just a dream.*

# Chapter 3

S erene had just stepped out of the shower when she heard the doorbell ring. She glanced at the clock on her nightstand.

*It can't be Sonia. It won't be four o'clock for another half hour!*

By the time she wrapped herself with a towel, the ringing had become relentless and had an actual rhythm to it.

"You're not ready yet? Let's go!" Sonia dashed into the apartment the minute Serene cracked open the door.

"You haven't changed a bit," Serene teased as she turned around and walked back to her bedroom. "We're in Mar Elias, relax. What's the hurry?"

Sonia followed her friend into the bedroom, threw herself on the bed, and exhaled wearily.

"There's this new recruit. An anesthesiologist I'm trying to impress. So, I need to find the right dress," she sang, swaying her arms in the air as if she was conducting an orchestra.

"You're a natural, my dear. Just be yourself, and don't stress," Serene said as she finished getting dressed.

She grabbed her purse and headed to the door.

It was a twenty-minute drive to get to Uptown. While Mar Elias was mainly residential, Uptown was the commercial center that served multiple neighborhoods over several kilometers. It had several restaurants and a variety of shops, each sporting the latest trends. In addition, it had a three-auditorium movie theater. Serene felt like she was revisiting her teenage years with her friend, when their parents would drop them off at a nearby shopping center on a Saturday afternoon. They would spend hours visiting their favorite stores, trying on clothes, and acting in front of dressing room mirrors. They would then eat dinner and go to the movies. Those outings were the highlight of her high school years. Serene would only buy the clothes Sonia deemed cute and sexy.

"The dress has to be simple. It has to outline your feminine curves and show off some spice," Sonia instructed her as they stepped into the first boutique.

Serene chuckled. "My spice has already been claimed."

"Does Kameel like white dresses?"

"He likes me in fitted clothes, like pencil dresses and tight jeans, which has been hard ever since I got pregnant."

Serene picked a white dress from the stand and headed to the dressing room. She hated the mirrors in dressing rooms. They always seemed to distort her image—or at least she hoped that was the case.

"How does it look, mamma?" Sonia whispered from behind the dressing room door.

"Like a mother fattening herself up to nurse." She stepped out of the fitting room to show the dress to her friend. "I seriously think it'll look better on you," she added.

"I'd like to try it on. By the way, how's Noura doing?" Sonia asked nonchalantly.

"I talk to her every evening. I wait until Kameel picks her up from either my parents or my in-laws. Sometimes she's so exhausted that she falls asleep in the car on the way home, and then I have to wait another whole day before I can talk to her again." She stepped out of the dressing room and handed the dress to her friend.

Sonia eyed her skeptically. "I gather you're not on good terms with either branch of the family tree."

"No, not really," Serene replied as she walked away, dismissing the subject altogether.

However, she could not shake off the haunting events from the day she left home.

**It's not** a cold day. It's a typical day in May, and the weather is temperate, but Serene is shivering. She has spent the day cleaning and organizing things around the house, wanting to make it more practical and simpler for Kameel to manage while she's gone. She's hesitant about the move she's about to make. Whether her leaving for recuperation will be beneficial for her and for the well-being of her family, or whether it will be completely ruinous, she doesn't know. However, a move of some kind is needed. A drastic change in her routine can help her regain the fleeting sense of normalcy in her life.

Noura must have felt her mother's restlessness. She's shadowing her from room to room, sucking on her thumb, and dragging her blanket behind her.

Serene looks the other way when Noura sucks her thumb, despite Kameel's disapproval.

"You keep letting her indulge in this ugly habit until it becomes deeply ingrained in her brain and very difficult to get rid of."

She hears him bellowing as he pulls Noura's thumb out of her mouth, and she thinks his reaction is harsh and unwarranted.

"She's ruining her smile and her teeth. Besides, it's not sanitary!"

At her father's angry outburst, Noura starts bawling inconsolably.

Serene is struck by a sudden stinging feeling. "She'll grow out of it. We just moved her bed to her room. She's adjusting to physical separation. And now that I'm leaving, it'll further exacerbate the issue. Besides, she's not always sucking her thumb—she does it when she's either tired or hungry. Why can't we resolve this problem after I get back?" She's half-shouting at this point as she pulls Noura up in her arms.

Looking astounded, Kameel turns around and walks away. "You're not helping. You never do," he says as he leaves the house, slamming the door behind him.

He comes back two hours later, looking pale and worn out. Serene's emotional unrest has been going on for more than three years, and over that period, Kameel's resilience has atrophied. His visits to the gym have become sporadic. His appetite for food has diminished to the bare essentials, and the skin of his once-young face has aged behind a web of wrinkles, layers of listlessness and ennui. He looks at Serene with bulging eyes. "Where's Noura?"

"Asleep in our bed." Serene has been working all day around the house. Her heart is racing, and her blood is boiling in her veins.

He walks into the bedroom, drops himself on the bed next to Noura, wraps his arm around her tiny body, and instantly falls asleep. Serene wants so badly to lie next to them, hold them both with all her might, and be cemented with them forever.

**"Was there** a dress you liked?" Sonia asked Serene as she popped her face in her friend's field of vision.

"Pardon?"

"You're shivering. Are you cold?"

"A bit," she replied, rubbing at her arms.

"I'm getting the dress and the two shirts. I always find good stuff here. Are you getting anything?"

"No, not really, not from here. Let's try another store," Serene suggested.

They grabbed the bags from the cashier and stepped out onto the street.

The bags that Sonia was carrying reminded Serene of the bags her mother showed up with at her doorstep on the day she was leaving for Mar Elias.

**Serene has** just finished packing her suitcase and sets it by the front door. Her mother is carrying two big bags of toys and clothes to surprise Noura with. She has promised to spend the night with Kameel and Noura to make the separation easier on them. She walks into the house with a big smile and spreads her gifts on the carpet in the family room.

Noura is so happy to see her grandmother and all the toys spread out on the floor that she starts jumping for joy. All four of them spend the next half hour laughing and talking, overpowered by Noura's exhilaration.

Serene catches sight of her mother staring at her, withdrawn in deep thought. "What's on your mind?" she asks her mother, seizing her hand.

"I'm worried about you and your family," her mother says. "I still don't see how you going away will help solve the problem."

Serene sighs. "God knows I tried, Mom. Nothing's worked. I have to give this a shot."

Her mother fumbles through her handbag and signals for Serene to follow her into the kitchen. She seats herself on a stool and gestures for Serene to do the same. "There's something you need to know … something your dad and I thought best to bury in oblivion."

Their faces are so close to each other Serene can break through the thick barrier that has risen between them as of late. Her mother has been shaped and reshaped through colliding, life-testing experiences, but *when did her face become so worn out? Were her eyes always so baggy?*

"Our plan did work for a while. We did not want to add fuel to the fire, but now that your anxieties and dreams are back, I think it'd be better for you to know." Her mother nods repeatedly as if to convince herself of her decision. She seizes Serene's hand. "Listen to me. You're a smart adult. Look how far you've come. You graduated valedictorian of your class, you married a decent young man who adores you and your daughter, and you hold a very nice and respectable job. You have a friend who would do anything to help you. You've accomplished what a mother and father would love to see their daughter attain."

She recites her lines breathlessly as beads of sweat form around her nose and on her forehead. She wipes her face with the back of her hand. "I would give anything for your father to be here with me, but I thought it best to spare him more emotional distress. You need to know that he believes in you. He always believed in your strength. You have proved him right in the past, and I want to see you do it again."

She lowers her head in deep thought, her fingers nervously fiddling with the buttons on her shirt. She shakes her head and says, "There were nightmares involving drowning, but even stranger were the stories you told of families, of people and names that neither of us recognized. You described scenes and places so well, as if you actually lived them."

She stops to catch her breath and looks at Serene with remorseful eyes.

"You talked about siblings and neighbors, you talked about a different mother and father, about how much you loved them and how much they loved you."

She pulls a small, weathered notepad out of her handbag.

"In this book, I recorded some of your dreams and stories. I didn't tell your dad about it until several years after the fact. He was against showing it to you, but I know he would not stand against me today, knowing what you're going through. Take it. It may help you find yourself."

**"Take this** one. I think it'll look beautiful on you. It has a bateau neckline and is gathered at the waist. It's worth trying. Fitting rooms are over there, to your left. You go ahead. I'll keep looking for you," Sonia said.

Serene took the dress and tried it on. Luckily, it looked decent.

She was not in the mood for shopping. She missed Noura so much, and she felt guilty for being away from home.

"I love it," Sonia said. "It makes your waist look good!"

"Can we go eat? I'm famished." Serene rubbed her stomach.

"I must've asked you three times if you were hungry, but you wouldn't answer me!"

At the restaurant, Sonia picked a table by the window.

The waitress greeted them and handed them each a menu.

**Serene takes** the book and turns it quizzically in her hands. "Why are you telling me this now, Mother? Why did it take you this long to share your notes with me? Instead of doing something about it, you decided to stifle my pain, pushing it back down inside me until it festered like a chronic disease." She will never forget her mother's distorted face.

"We didn't know what to do with this information. We didn't know whether your nightmares were just a reflection of your fears as a child—or whether they represented something much bigger. We didn't know if your stories were based on your dream visions or your imagination. Believe me. We didn't know what to do with all this information. We thought time would take care of it. So, we raised you on high alert throughout your childhood. You should appreciate how difficult it was for us now that you have a child of your own."

What Serene tells her mother next, that evening, her boiling fever of rage rising, is what Serene will catch herself saying out loud on several occasions as she walks around her apartment in Mar Elias. "Why didn't you and Dad try to really pay attention and decipher what was going on inside me? What was scaring you? I'm the one who was always scared. Those accomplishments you're talking about, none of them came easy. I overcame self-inflicted obstacles on a daily basis. And what strength were you talking about that you and Dad believed in?"

Her mother covers her face with her hands and shakes her head from side to side as she cries.

"Do you remember in sixth grade when you took me to the school's year-end party?" Serene continues. "Well, it was one of the scariest moments of my life. Everybody thought I was having fun, including you and Dad, but I really suffered. When they dumped the bucket of water on my head, I could not feel the ground under my feet. I panicked. I couldn't see the faces staring back at me. I couldn't even hear my own voice when I called you for help. I could only hear the roaring of water inside my head. And when everybody finally moved on, I just stood there confused, too scared to move. I hid in the girls' bathroom for the rest of the day. It was horrible!"

Serene stands up and starts pacing nervously around the kitchen. She's sobbing.

"Oh, honey, I am so sorry!"

"You thought of me as a Gordian knot. I heard you say it to Dad once," Serene responds, her voice crescendoing. "I'm old enough now to take charge and undo my own knot. I knew that you and Dad preferred me to stay on the normal course of life and be the normal child my brother was. I tried very hard to be your good girl. All along, I was stumbling. You must have seen me stumbling! You never encouraged me to slow down and figure out what the hurdle was. And now that I'm married and have a child, I cannot help but ask: What have I done? Do I deserve Kameel and Noura? How can I be a good mother and a good wife when I don't even know who I really am? What's vision and what's reality?"

Serene has been rehearsing this conversation over and over in her head for as long as she can remember, but she has never had the courage to bring it forth. She is neither confrontational nor truculent by nature. The last thing she wants is to burden her parents with the responsibility of her anxieties and sleep problems, but on that day, something happens for the first time. Her decision to take charge of her life has somehow pulled her out of her conventional matrix and dissolved her conformist impressions. An unpleasant feeling is stirring inside her, bringing with it an intense feeling of resentment over all that is lost. And when she finally regains her composure, she pins her mother with a suggestive look. "Was it an issue of faith—or more of a social concern to you and Dad?"

Her mother effaces Serene's words with a brisk shake of her head. "No, no, no, honey. It was never about us. We wanted a normal life for you. We thought you would outgrow these nightmares for good."

**"Can you** please snap out of reverie and tell me what you're drinking?"

Serene sat up straight as she realized she had slowly shrunk into an unnatural hunch.

Sonia was looking intently at her with tender and worried eyes.

"You pick. I trust your taste," Serene replied, flipping open the menu.

"Did I tell you Nader is vegetarian?"

"Who's Nader?"

"The new anesthesiologist. Where have you been for the past two hours while I was rambling on about him?"

"Well, no, you didn't say anything about his food habits. What else are you keeping from me?"

"I think he might be the one I've been looking for. I mean it this time."

**Serene knows** her mother means every word she's saying. She knows that what her parents have done is to the best of their understanding and to the utmost of their endurance. Why burden her mother after all these years? Her father didn't even know who she was when she last visited him at the nursing home. Hasn't she caused them enough hardship and stress? Hasn't she given them enough sleepless nights already?

That afternoon, Serene gets in the car heartbroken. She's devastated about leaving Kameel and Noura. How is she going to survive without them? How is she going to be able to look inside herself and face whatever is eating at her like a parasite? The confusion of what is real, and what seems real, makes her skeptical of her cognitive abilities. The fact that her parents have consciously suppressed her thoughts might have led to this misconception of who she really is. Can her mental distress be the outcome of some past physical and emotional anguish? Couldn't her mother and father have taken an initiative in helping her understand, rather than suppress, remember, rather than erase? It's too late at this point to burden them with any blame. Her brother's sudden death has caused them to wither swiftly. They look years older every time Serene sees them.

**"In a** matter of few hours, you'll meet all the people of Mar Elias at the summer festival. It'll be good for you, you'll see," Sonia proclaimed. "I'll introduce you to all my colleagues, including Nader. I'll make sure he goes. You'll unwind and have fun."

The waitress came back with their food: a chicken sandwich with garlic aioli for Sonia and a grilled eggplant sandwich with avocado and sprouts for Serene.

"Your favorite sandwich," Sonia said, gazing into Serene's eyes in search for answers. "Go ahead and eat. You look pale. We should just go home after dinner. We need to rest for tomorrow."

Serene's emotional entanglement was stifling; she could not unwind. As Sonia was driving them back to Mar Elias that evening, Serene kept groping her purse for the book her mother had given her, debating if and when she should read it. Why was her father against showing it to her? Was she better off without knowing? And why did her mother decide to give it to her on the day of her departure? Wasn't she leaving home to try to detach from whatever was ailing her?

"What are you looking for?" Sonia asked, pulling Serene out of her reminiscence. "Did you lose your keys?"

Serene looked at her friend, her hand still fumbling nervously inside her purse.

"Pardon?"

"Your purse. What's in your purse?"

"Oh! Nothing important," she said, dropping her shoulders and exhaling the air that had been straining her neck all afternoon.

Sonia smiled at her nervously.

"I'm really sorry. I've just been trapped in my thoughts."

"It's all right!" Sonia assured her, keeping her gaze on the road. "Try not to dwell on the past too much so that you can move forward."

It had been a month since her mother had given her the book, but she still hadn't opened it. Why hadn't she? Was it a conscious decision so that she could move on? Was she in control of her own situation— or was that control an illusion? In any case, she needed time to rest, which was why she left home in the first place. She needed time to reflect on her life and realign with her present. Back at the apartment, she took the book out of her purse and shoved it in the lowest drawer of her closet, out of sight, under a pile of clothes. She would come back to it when she felt ready. She slammed the drawer shut, put the fan on high, and threw herself on the bed, feeling exhausted.

# Chapter 4

Time seemed to slow down in Mar Elias, and its people, satisfied with the simplicity of their lives, sought to seize every moment of the day. Casting aside any sense of urgency, they socialized over morning coffee and afternoon tea. They seldom watched a television show without friends and family, spending the following days discussing what they saw. The community lived in harmony and in agreement with the nature surrounding it. Everybody knew everybody. Honesty and integrity were the quotidian way. No pretenses and no social layering to veil their core. Surprisingly, the advent of the hospital did not break through the fabric of the town. Staff, patients, and visitors found it inviting to assimilate and convalesce.

On the day of the festival, however, the town experienced a different dynamic. The mood was enlivened and electrified. All shops closed down early in the day. Kids on their bikes rode up and down the streets unattended, bursting with excitement. Neighboring towns were drawn to the celebration too. People brought their picnic gear and plenty of food and games with them. They came as early as they could to claim a good and encompassing spot, where they could gather with friends and family and still be close to where most of the action was taking place.

There was something for every member of the family: foods, games, competitions, music, arts, and crafts. All ages aggregated in high spirit. Young men and women were happy to intermingle with old friends and kindle new relationships. According to Sonia, two marriages came of last year's summer festival. This was actually its original purpose. It explained why the tradition called for black slacks with collared shirts for men and white dresses for women.

Serene had asked Kameel to bring Noura to Mar Elias for the weekend so that the three of them could attend the festival together, but Kameel dismissed the idea under the pretext of being too busy with his job. He said he needed the weekends to prepare for his upcoming high-profile meetings. He had accepted a job promotion about two months ago. The heightened responsibility that came with it had brought on a new level of tension between them.

She remembered how their regular evening stroll to the park had started to dwindle under the same pretext. Kameel was bringing paperwork home, and evenings were the only time he could take care of it. Serene did not like taking Noura to the park alone for fear of having to socialize with others. She used to rehearse conversations and scenarios, preparing herself in case she needed to use them. The constant wondering of who was thinking what of her was disquieting. She always forgot people's names and faces, as if her subconscious mind naturally dismissed them as peripheral. People felt her tension; she could tell by their reactions toward her. Their wistful smiles accompanied a glint of pity. Oftentimes, she was omitted from conversations and dialogues altogether.

"My boss and his new wife are in town this weekend," Kameel told her while they were having dinner one day. "What do you say we meet up with them for dinner somewhere?"

Serene did not answer.

"It's good for my job. It's imperative to network," he added without lifting his gaze off of his plate.

"You can go. I'll stay with Noura."

He lifted his head and looked her straight in the eye. "We shouldn't do that. It's not good for my work, and it's not good for our relationship. We haven't gone out since Noura was born. We really cannot continue like this." He spoke slowly, so that each word had enough time to set in.

"You know very well how Noura cries when neither one of us is around," Serene argued as she got up to clear the table, trying to find a good and noble reason for her answer.

Deep inside, however, she knew all too well that she needed to compromise.

Kameel ended up reserving dinner at a bistro downtown, and the ambience was relaxed and casual. Serene was able to recline behind the commotion and shield herself behind the loud music. She sat observing the people around her. Their joyfulness seemed fake to her. Their high-pitched voices were grating, and conversations seemed disembodied. She smiled every once in a while and chimed in only when she deemed it necessary for the conversation to carry on.

The summer festival in Mar Elias was more elaborate and organized than Serene had anticipated. A live band struck up happy tunes. Shady, aged trees of oak and pine were surrounded by a variety of orchards. Along one side stretched an expansive orchard of peaches and plums, where rows of white, pink, and red flowering trees with expanding branches canopied in a fiery sky of blooms. On another side stretched rows of citrus trees, their intoxicating aroma infused the evening's cool breeze. The grounds were carpeted with a satiny rug of pastel green grass that felt like silk under her feet. In the distance, there rose a rolling hill covered with a spectrum of wildflowers, a walking trail of grass running through it.

*What a heavenly piece of land!*

Strands of paper lanterns connected trees and poles. As the rays of the sun gave way to the darkness of the night, the dim light of the lanterns felt increasingly magical and cast a soft shadow on the ground.

As Serene roamed in wonderment through the crowds, everybody greeted her. Men nodded their heads in her direction, and patients of hers greeted her warmly. Nadia, the receptionist at the clinic where she worked, was so happy to see her. Just like Sonia had told her, women were dressed in casual white dresses. Dresses fluttered in the wind as laughter filled the air. Under a centennial oak tree, a marionette show was taking place on a stage. She walked to the stage and watched the show. Kids of all ages had gathered around, mesmerized by the talking marionettes.

Serene felt a sudden wave of happiness. She looked up to the sky. Hundreds of stars speckled its black vastness. She imagined herself standing on one of the stars and looking up into the sky. Would it still look limitless? The crisp air felt so refreshing on her face and arms, and it carried with it a profusion of jasmine, citrus, and peach. It was a perfect night. She couldn't imagine a better setting. In nature, Serene found her comfort zone.

She realized she was still holding the plate of homemade baklava she had promised to bring. She headed to the food tables to set down her plate. The tables were covered with cloths of all colors and laden with all sorts of foods. She felt her stomach rumble.

"Hey, Miss Perfect, which plate is yours?" Sonia exclaimed as she ran up to her friend, her face beaming with joy.

"Well, the baklava of course. Go ahead. Try it."

"No, not now! Follow me. There's a lot to do," Sonia shouted above the crowd as she darted ahead of her friend.

Sonia's long, curly brown hair bounced weightlessly as her body floated to a happy gait. Her white chiffon dress with its fitted bodice hugged her down to her tiny waist, the bell-shaped skirt floating in the air behind her. She looked like a princess from a fairytale. Everything about Sonia exuded happiness, so Serene acceded contentedly, allowing the festive energy to channel into her. The wholesomeness of it all started to fill her up.

They met up with Sonia's friends, a group of incredibly smart and charming young doctors with well-cultivated manners. Sonia had already introduced Serene to a few of them, but there were several Serene had not yet met. They seemed to her a group of blessed people, in control of their own destinies and the world around them.

"This is Nader, our new anesthesiologist," Sonia said, curtsying and pointing her hands in his direction. "Besides knowing how to put people to sleep, he also knows how to keep them up all night." She patted him lovingly on the shoulder and winked at her friend.

*My friend has finally fallen in love.*

"I've heard a great deal about you, Serene. It's a pleasure to finally meet you," Nader added, shaking her hand.

"Thank you. The pleasure is mine. Sonia is the sister I never had."

Sonia led everybody to an area where several dartboards had been set up. She split them into two groups, with Nader and Serene on her team, and for the next hour or so, they were taken by the amusement and pleasure of the game. Serene had never doubted her friend's ability to surround herself with amazing people. Sonia's resolve and cheerful attitude helped her realize her dreams. Serene could see that Nader was completely dissolved in her friend's charms. He had an ebullient personality that allowed him to keep up with her overflowing enthusiasm, and his laughter seemed capable of cheering up anyone around him. Serene did not want the night to end. Everybody ate, drank, and had a great time.

At midnight, when everyone stampeded to the river to watch the fireworks, Serene stayed at the outskirts, watching from afar. The air was getting misty. The droplets of water danced weightlessly in the air, glimmering like the Milky Way under the projected lamplights. She started to feel nostalgic. Nostalgic for something she could not define. Nagging questions started to infuse her mind with doubt. Had she still not found what she longed for? Was there something else in life waiting for her? Was she on the wrong path—or was her mother right when she told her she had accomplished considerably so far? What was going to solidify her, settling her body, mind, and soul? She felt like those droplets of water, floating in the air, balancing between the whims of the wind and the pull of gravity, on a long and indefinite journey.

A chill ran through her. At one end of the gardens, right before the grounds sloped down to the river, stood a charming golden weeping willow. She always loved that tree and felt it grand in its modesty. She walked to it and stood under its graceful branches, allowing them to fall over her head. She leaned her back against its solid trunk and looked out on the night.

"Excuse me, miss? I was asked to give you this," a young lady said, handing her a shawl. "It gets pretty nippy in the evening," she added before turning around to walk away.

Serene took the shawl and thanked her. She looked around to acknowledge the person who had noticed she was cold and shivering, but no one seemed to be looking in her direction. She wrapped the shawl around her shoulders and felt its warmth seeping into her. She brought it to her face and nestled her cold nose in it. It smelled of a pleasant perfume. She felt comforted by it and stood there until the last sparkle of fireworks shot up into the sky.

"Here you are! Where did you disappear?" Nader shouted, running up the slope.

He was barefooted, his clothes were wet, and his pants were rolled up to his knees. "We're all down there looking for you. Were you able to see the fireworks from up here? Give me your hand."

He grabbed Serene's hand and started pulling her down the slope, through the crowds. She tried to free herself from his grip, but he wouldn't let go of her. She realized everybody was watching her, and she did not want to make a scene. She started to panic.

"The river is pretty shallow. The water feels so good. You should've seen the frenzy of water splashing. Look at my clothes!"

And, before she could say another word, her feet were submerged in water. Her heart was pounding. She could not catch her breath. She looked down at her feet, but the water was already up to her knees.

"Don't look down," Sonia shouted, wading in her direction. "Grab my hand."

Serene's body was shaking. "Please don't let go of me," she pleaded as she tightly held on to her friend's arm.

"I won't let go of you. You're going to be fine. Breathe deeply. Look up. I won't let go. Trust me."

Serene took a deep breath.

"That's my girl," Sonia said. "Just relax, we're getting out."

"I'm sorry," Nader said. "I didn't know you hated water so much."

"I'm fine. Don't worry about it," Serene said, sensing his genuine remorse. "The water is freezing." Serene remembered the promise she had made to herself. The promise to face her fear of water head on. *So why not start now?* "Thank you, Sonia," she whispered, her teeth chattering. "What would I do without you?"

It was two o'clock in the morning when Serene finally decided to leave the festival. Sonia and Nader offered to walk her to her apartment. The streets were still lit up and alive.

"I love the spirit of this town," Nader said, blowing hot air on his frozen hands. "I could really see myself settling down here."

"It's not too remote from the city, but it's far enough to be surrounded by nature. The hospital is state-of-the-art, clean, and brand-new. The people are amazing, and the weather is beautiful and smog-free. It's truly a piece of heaven," Sonia concurred, her bottom lip twitching.

"Here, you can share this shawl with me," Serene said as she extended one end of it to her friend.

"Thank you. I need it. This festival keeps getting better and better every year." Sonia wrapped one end of the shawl around her shoulders. "They used to set up for it in a clearing by the river, but the area wasn't big enough to accommodate the growing crowds of recent years."

"The gardens were breathtaking," added Nader. "The landscape is that of a dream."

Sonia said, "The whole piece of land is privately owned. It's actually a side garden of a residence. The owner has been offering it as a festival ground for the past three years. He's quite the punctilious man. They say he hires people way in advance to attend to the grounds and comb them for weeds and small rocks."

"That's nice," remarked Serene.

"Apparently, he did it all for his wife. She loved this town and the idea of the summer festival. Sadly, when she fell ill, she couldn't walk all the way down to the river. He used to bring her out to the garden, where she could sit and watch the whole event."

"Which residence? I don't remember seeing one," Serene asked, squinting as she tried to tap into her memory.

"Do you remember where the blooming peach and plum trees were?" Sonia asked. "Well, right behind them, there's a huge house. You probably couldn't notice it because of the dense row of cypress that's fencing it," she continued. "Actually, it's a beautiful house of stone, white marble, and stained glass windows. I've walked around it once, but I've never seen it on the inside."

"Are they locals?" asked Nader.

"No, they're not. No one knows why they decided to settle in this town. Different people tell you different stories, but people like them a lot. They've shown their love for this town. They've repeatedly contributed to the community. They own a good portion of the land around here. Anyone selling a lot for cash still goes to him for a quick and easy transaction."

"How do they make their money?" interrupted Serene.

"I heard they have businesses everywhere. He's the founder of several nonprofit organizations and of Mar Elias General Hospital. Someone told me the other day that had it not been for him in particular, it would've been close to impossible to find investors interested in building such a big hospital here. Not only that, he's currently lobbying against commercializing the town, fighting to keep it unadulterated and full of open space."

"Where are they now?" Serene asked.

"He's around most of the time," Sonia answered. "He travels a lot though. His wife passed away about five months ago. She had oral cancer. By the time it was discovered, it had metastasized to the lungs. People who know him say he rarely speaks of her and that he's still in deep mourning. He lives alone in the house now … except for the housekeeping staff."

"So, no kids?" asked Serene.

"No. They have no kids."

"Was he at the festival tonight?" asked Nader eagerly.

"No. He's quite an enigma. And, believe me, I would've noticed him immediately had he been. He suffers from a spinal cord injury. He uses a walking cane, and lately, he has been seen in a wheelchair."

"Interesting! What's his name?" Serene asked.

"Mr. J." answered Sonia.

"As in the letter J?"

"Yes. It's his last initial."

"Hmm, I see," responded Serene. She kissed her friends good night and entered the apartment building. "Thank you for walking me all the way here—and thank you so much for insisting on taking me with you tonight. I had a good time."

"I knew you would," Sonia responded, wrapping her hand around Nader's arm. "Have yourself a good night's sleep. Sweet dreams!" She leaned her head on Nader's shoulder and disappeared into the night.

Serene could not take Mr. J.'s story out of her mind. She couldn't help but feel bad for him. A cold draft of wind greeted her as she stepped into her apartment. Had she left the window open? She stacked some wood in the fireplace, and sat watching the fire, its blue and orange plumes bending with the wind. It was the first time she had ever used a fireplace.

She stepped into the kitchen and poured herself a glass of wine. Back in the living room, she sat facing the fire, the shawl still wrapped around her shoulders. She pulled it off and looked at the tag: "100 percent cashmere." It still felt wet in several spots. She laid it on the sofa next to her to dry. After all, her night was not so bad. She made it into the river, met Sonia's friends, and saw several of her patients, as well as people she recognized from around town. And the taste of the delicious food was still lingering on her palate. She sipped on her wine. It tasted good. Sonia had given her the bottle when she first came to Mar Elias.

"Sonia," Serene muttered, "nothing this girl is not good at."

She grabbed the shawl again and wrapped it around her shoulders. With the wineglass cradled in both hands, she forgot herself in the reflection of the flames as they danced on the walls around her. The cracking sound and the smell of burning wood gave her a sense of earthly serenity.

She woke up the next day feeling rested. She had fallen asleep on the sofa, the shawl crumpled in her hands. She had forgotten to turn on the ceiling fan, but she still managed to sleep through the night.

# Chapter 5

On the day Serene met Mr. J. in person, his medical dossier was in the stack her assistant had piled on the front desk to be reviewed. His appointment was set up for three o'clock that afternoon. Finishing her morning sessions earlier than anticipated, she decided to go eat lunch at the corner café and familiarize herself with his medical history. She grabbed his dossier and her purse, and she stepped out of her office.

"Are you going out to lunch?" asked Shatha, running after her as she passed through the lobby.

"Yes. I thought it'd be nice to be outdoors on a beautiful day like this," Serene answered as she exited the building.

"Can I join you?" Shatha persisted before Serene could walk away, catching up to her steps.

"Sure."

Then, remembering the dossier she was carrying, she added, "Give me one second. I'll be right back." She dashed into the building, went to her office, and laid the dossier on her desk. *I'll review it on my own later.*

"I've been wanting to go out to lunch with you for a while now, but I haven't had the chance to. What did you have in mind? Did you want to grab a quick sandwich or have a hot lunch?"

"A quick sandwich will be fine!" replied Serene, thinking the shorter the break the better.

Shatha reminded Serene of Paula, a colleague she had met in

college. She was nice and friendly on the outside, but she was stingingly jealous and competitive. Paula sought her and others, as Serene later came to realize, to pry into their affairs. She always asked questions and never provided answers. Paula always managed to find out what other people's grades were, measuring herself up against them. On several occasions, Serene had noticed Shatha watching her while in sessions with patients. She had even suspected Shatha to be eavesdropping on her conversations with them.

They picked a table on the patio of a café overlooking Hamra Street. A lady with a cute little girl sat at the table next to them. The mother was patiently taking small pieces of her sandwich and feeding them to her daughter.

**"Let the** child learn to eat on her own, for God's sake!" Kameel grunts while the three of them ate at a restaurant a week before she's supposed to go to Mar Elias.

His tone is so petulant it makes people around them turn their heads. He doesn't care if half of the pasta ends up on the floor or if Noura's face and clothes are smeared with tomato sauce. "You're too smothering. Her motor skills need to develop properly."

"That's not smothering. I want to make sure she actually eats her dinner." *Don't all kids end up eating on their own? Why should there be a time constraint on growth and development?* But she's not going to argue because it won't get them anywhere. Persuasion is an art, and she knows that Kameel is usually pretty talented in that department.

**"Have you** ever eaten at the Local Eatery across the street?" Shatha asked.

"No, not yet. Is the food any good?" Serene asked, feigning interest.

"It's actually the best. You mainly see hospital employees or high-profile hospital visitors eating there. Every time I go there, the menu's different—and so are the prices for that matter."

"Here you go, ladies. One roast beef and one veggie. Enjoy," said the waitress as she set the plates on the table.

"Are you vegetarian?" asked Shatha, glancing at the olive and avocado sandwich Serene had ordered.

"I aspire to be."

"Believe me, nothing's wrong with eating meat. I was raised on it and I'm really healthy," Shatha said proudly, taking a considerable bite out of her roast beef sandwich.

Serene felt a wave of hostility emanating from Shatha. *Why do Shatha and society in general view nonconformists as a fissure in their aggregate? Being vegetarian is humanitarian at the core and benign in essence. It should not be perceived as threatening. Besides, Shatha is too quick at drawing conclusions from a one-time observation. Or maybe she has been watching.*

"How do you like Mar Elias so far? Are you going to stay through the summer?" Shatha asked as if she were going down a list of pre-meditated questions, checking them off with a pencil as she moved on.

"I really don't know yet. Most likely not."

"Well, there's a physical therapy department at the hospital … if you ever grow bored with this one."

Serene nodded and busied herself with her sandwich, hoping Shatha would do the same and stop asking her questions.

"Have you met all of our regulars so far?" Without waiting for an answer, she added, "Have you met Mr. J.?" Shatha's smile did not destabilize her piercing gaze.

"Not yet. He's scheduled for this afternoon," Serene said, knowing very well that Shatha was already aware of the fact.

"Well, that doesn't mean he'll show up."

Shatha sat up straight, leaned forward, and rested her elbows on the table. She sipped her juice through a straw, deflating her cheeks down to the bone. "He's been skipping his appointments lately. He's notorious for being irregular!" After a few seconds, she added, "Spinal cord injury, L3. He was seventeen."

Serene felt her stomach hollow. "How much of a recovery?" she asked.

"Most of the sensation is back. His motor skills have been partially compromised though. He wears braces. He needs a cane on normal days, and he still uses a wheelchair on others."

"It must've been dreadful," Serene said, "being young, full of energy and big dreams, and then having to succumb to such a handicap for the rest of your life."

"His wife passed away five months ago. I think he's still grieving, which has only aggravated his impatience with his rehab process."

Back in her office, Serene went over Mr. J.'s long medical record and familiarized herself with his history: incomplete spinal cord injury at L3; misaligned lumbar vertebrae; posterior cord syndrome; loss of bladder and bowel control; loss of sensory and motor functions of pelvis, different areas of legs, ankles, and feet; respiratory function intact. She also skipped through his rehabilitation progress: natural healing of spine with use of traction; spinal fusion; supportive rehab; partial motor recovery. She realized that he had been to hospitals around the world for diagnosis, treatments, and rehabilitation.

Serene flipped through his thick dossier, going over his most recent rehab regimen. There were names of staffers who had worked out of this office, but no longer did. It looked like Shatha had been the one he had seen the most. He hadn't showed up for a single treatment at this physical therapy center for the past six months, with no record from any other clinic or hospital spanning the same period. *Maybe it's because of his wife's illness and death*, she thought. She shook her head. *He's most likely seeing therapists elsewhere.* She remembered Sonia telling her that he traveled a lot for work, which could explain his absence, but the way Shatha was talking about him at lunch, how she seemed agitated, made her think she was hiding something from her.

She stood up and walked to a framed mirror on the wall. Despite the emotional and mental uprisings she had been experiencing lately, her face looked strangely rested. She ran her fingers through her hair. Did he ask for her in particular, or did Nadia, the receptionist, recommend her to him? But why would he ask for her to start with? Serene knew very well that Shatha was excellent at her job. Did he expect Serene to do even better? A fleeting wave of apprehension streamed through her. She finally went back to her desk, sat down, and flipped through his file.

"Mr. J. is here. He's in the lobby," Nadia announced, poking her head through her door.

"Thank you, Nadia. Please offer him a cup of water. I'll be there in a minute." She got up nervously and walked straight back to the mirror. Her cheeks were red. She took a deep breath, and then she stepped into the lobby.

He was facing the large window overlooking the parking lot. The waiting room was uncharacteristically quiet. Nadia was busy at her desk. There were no other patients or staffers around. His presence felt commanding. With his back to the room, he stood looking through the window. He stood tall, except for a slight tilt in his body. He was resting his weight on a cane. He reminded her of the tower of Pisa; although leaning, it exuded preeminence. His hair was a cascade of black, shiny silk. He looked elegant in his expensive suit. Serene walked up to him.

"Hello Mr. J.," she said.

After a few seconds, she wondered if he had heard her. Then, slowly, he turned around to face her. Their eyes met. Time froze. She blinked repeatedly. His smell. His perfume. He did not blink at all. His gaze was fixed on her. Her breath stalled even though her heart was racing. She didn't know what was happening to her. She knew she needed to calm down before she broke into a sweat. She took a deep breath.

*Calm down.*

"I'm Serene Doory," she said, trying to steady her breath.

Her trembling voice only exacerbated her anxiety.

"Nice to finally meet you, Ms. Doory," he responded with a sweet smile.

Elegance was at his core. His face had a radiant beauty Serene had never imagined. Manly, yet delicate. His features were an artist's dream. Big, hazel, almond-shaped eyes sheltered by softly angled eyebrows, where each hair was aesthetically placed as a final brush of elegance to a face that was meant to dazzle. His long lashes guided her straight to his sweet eyes. She could easily get lost in those eyes, in their infinite mystery. His straight-edged nose gave him a sense of nobility, emphasizing a wide and beautiful smile that seeped into Serene effortlessly, like water seeping through dry soil. He didn't look like anyone she had met before, yet he seemed so familiar.

*Who's this guy?*

"I'm unable to have a session today. I'm actually on my way out of town due to some pressing business issues. I just stopped by to apologize for the cancellation, but I'll make sure to reschedule at my earliest convenience." He was still smiling.

"All right. No problem. Thank you for stopping by."

"I'll be seeing you soon, Ms. Doory."

He bowed his head, turned around, and limped his way to the door.

Serene watched him walk away. She did not want him to leave. She looked at the door as it shut slowly behind him, bewildered by what had just happened to her. She took a deep breath of his lingering perfume. It smelled good. She walked to the window.

He was slowly stepping down the flight of stairs that led to the parking lot. He stopped for a second and lifted his gaze to the sky before heading to his car. A metallic Mercedes-Benz was parked at the curb, and his chauffeur was holding the door open for him. He handed him his cane, and carefully eased his body into the car.

"That sure was the shortest session I've ever seen!" Shatha said, clapping her hands as she walked up to Serene.

"Mr. J. is heading out of town. He stopped by to cancel his appointment."

"I told you!" she added with a wide, sly smile drawn on her face as if she was settling an old score. She then exhaled, turned around, and walked away.

*Sadly obtuse. How can she overlook the fact that he could've easily called the office to cancel? He even could've sent in his chauffeur to do so.*

As she stepped into her office, Serene caught a reflection of herself in the mirror. Her face was crimson red. She lifted her right hand to her face and smelled his lingering perfume on her skin. She sat at her desk, trying to suppress an urge to cry. She did not want him to leave. What had just happened to her? Why were her hands trembling? She couldn't comprehend why her heart was racing. Did she hear him say, "Nice to finally meet you"? His voice was irresistibly attractive. Masculine, yet soft and appealing.

She was supposed to accompany Sonia and her friends to an Italian restaurant in Uptown that evening, but Serene had no desire to go anywhere. She could not see herself dressing for the occasion—or socializing for that matter. She doubted Sonia would have any explanation as to the feelings that had stirred inside her at the clinic that day. She was certain her friend would just dismiss them as inconsequential. It would be horrifying to have her friend think of her as susceptible and naïve. How could she tell her that she felt attracted to a total stranger? How could his pleasant voice have touched her so deeply? It was still echoing in her ears.

That evening, she walked miles around her small apartment, restive, a somberness wrenching in her heart. His stunning face would not leave her mind. High-density sentiments trapped deep inside her core suddenly felt buoyant and surfaced to the top. Feelings she had never experienced before jolted through her like an electric current.

*His smile.*

*His smell.*

*His voice.*

She opened the window in the living room and turned the fan on high. And, when she finally dropped herself on the couch, she unleashed her urge to cry.

# Chapter 6

Serene's second encounter with Mr. J. wasn't until two weeks later, on a Sunday afternoon. She had just returned to Mar Elias from her dreadful visit back home, and she was about to step into the shower to recover from the three-hour drive when she heard a knock on her apartment door.

"Sonia, could you please get the door? I just undressed," she called to her friend, wrapping herself with a towel.

Sonia had run errands for her friend and was in the kitchen working on her latest concoction she had promised to prepare for dinner.

A few minutes later, Sonia walked into the bedroom carrying a bouquet of flowers with both hands, a searching look drawn on her face. "Someone had this hand-delivered to you," she told her.

Serene took the bouquet and sat on the edge of her bed. The two dozen white roses accentuated with white freesias and white carnations looked beautiful.

"I'm deeply sorry for your loss. May you find peace and comfort in the difficult days to come," she read.

"Who is it from?" asked Sonia as she dropped herself on the bed next to her.

"Well, this is odd. It's signed A. J.," Serene said, turning her head to face Sonia, her eyes wide open. "He's truly mysterious, this guy!"

"When did you guys meet?"

"He had an appointment to see me at the clinic, but he had to cancel last minute. He stopped by to do it in person."

"Why did he cancel?"

"He had to leave town on business."

"Maybe he called the clinic to reschedule and was told you had to leave town and why," Sonia opined matter-of-factly. "He's just a nice guy."

Serene got up with the bouquet cradled in her arms and headed to the console table in the hallway to grab the vase. She then followed Sonia into the kitchen and sat at the table, unwrapping the bouquet. "Something about him. Something I cannot explain. Since his visit to the clinic, I cannot seem to get him out of my mind."

"Are you in love, my dear?"

Serene shook her head. "No, it's not that," she said, getting up to carry the flowers to the coffee table in the living room. "It's such a weird feeling though." She set the vase in the middle of the table, reached to smell the flowers again, and turned around to face her friend. "Did you ever meet people when, from the very first time you met, you wanted nothing to do with them? Just like that, for no real reason?"

"Yes, actually. Several times," Sonia responded, fixing her friend with a curious look.

"Well, this is similar. Only I'm strangely attracted to him. I want to get to know him. I sense something in him that's positive and inviting."

"Like what?"

"I wish I knew."

She went into the bathroom and stepped into the shower. As warm water ran down her shoulders, hot tears came to release her seething sorrow. Images from her trip home replayed in her head.

Serene had planned her first trip back home before she even left for Mar Elias. She was supposed to visit with her family last weekend to celebrate her twenty-seventh birthday. Kameel had called her the Wednesday before, urging her to make the trip as soon as possible. He said her father had slipped into a stroke-induced coma. A trip that was supposed to be a three-day weekend of fun turned out to be ten days of loss and grief.

When Serene arrived at her parents' house, the whole family had gathered to discuss and plan the days to come.

"Oh, Serene!" her aunt exclaimed mournfully as she opened the door for her. "Your father is leaving us!"

Serene hugged her aunt and darted into the family room where everybody had gathered. When she saw her mother, she was struck by how old and shrunken she looked. Everybody was happy to see her and eager to hear about her stay in Mar Elias.

Noura came running into the room and threw herself into her mother's open arms.

Serene held her and kissed her like there was no tomorrow, trying to satiate her longing for her daughter. Her aunt's husband and two sons, as well as her uncle and his family were also there. She was relieved to see the family gathered around her mother during yet another dark moment in her life. Tears of mourning for the loss of her brother had not yet had the chance to dry.

Kameel stopped by her parents' house later that evening. He looked well put together. He was wearing a nice suit that she did not recognize. His face looked rested but withdrawn, and his welcome to Serene was cold. It was obvious that things were no longer the same. Their relationship had not been at its best when she left, but, he was still her husband, the father of her child, the person whom she planned to live the rest of her life with.

Back at their house, she bathed Noura and sang her to sleep. She couldn't wait to be with Kameel, to tell him all about Mar Elias, but when she entered the room, he was already sound asleep, curled up on the edge of the bed with his back turned to her.

Serene could not sleep all night. He was only an arm's length away from her, but it felt a thousand leagues farther. Should she have never left? Could they have both tried harder? Was her depression the sole culprit—or could Kameel have been more supportive and understanding? How could she eradicate this uncertainty and the many others that were engulfing her? How could she squeeze them, beat them to death, flatten them under her feet so that she could breathe again?

Her heart was pounding. She couldn't fall asleep no matter how many sheep she counted. Her father was dying. How could life suddenly feel so short? She couldn't breathe deeply enough or quickly enough to steady her heartbeat. She had to get out of bed. She walked to the kitchen, gasping for air. She felt as though her lungs had collapsed on her.

**"I can't** breathe," she begs, looking to the anesthesiologist standing behind the delivery bed, cupping her head in his hands.

He looked straight down at her. "You're breathing just fine. You're doing great. Just try to relax."

**As Serene** stumbled into the kitchen that night, the same feeling revisited her. She grabbed a cup of cold water and sat at the kitchen table, drawing deep breaths. Several photo albums, including a couple from her wedding, were spread on the kitchen table. She was certain she had arranged those albums in the linen closet before she left for Mar Elias. She imagined Kameel sitting in the same chair every night, sipping on his favorite wine, and turning through them. What went through his mind? Did he miss her? Did he miss their dinners and evenings together? In these pictures, everybody looked happy, especially her brother. He was seventeen years old at her wedding. Every time the camera froze a glimpse of him, he was smiling. The difference between the two of them was that he was able to experience true happiness, whereas hers was always ephemeral, lacking any palpable depth. His death, compounded with her father's critical situation, felt insufferable, and every iota in her body ached for him.

His fate was sealed way too soon. It's strange how things happen in life. People went to wars, raced cars, and climbed mountains—looking death straight in the eye—yet death spared them. Her brother, on the other hand, the love and care of her parents, was taken without any warning. As she leafed through the albums on the kitchen table, a strange feeling seized her, and she suddenly felt drenched in sweat. She could feel something big and frightful lurking in her future. A premonition so overwhelming, she could not put it into words.

Ever since Serene and Kameel married, their lives were plagued with unfortunate events. The sudden death of her brother shattered her hopes and aspirations. Getting out of bed in the morning became trivial. Happiness seemed hollow and more unattainable than ever. *Why plan? We are so fragile, and so meaningless to this superpower that kneads us, tosses us in the air, and sits back to watch us fall and shatter into a million little pieces, mocking our stubbornness and resilience as we try to gather our strength and stand up again.*

Her brother was happy and full of life one day, helpless and dead the next.

"Come down. Food is ready," her mother had called out to him, one last time, as she finished cooking his favorite dish.

"Give me ten minutes, Mom. I'm dropping off my friend at his house down the road."

Four years later, her mother was still waiting.

One thing Serene knew for sure was that her mother and father died that day. Their minds were shattered. Their hopes and joys were shattered. Their family holidays and dinners were all shattered. Shattered beyond repair. He was their continuance, their avatar, and without him, they reached a dead-end. Their final shape had been assumed, and their verdict had been sealed. Nothing and no one could reshape them or help them rebound. They were fixed, calcified in time and place. Her father resorted to smoking and drinking, and her mother retreated to her room and her doom. Their house suffocated from despondency and staleness, from darkness and death.

Serene too was fixed in a state of extreme grief. She mourned the loss of her brother and also that of her mother and father. She was five years old when her brother was born. He was everything a child should be and more. He was happy. The one who woke up with happy dreams. With a joyful "Good morning." The one who challenged her father to a game of chess, brought friends home, and turned it into a fun playground. The one who told jokes, sang songs, and played sports. The one who chose what he wanted because he felt free to do so. The one who made Serene look and see, distracting her from her engrossment.

As a recompense for everybody's loss, Serene got pregnant, but nothing was the same anymore. Although her parents seemed happy with the news, it was a reluctant, reserved happiness. They no longer trusted life as fair. They had been wounded beyond repair. As for Serene, she was just doing what she had always done, following the "natural course of living." She had gone to college, gotten her degree, gotten married, and given birth all under the same banner. How splendid was her life when she lived it like she was supposed to—not like she wanted to? But what did she really want from life? Wasn't it to feel happy? Wasn't it to escape the mental and emotional shackles that made her struggle when others navigated instinctively?

*Neophyte Artists, Outstanding Arts* was the title of the art exhibition where she met Kameel. The convention center hosted the event once a year. It attracted hundreds of people with arts ranging from paintings to sculptures and ceramics. It was a fun and unassuming night to be out in the city. Even the streets and sidewalks surrounding the convention center were packed with artists displaying their work.

Sonia's mother, a painter herself, accompanied them to the show that day. Serene had always gravitated toward paintings of nature and animals, in particular those that displayed horses. Abstract art did not mean much to her.

"What a wonderful creature!" she heard someone whisper as she stood admiring a particular horse piece. "Imbued with vigor, yet extremely gentle," the same person continued.

Serene turned around to see the source of this soft voice. Behind her, she saw a man, not much taller than herself, with a handsome face. He smiled gently at her.

Later that night, as they waited in line at a popcorn kiosk, Serene ran into him again. He was conversing with a nearby group of people.

"This guy over there is fond of horses," she whispered into Sonia's ear, nudging her with the elbow.

Sonia stretched her neck, immediately turning around. "Which guy?"

"That one over there. He's the one with the white top," Serene responded, jutting her chin in his direction.

Sonia's face lit up. "Really! He's handsome too! He's looking in our direction!" At that, Sonia walked up to him. After a handshake, a few head nods, and some feather-light words, he walked back with her to meet Serene.

As they all sat down at a bar for a cold beer, Kameel kept stealing glances at Serene. He came across as a well-learned, unpretentious man with a straightforward and transparent mien. He asked for her number and quickly jotted his down on a napkin. The following day, he invited her to the movies. The day after, the two of them went horseback riding. He was Serene's first real boyfriend. Her life seemed to have finally ironed out its wrinkles, and she found herself enjoying the simple pleasures of life. Until her brother's car accident.

He crashed into a tree on the side of the road, two blocks away from home. How many times had they all walked by that pine tree or driven by it? Serene passed it again on her drive back home from Mar Elias. The pine tree still stood tall, unshaken by the accident.

On his way home from work that evening, her father saw the accident. He saw the totaled black car and the paramedics as they tried to pull the lifeless body of a young man out of the wreckage. Streaks of blood were trickling from under the car, like the evil fingers of a merciless death. He could taste blood in his mouth as he sat watching, motionless. That young man was his son. How could that be? It did not add up. It did not make sense. The whole thing was a mistake. There was a dinner waiting at home. A mother and a sister, a high school diploma, a graduation ceremony, a career, and a family. All were waiting for him. Too many promises to forsake.

Four years later, Serene and the whole family gathered at the same church. It was a beautiful and sunny spring day at her father's funeral. Her father's coffin was left open. She could see him sleeping in peace, buoyant above all that tried to sink him. Her brother's coffin, on the other hand, had been sealed tight. His destiny maliciously framed in a box. There was no peace in his death. On his day, heavy clouds had billowed and quaffed every hue of life from the sky.

Back in Mar Elias, she allowed her tears to flow freely as she stood in the shower. Scenes from her pained past were unfolding under her eyes. She had been pushing them down for the past ten days. She needed to be strong for her mother's and daughter's sake.

"Are you all right in there, Serene?" Sonia called from behind her bathroom door. "Food is ready!"

Serene finally turned off the water. She caught a glimpse of herself in the mirror as she stepped out of the shower. Her face was swollen, her eyes red. She felt famished and exhausted. She was looking forward to eating a quick dinner with Sonia so that she could make up for the sleepless nights of the past two weeks.

"Look at the beautiful shades of this twilight sky," Sonia said as Serene entered the kitchen.

Sonia was facing the kitchen window, a wineglass in her hand. "The view you have from your kitchen makes me want to cook all day."

Serene did not respond. She sat at the table, reached for a lettuce wrap her friend had just prepared, and took a bite.

Sonia grabbed the chair across from her. "Are you with me? How do you like the lettuce wrap?"

"I love it. Thank you."

"You have enough food in the fridge to last you a week. I spared you a couple trips to the market so you can focus on yourself."

"Thank you, Sonia. What would I do without you?" She reached across the table to touch her friend's hand. "Did I tell you my mom accepted Kameel's offer to move in with him and Noura?"

"That's awesome news. It'll be in everybody's interest."

"Yes, I know. It's good for her to be away from home for a while, and good for Noura as well, since Kameel is always traveling for work now."

"That should give you some peace of mind."

But how could Serene understand what that meant? After burying her father and returning to Mar Elias, she started mourning the loss of her brother all over again. She couldn't explain how his loss, four years ago, could overshadow her father's. Her brother's death was associated with something deeper. She couldn't get him out of her mind. His voice rang in her ears, and it made her turn her head on several occasions. She resorted to keeping the hallway light on at night, because at times, she could feel him hovering around her apartment. Her days became endless. Sleep became light and intermittent, despite her extreme exhaustion.

At work, she booked her schedule with back-to-back appointments. She signed up for extra hours at the hospital on the weekends. In the evening, she walked home exhausted, happy to grab any form of food from a nearby café before racing home. Although a good book had always been a reliable distractor, that too started to fail her. She could no longer concentrate on her reading. On nights she grew restless with her situation, she took long walks around town, mindless of where she was going or of the stark darkness outside.

"I brought you this magazine from the hospital's library. I thought you'd like to read it," Sonia said at lunch one day.

Serene took the magazine. On the cover was a full-length portrait with a caption: "A. J.—A Lifetime of Philanthropy." The magazine would land on the coffee table, in the living room of her apartment. She would leaf through it every now and then and read the article as if it were for the first time. He was portrayed as an influential man, a man of several nonprofit organizations, founder of the A Future for a Child and Trees for a Tree foundations, an environmentalist at the core, and a public speaker. He traveled the world, but he always came back to his home in Mar Elias.

# *Part 2*

Growing up is losing some illusions in order to acquire others.

—Virginia Woolf

# *Chapter 7*

R eflections

Who am I?
I am mind and soul.
I am all past.
I am all future.
I am an expression.
I am a word.

# *Chapter 8*

"The cruel punishment of life," my mother said every time she was reminded of the story of my birth. "All elements of nature conspired to mock me," she would passionately add.

A story I must have heard a thousand times over the course of my childhood. Everything about that day was gloomy. The skies had not cleared for a whole week. The earth was soggy, and the serpentine road to our village was so dangerous to drive that my father did not bother to head home from the city that evening, regardless of my mother's intuitive insistence that I was due any minute.

"As the contractions sliced through my inner core, the thunder roared through the dead silence of that evening, and lightning carved out the skies with magical laser beams."

She was always good at embellishing her stories.

I silently thanked my stars for being a boy. I could imagine my mother's screams, muffled by the sounds of raw nature gone wild. Even Nana Thabita agreed that the night was heavy. The roaring thunder resonated endlessly in her ears; she couldn't hear the interim silence. My brother Aslan, who was one year old at the time of my birth, would nod in agreement.

"Of course I remember. I remember how Mother almost died giving birth to you."

His delivery had gone "just as expected."

And so, the story of my birth found its way through many

conversations, under a wide range of contexts. My mother used it to define her heroic delivery, considering the absence of a doctor or that of my father by her side, almost boasting her physical strength as a testament to her genetic superiority. And while my brother used it to provoke me at times and intimidate at others, Nana Thabita knew how to lift me up and lighten my mood.

"You made it against all odds! You are a miracle!" she would say.

Nevertheless, the burden of my unfortunate birth weighed on me silently, and on impulse, I strove to please.

I was the good kid around the house. As Nana Thabita twirled endlessly around the kitchen, preparing family meals, I sat on a stool and read to her out of my storybooks. *A Thousand and One Nights* was by far her book of choice, and "Ali Baba and the Forty Thieves" was her favorite story. She never had much of a childhood herself, and she became forever a child on the inside. She fervently longed for magic and fun, and she filled her inner desire through her imagination, tales that allowed her to sail through the kitchen window to worlds she knew were physically unreachable to her. And I loved it, my effect over her, the way I made her laugh, close her eyes, and act the parts of the story, with a rolling pin for a dagger and a pot for a crown. She made me feel important. She listened to me when my mother was busy maintaining the social status of our house and my father the reputable status of his profession.

Nana Thabita was older than our house. My grandmother had adopted Nana into the family when Nana was fourteen years old, not as the daughter she longed to have, but as her help. Soon after Nana came into the family, my father was born. Nana became the only person my grandmother entrusted with her baby, and about thirty years later, she became a nana to my brother and me. Nana's devotion to the family had earned her my grandmother's unwavering trust, and so she became her confidante, and years later, the guiding force that made our house run smoothly. Although she did not read nor write, she was very smart, quick on her feet, and above all, wise. Her days were long, yet no one had ever heard her complain. The kindness in her eyes was an honest reflection of a heart of gold, beating to cater and care for everybody. She seemed to like everybody equally, respected everybody equally, and played dumb and deaf to any wrongdoings or arguments that arose around her.

It was my grandfather who built the house I grew up in and discovered this valley to start with. A young man of twenty-two, his father used to send him on trips, accompanied with two of his men, to trade horses. My grandfather loved nature and found it wonderful. His love for horses led him on weeklong journeys up and down the coast and into the rugged inland. He often took his trips off the beaten path in search of hidden, unadulterated lands.

That was how my grandfather chanced upon this beautiful valley. Situated between two mountain ranges stretching north to south, it was full of epic scenery and untamable wildlife. He discovered something different every time he came back to visit. The variety of birds inhabiting the land, each playing their own games and singing their own songs, kept him entertained for hours, and the earthy, invigorating aroma that filled the air left him spellbound. He knew from the moment he passed through this valley that it would be ideal for agriculture and farming. He set to buy as many lots of land as he could afford. Eventually, he built his family a huge estate that would keep distending until the last day of his life. He called this valley Crescent because the crescent moon was gloriously bathing in the river as he kneeled down to drink from its running water.

Our house occupied, by far, the best piece of land in the whole village. Perched on a hill, it had an all-around view of the valley and the mountains surrounding it. It was built of natural stone, cut by masons from the edges of the river, and carried on horseback uphill to the building site. There was nothing like it around. My grandfather's heart and mind were in developing the land into a haven of fruit and nut orchards, which became his lifelong endeavor. On the other hand, my grandmother's vision was for the house itself.

Her original plan was a two-story house. It had a well-insulated ground floor where the family could spend the harsh winter days. It was equipped with a chimney in every room and furnished with wool carpets and multilayered curtains. In addition, it had a second floor with vast windows to let in full summer light. However, both of my grandparents knew that their house would eventually expand in size since they both wished for a big family. Little did they know that my father would be their only child, a miracle child, for my grandmother could no longer get pregnant, regardless of the prescribed drugs or potions, visits to pilgrimage sites or temples, and computed additions or subtractions.

When time came for my father to find my mother, my grandmother took the endeavor upon herself, and she took it very seriously. My mother had to fit a list of requirements. She had to be from a prominent and wealthy family herself. She had to be pretty, tall, and strongly built, without any family predisposition to illnesses. So the questions piled up on my grandmother's list. My grandmother was not only adamant to meet the immediate family of the bride, but also all the aunts and uncles, grandparents, and cousins for the lineage to be established and cleared. That was how my mother was sifted out of the whole list, and that was how she had adamantly intended to remain.

Having both my brother and me solidified my mother's case over that of my grandmother's. Deep inside, however, Mother too had wished for many more children, but how could she wish for the impossible? Several elders, including her mother, had told her that the problem clearly lied in the family's male seed. It just was not as strong as one could hope for. So, how probable was it for her to have more than two successes, regardless of her robust makeup?

Contrary to my grandmother's belief, my mother thought the size of the house to be totally independent of the size of the family—and directly proportional to the family's social standing. So, the family house became her ongoing project of aggrandizement and

glorification, sedimenting along the way her felt sense of social betterment. The construction started at one point, and it did not have an
end date for many years. Her creativity was endless, and my father's
wallet was accordingly fat. Her incognito motive was to build around
what my grandmother had started in order to completely mask it and
turn it into a pit that is buried deep under a thick layer of colorful
and fatty mesocarp. She used the top floor as our main residence. The
exquisite marble and stone she picked while vacationing in Italy covered the floors and the columns that dispersed throughout the house
like gigantic chessmen. She personally designed each bathroom and
bathtub in the house and hired the best craftsmen to coat it all with
colorful mosaic stone.

Although our house was incredibly big, it was welcoming. It
blended engagingly with nature, and from almost every room, one
could see breathtaking views of the mountains and the valleys surrounding the house. The walls were covered with floor-to-ceiling beveled panels of tinted glass that diffracted light into millions of pieces
and hues, creating a continuum with the landscape outside. For that,
my father loved it. Just like his father before him, the more a house
indulged his craving for open air, the freer he felt. He loved the house
even more for the fact that it had kept my mother busy.

A very busy man himself, juggling between the family business
and his post as mayor, my father was barely home. He had built himself an office in the center of the village, on the main street, about
two kilometers away from our house. It was at this office where his
days in Crescent were spent. The majority of his business was not
conducted from Crescent, however. His trips to the city and abroad
were numerous. He always looked forward to his trips, for although
he loved Crescent, his persona was much bigger than the valley and
its inhabitants.

Growing up, my father had to attend school two towns away, for
Crescent did not have its own. He always dreaded riding in a horse
carriage on bumpy roads, especially early in the morning on a snowy

day, just to get to school. Not being studious, my father used to throw tantrums in the mornings, to which my grandmother turned a deaf ear. To her, school was necessary, and only fools dropped out. When my parents married and the prospect of children started to materialize, Father took it upon himself to establish a school in Crescent.

Since its inception, the school had enlivened Crescent and the surrounding area. Real estate as well as small businesses had assumed a new dimension, creating along with them new job opportunities. New merchants started settling in Crescent, and new families were introduced into the tight-knit community. Crescent was no longer a dead-end village, but a connecting town. For all those reasons, Father believed it to be more professional for a mayor to run his affairs from a business office and not out of his house, like his father before him.

Certain summer afternoons, Mother felt compelled to take us on an afternoon stroll through the streets of Crescent to visit the office. She made sure we always dressed up in slacks and shiny shoes for the occasion because "everybody on the street knows who we are." She always had a long summer dress herself, with white lace gloves and a lace umbrella to protect her fair skin from the afternoon sunlight. She kept a soft smile on her face, nodding her head to the left, and then to the right, as people hastened to greet us. Quite often, people mistook me for my brother and sought to shake my hand first, for although he was a year older than me, I was a few inches taller. Aslan did not appreciate being acknowledged second or having to straighten out the confusion. As a result, he resorted to walking several steps ahead of us, with his head lifted and his chin protruding, and made a habit of initiating the handshake himself.

Aslan's behavior felt obtruding, yet the pride that swept across my mother's face was undeniable. Her nostrils flared open, and a smile rippled the corner of her eyes at the sound of Aslan's voice introducing himself with his full name. He always cleared his throat and assumed a deep and manly voice when he spoke to adults. I was happier when he no longer walked by my side. He was always pushing me around, pinching me in the arm, and blaming me for things I did not do. He loved to see me get in trouble. Above all, he always found something to criticize about my looks and strove to abolish my self-esteem. Although it was his face that bore a rough adolescence, I never found it in my heart to make fun of him. Mother seemed blind to his evildoings, and when our arguments grew out of control, she reprimanded the two of us equally.

"Boys, your father is a very important man," she would say, pointing her finger to the huge sign hanging on the door of my father's office. "You can't be fighting like that in public."

The sign on my father's one-story office building read: "Jacob Jacob," in big font, and right below it in italics: "Mayor."

While walls erected around the house and gardens changed shape, the physical and social divide that separated our family from our neighbors became unbridgeable. Our skin color was a few shades lighter than that of the rest of the kids. Unlike most of the kids around us, we were not expected to work in the fields or tend to farm animals. In the summertime, we traveled around the world, but for the few days we were in Crescent, our time was well planned. Our horseback riding lessons were always in the morning when the sun was most pleasant. We then had tutors for every conceivable subject, from math, to piano and chess, to keep our "minds well lubricated over the course of the summer." An afternoon nap was also a part of the daily routine. Therefore, we were barely left with two hours in the afternoon for outdoor playtime. Knowing that we were still supposed to factor in a bath before we could sit at the dinner table, I hated to waste my time napping, and I made my showers quick. Aslan did not care to play outdoors, and so he took his nap very seriously and made his baths very lengthy.

Kids from all over town showed up to our house for outdoor play in the summer afternoons. They waited so patiently behind the gate for Aslan and me to emerge from the house, their thin fingers wrapped around its iron bars. It was always I, however, who ran out and unlatched that gate. The sight of them unfalteringly wrenched my stomach, and so did the gate's stone pillars, its intricate ironwork, and the "Jacob Estate" inscribed on a big plaque. I always thought that the gate imposed boastfully on all that lay on the other side. I never understood why Mother preferred the gate shut during the day. I loved my friends. They were always smiling. They laughed at my jokes. They were smart too, and they knew all about Crescent and nature. They knew the names of every tree and every animal.

Aslan usually walked out of the house much later, looking blasé and bored. None of the boys or girls really cared for him. Their bodies stiffened, and their voices hushed when he was around. He never shared his toys or bike with anyone. He mostly lingered around, listened to our conversations, and injected his venomous opinion whenever he felt like it. On the few occasions when he actually got into the game, his twisted rules made him come out on top. No one dared to argue, and the few times I did, his eyes bored into me as he hissed threatening remarks. I learned not to let his behavior bother me. It was the only time I could somewhat break away from his dominance, and I was not going to let him ruin it for me. I knew how much a bike ride around the gardens would mean to kids who had never owned one, so I strove to please. Seeing my friends happy brought happiness my way. The bruises on my shins and the scrapes on my elbows stood witness to time well spent.

Oftentimes, incidents or conversations from those afternoons resurfaced at the dinner table, twisted and exaggerated. Mother would look at me with unblinking eyes, as if I were a sad case.

"I really want you to have a good time," she would say with a gentle tone, "but please don't ever get too close to any of those kids. We need to keep the house lice-free."

I learned to accept her bias, and I did not let it get in my way.

*Let there be lice.*

In the evenings when Father was in town, our gates spread wide open, and families, mainly on foot and sometimes by car, flocked over.

Some came to discuss issues such as water rationing for agricultural purposes, grazing sites for cattle, business propositions, or whatever they thought my father's influence could help them iron out at the time. Most of the regular visitors were cousins, although it was impossible for me to keep track of how exactly we happened to be related to all of them. Regardless of the nature of their visit, everybody stayed for hours and left happy.

Throughout the evening, Nana Thabita would replenish serving trays with finger foods and desserts. Pots of tea boiled on the stove, and incense burned in every room. I would bring out my board games and play with the kids as we ate, watched television, and told stories. Aslan, however, never mixed with us and preferred to be with my father and the rest of the men on the other side of the room, joining in on their conversations. As to Mother, she always sat surrounded by the women and enjoyed the praise and gossip that came her way.

No family ever came empty-handed. Baskets of freshly harvested fruits and vegetables, or whatever the women baked fresh that day, would cover the kitchen table. What I liked the most were the handmade crafts my mother often received from neighbors and friends. There were handcrafted ornaments, hand-embroidered silk throws and shawls, and handmade candles of all scents and shapes. Mother was generous and always gave them a "little token of appreciation," a number of money notes sealed in an envelope. Father had a prefilled stack of those envelopes ready in his top desk drawer at home.

One summer night, I asked my mother to show me the gifts she had gotten as she was unpacking them and displaying them on the dining table.

"These are not gifts, idiot. These people bring them so that Mother will give them money," Aslan argued.

"No, they don't," I said, remembering their faces and how eager they were to please my mother. "They like us. And besides, Mother loves their crafts because they are all handmade. Do you know how long it takes them to come up with all this?"

"How can you be so sure of that? What do you think would happen if Mother just stopped paying them? Do you really think they'd keep bringing us gifts?"

That summer night, what followed was totally unexpected. With one slow and fluid gesture, Aslan swept the gifts off the table, sending them shattering to the floor. Aslan was seventeen years old that summer. I was sixteen.

"Why did you do that?" Mother asked with a tone that did not quite rise to the intensity of the moment.

"Well, because I wanted to," he replied with a spiteful voice, and then he turned around and walked away. "Besides, you weren't going to use them anyways, Mother, so why hoard them?"

"You can't just do that and walk away," I said, baffled by his malicious behavior.

I went down on my knees to gather the pieces.

Mother did the same.

"Was Aslan right, Mother? Do these people bring you gifts to get money in return?"

She did not answer. Her hands were collecting the pieces, but her thoughts were already somewhere beyond the room. Her face was no longer hers. How could these people not like my mother? It did not make sense, especially because she always talked about how deeply sincere and kind these people were.

# Chapter 9

It was an ordinary summer day when Dog disappeared.

"Good morning, Nana. What's for breakfast today?" I asked, skipping into the kitchen.

"Well, good morning to you, sunshine," she said. "Look what I got for you!" She held up what seemed to be a bigger-than-normal dark brown egg.

"It's an egg!" I said. "A huge one. Unless it's not a real egg. Nana, you know I don't like eggs!"

"Well, this is no ordinary egg, Adel. Inside it, there's a little magic. This one has not one, but two yolks."

"Well, that doesn't change the fact that it's an egg—or maybe two—which makes it even worse."

Nana laughed. I loved the way she laughed. Her whole body shook, and her belly danced.

"Your mom said any version of eggs, as long as you eat your eggs today. So, what should it be: an omelet, pancakes, or simply boiled eggs?"

"One of each," interrupted Aslan as he walked into the kitchen, stomping his way to the breakfast table.

Like usual, he fell clumsily into his chair, tilting it backward on its hind legs, and then swung it back and forth, each time dropping it loudly to the floor.

"And I'd like them today, not tomorrow. So, let's get going!" he said, eyeing Nana while tapping his knuckles on the table.

"Why do you have to be so mean?" I whispered to him as I took my seat at the table, skipping two chairs in between.

"Mind your own business, Mr. Good. And by the way, I should just call you chump from now on because that's what you really are. A true chump!"

So many times, I wished I could just punch him in the face and break his ugly nose. That morning, I came so close to doing just that. His verbal abuse had been more hateful as of late, its caustic effect settling in my stomach like a heavy rock. The two of us had gotten into so many fights, and every single time, he ended up hurting me physically. Although I towered over him by at least half a foot, and I confidently knew that I could knock him down in an instant, I just could not hurt him. It only took the slightest provocation to turn him mad. At times, he would grab my arms with his hands and bury his nails into my skin, his face burning with rage. I would walk away every single time with a new set of welts to add to my collection. I saw it all along. His fury spiraled from madness, and it was imperceptible to my parents and most people around me. His fury blinded him, but it opened my eyes to vexing nuances.

Nana was too wise to show any sign of discomfort at Aslan's unkind and rude behavior. That morning, she preferred to turn her face to the window and busy herself with pots and pans. His words had undeniably ached her deep inside. Her shoulders stooped, a subtle lassitude sweeping through her body. Just a moment ago, she was jubilant and full of energy. Aslan had always been impolite and unrepentant, for as far as I could remember, but not this bluntly, especially to Nana!

Nana brought the food to the table. My plate was simple. She had my double-yoked egg sunny-side up, with a sprinkle of cumin on top, chopped heirloom tomatoes and a piece of bread. To Aslan, however, she brought a whole tray with different plates on it. Exactly what he had asked her for, one of each. I thanked her for my breakfast. She nodded in my direction as she poured our fresh milk.

Aslan had already guzzled half of his food, digging his fork into all three of his dishes at the same time, before I even took a bite of mine. He had this annoying habit of humming while eating. I couldn't stand it, which he was very well aware of.

"Is this egg going to taste any different?" I shouted out to Nana as she stood at the sink, clearing away the mess the breakfast had left.

"It should taste just the same," she answered without turning around to look at me.

Suddenly, Aslan felt alarmed. He stopped humming.

"Why? What kind of egg is it?" His head was bent over his food, his eyes knotted with a frown. He looked up to stare maliciously at me.

"A special double-yoked egg," I volunteered teasingly.

"Why didn't I get one, Nana?" he asked, still staring at me.

"I only had one such egg. I found it this morning in the chicken coop. I'm sure there will be more of them soon," she responded with her back still turned to us.

"Will there?" he asked flicking his food.

He started humming again.

Once he finished eating, he leaned his body against the back of his chair and crossed his arms behind his head. He was watching Nana with squinting eyes. "How come I have never heard of such a thing?"

"Haven't heard of what?" asked Nana.

"The egg with two stupid yolks."

"Well, because it doesn't always happen. Very few chickens lay these eggs. Maybe you can ask your tutor to explain it scientifically to you. I think it's just like having twins."

"Does the chicken itself look different? Do you keep it in the main coop? What color is it?"

Nana turned around to look at him. Her face suddenly looking disturbed. She did not answer his questions; instead, she started filling the coffee pot with water.

I got up to take my plate to the sink, hoping to put an end to his endless and drilling conversation. Then I heard Dog bark.

Malec poked his head through the kitchen balcony door. "Spring water for the kitchen today, Nana?"

"Well, sure, Malec. We need four of the jars for now, please."

Malec came from a poor family that lived in a small house by the river, straight down the hill from our house. He lived with his mother and two sisters, Eeman and Mona. His father had recently passed away. His mother worked as a seamstress to support her three kids. Malec had taken it upon himself to help his mother put food on the table, picking up various summer jobs around town. Although Malec was a year older than me, he looked years younger. He had a small and frail figure. His skin was dark, and his face bore no sign of puberty. He had big brown eyes that lacked the luster of youth; instead, they were laden with a kind of fatigue that conspired heartlessly against his tender age. It was the fatigue of desolation, boredom, and hopelessness.

Nana had known Malec's family for years. Ever since his father died, Nana had done all she could to help him. She usually invited him into the kitchen and gave him breakfast before assigning him odd jobs for the day, but not today. Aslan's presence was imposing and distressing. So, she just sent Malec straight on his water mission. Nana had always kept fresh spring water in clay jars on the kitchen table. She preferred the taste of it to water from the tap. She did not pour the water into a cup to drink. Instead, she held the jar above her head and poured the water into her mouth. I had yet to master her drinking method.

"Malec, wait," I said. "I'm going with you. I have to talk to you." I wanted to go with him to the spring to help with the jars so that he did not have to make the trip twice. I had thought of doing that on the weekends when I did not have a riding lesson in the morning. Nana thought it was a good idea. I didn't want Aslan to know of my plan since he would undoubtedly make a big deal out of it. I knew he would tell Mother that I was helping Malec carry the jars of water from the spring, and the whole mission would indisputably come to an end.

"Talk about what?" Aslan asked as he stood up, flexed his wrists, and stretched his fingers.

"Nothing."

Aslan lingered for a few minutes around the kitchen and then walked away.

"Bye, Nana, and thank you for breakfast," I said, hugging her.

"Why can't he be nice like you?" she said. "Give this to Malec." She handed me a paper bag with a sandwich and three boiled eggs. "Be careful out there. It's snake season. And don't be late."

I went out the kitchen balcony door, down the long flight of stairs, and then out the back gate.

Malec was sitting on a rock, waiting for me, and Dog was lying on the ground right next to him. I loved Dog. A herding Canaan, he had been in Malec's family for as long as I could remember. He was friendly, loving, and very intelligent. His fur was the color of rich, golden honey. Upon seeing me, Dog's furry tail wagged happily, his almond-shaped eyes lighting up as he gracefully lifted his head. He pricked up his ears in anticipation.

"Why don't you just call him Honey?" I asked Malec for the millionth time as I petted him.

"Look at him. He's in heaven right now. Dog really likes you, Adel!" Malec had always been adamant that Dog was his name. That was what his father had always called him, and he did not intend to change it.

Malec's father had died a year ago. I remembered him very well. He was a gaunt man whose skin had been irreversibly tainted by the unrelenting summer sun. He was a goat herder, and Dog was his best and most useful companion. The two were inseparable around the clock. He held a crook in his right hand on which he rested the strain in his back. His movements were systematic. He could herd blindfolded, his eyes always set beyond the bushes and the ditches in his trail, beyond the farthest tree on the highest hill. He had been on the job for decades; he himself could not remember the exact number of years.

Malec's face brightened at the sight of the bag in my hand. I loved Malec. Most people thought he was simpleminded but not I. He was the kind of person who was always appreciative and obsequious. He threw the boiled eggs to Dog, unwrapped the sandwich, and took a big bite.

"Thank you," he said, covering his full mouth with his hand.

Dog barked for more.

"This is for you," Malec said as he handed me a small bag of wild berries.

I loved wild berries, but I never got to pick them myself.

We ran to the spring. Dog hovered around us in delight. Cold, pristine water poured out of a gash in the rock, about four centimeters wide on the side of the hill. The water streamed out of earth's belly at an arch, hitting the rocky ground a meter below with an eroding force and sending a colorful mist in the air. The stream flowed infallibly year-round. I put my cupped hands in it and splashed my face with its cold water. The whole village drank from that spring. It was a landmark around town, a meeting place for friends and families. Sometimes we had to line up and wait our turn. With its therapeutic sound and invigorating mist, this water diluted people's problems, brought out laughter, and lifted spirits.

We filled up the clay jars, two each, and headed back. Carrying those full jars uphill was a completely different experience. They felt callously heavy at two gallons each. Struggling with the heavy weight, Malec and I pushed on, counting our steps uphill. Those jars had no stoppers, and too much movement could empty out a lot of water.

"I've been walking up and down this hill for as long as I can remember," Malec said. His frail body looked even more shrunken with his back stooped and shoulders hunched. "I know the path so well I could walk it blindfolded, with its every bend and mudslide." He saw me looking at him and flashed a smile at me. His white teeth looked ghostly against his sunburnt face.

"Yet, it never gets easier on you, right?"

"It's tough. One slip of the foot could spill an entire jar."

We both knew very well that climbing the back of the hill, with its inherent ruggedness, was rewarding. We discovered charming scenic views as we stopped to rest along the way. The town below, the mountains surrounding it, and the endless skies were all set in a panoramic, breathtaking medley of shapes and colors. That summer, I came to revere the beauty of nature and our town. Even though I had always lived in that beautiful landscape, I had never paid attention to it.

As we approached the last bend, we stopped to catch our breath.

"This hill seems much shorter when you walk it with me," said Malec. He wiped the sweat off his face with the back of his sleeves.

"Where's Dog?" I asked, suddenly realizing he was not around.

"I don't know!"

A sudden fear electrified his body. He looked around frantically in all directions. Dog had never left Malec's side. He had become Malec's shadow just the same way he was a shadow to his father.

"Dog! Dog! Come here boy! Where are you?" He started shouting hysterically. He set the pitchers on the ground and took off downhill. His voice echoed off the mountains. I stood by the back gate for a while, hoping he would find him sauntering a few steps away, but Malec did not come back.

Malec did not show up at the kitchen door the next day, or the day after. He stopped showing up at our gate in the afternoons. I asked my friends about him, but no one had seen or heard from him for the past few days. I finally decided to go to his house to check on him. His sister Mona answered the door. Her shy smile disintegrated when I asked her about Malec.

"We don't see him all day. He leaves at the crack of dawn and doesn't come home until it's pitch-black. He goes looking for Dog."

"He hasn't found Dog yet?"

She shook her head.

"Can you tell him I need to see him? It's important. Please," I urged her, not knowing what else to say.

On the fourth morning, I saw Malec again. My heart skipped a beat at the sound of his voice.

"Spring water for the kitchen today, Nana?" he asked, his voice listless.

"Well, yes, Malec! Where have you been?"

"Looking for Dog, Nana."

"Well, did you find him?"

"Yes, Nana."

My heart jumped. I stood up to run to the kitchen door, feeling the joyful urge to scream.

Aslan said, "All in one piece?" He was sitting at the kitchen table waiting for his breakfast.

Nana and I looked at him bewildered, and then something fiendish happened. He broke out in a satanic laugh that froze me in place.

"What are you doing?" I yelled. "Why are you laughing like a maniac? What are you talking about?"

"Nothing. Isn't the word *nothing* your favorite answer?" He was pursing his lips and grinding his teeth. "Every time I ask you a question, you say, 'Nothing.' So here you have it. I'm talking about nothing."

That was the day when I realized he was insane, that something in him was beyond evil. I felt really scared. He must have scared Nana too. That time, she could not hide it. She stood aghast and speechless.

I looked at the door, but Malec was no longer there. I ran to the balcony, but he had already skipped down those treacherous steps and disappeared through the back gate.

# Chapter 10

Dog caused quite a stir in town. Not only because of his death, but also because of the way he died. His body was thrown in the fields about a kilometer south of Malec's house. What made the incident ominous was the fact that he was completely butchered. His ears were missing. His tail was cut off and left hanging on the branch of a nearby tree.

Dog's killing was a message of horror. It dominated conversations for weeks, both in our living room and all around town. The town had never witnessed such a cruelty before. The consensus was that it had to have been a stranger passing through because Dog was the whole town's pet. Everybody knew him and liked him.

I disagreed. A stranger did not kill Dog. Dog had strayed from Malec and me that morning without even a bark. And I worried about Malec because he abandoned his normal self and daily routines and disappeared for days. I sent him messages with his sisters, Mona and Eeman, urging him to come see me. I had so much to ask him.

His sisters worked in our downstairs kitchen during the summer. It was where the bulk of cooking took place. Nana had two permanent assistants helping her year-round. Even more joined in the summertime when they were needed. They were in charge of sorting out fruits and vegetables, sending some upstairs for Nana to cook and serve, and using the rest to make jams, pickles, and dried foods, our supplies for wintertime. There were barrels of dried peas and beans, and canning jars of all shapes and colors. All were labeled and stored neatly. Nana distributed whatever produce was left over to needy families. It was there where olives were pressed and pine nuts and walnuts were hulled for as long as I could remember.

I started feeling apprehensive over the cruelty and unfairness of what had happened to Dog. His story gave me nightmares. I would wake up in the middle of the night with Malec's frantic cries for Dog echoing in my head. I tried to share my concern with Mother one morning.

"I don't know who could have killed Dog, Adel. Strangers pass through our town every single day," she answered.

"Why can't Father hire someone to look into the crime?"

"You can't hire someone to look into the death of a dog."

"It was a crime, Mother. He was mutilated. Just imagine his suffering."

"It's just an animal, Adel. Just let it go. Please!"

"Well, Marjana is an animal," I replied. "What would happen if someone did the same thing to Marjana?"

"He's not going to kill Marjana—there is no way he would."

It seemed, at that moment, that my mother was taken aback by her own words. She squinted her eyes to a slit, bit her lower lip, and frantically scratched the side of her face. She then turned around and walked away.

"Who is he, Mother? How can you be so sure he was not on a killing spree?" I shouted.

"I don't know what I'm saying anymore," she said, shaking her head defensively. "Go have your breakfast and get on with your day at once." She disappeared into the hallway, but I knew she was hiding something from me.

"I'm going to Father's office," I shouted from behind her bedroom door.

She did not respond.

I went to the kitchen. Aslan was not there. I kissed Nana good morning.

"I'll be back for breakfast," I assured her as I grabbed a handful of dried figs off the table, went out the kitchen door, down the flight of stairs, and ran straight to the stable.

The stable was as old as the house. It was a freestanding rectangular structure with a vault ceiling, completely made of natural stone carried from the river. A total of twelve small windows ran along the walls, enough to catch ample sunlight. It was partitioned into ten stalls running along each of its walls, accommodating a total of twenty horses and mules.

As I approached the stable, I could see Marjana's beautiful head sticking out of the window. Bathed in morning sunshine, her color assumed a stunning dark coral shade, hence her name Marjana, the Arabic word for *coral*. I knew her name the moment I saw her. She was unmistakably the most beautiful horse I had ever seen. A white stripe of hair ran down her face, forming a diamond shape over the jibbah, narrowing between her large eyes and widening again as it descended over her nostrils. Her markings endowed her with nobility. I shoved my face in her warm neck and ran my fingers through her silky mane.

"Good morning, Marjana," I whispered. "Let's go for a ride."

Marjana loved it when I took her on a ride. Her gentle disposition detached me from my worries and tied me closer to nature. She was my parents' gift to me for my sixteenth birthday.

"She's an Arabian with incredible energy and unmatchable intelligence," Father said as he handed me the halter for the first time.

Although I had only had her for two months, it felt like she had always been a part of my life.

That morning, I rode Marjana down the hill to the river. I wanted to go to Father's office. There were so many nagging questions I needed him to answer, but I decided to stop by Malec's house first. Malec's house looked even smaller from atop Marjana. It looked sunken. The cowshed that stood next to the house was empty and derelict except for a few chickens sauntering around. A huge and ancient cedar tree overshadowed the house with its far-reaching branches, dwarfing the structure and accentuating its flimsiness. The front door's glass panels had cracks running through them.

I knocked on the door and called out Malec's name, but no one answered. So, I set off down the road to Father's office, thinking I would try again on the way back. I could not remember if I had ever visited the office so early in the day. When I got to the building, there were about ten people gathered outside the front door. They were engaged in what looked like a solemn conversation, pained expressions weighing on their faces as they drew heavily on their cigarettes. Upon seeing me approach, they elbowed each other and stopped their conversation altogether. I nodded in their direction and dismounted Marjana. I tethered her to a tree and entered through the double door. The waiting room was congested with even more people, the same weary and morose look drawn on their faces. Though some were sitting, the majority was standing, gesticulating, nodding agreeably, or nudging refutably. Their muffled voices stopped as they saw me enter the reception area.

"I'll let you know when your father is ready to see you," the receptionist said. "Help yourself to some refreshments."

I did not realize how thirsty I was. The dried figs were so sweet they made my mouth dry and sticky. I poured myself a cup of cold lemonade.

"What's the matter with all these people? What are they all here for?" I asked the receptionist, whispering as I leaned over her desk.

"Your father's job is to listen to people's concerns and help them in every way he can," she answered. "They're worried about the animal killings that have been taking place in Crescent."

"You mean Dog?" I asked, startled.

"Very similar, Adel," she said. "Since then, another dog has been found mutilated. And there's talk of other animals too."

I left the building a half hour later. At one point, Father had stepped out of his office and sternly looked around the waiting room. His eyes caught sight of me, but they never lingered, and only after they moved on did a quizzical look wash over his face. I waved at him, thinking he might not have noticed me, but his eyes never circled back my way. He called up his next visitor and disappeared again behind closed doors. I wasn't going to wait my turn, so I got up and rode back to Malec's house. His house looked just as empty. I dismounted Marjana and knocked on the door. The inlaid glass panel rattled under my knuckles.

His mother opened the door and reluctantly invited me in. I had never been inside Malec's house. Once inside, I could see the entire house, without even turning my head. A two-dimensional representation, lacking any hidden depths, amplified the simplicity of their living situation. The central room had a shabby sofa and a ragged chair, probably as old as the house itself. A table was pushed back against the wall. On it sat an old sewing machine, cut-out papers, and several pieces of colored fabric.

A door to the right gave way to a tiny kitchen. Two metal pots stood on a shelf above the sink. The pots had long lost their even shape and smooth appearance. Their hammered surfaces reflected the surroundings in puzzle pieces. A puzzle with so many pieces gone missing, it underscored the salient perforations gnawing at the backbone of this structure. A ramshackle structure. Nana would not even fit in that kitchen.

A door to the left led to what appeared to be the bedroom, but there were no beds in that bedroom. A distorted mirror hung on the wall across from the window, contorting all proportions surrounding it, and withstanding courageously all that was real. Four straw mats stood rolled up against the wall.

I had always known that Malec's family was poor, but I had never imagined what that really meant. *How could people live on so little?*

"I'm worried about him, Adel. I'm working very hard at supporting my children on my own. We went through bereavement for a long time after the loss of my husband. It was hard carrying the family through such intense despair." She tried to swallow her tears. "How can I save Malec from his misery now? Dog was his companion, the only friend he ever had."

I wanted to jump and say that I considered myself to be Malec's friend, but words wouldn't come out. I wanted to say that I was as distraught as Malec was by the loss of Dog. It felt trivial to compare my loss and grief to that of the person standing across from me, who was no more than the straw mat, flattened and rolled up, supporting her back to a wall so full of cracks it could crumble with the next storm. Disheartened, I turned around and left.

That evening of my sixteenth summer, something different happened at our house. Only a few people showed up in our living room for evening tea. My mother looked worried, and my father seemed tense.

As I was walking to my room to ready myself for the evening, I caught a glimpse of Father heading down the hall and into Aslan's room. He half-closed the door behind him. I could only see his back, his body completely overshadowing Aslan's. While Father and I could almost see eye to eye, Aslan was about fifteen centimeters shorter. Aslan's facial and body features were more like those on my mother's side of the family. I could tell that the conversation was not pleasant, and Father's arms were gesticulating in all directions.

Later that evening, Aslan emerged from his room looking calm and confident. He was wearing a suit. I didn't understand how he could be so guiltless and shameless in the face of Father's indignation. We never had to dress up in a suit for the evenings; usually only long slacks and a dress shirt would cut it, but there he was nodding to people with a smile on his face. Charming. Slyly charming. Even hypocritical because I knew the contempt he held for my parents' visitors. I could read his body language very well. He was shaking hands with his arm fully extended to maintain a good distance between himself and others. He looked grandiose, especially when he was not standing right next to Father. That was why he stood on the other side of the room, splitting space in two, measuring his stature to that of our father and counterpoising his high standing. He looked arrogant. His eyes were piercing. I did not like the way he looked at me. I did not like his hair or his smile. His tie was too tight around his neck, which made his chubby face look even chubbier.

"What are you looking at me for, chump? Go play with the kids."

The next morning, Aslan walked into the kitchen freshly shaven, dressed up in a full suit with a blazer and a tie.

"Did you sleep wearing your suit?" I asked teasingly.

"What's hurting you, chump? Are you jealous?" An eerie smile distorted one side of his face.

I instantly regretted teasing him. I knew how insidious he could be. He would make me pay for it sooner rather than later.

"Starting today, I'm officially being trained to run the family business. And when I do end up running the family business, things will be so different. Things that you, chump, won't be able to wrap your head around."

Things had already long been on a different road. I could tell that Father's business was starting to assume a new dimension. Recent conversations seemed to have shifted their focus from agriculture to construction materials, contractors, equipment manufacturers and suppliers, words I had never before heard in our living room.

The deal was that Aslan would start shadowing my father at the office three times a week until the end of the summer. I was actually relieved that he would be out of the house since it gave me more freedom to be myself and not have to worry about him judging and threatening me. I could maybe even invite a few friends into the house to watch movies in the afternoons or allow some to ride around on Marjana. And maybe summer would be back to normal, and the friends who had stopped showing up since Dog disappeared would come back again. I read two chapters of *A Thousand and One Nights* to Nana that morning.

"What happened to the double-yoked eggs, Nana?" I asked as I brought my plate to the sink.

She sighed. "She stopped laying them."

"She can do that?"

"She can do whatever she wants—they're her eggs!" She took my plate, poured soap on it, and started washing it.

"Thank you for the delicious breakfast," I said.

I always knew where to find Nana when I needed her. I stopped for a moment to watch her methodical movements around the kitchen before hurrying on with my chores. My days suddenly felt short.

# Chapter 11

Summer finally started to feel like summer to me. The foggy atmosphere engulfing our house as of late had at last dissipated. I could breathe again. I was much happier on Mondays, Wednesdays, and Fridays when Aslan left in the morning and didn't come back until the evening. The best of all was that his daily routine no longer overlapped with mine, even on Tuesdays and Thursdays, when he did not go to the office. While I still had my riding lessons in the morning, he had his "special" tutoring lessons, which caused our activities to diverge for the rest of the day. That additional hour of tutoring in the morning had also shortened his outdoor playtime, and he, at times, skipped it altogether. My parents must have planned it that way. It was too good to be true.

"What's this special tutoring lesson in?" I asked him once, curious about what he was learning behind closed doors.

"None of your business," he said. "Why don't you go play with your stupid friends? Oh! Silly me! You wouldn't know your friends are stupid because you're just like them," he replied with a smile that clashed with his words.

His "special" tutor was not local, and he did not show up with books in his hands. He was too serious for a summer tutor, always wearing a suit. He looked funny, his slacks a couple of inches shorter than standard, and the color of his bow tie was always obnoxiously bright. He carried his car keys and a folder with a pen attached to it in one hand, and in the other, he held what looked like a small radio or tape recorder. He looked at me with penetrating eyes that seemed to be digging layers beneath my skin. I tried to avoid his eye contact completely. He met with my mother in the main living room for about fifteen minutes after each lesson. He did all the talking, his eyes barely blinking, and his voice barely audible.

About a week into the new routine, Aslan's demeanor around the house began to change. Since his riding lesson started when mine ended, our paths crossed daily at the stable. Although he had been told time and time again that his horse was well trained, he had always felt the need to do his own training. Surprisingly, his attitude toward his horse also changed as of late. Aslan no longer rode his horse like a war tank. He no longer pulled on his collar and shouted, "Down!" to wake the whole neighborhood, along with the dead. He stopped whipping him ferociously and kicking him at the legs, forcing his knees to buckle down, as he eventually fell over. He even stopped using the harsh bit he had personally designed for him.

I always felt sorry for Aslan's horse. He never gave him a real name, and he didn't allow anyone to call him by one. "He's a confused animal, acting most of the time like a mule, why does he need a name?" he would argue.

Marjana was a much happier horse. She had a calm, friendly look in her eyes. While she was always alert and ready to cooperate, Aslan's horse always seemed reluctant and nervous. He held his head tensely while grinding his teeth; he stall-walked, and barely ate. I had brought the issue to my parents' attention several times in the past, but my words always fell on deaf ears. Maybe my parents finally realized the severity of the situation since the veterinarian was called in for an urgent visit to check on Aslan's horse.

Another thing I realized was that Aslan faded somewhat into the background. His mind seemed preoccupied, and he was noticing me less. I began seeking Malec again. I wanted to prove to him that he was my friend. We went back to the habit of fetching water from the spring, and I gradually started seeing a smile on his face. We stopped taking the back road to the spring, for although it was shorter, our driveway was an easier way uphill. With Malec, I discovered the joy of giving. I gave him toys and books. I gave him shirts and pants. I found reasons to give him several pre-sealed envelopes I had snuck out of Father's top desk drawer. My mother did not seem to notice the missing envelopes, and if she did, she never asked.

"With this money, you should eventually be able to buy the best herding dog ever," I told him. "You could also buy him a kennel."

"I can almost buy a horse with this money," he said with a chuckle. "Besides, why should I buy a kennel? I can build one myself."

New faces began to emerge in the afternoons. Even Mona and Eeman started to show up. With Aslan not in the picture, I was playing freely and screaming freely. I no longer had to witness his belligerence on the playground.

Although we all went to the same school, it was almost impossible to intermingle with most of the town kids after school ended. Our lunch break was only half an hour long, which was barely long enough to eat lunch. Besides, our driver always picked us up right when school ended and brought us straight home. The school did not have any organized after-school sport or activity, and we were not expected to walk home like all the other kids in town.

Aslan, however, did leave school on a whim several times, not bothered with the consequences of his impulsive behavior, claiming school was not teaching him anything interesting. No one knew where he went or what he was doing. He would disappear for hours before heading home.

"What do you do all day at home?" Mona asked me one afternoon.

Mona was my age. She was a year younger than Malec and two years younger than Eeman. I found her graceful and very attractive. Her silky, shoulder-length hair gently hugged her beautiful face, and her broad cheekbones highlighted her delicate chin.

"My schedule is actually always full. Leave it to Mother to know how to keep me busy."

She laughed. Her eyes were sweet and full of expression. I had caught her staring at me several times, and every time our eyes met, she hit me with a warm, captivating smile. Until my heart leapt unexpectedly one afternoon. Maybe her eyes caught me by surprise or maybe I finally sank in their charm. Her image of me was a good one. I saw its reflection in her gaze and in her body language. I felt happy when she was around.

"I've been thinking lately that maybe we could put on a show for the town," she said one day.

"What kind of a show?" I asked curiously.

"A play, maybe. We can pick a few friends—you can actually pick them yourself if you prefer—form a cast, and put together an acting show for the town."

I could hear the excitement in her voice.

"Brilliant idea!" I exclaimed. "I'm bored of the games we've been playing anyways. Do you want to start tomorrow?"

Her face lit up. "You mean it?"

"Of course I do. We should first pick the play and then worry about the cast. Don't you think?"

She stood staring at me. "Let's do it then," she replied.

That day, it took me a long time to fall asleep. The night started off pleasant and light. I lay in my bed in complete darkness, windows wide open, the air cool and crisp, but I could not unwind. I got up and walked around the room, only to lie back down, more awake than before. My mind was spinning. I was finally discovering the town I had been born in and had lived in since my birth. The town of Crescent had never felt so real and exciting. I finally came to realize that summers could be a lot of fun just spending time with my friends. Our family had always traveled in the summer. "Let's explore the world," my mother would say. *Shouldn't we explore our own town first?*

I was glad we ended up staying in Crescent that summer. Father had started an "exciting" new business that demanded his undivided attention and his physical presence. "Rock excavation," I heard him mention over and over. It had something to do with blasting and drilling. I was getting a mixed feeling about the subject of rock excavation. What's the harm in drilling rock? Father wasn't the type to harm anyone, yet I could sense resistance to the idea, even from my father's closest advisors and friends.

The chirping of crickets outside my window was getting louder and louder as I lay in bed, until the sound filled my head. It seemed that my heartbeat had synchronized with their chirping. What did the teacher call it? Stridulation? It had to do with rubbing wings and emitting sounds, singing sounds, to attract mates. Those wings must move very fast for sounds to emerge. Hundreds of times per minute. It was dizzying to watch them beat. It was straining to try to count their beats per minute. *At least the crickets have figured out how to attract their mates. I have yet to figure out how to attract Mona.* I liked her a lot. I needed to tell her how I felt. I needed to think of a play for our project. One that would impress her. I could see her walking up to me, an intent gaze in her eyes. I could feel her breath on my skin. Her hair brushed against my cheek. Warmth was radiating from her body. Then I felt her lips touch mine. Her eyes were closed, but the second mine did, they popped right back open. I was still sleeping in my bed. I must have dozed off. I touched my lips. My heart was beating faster than the chirping. I sat up to catch my breath.

I tried to keep my distance from Mona the following afternoon. For some reason, I could not find the courage to approach her after dreaming of kissing her the night before.

"So, Adel, do you have any recommendations for the play?" she approached me as I stood with the guys, trying to fire rocks with a slingshot.

We had each designed our own slingshot, and we were testing whose creation proved better at reaching an empty soda can on a wall. I had made mine with a Y-shaped branch and a thick rubber band.

"Well, shouldn't we establish what genre we want to consider first?" I replied, avoiding looking at her by aiming at the can with my slingshot.

"I thought about it last night. I think comedy will be fun and good for all ages. What do you think?" She was standing close to me, too close actually. She was looking over my shoulder, focusing with me on the target. Did she really believe I could ever say no to anything she suggested?

"I think comedy is a great idea," I replied.

"Why don't you go for it already?" asked one of the boys.

Reluctantly, I fired. The rock came up short of the can by a couple of feet. I did not realize I had been standing there for a while, aiming at the can on the wall.

I turned and faced her.

She smiled. "What do you think of Molière?"

"I think he was an excellent playwright. All I read though is *The Imaginary Invalid,* the one Mr. Joseph had us read in class last year. Have you read more of his plays?"

"I read several of his plays. They are all funny!"

"Which of his comedies did you like most?" I asked.

"I prefer *The Miser* out of all his plays," she replied. "I still have the book if you'd like to borrow it. Mr. Joseph lent it to me, along with several other of Molière's plays, to read over the summer."

"I'd love to," I admitted. "Can I get it today? I like to start reading it so we can get going."

She laughed gently. "I'll bring it with me tomorrow morning when I come to work in the kitchen downstairs. Why don't you stop by and pick it up?"

And so I did.

I sought her in the downstairs kitchen. From yards away, the roasting of chicken and lamb intoxicated the air. The smell never failed to make my stomach bubble with hunger. Although the downstairs kitchen was not the main kitchen of the house, it was sizeable and fully equipped. Shiny copper pots and pans of all sizes stood neatly on the shelves. A wall-to-wall kitchen cabinet housed enough serving plates and utensils to accommodate my parents' lavish holiday dinners. In one of the corners stood a high-domed wood-fired oven. It was built of firebricks and connected to a chimney to pass away the smoke. The smoke chamber and the flue, all laid in beautiful multicolored natural stone, radiated welcoming heat and color from the blazing fire inside. I loved the smell of burning wood. Folk music from the radio was playing on high. Happiness and harmony floated in the air as conversations carried in all directions. I thought of Nana and how efficient and dedicated she was, taking care of the family upstairs while overlooking this operation downstairs.

A huge central table was boasting heaps of fruits and vegetables that Mona and Eeman were busy sorting. Mona's hair was tied to the back with a scarf, exposing her delicate neck. Her face was red from the heat of the oven, and her forehead sparked with a few trickles of sweat. She looked like a morning flower kissed with sunshine and drizzled with morning dew. I walked up to her.

"Oh! Hi," she said. She looked surprised to see me.

Did she not think I would follow up on my promise? "I came to get the book. Did you remember to bring it?"

"Yes, I did." She hurried to the sink to wash her hands. She dried them with her apron and then went to the bench by the window where she opened a fabric bag. She pulled out the book. "Here you go," she said with a sincere smile. "You can finish it in one day. It's a page-turner."

And so I did.

I went home and buried myself in the book. I must have read for five hours.

"I can see why you picked this play," I told her when she came over to hang out that afternoon. "I have a feeling the town will love it!"

She was untangling a jump rope. She put it down and looked at me with a glint of delight in her eyes.

"I think Molière's approach at using satire to condemn greed is very effective. It's actually captivating," I proclaimed, so sure of myself.

"It sure drives the message home," she added. She put down the jump rope and slipped her hands into the pockets of her denim. "A seventeenth-century satire of greed. It was 1668 when it was performed for the first time. Did you know Molière played the role of the miser, Harpagon?"

"I didn't know that."

"It's even said that the two personalities had several characteristics in common."

I followed her as she started walking. "How so?" I asked.

"Some argued that Molière was parsimonious himself. Also, Molière was married to an actress who was half his age. The two were having marital problems at the time of the play. And now that you've read the play, you should know that Harpagon wanted to marry Marianne, who not only was half his age but also in love with his son Cléante."

I stopped walking and turned to face her. She did the same. I had never stood facing her so close before. She smelled of roses. We were standing under the oak tree. A fading beam of sunlight had somehow escaped the staggered deep green leaves of the branches and settled on her face. A sublime light resting on a sublime face. Everything about her impressed me.

"How do you know all this?"

Her lips trembled slightly. She looked up, distracting herself with a bird perched on a branch above us.

"I borrow books from Mr. Joseph."

She looked at me again. Our eyes locked for a few seconds, carrying my mind a light-year away. She did not smile. She timidly tucked her hair behind her ear, turned around, and started walking back toward the other kids.

"You can do the same, you know," she said as I followed her. "You can go to Mr. Joseph and borrow as many books as you want. Several students have gone to him for books already."

She picked up her pace.

"Did you know he borrows the books himself from a public library about ten kilometers south of Crescent?" she asked.

"No, I didn't."

"I wish we had a library at our school—or anywhere else in this town," she added.

"Don't you love the smell of libraries and bookstores, the smell of new paper?" I asked.

She shrugged. "How would I know? I never smelled a library or a bookstore before," she replied, sounding solemn.

"Can I play the role of Harpagon?"

"Of course you can," she said, smiling all over again.

"Which character did you like the most?" I asked.

"The most sensible of them all is Élise, the daughter of Harpagon. She is animated by her love for Valère and her wish to marry him, and is so keen on making her father accept him," she said. "But still, she's my second choice."

"Who then?"

"Cléante, of course. Unless you think we shouldn't cross genders."

"Cléante? Harpagon's son?" I asked, intrigued by her choice.

"Well, Cléante is the most passionate character of them all. As you read, Cléante and his father are rivals in love for Marianne. While Cléante really loves Marianne and tries to borrow money to help her provide for her sick mother, his father is looking for ways to benefit monetarily from marrying her. Ultimately, Cléante risks disinheritance from his father's wealth and makes it clear that love is stronger than money."

"So, you really believe love is stronger than money?"

"No doubt," she said.

"And you don't care that he's a boy?"

"It's all in the character—not the gender."

And she smiled.

# Chapter 12

For the remainder of that summer, there was not one day when Mona and I did not meet to work on the play. Sometimes she came over to my house after her kitchen chores were finished, but mostly, it was I who went to her house in the afternoons. The simplicity and fluidity of her life allowed a sense of ease and satisfaction to seep into mine. Her contentment intoxicated me. I experienced humility. I discovered love and harmony. I saw the simplicity in happiness and the happiness in simplicity. And I was drawn to her house. It became the light, and I was a desperate heliotrope.

As I started to venture into town, I became acquainted with new ways of life. I got to know more people, and I witnessed a side to their social mingling that somehow had never made it uphill, onto our driveway, and through our gates. Houses left their doors wide open. Everybody shared with everybody.

"You're Adel, right? You're a good boy," people said when they saw me.

I was never asked about my brother or my parents. Conversations stopped after the introduction, a handshake, and a few nods.

Outside our walls, the town had a completely different attitude. Faces looked anxious and overwrought. The new rock excavation project that my father was trying to promote was consuming people's minds and exhausting all conversations. It was clearly igniting fears and concerns. The excavation site had already been chosen. Young men from Crescent and surrounding towns were being recruited to work on the project. Malec was among the recruits. I stopped seeing him altogether.

At Mona's house, I knew what to expect. There was a sense of sameness that was the ground for their unity as a family and the solidarity of their principles. Mona's mother was always in the far end of the room, hammering at her sewing machine, seldom realizing my presence. Piteously dressed in threadbare clothes, she tailored new and crisp cloths into dresses, shirts, and other pieces for town customers. Although she was around my mother's age, she looked worn out, encumbered by years of onerous duties and pulverized by poverty. Completely absorbed by her work and driven by destitution, her right foot pounded at the machine's pedal, at times slowly, but mostly with a nervous cadence. The sound of that pedal became our metronome. Our conversations in the adjacent room undulated to its tempo.

I spent the afternoons with Mona sitting on the straw mat, working out the details of the play, and messing around. At times, it was a struggle to focus on the play and not on her body next to mine—and her breath brushing against my face. Eeman joined us every now and then to go over her part, which was Élise, Harpagon's daughter, but she could not spend too much time with us since she was in charge of the household chores and cooking dinner for her family. It was mainly Mona and I who worked on establishing every line to be memorized and recited, every gesture, and every expression. We agreed on which scenes to play and which we could totally omit. I felt in charge. I became creative.

Eeman was pretty too. She was a few centimeters taller than Mona, with slightly darker skin, dark brown hair, and big brown eyes. Although two years Mona's senior, she looked much older. She had just graduated from high school, but I had never heard her talk about college. A residual somberness veiled her face. She shared her mother's seriousness; it was as if it helped alleviate her mother's burden. She rarely smiled, and when she did, it did not wrinkle her weary eyes. Eeman's cooking used to unfalteringly fill the house with an appetizing smell. It consisted mainly of fresh vegetables and legumes. Every single time they invited me to have dinner with them, and every single time, I had to turn down the offer. I was always expected home for dinner.

One afternoon, I was rehearsing Harpagon's famous monologue, acting crazy and distressed, since Harpagon had just discovered that his money was stolen. I was acting the role, walking aimlessly around the room and screaming in despair:

> Thieves! Thieves! Assassins! Murder! Justice, just heavens! I am undone; I am murdered; they have cut my throat; they have stolen my money! Who can it be? What has become of him? Where is he? Where is he hiding himself? What shall I do to find him? Where shall I run? Where shall I not run? Is he not here? Who is this? Stop!

And then to myself, taking hold of my own arm:

> Give me back my money, wretch ... Ah! ... it is myself!

I fell to the floor laughing hysterically, as Mona and Eeman fell beside me, cheering and clapping their hands.

And then we heard it. The sound of a loud call bell. Mona and Eeman looked at each other and gasped. They got up hurriedly and raced to the door, with me in tow, curious to see what was going on. It was Mr. Ramsey's wagon. Tall, thin, and dark-skinned, Mr. Ramsey was a peddler. He roamed around nearby towns, selling articles he deemed essential to town folks. A donkey pulled his wagon, which jingled as he led it across the cobblestoned streets. The wagon was always overflowing with rolls of fabric, hats, shoes, accessories, pots and pans, and several odds and ends. Although small shops had sprouted here and there around Crescent, his stuff was cheaper. His wagon incited a sense of wonderment in children and curiosity in adults. Mr. Ramsey's call bell had proved, over the course of that summer, to be a good example of Pavlov's classical conditioning theory on reflex responses. I started to react to its sound just like Mona and Eeman did: a gasp followed by a race to the door.

It was in the shade of the cedar, right outside Mona's house, where Mr. Ramsey always stationed his wagon. He would ring his bell and wait for the flocks to arrive. He stood surrounded by grown-ups and kids alike, all reaching over each other to touch this or feel that. He stood alert, his eyes on his merchandise, talking with some and negotiating with others. He was a man on the move, a messenger from towns beyond. Along with his merchandise, he always carried a story or two about who was marrying whom, who had passed away, and who had bought what from him. All one needed to do was ask, and he gladly provided the answers. Moreover, people could express their need for any item and be sure Mr. Ramsey would have it on his next visit to town.

"Say, Mr. Ramsey, we're planning an open-air stage comedy for the whole family. We don't have a set date yet, but we're shooting for a weekend next month. Will you be able to spread the word to neighboring towns?" I asked on one of his visits.

Mona's face brightened, and her jaw dropped. "Brilliant idea," she shouted as she started jumping.

Did she know that her enthusiasm was my inspiration?

"We'll have food and drinks for everybody. It'll be a splendid night out!" I added, so sure of myself.

"Am I invited?" asked Mr. Ramsey smiling, unveiling a set of crooked teeth.

"Everybody is. The play isn't ready yet though, Mr. Ramsey. We'll hopefully give you a date on your next visit. In the meantime, you can start spreading the word," Mona interjected fervently. She grabbed my hand and pulled me back into the house. "Let's go! We have a lot of work to do."

At times, Mona and I took the play to a clearing by the river. We rode Marjana up and down its banks. I felt emboldened by her familiarity with the terrain, and I allowed her to navigate us through a Crescent I had never experienced before.

"The sound of rolling water inspires me," she told me once. "The moisture the river sprays in the air is quite refreshing."

"Did you ever swim in the river?"

"No! I'm actually too scared," she confessed. "Look how fast it's going!"

"I'd love to teach you, but my mother will kill me if she finds out I swam in this water. She thinks it's full of bacteria and parasites."

"Well, no one has died from it yet," she said with a shrug.

At least I was able to teach her horseback riding. She loved Marjana, and Marjana loved her in return. Thankfully, her resolve to see the play materialize kept us focused on our mission. Our thoughts solidified into something big. I gradually came to realize that my father's consent and help were crucial to the success of the idea, and I started devising a plan on how to approach him and my mother with the issue.

I carried the thoughts and events of the afternoons with me to bed each night. In the darkness of my room, I replayed conversations from the day in my head. For the most part, the flashbacks were invigorating. They nourished my imagination and revealed endless possibilities. However, there was one incident that, since it had happened, kept reemerging in my mind, darkening my thoughts. It scared me. I was not necessarily scared for myself as much as I was for Mona, Malec, and the rest of their family. The flashback of that otherwise routine afternoon at their house became a nightmare. Mona, Eeman and I had spent most of that afternoon telling stories, laughing, and playing games. Right around the time I usually left to go home for dinner, we heard a loud thump at the door. Mona looked at me with questioning eyes. She then got up, went to the front door, and pulled it open. We heard her scream, but by the time Eeman and I caught up to her, she had already slammed the door shut. She stood there motionless, her face blanched. The door's glass panels were smeared with blood. I felt horror-struck.

"What's the matter?" shouted Eeman.

Mona's mother came running from her sewing table, stumbling on her bone-thin legs, kicking her shoes in front of her, and trying to slip them on as she hurried to the door. I grabbed Mona in my arms and held her tight for a moment. It was the first time I had ever hugged her like that. She was shaking. Reluctantly, Eeman reached for the door and pulled it open. Mona furrowed her head deeper into my chest.

"Someone beheaded one of our chickens and flung its head at our door," Eeman said, her face turning red. "The headless chicken is still running around."

My heart sank. I let go of Mona and stepped outside to see for myself. Blood was everywhere. The sight of the headless and twitching body frightened me. I looked around to see if I could spot a culprit. There was nobody, not even a sound.

Mona's mother picked up the dead chicken.

"I can still pluck it. We'll eat it tomorrow." Eeman grabbed the dead chicken from her mother's hands and shuffled dejectedly into the kitchen.

I could not eat dinner that night. Father sat at the head of the table like usual, wearing a smile on his face. Mother sat on his right, channeling his disposition with a gratified face. Aslan sat on his left and was tackling his food with a gluttonous appetite. No one seemed to mind his pestering hum and the clatter of utensils against his plate. I could not get myself to eat. I could not get the sight of the chicken out of my head. The thought that someone had meant to scare Mona and her family disturbed me.

"Well," I finally said, "someone slew one of our neighbors' chickens this afternoon and flung its dead body at their door. The family was terrorized. There was blood everywhere." My eyes were fixed on my plate. I did not look up to see the impact of the news on their faces. I did not know how Father would respond to such a negative announcement at dinnertime.

"Here you go again, Adel," Mother responded forcefully, slamming her fork onto her plate.

Her reaction was instant, as if she had known what I was going to say. Her plate broke in two. The tomato sauce of the bean stew seeped through the crack and onto the table. It looked like the chicken blood I saw earlier. I felt nauseated.

"How many times have I told you to drop this subject?" she shouted. "I don't want to ever hear a word about the stupid animal killings!"

Silence ensued. Father was taken aback by Mother's scathing reaction. As for Aslan, what had just happened did not seem to interrupt his eating in the slightest. On the contrary, it drew a sarcastic smile on his face. It took Mother a long time to take her eyes off of me. She drew in a deep and exaggerated breath, and then exhaled it vigorously, as if she was trying to blow away the dark, heavy cloud hovering over our dinner table. She pushed her chair back to let Nana Thabita clear away the mess. This had been her reaction to the animal killings since the beginning. I did not know how to classify it. Was it vehement denial or a rational attempt to protect us from such unfathomable cruelty? She finally turned to my father. "How was your day at the office? Have you acquired any new investors?"

Father never answered her question. He kept his steady, slow pace of digging his spoon into the stew on his plate, bringing it up to his mouth, and chewing endlessly before swallowing. I doubted he could taste the food that evening.

I was petrified by my mother's caustic behavior. I did not dare utter another word. Nana Thabita had set a new plate in front of my mother, who did not so much as look at it for the rest of dinner.

Aslan finished his plate and asked for seconds. He was looking at me, his head wobbling left to right. A disdainful smile pulled the right corner of his mouth up to his ear. He winked at me the second my eyes met his.

"Hey, chump, are you eating chicken with them tomorrow?" Aslan called out to me later that evening as I walked to my bedroom.

I hurried down the hallway, into my room, and closed the door. I heard him break into a wry laugh.

"I'd hate to see the chicken go to waste. Maybe I'll show up for dinner too. Will your girlfriend have enough for two?"

"She's not my girlfriend. We're just friends."

"Are you getting agitated, chump?"

I was so mad at him. Could he be behind the killings? How about Dog? And all the other animals? These questions baffled me. It couldn't be true. Why would he do that? My heart was pounding out of my chest as I tried to go to sleep that night.

I woke up the next morning to a loud noise in the hallway. It was the same noise that had been waking me up early for a week or so. Aslan's interest in the unfolding rock excavation project had become an obsession. He started leaving for the office before dawn, and he did not come home until after Father showed up in the evening. All he talked about was the project. He started missing his tutoring and riding lessons on a regular basis. His special tutor became concerned, and for the past three times, insisted on waiting for him, despite my mother's assertion that he wouldn't be back on time for a lesson.

"You're to stay home and go through your regular chores. You don't need to go to the office today," Father said to Aslan that morning, still wearing his pajamas.

Aslan sat at the breakfast table, waiting anxiously for Nana Thabita to produce his breakfast. "Why?" he asked, sounding irate.

"You heard what I just said. Your morning sessions are very important. You have missed several already. Also, you go back to school in a few weeks, and you need to get ready academically." Father was leaning with his arm against the back of Aslan's chair, his other hand on his waist. Their heads were almost touching. Father was looking intently at Aslan, but Aslan was gazing straight ahead.

"These sessions are stupid. All this guy does is ask me questions and write down notes. I say he's learning from me and not the other way around. Besides, he doesn't know that most of what I tell him isn't true anyways."

"What do you mean? Are you telling him lies?" Father was fuming at this point. "The guy is here to help you. He won't be able to do it if you're not telling him the truth about everything."

I felt compelled to get out of bed to see what was going on. I was heading to the kitchen when I saw Nana Thabita heading away from it.

"Good morning, Nana!"

"Good morning to you, angel. Did you want your breakfast now—or can you wait a bit? Your father is in the kitchen with Aslan."

"Of course I can wait. It's too early for me anyways. I'm not even hungry," I answered, walking straight into her open arms.

Her hug was the only soothing part of that thorny morning in June. As I got closer to the kitchen, the arguments were getting more heated. Neither Aslan nor my father was willing to concede to the other. Aslan was chewing on his breakfast with Father bent over him, shouting straight into his ear. I knew better than to walk in on them at that moment.

I headed back to the living room and sat down. Their voices by then were rumbling across the hallways and through the walls. Contracts, rock excavation, shift rotation, and liability insurance were a few of the exchanged words that confused me.

A few minutes later, they started walking toward the living room. Aslan, his face a deep crimson, was seized with an increasing frenzy. He was screaming, sending his arms hysterically into the air, and throwing threatening stares at Father. "I'm not going to boarding school. I'm not going to boarding school," he kept ranting as he walked past me.

I didn't know what to make of any of it. *Who's going to boarding school? What's he talking about?*

At that moment, my mother came running in. She was wiping at her forehead and trying to reach Aslan's back as she chased him across the room. She looked frightened and disoriented as if she had just been awakened from an episode of sleepwalking. "What's gotten into you two at five o'clock in the morning? What's the fight about?"

Aslan circled a couple of times around the room and then walked to the French doors leading to the balcony. He stopped there for a while and looked through the glass door into a hazy early summer morning, his hands digging deep into his pockets. All of a sudden, he started to unbolt the door locks frantically.

"You can't walk onto the terrace. It's still under construction. It's not safe," Mother said, looking horrified. She tried pulling on his arm to stop him, but Aslan kept shaking her off. Then, using his body, he shoved her backward.

The terrace outside the main living room was designed to be massive. It was round with a twenty-meter diameter. It jutted out from the upper floor of the house, standing three stories above the lush gardens below. It was one of Mother's latest additions to the house, and on that June morning, it was still under construction. With steel poles and scaffoldings extending from several spots, it was perilous to walk onto. There were big gaps between the flooring wood planks, and its guardrails and balustrade were missing, but nothing could stop Aslan. He stepped onto the planks overlooking all danger and walked haphazardly to the far edge of the balcony.

My parents and I froze.

"What's he doing?" Father mumbled through his teeth.

Aslan did not stop until he got to the very edge. He then turned around to face the house. Surprisingly, the rage in his eyes was completely gone and was replaced by a wide, genuine smile. He actually looked excited.

"Come back inside. Please," Mother implored tremulously, her entire body shaking.

"It's actually nice out here," he shouted back with a mischievous laugh, stretching out his arms. He looked as if he was floating on the clouds of the morning fog. "And to think that one wrong step could be my last! I like it."

"Stop messing around and come back inside," Father said authoritatively. His fists were clenched, and his lips pursed with anger.

Aslan did not listen. He started walking along the edge, engrossed in his wrongdoing.

Mother stood with her hand over her heart. She was watching Aslan with bated breath.

"Come back inside. Now!" Father shouted.

"Not until you promise there will be no boarding school," Aslan shouted back.

"I thought we agreed to wait until the end of the summer to tell him," Mother muttered.

"Oh, and also, I want to manage the excavation project," Aslan added.

"Why don't you come back inside so we can talk about it," Father replied.

Finally, Aslan started walking back toward us, his arms extended in a balancing act. "Good job on this terrace, Mother. I really like it." He stepped into the living room, grinning maliciously.

Mother slammed the door shut behind him.

"I'll head to the office now. See you later, Father." He exaggerated a bow in Father's direction, then again in Mother's, dismissing himself with long, victorious strides.

The whole scene looked theatrical. My parents stood watching him walk away, then eased themselves onto the sofa. Father bent forward, and with his elbows resting on his knees, he took his head in his hands. They were both breathing heavily, trying to recover their composure. Their reaction fed right into Aslan's manipulative behavior.

"Go on, have your breakfast, and get going with your day" Mother said to me, finally realizing I was there all along. She stood up and headed back to her room.

I could not move for a while. I stood watching Father.

He was motionless, staring vacantly at the ground between his feet. He looked like a feeble man in the face of a tempest. I had never seen that side of him, and suddenly I felt sickened. A choking sense of foreboding weighed down on me for the rest of the day.

# Chapter 13

As the day of the play was drawing near, a festive feeling started lingering in the air. The town was thrilled at the prospect of the event. We dreamt big, and I sought to realize our dreams. At times, our mission felt impossible, but Mona's captivating personality and intense devotion drew me so passionately toward it. Mona's mother sewed our costumes, and her uncle took charge of building us a stage. The stage was to be an elevated plank ten feet long and five feet wide, with steps on both sides. We picked the perfect spot for it at a clearing by the river, between two pine trees that stood about five meters apart. We intended to use the trunk of those trees to hang the stage curtain.

Mr. Joseph, our high school English teacher, was so delighted with our endeavor that he promptly became absorbed in every aspect of it, from modifying the dialogues to staging. We spent countless hours in his office on campus, rehearsing and laughing. Mr. Joseph had devised a plan to effectively spread the word to neighboring towns. He suggested sending promotional flyers aboard Mr. Ramsey's nomadic wagon, having him nail some to tree trunks along roads he routinely traveled, and leaving some for local businesses to distribute.

I took a sample of the pamphlet to Father's office one afternoon to get his opinion on the issue. As I tethered Marjana's halter to a tree outside the office building, I prayed that Aslan would not be inside. For one thing, there were no crowds gathered outside the main entry.

I rejoiced at the fact that he was nowhere to be seen or heard as I entered through the double door and into the lobby.

"You can go right ahead," the receptionist told me. "Good timing! Your father has no visitors at the moment."

I had been in my father's office only a couple of times before. Aslan and I used to mainly linger around the waiting room during the few visits we paid him at work. What I remembered the most were the floor-to-ceiling shelves filled with his favorite books. The back wall had two wide windows that filtered in abundant light.

I knocked on the door and entered. His office was bigger than Mona's entire house. Father was sitting behind his desk, with my grandfather's portrait, in real size, centered on the wall behind him. Both men exuded haughtiness. They filled the central space. My grandfather felt omnipresent, floating in spirit and shadow, only brought to perspective by the gilded frame hanging on the wall. He stood tall, hands resting on an ebony cane with a silver lion's head. His own head was slightly turned to one side, aligning with the lion's head on the cane and emphasizing the sharp contour of his profile. He was not looking directly at the camera, too conceited to even grant the photographer full attention.

Sitting at his desk, Father was carrying the weight of my grandfather's heavily gilded legacy on his shoulders. He was sitting with his feet stretched out on his desk, his face buried behind a newspaper he held wide open. His shoes were clean and shiny.

*Does he ever step outside in them? When was the last time he walked around town?*

Upon hearing his door open, Father set the newspaper on the desk. He lowered his spectacles, stretched his arms open wide, and locked them behind his neck. He seemed bored. He gave me a quizzical look. "Adel! What a surprise, young man! Sit down. Sit down, please. What brings you here today?"

I grabbed the seat straight across from his desk. It seemed lower than usual, and I felt swallowed by it. "Good afternoon, Father. I have a question regarding the play."

"I thought all concerns were settled. I already asked my assistant to make sure you have fifty chairs for your spectators, and your mother's making sure you have enough food for fifty people. Or was the money I gave you not enough to get what you need?"

"Oh no. It's all great," I said. "That's not why I'm here. I came to show you the flyer we'll be handing out in the next couple of days, upon your approval of course. We're hoping to include neighboring towns."

"Hmm. What flyer? Show it to me," he said.

I handed him the paper.

**Come celebrate with Crescent and its people.**

**Come laugh at The Miser of Molière and enjoy an afternoon of food and fun.**

**Play starts at five o'clock, in the afternoon of Saturday, August 2.**

He set the flyer on the desk and gave it a loud tap.

"I like it," he said, contemplating the idea.

I silently sighed in relief.

"Does it mean you're expecting more than fifty people?"

But before I could answer, the door was violently pushed open.

My heart sank.

"Well, well, well! Look who has finally manned up! How did you gather all that courage?"

Aslan's tone was acerbic.

A wrenching stiffness seized me, and I couldn't turn to look at him. Had it not been for the doorstopper, that door would have easily gone through the wall.

"Sit down, Aslan. Your brother is thinking of opening up the play to neighboring towns," Father divulged in one breath. "What's your take on that?" He handed Aslan the pamphlet.

*Why didn't he say anything regarding Aslan's impenitently conde-scending remarks? Did he not hear him? Or was he in denial like Mother?* I felt betrayed sitting in the office that summer afternoon, left exposed to Aslan's harassment.

"It's your decision—not his!" I jumped to say.

I anticipated nothing less than malignity from Aslan.

"All the same," Father said without even looking at me, drumming his fingers on his desk.

I was cornered. It was totally unfair to have Aslan interfere with my project. Aslan took the pamphlet and looked at it for a while. He then stood up and walked to the window, his hand thrust in his trousers' pocket. He looked important in his suit. He stood there for a minute, his back to us, looking through the window. He belonged in the same tableau as my father and my grandfather. Aslan however, was free from preordained expectations. Completely detached. His mind was already floating away from the family space, through the window, and out into the far beyond. Their inner drive was nevertheless a common ground. Three generations of love for power. An innate trait. Or was it acquired? Nature or nurture? I believed it was a combination of both, brewing over and around. The emerging outcome could very well be an explosion, and Aslan was explosive.

We sat and waited while Aslan looked down at the paper and then up through the window, as if the answer lay hidden beneath the trees. He finally nodded his head and turned around to face Father.

"I think it's a very suitable idea," he responded, snapping me back to real life. "We should go for it, Father. It'll be a good opportunity for us to drive our excavation project forward."

Aslan's suggestion awakened Father from his languorous state. A swift eagerness seemed to have aroused his senses. He lowered his legs off the desk and swiveled his chair to face Aslan.

"Elaborate!"

"Well, let me remind you, Father, that your popularity as mayor has taken a dip with the advent of the excavation project. You can seize this opportunity to conduct your campaign. Mobilize as many people from Crescent and adjacent towns as you can to the event and sell them on the idea."

"By addressing them with a speech," Father said, materializing the proposal.

At that, Father stood up, slipped his right hand into his pocket, and walked up to Aslan. He stood facing him. They looked like mirror images, only one was taller than the other.

"Exactly. And mind you," Aslan said, poking Father in the chest with his index finger and fixing him with an exaggerated gaze, "it's not to get their opinion or approval, but to make them believe that they are engaged in the decision-making. That their sentiments matter. It sure will feed their pride."

I was confused about what had just happened. Another theatrical spotlight for Aslan. How did the conversation go this far? Neither of them was looking at me after that; it was as if I had just fallen off a cliff and disappeared. Clearly Father was so taken with Aslan's proposal that he completely forgot about me. I quickly got lost in their convoluted webs of business and political jargon. What does a play by Molière have to do with campaigns and reelections, government subsidies and Swiss bank accounts, land erosion and water contamination?

"Swiss bank account? What Swiss bank account?" Father interrupted suddenly.

A sly look washed over Aslan's face. "Ours of course," he answered.

"You've been going through my files, haven't you?"

"Well, do you expect me to work in this office without knowing what I'm working with? That's no deal, Father!"

Father coiled around himself. He seemed to have lost his six-inch advantage over Aslan. He walked back to his chair and dropped down in it.

"I think I heard enough for now, Adel," he said to me with a subdued tone. "Don't act yet on the flyer. I might have to make some changes to the announcement. I'll go over it and give it back to you tonight."

"No, Father. We're not going to change the announcement at all," interjected Aslan with a hoarse tone. "You lure the people to the play, and then you infiltrate your message stealthily. Make it all look spontaneous, not premeditated. We give them free food, a play, and fun for the family. This way, they can swallow your message easier and won't know what hit them!"

"I still want to think this through," Father insisted. He turned to look at me, but his mind had already soared way above my head. "You can go now. We'll discuss after dinner."

I stepped out of the office and shut the door behind me. I leaned my back against the door for a while, transfixed by what had just happened. Or was it still happening? I could hear the hushed conversation still going on the other side of the door:

"You don't have to divulge the complete excavation site yet. You can just say we're interested in the southern foot of the mountain, where we have already started. Don't talk about expanding the site."

"That doesn't cut it. Soon, we need to start working our way north."

"And we will."

Father must have realized, at that point, that Aslan was a few steps ahead of him in the scheme of things. "What do you have in mind?"

"Well, the summer heat will be scorching. Fires will eat homes and trees—not just shrubs. And when that happens, the people will have to relocate, and the grounds will be cleared and ready."

"I'm more than willing to help them relocate."

"If you feel so obliged, Father."

"A nature-coerced evacuation is what you're thinking of?"

"Something of the sort."

A well-designed drama, and the title was *The Insatiable Greed*.

Fires eating through the meager belongings of people confined to the bottom of the social pyramid would be the climax, followed by confusion and struggle to deal with such a crippling blow to the spine, the falling action. The dénouement of the drama was to be where my family would step in to rescue and refurbish. Conflicts would be resolved, and catharsis would come to release, along with the tension, the second phase of the excavation project.

My mind was disoriented. I was disgusted with both of them. How could they be so ruthlessly covetous? What was I to tell Mona and Eeman? What was I to tell Mr. Joseph? That it would no longer be about the play, the art, and the fun? That it would all be about the Jacob family business and greed? I felt discomposed. Stripped from my dignity. How would they feel?

I mounted Marjana and galloped straight home. I could not face Mona that afternoon. I needed to ruminate on what had just happened. I took a long shower and spent the rest of the afternoon in my room. My body ached. My shoulders sank. I had never experienced fear so vehement. Nightmarish thoughts clouded my vision. So much to grasp. Who could I talk to? My mother would not hear any of it. I was certain of that much.

I must have fallen asleep for a good hour. I woke up to Nana Thabita's gentle knocking on my door.

"Adel, are you in there? Are you all right, honey? Dinner is ready," she whispered gently from behind my door.

"I'm fine, Nana. I'm coming!"

Like usual, the table was laden with dishes tailored to satisfy the appetite of each one of us. Nana had also prepared my favorite dish of pasta in garlic and tomato cream sauce. Such an array of food usually made my mouth water, but that evening, it looked excessive. I could not eat.

Aslan had his plate full already, and he was impatiently waiting for me to claim my seat. He immediately resumed his revolting habit of humming while chewing.

Mother, on the other hand, was her usual self, barely lifting any food onto her fork and chewing until her teeth bit into an empty mouth. She always filled up on water, tricking herself out of hunger. Father, however, did eat. He too chewed forever. I had tried several times to do the same, but food just slipped into my throat way before his did. By at least five seconds.

Nana had served me some salad, but Aslan was already going on seconds before I even took my first bite. Where did he put all that food? My parents did not seem to notice his humming, but they definitely took note of it when it stopped. They inadvertently looked at Aslan and smiled.

"Why aren't you eating, Adel?" Mother asked with a sweet and concerned tone.

"I don't feel good."

Aslan suddenly stopped humming and looked at me with mirthful eyes.

"You could be coming down with a cold." She stood up, walked up to me, and lovingly pressed the palm of her hand against my forehead. "You do feel warm, honey. You've been working very hard on the play. Why don't you take a break for a day or two?"

"I'm not physically tired. I like what I'm doing." I tried to eat what was on my plate.

Father had finished eating and was patiently waiting for the rest of us to do the same. He had his hands on the table with his fingers interlocked. He was mainly staring at me as I struggled with the last few bites. "Now that we're done eating," he announced, "we need to discuss the play." His eyes were still on me.

I did not respond.

"Adel, tell your mother what you had in mind regarding neighboring towns."

I swallowed my saliva a couple of times in an effort to suppress my anger and steady my voice. I could not play their game. I drew in a deep breath and tried to untangle my thoughts. "All we were trying to do was open the invitation to neighboring towns so that maybe, in the years to come, we could turn this event into a festival. My teacher, from last year, suggested sending out a flyer with the information. A fun event, that's all we intended it to be."

Mother's face contorted to my tremulous voice.

"Smart teacher you have! Is it Mr. Joseph?" Aslan asked, faking a loud yawn.

It was his innate tendency to patronize. I did not look at him.

"And that's exactly what you should get, a fun event," Father said to me softly, totally ignoring Aslan's comment. "We'll make sure to expand the invitation to several towns, but mainly, we should aim at getting full attendance from Crescent. We'll keep the flyer as you have intended it to be, but let's make the event more enticing. Any suggestions?" He looked at each one of us. Clearly, Father had decided to capitalize on Aslan's idea.

"Excuse me! I have already thought it through," Aslan interrupted. "We'll promise each attendee a free raffle ticket, and we'll make the grand prize a good plowing horse."

Father's face lit up. "Excellent idea, Aslan. Excellent idea!" He pounded so hard on the table that the plates jumped up a few inches.

Nana Thabita came running, holding a rag and a dustpan.

Mother sat up straight. Her nostrils flared as she looked at Aslan in complete awe. All three seemed to be orbiting around a common and solid core.

At that point, I was completely aware that I did not wish to be caught in their current.

"Food for everybody? Better start cooking!" Mother proposed jokingly.

"Yes, of course. Make sure there is plenty!" Father added.

"We should have it on our grounds. It's only logical since we're providing for every expense," Aslan said.

"We've already decided on the location," I interjected, knowing well it wouldn't get me anywhere. By that point I felt infuriated, my fists clenched in rage under the table.

"And where's that place that's big enough for everybody, chump? Mona's house?"

"Aslan, be nice to your brother!" Miraculously, Mother finally noticed my predicament.

Aslan pounded his chest and trumpeted a belch.

"We should have it here. I totally agree." Father looked at me. "Adel, I will send you help tomorrow morning. Put the men to work for as long as you need them. Make it look festive."

"We should build a stage," suggested Aslan.

"We already have a stage!" I shouted.

"We will need a bigger one, with microphones and speakers to cover the entire grounds. We also need good lighting. People will stick around until after nightfall," Aslan instructed.

I could not hold myself any longer. I stood up, brimming with rage, cheeks burning from the furious fire that had been blazing inside me since my visit to the office. "That was supposed to be my project—with my friends!" I screamed with all my might.

Aslan looked amused.

My parents watched me with astonished faces. They were the marionettes that Aslan took pleasure manipulating. Their faces looked funny, as if Aslan had pulled on strings attached to their eyebrows, rounding their eyes in surprise, and pulled down on others attached to their jaws, stretching their mouths wide open. They froze for a while. They never expected their good son to scream in their faces at the dinner table. Why would they? I never gave them any reason to. I was never their source of worry or anxiety. So, they went ahead and stepped all over me—without reservation.

"Go to your room and sleep it off. You look exhausted," Mother said.

I woke up later in the night, my hands numb. I had crashed on my bed facedown, my head weighing on my hands. The sheets felt wet, my nose felt congested, and my head felt heavy. It took me a few seconds to realize why I wasn't in my pajamas sleeping soundly under my sheets. And then I remembered how terrifying my day was. I got up and went to the kitchen for some water. The house was dark and quiet.

As I opened the cupboard, I heard shuffling coming from the kitchen balcony. My heart jumped out of my chest. I hadn't realized the balcony door was wide open. And then I saw Nana walking through the door, wearing a long white dress.

"Adel? Are you all right?"

"Oh, Nana, you scared me! I came to get some water. Why are you still up?"

"I never go to sleep before midnight. I finish all my chores and wait for everybody to go to sleep before I take my shower. And then I sit on the balcony to braid my hair. It helps me relax before I lay myself to sleep. Come sit with me and listen to the peaceful sounds of this beautiful summer night."

I grabbed a chair from the kitchen table and set it next to hers. The sky was dusted with hundreds of scintillating stars. The moon, fully lit, bathed the landscape with its white ghostly light. It was a light strong enough for my eyes to see the silhouettes of trees, but it was subtle enough to seep through the branches without casting a shadow. I looked at Nana. The sight of her bathed in that light made me feel sad. "Nana, your hair is all white!" I had never seen her without her scarf before.

"One only grows older, and I'm very old!" she said, a sweet smile radiating from her sweet face. She had parted her very thin and long hair in the middle all the way back to the nape of her neck, and she was brushing both sides down her chest. "I had much more hair back in the days!"

She smiled. Her comment held no remorse. She was at peace with herself.

"All you do is work, Nana. I never see you take a break."

"And do what?"

"Anything Nana. Anything other than work. Maybe go somewhere. You never go anywhere."

"I like working here, Adel. Besides, where can I go? I have one brother who lives two hours away from here. He works very hard to take care of his family. The last time I saw them was five years ago."

"Do you miss him?"

"Of course I do, silly!" she said as she ruffled my hair.

"I wouldn't miss Aslan for a hundred years!" I snorted.

She looked at me and smiled wistfully. She took my right hand in both of hers and rubbed it gently.

"You won't have to deal with him for too long. Just stay out of his way and stay the way you are. And most importantly, don't let him get to you."

Her advice was motherly. Her voice sincere. I hugged her. She felt warm and soothing. She kissed the top of my head and caressed my hair.

"Nana, I'll always be here for you," I whispered as I hugged her stronger.

"You'll always be in my heart," she whispered back.

I loved the smell of her clothes.

"Nana?"

"Yes, darling?"

"What do you think of Mona?"

"I think she's a lovely young lady. Good-hearted and very bright."

# Chapter 14

On the day of the play, everybody was in high spirits. It was one of those late summer days that felt like spring, gratifyingly bright and pleasurably warm. Our house woke up uncharacteristically early that morning, and our doors were left wide open all day as workers dashed in and out, setting up for the event. Yards of drop string lights were being hung from poles and trees to keep the grounds bright and festive after nightfall. Outdoor speakers were dispersed to bring music and stage to every spectator. Rows of tables were set up to showcase the tens of savory and dessert platters that Mother and Nana had decided on. Ever since the decision was made for the play to be on our grounds, many workers were summoned to clear the soil "from every weed and pebble," as per Mother's instructions. "I want everything to look lush and healthy. If it means replacing every single plant, so be it. Let there be flowers everywhere."

People started showing up around at three o'clock in the afternoon. They came mainly on foot. Crescent had two school buses that were put to use that day, transporting people from neighboring towns. People dressed in their best clothes for the event. Nana Thabita was very excited and was happily overlooking the buffet, making sure there was enough food for everybody. Father had positioned himself by the main gate, and he was greeting everyone with a handshake. Mother was nowhere to be seen. She did not show up until a few minutes before the play started, and she evaded as many handshakes as she possibly could.

Dressed in a suit, Aslan was strutting around, saluting and joking, with children and adults alike, in his usual glib way. He shook everybody's hand, purposefully calling people by name and asking for the names of those he did not know. For how short he was, he somehow managed to make himself look big. People spotted him easily and gravitated around him. He had appointed himself to be the master of ceremonies.

Mona said, "It really doesn't bother me at all, Adel. Just let him do whatever he wants. Why do you want to fight him over something that seems trivial?"

I never shared with her the real motive behind my parents' involvement with the play, although she had questioned me several times as to why my parents had decided suddenly to take the event to an unforeseen level. She was feeling apprehensive about the play not measuring up to my parents' expectations.

At five o'clock sharp, Aslan took to the stage and introduced the evening. He addressed the audience as "friends and family" and welcomed them to Crescent and Jacob's estate. "What a pleasant evening! Seeing neighboring towns eager to celebrate the end of summer, a summer of good harvest, with Crescent and its people, is ingratiating. This is only the beginning, my friends. Our intention is to grow this event to a yearly festival, and our vision is to improve on it year after year."

A wave of cheer and applause rose from every direction.

"Crescent will always remember its good friends and value their alliance. Our valley is rich with so many resources, the most important one being the people and their willingness to grow and improve. Crescent is destined to be the leader in growth, and Mayor Jacob is unwavering in his fight for the valley, Crescent, and beyond."

He stopped again, inviting the audience to express its gratitude.

"We'll start the event with a play, *The Miser* by Molière," he proceeded, "that a group of our youth put together for our enjoyment this afternoon. I hope you find it entertaining. The play will be followed by food and music and will conclude with the raffle drawing. Our grand prize is a nine hundred-kilogram draft horse, sure to please anyone. It is strong, docile, and capable of heavy tasks. Enjoy the evening—and thank you for coming."

Aslan did not stammer once. He spoke slowly and eloquently. I was impressed by his fearlessness. He stole the show before it even started. Mona applauded him. My mother and father, sitting in the front row, kept nodding approvingly throughout his introduction, and they applauded him fervently. My eyes were watching them throughout Aslan's address from behind the stage curtains. I had made sure to reserve four front seats for Nana, Mona's mother, Mr. Joseph, and Malec. They too applauded him, impressed by his gran-diosity. Although I could only see Aslan's back from where I stood, I could see right through his arrogantly erect posture, spotting the disingenuousness behind his charming voice and generous offer. He was a deadly nightshade plant that stood with an upright habit, all laden with berries. Poisonous berries.

Mona, Eeman, and I played the three main characters of the comedy. Our roles were executed to Mr. Joseph's utter satisfaction. I played the character of the protagonist Harpagon, the miser who was consumed by a gnawing fear of using and losing his money to the point of ignoring basic necessities, such as feeding his horses. I was dressed in ragged slacks and a blazer dusted with holes and patches to deride and denounce the character of Harpagon. I also wore funny-looking spectacles that kept sliding down my nose. Mona played the role of Cléante, Harpagon's son, who had a defiant attitude toward his father and believed in the power of love over that of money. She had her hair pulled back in a bun, which she concealed with a hat, and wore a pair of tan slacks hanging loosely around her slim waist. Elise, the daughter of Harpagon, was played by Eeman. Elise was on a mission with her brother Cléante to break free from their father's obsessive control over their freedom. The seventeenth-century farce portrayed the universality of Molière and his comedy.

The play lasted nearly an hour. My father was the first to stand up and applaud at the end, and he was soon joined by everybody else. He was smiling and nodding his head in admiration.

Greatly elated by the success of the play, I turned to face Mona and hugged her. "I can't believe we actually did this. Thank you for such a wonderful idea. This was all you," I tried to scream above the noise.

"Thank you for believing in it," she screamed back.

She was glowing with happiness.

"I love you," I shouted in her ear, not knowing where it came from.

"What did you say? I can't hear you!" She was pulled away by a group of young girls who were surrounding her, so eager to get close to her. She turned to look at me and flashed a smile.

Nana hugged me tight. "My goodness, Adel! You did great! I am so proud of you! I loved the play. When did you prepare all that? Get ready to read the book to me around the kitchen. I think I just found me the second best to *A Thousand and One Nights*!"

My parents also sought me. Mother looked pale in her flower dress that hung from her shoulders. She had her hair tightly pulled back in a low bun, exposing her slender neck and making her look even slimmer. She too hugged me. As for Father, a pat on the shoulder was the extent of his embrace.

"Job well done, son," he said, and then he proceeded with his social mingling.

"Great play, Adel!" Malec was smiling from ear to ear.

I had not seen Malec for six weeks, ever since he started working at the excavation site. He basically worked from dawn to dusk, including weekends. He had grown so much during that time that he looked different when I saw him that evening. He looked taller and darker. His shoulders looked rounded. Above all, he seemed happy. Mona and I had discussed visiting him at his work one day, but Eeman had always been adamant that we wouldn't like what he was working on—and that we would grow to regret it.

I ran up to Eeman and congratulated her on her excellent portrayal of Elise.

"Thank you, Adel, really, for making this happen. It was a fun experience. It brought everybody together. The town needed it!"

"Congratulations!" Mr. Joseph said gleefully as he walked up to us. "You have just paved the road for a wonderful and inspirational annual event. Imagine all the things we can include in this event if we start planning as early as January next year. We might even be able to make it an exposé for the arts and music as well."

I loved Mr. Joseph's idea, but I could not get too excited at the prospect of it. I could sense a crocodile lurking beneath what seemed to be a clear and friendly surface. I looked around for Aslan, but he was nowhere in sight.

The smell of food and grilled meat had been lingering in the air for a while, and my mouth was watering. Nana oversaw all the cooking that had been taking place for several days. All sorts of stews and appetizers, pies and casseroles, and a wide selection of fruits and vegetables were prepared. A crew of five men, dressed in white aprons, was grilling chicken, beef, and lamb skewers. My stomach was growling. I grabbed Mona's hand and tried to inch our way to the food. I couldn't help but notice how people gave us furtive glances as we passed by, elbowing each other and jutting their chins in our direction.

"Why are people looking at us like that?" I asked.

"Maybe because they find it odd that you're holding my hand." Mona was smiling radiantly.

We filled up our plates and found a relatively quiet spot under the oak tree where we sat down to eat. We were both famished. The last two weeks had been exhausting.

"Do you like the food?" I asked, turning my head to look at her. She had stopped eating and was watching me devouring what was left on my plate. She smiled. "What were you trying to tell me on stage?" she asked me dreamily.

I hesitated for a second, and then I went back to eating, hoping she would do the same.

"Adel, you were telling me something on stage. What was it?"

I took a sip of water to dislodge the food that seemed to have gotten stuck in my throat.

"That I love you," I said without looking at her.

We both froze for a while.

*Why won't she say something?*

I finally looked at her. A curious expression was drawn on her face. The longer I looked, the more I saw the unmistakable hint of dolefulness residing in her eyes.

"I can't stop thinking of you. I sleep and wake up wanting to be with you," I finally added.

I was surprised at how easily the words had spilled out of me.

She took a deep breath. Her face then relaxed, and she smiled. "How can someone like you, Adel Jacob, be interested in a girl like me?" she teased. The witty gleam I saw in her eyes at that moment came to release the strain in my neck. She drew me to the moment, to the two of us sitting under the oak tree, that unforgettable summer night.

"It's very simple," I said.

Our eyes locked. I plunged into a well of honey. I wanted to hug her and kiss her so badly, right there and then. How could my pounding heart knock the air out of my lungs when my body had not even moved an inch?

"Attention please," I heard my father's powerful voice echo through the loudspeaker, at a hundred decibels louder than my heartbeat. "Brothers and sisters," he continued in perfect alignment with Aslan's introduction.

My body went numb. It felt like someone just emptied a bucket of ice water over my head. *This is it. The moment of truth.* My eyes flinched.

"Are you all right?" Mona asked, noticing my predicament.

"Yeah, I'm fine. I just wish you and I could get away from here, go for a walk or something."

But there was no running away from Father's address. His voice could be heard kilometers away. He had propped himself up on a chair, at the center of the crowd, not too far from the stage, yet not on stage. He carried on with his plan through a loudspeaker held closely to his mouth, so that not a single word would escape. The setting looked spontaneous, unpretentious, and unrehearsed, inspired by the loving crowd that had been orbiting around him throughout the evening. And now, even the ones who had sat down to eat rose to their feet, cranked their necks, and opened their mouths.

Mona and I were getting pulled by the same centripetal force and went orbiting with the rest. I was gripped by fear. I stole quick glances at Mona to try to read her reaction. Her face was blank. Later that night, and for many nights to follow, my father's voice would reverberate in my ears, and faces from the crowd would haunt me in a series of black-and-white images.

"I'd like to thank each and every one of you for coming out to support our children and congratulate them on their wonderful initiative at organizing this event. In the meantime, it's a delightful idea to celebrate the close of yet another good summer harvest. We take pride in our earth that has cradled us and sustained us for so many years. We're all united by our love for this valley—make no mistake about it! It's come to be a symbol for organic and healthy living, a rare commodity nowadays with transforming industrialization and competing markets," Father said.

The sound of applause swept like ripples away from where he was standing. He adjusted his feet on the chair.

"We cannot, however, turn a blind eye to this sweeping growth. At this point, we can either be malleable and go with the flow and move with the change—or stand our grounds in a manner that will only leave us broken into pieces by the unrelenting stampede."

He stopped again. This time, he looked around to assess the impact of his words on people's faces.

"Tomatoes and cucumbers and summer squash, and the rest of our summer harvest, although organic and healthy, are being sold for nothing. The drop in prices will catch up with our main produce: olives and nuts. It's only a matter of time. As we all know, this year's olive tonnage will be less than half of last year's."

At that point, I noticed a shift in the mood around me. People started to stir. I heard whispers throughout the crowd, and some even turned around to walk away. They did not anticipate a crash course on how markets and the economy work. They understood earth's cycles, just like their fathers before them, and maintained their optimism when nature became capricious.

Cleverly, my father's tone of voice was agreeable and managed to remain as such throughout the speech. Was my father's soft voice ever a genuine reflection of his gentle heart and lucid mind?

"Brothers and sisters, we're at a point where Crescent, and the valley beyond, need more resources to sustain themselves. We don't want our children to go off in search of opportunities. We want them to stay here. Our society will be torn apart and dismantled, and unless we become proactive, there's no way to stop it. It's urgent that we start thinking along those lines. We need to create jobs for them. I built the school to keep them here, for their own comfort. With the excavation money, we can plan to build a college. We can start by building a health clinic and expanding it slowly into a hospital. Then our kids won't need to leave this valley. There will be plenty of job opportunities for them, right here, in their own backyard."

He stopped to catch his breath. He then launched into his assertive speech about his linkage to the land, and that of his father before him, as a reminder to everybody of his entitlement over it.

"We cannot sit idly. Our farming won't sustain us much longer. We have to do something about it, and we have to do it immediately."

He cleared his throat.

"Let's not wait any longer. Let's gather our forces today and proceed with the rock excavation project. I see good things coming out of it. Many roads will be built, and fields will have easier access. Consequently, land will appreciate in value. We need to come together and do what needs to be done to survive. It'll bring us comforts and wealth we never dreamt of having. For those who might feel cheated out of their land, I say the compensation will be worth it. I assure you all measures will be taken to control land erosion and prevent any contamination to our clean spring water. I, and my father before me, never let anyone of you down. I'll always be here to share your pain and happiness."

It took the audience a moment to realize the speech had just ended. Everyone was staring at my father with open mouths and wide eyes. For some, his words lay far beyond their field of vision for tomorrow. They were incapable of distrusting and uncomfortable with questioning. For others, the excavation project meant the endangering of the people of Crescent, the expropriation of their land, the erosion of their mountains, and the contamination of their water. It meant an earthquake under their feet, the destruction of their most valuable commodity, and an unearthing of their agricultural resources. These were the hidden treasures that had sustained them through the years. So, they walked away feeling indignant.

Aslan, most likely sensing the tension in the crowd, proceeded immediately with the raffle he promised.

Father, however, disappeared the moment he stepped off the chair.

# Chapter 15

Time seemed to have slowed down after the night of the play. Aslan was never around the house during the day, especially since my parents bought him a car. He drove it everywhere, including the one-mile distance to the office. He began walking around the house ostentatiously, with his car keys jingling on his belt loop. I was happy it kept him occupied.

There were three remaining weeks of summer vacation. I tried to spend as much time as I could with Mona. We toured the whole valley on horseback, crossing streams of limpid water, listening to the voices of nature, and taking in its scents. I let her ride Marjana, while I rode Aslan's horse. With nature in the background, and Mona by my side, summer never felt better.

"Did Aslan agree to name his horse?" she asked me one day.

"No, not yet. I don't know if he ever will. What would you name him if he was yours?"

"Well, I must admit, I've been thinking about it for a while. When I look at his beautiful bay color and his high crest, the name Godo comes to mind. It's short for Godolphin Arabian. I think it'll fit him perfectly."

"What kind of a name is that?" I asked.

"The Godolphin Arabian was one of three oriental stallions that were the start of the modern thoroughbred. He was born in Yemen and given to King Louis XV of France as a gift. To make the story short, he ended up in England and was bought by Earl Godolphin. All of his offspring carried his features and were fantastic on racetracks."

I was surprised she knew all this. She realized I was looking at her in admiration and blushed.

"What? Horses have always been special to me. I read about them every chance I get."

She shrugged her shoulders, her smile suddenly draining. The sound of rock blasting had been reverberating through the valley for several weeks, but it was never this loud. She took a deep breath.

"What's the matter?"

Mona squeezed Marjana with her heels and took off ahead of me.

"Follow me," she shouted back. "I need to show you something."

We rode across orchards of fruits and nuts. The weather was beautiful. Along the way, several farmers were toiling with the earth. I recognized most of them, thanks to the days I spent with Mona. They unhinged their backs to greet us. I was shocked to see children, as young as thirteen years old, working diligently alongside their parents. Several of them were among those who came over to my house to play in the afternoons. There was a silent agreement between them and the earth they stood on. They agreed to backbreaking labor. They dug deep into the earth that fed them, sifted it, aired it, infused it with their sweat, and carried it around all day and night deposited under their fingernails, trapped in their ears and noses. In return, the earth gave a bountiful harvest. It listened to the stories they told—or forgot to tell. It was always there for them, solid under their feet. Its predictability gave them peace of mind, and its spontaneity humbled them mercilessly. Mercifully, however, it was there when their bodies finally gave up on life.

When we arrived at a clearing, I had to stop, shake myself out of my reverie, and try to make sense of the breathtaking landscape that surrounded us. An endless stretch of terraced plains was supported by stone walls that belted the slopes of the hills, emphasizing their bends and curves, and cascading a whole spectrum of gracefully hued shades, a kaleidoscope of red, orange, yellow, and green. The wealth of colors, depths, scents, and sounds compelled me to stop and acknowledge nature's intricate beauty.

Mona turned to face me and said, "Come on. Catch up. We're not there yet."

I was engulfed by a warm feeling. My stomach clenched, and I felt my heart jump in my chest. "Mona, wait a second."

I eased Godo next to Marjana and grabbed Mona's hand. She did not move. She looked at me with longing in her eyes. Her gaze was a silent and gentle confession. Her face blushed pink as she held her breath. When she finally exhaled, she pulled back her hand, dropped her shoulders, and smiled shyly. She reached to caress Marjana's mane, and with a stolid face, she turned around and started on her way back to town.

"Wait," I said. "You were taking me somewhere."

"I changed my mind," she shouted over her shoulder as she tried to trot away.

"You can't change your mind just like that. Please."

She turned around and trotted past me, her face assuming a serious look. "I wanted to save you," she said when she got close to me.

I followed her down a winding trail for about a quarter of a mile, matching her speed as we passed through farmlands and dispersed houses. A humming sound of machinery was echoing through the valley, a sound that kept getting louder.

Finally, I realized why she had brought me here. We had reached the southern border of Crescent. A dozen small, shabby houses scattered across the plain, each surrounded by its own lot of land. The site of the mountain rising high above them, however, was ominous. It did not fit the rest of the landscape. It looked like a cut-and-paste picture that a child would make in rebellion against a teacher or a parent. A picture of a desert pasted in the middle of the Amazon Forest. It reminded me of Aslan when he colored the moon blue and told the teacher that it was indeed blue and that she was colorblind. Guiltless. Unabashed.

The edge of the mountain had been eaten away by explosives. Gentle slopes turned into steep cliffs. Earth's depths were shamelessly exposed, desolate and naked. It was a deplorable act of desecration. And the tall trees, higher up on the mountain, aged with white dust. They stood as incapacitated witnesses to the destruction below, anticipating their own demise with the least downpour of rain.

The site looked overwhelming. Workers buzzed around overseeing different tasks, staunchly set on their course. Some were on foot, some behind big machines, while others transported rocks in carts, whipping up the mules that wheeled them from site to site. To one side, a group of men with hammers in their hands were hitting revengefully at the rocks. A procession of blows, where one relied on the other to proceed. A unison and orderly labor creating such a chaotic and disruptive sight. These men were all small elements cemented in one tableau. Fragile figures in combat with a juggernaut. I was eager to spot Malec among them, but he was not easy to spot. He could have been any one of them.

While joints were grinding under the strain, melting away a drop at a time, yellow machines stood armored and lubricated, reflecting back all sunlight with their shiny facets, clawing effortlessly at what took eons to put together. A group of five men in overalls of the same yellow color—with yellow helmets and big black boots—stood on one side, busy taking notes on the thick pads they were carrying, pointing to this and that. In the middle of their circle stood Aslan in his office suit and white helmet, gesturing at times while nervously scratching his face at others.

Why is it considered a milestone to tame beast and nature and a catastrophe when a natural disaster occurs? Is it not the balance of forces that drives every planet in the universe and every speck of dust in the atmosphere to assume its perfect spot? When will people learn to accept that everything is well-balanced—even if it appears to be in total chaos? That everything is well measured—even if it appears to be infinite and indefinite? Some people have proved to be wicked, even to fellow humans, and covetous over nature's resources. In the immediate time, nature keeps giving, to the point of exhaustion, feeding an inexorable greed. It is also natural for the balance to shift, to readjust somewhere in the middle, where its needle reassumes equilibrium.

Malec didn't even notice us. His focal point was on the rock between his feet. He didn't even lift his head to take note of the lifeless trees higher up on the mountains. The trees were swaying as the land shook to expose their roots in open sunlight, burning them from bottom to top.

"Let's just leave," said Mona. She started to become restive.

"How horrible. It's an Armageddon," I thought out loud.

"I was here yesterday. I was sickened when I first saw it. I guess that's why Eeman didn't want us to come here after all."

I vowed to not remain silent. I vowed to do all I could to put an end to this crime, but I needed time and a good plan. A smart plan—one to outsmart Father's and Aslan's plan. I knew it wouldn't be easy, but I was ready to try. I knew my father could have considered other choices had he tried harder. Should the project proceed, it would put my grandfather to shame. It would destroy the very land he once fell in love with. "What do you think I should do?" I asked as we approached the stables.

"You can start by talking to your father. Tell him how you feel about all this. Tell him that you've been hearing things around town, that even people who signed up for the job see it as a necessary evil, that they're doing it for the money, but that one day they're going to wake up and say no more. I hope they wake up before it is too late. The rainy season is here."

"I'm concerned too, Adel. I was sincere when I said I was doing it for the good of the people and the prosperity of Crescent," Father told me the following morning.

I had planned to catch him during his breakfast, knowing that

Aslan would have long been gone to the office, and my mother would still be sleeping.

He sipped on his hot coffee. "I needed to go along with this, Adel. It has kept your brother busy for the past two months. He's doing a great job in the field. I'm very impressed by his diligence and his complete devotion to the project," he assured me, almost in a whispering tone.

He then rested his fork on the plate, leaned his back against the chair, and stared at me. It was the way he spoke when words could in no possible way relay his complete message. A convoluted maze of uncertainty was concealed behind his cloudy eyes. He looked worried.

"I'll tell you what. I want you to think seriously about what I'm going to say. I want you to find out what could be a good project for Crescent and its people. You might want to ask around and get me the general consensus on this matter. Perhaps what their main concern is. You'll be my reporter from the field. How about that? I'll be meeting with my business consultants next week down in the city. We'll be ascertaining the kind of business we'll be taking on next. I believe you're ready enough to come with me to the meeting, for down the road, I see you in charge of Crescent."

*In charge of Crescent?* I had never contemplated things along those lines.

"So, what do you say? Do you think you're ready to do what I just asked of you?"

"Yes, Father," I said, totally aware that it was the only way I could perhaps change things around.

He stood up and adjusted his tie. "I have to go now. Go on with your morning routine. I'll have Mr. Salem take you shopping for a couple of suits. He will be here at ten sharp. Be ready for him."

He made a sign for me to follow him to the door.

"You know, Adel, our family doesn't need to invest money locally. We have several good investments in the city and abroad, in several countries, as a matter of fact. You need to trust my intentions. And for your information, this project is well studied, with a professional team of engineers working very hard to make everything right. Just think about it, Adel, a good majority of the people working on the job is from Crescent."

"What does that tell you, Father? People of Crescent are young and desperate for jobs. To Aslan, it makes a lot of sense to hire them. They're cheap labor."

"Do as I told you for now," he said as he rested his hand on my shoulder. "We'll take it a day at a time."

# Chapter 16

It was a summer of instigation. It felt as if I was experiencing gravity for the first time. I had always had a bird's-eye view of the world around me. I floated on an imaginary cloud where my family's pull counterbalanced any gravitational force exerted on me. My life on the cloud was blissfully elating. I had always had all I needed—and more. Aslan and I were the only kids who missed school to go on family vacations around the world: snow excursions in the winter, tropical resorts in the summer. No dictum couldn't be bent, no situation couldn't be maneuvered, no food couldn't be eaten, and nothing couldn't be bought.

Falling off from the imaginary cloud was not randomly timed. It was not an accidental bolt of lightning that flicked me into the open, into a twirling funnel that swirled me, dizzied me, and confused me before throwing me helpless on the ground, where I was left to learn to stand up and walk all over again. It was, instead, a series of blows, in perfect sequence, and in accordance with every physical and chemical principle.

Isn't love both chemical and physical? How about hatred? What causes a boy to race against his watch blasting the heads off of innocent frogs with his slingshot? What causes him to come back the next day, and the day after, to kill more frogs, dogs, and chickens?

Could it all be blamed on the rain?

The path to destruction has its own momentum. It is a spinning gyroscope behaving in the most surprising ways, defying gravity and resisting any challenge for change. It is propelled by the impulse to subjugate, whether be it the subjugation of human, beast, or nature, only to raise within the oppressed an oppressor, widening the spinning wheel and, in its wake, expanding devastation.

When the momentum for destruction materializes, what stops it? When a cell undergoes a series of well-timed mutations, what could revert its doom on the path to malignancy? Any attempt at stopping it is by itself invasive. Any attempt has to destroy to stop destruction. It's the side effect; it won't kill you, they say.

It sure killed his mother. It killed his sisters, and it killed me.

"Who gives you the right to destroy our hills and crumble our roofs over our heads?" came the angry interrogation.

A zealous accusation that was shelved shortly after its inception.

"We could not have foreseen such a catastrophe. We could not have predicted the sudden heavy rain we got last week. And while we took every precautionary measure to protect our employees by sending them home for three days, there was no way for us to have prevented what happened. The cave-in happened incredibly fast. It was a stroke of bad luck," came the undisputed rebuttal.

Was it luck or was it cause and effect? Didn't Emerson, the sage philosopher, say, 'Shallow men believe in luck. Strong men believe in cause and effect'?'

It came three days after the rain had stopped. The sun, although in September, was glorious and incandescent. The sky was a rich blue, speckled with cumulus clouds so white and bright they lifted me on a high-altitude joyride of shapes and colors, illustrating tales of unicorns and dragons, Zeus and Heracles, the gatekeeper of Olympus.

Hades, however, the god of the underworld, sensing hunting grounds, was lurking around the hills, violently shaking with his own hands the trunks of the trees, plucking them from their roots, sending their soil on an avalanche of death. The whole village trembled. Men started running in all directions, horror drawn on their faces, screams of panic bursting from their lungs. Dogs barked, and horses screamed and bellowed in terror. The people of Crescent would never be the same again. The earth that day interred every man's buoyant hope and shadowed his brightest expectations. Nature struck to remind us who's boss, who has the last say in the realm of things, and who's dominant on the scale of things.

No one could have foreseen Hades's presence that morning—no one but Malec's mother.

"Are you sure the site is safe? Why not wait another day? I really don't feel good about you working today."

"Don't worry, Mom. I won't stay long. I promise. I'll be back before sundown."

Promises.

Didn't her husband promise to take care of her and their children forever?

Didn't Aslan promise her and her son that the site was safe?

Should she believe any more promises? No. She was tired of believing. She was tired of waiting. Promises started to scare her. Even the promise to live another day became burdensome. So, she stopped living. The mere act of existing had kept her above the turf that covered her husband—and now so mercilessly encapsulated her son.

When the end is as miserable as the beginning, the journey becomes stagnant. A breeding ground for misfortunes. It was all she could take in. She felt heavy. Her heart was carrying a massive weight, more than it was designed to carry. Everything became compressed and distorted. Even time and space became distorted. A black hole engulfed her and trapped her. She could never escape from the black hole.

The town was dragged into mourning. People had little experience in dealing with the sudden loss of three of their young men. It took two days to retrieve the bodies.

Mona, Eeman, and their mother would walk to the site at the break of dawn and not come back home until past sundown. They seemed trapped in a daze. Mona's mother often resorted to wailing out of control. Watching her cry was heart-wrenching. She looked even smaller and more emaciated, as if it was possible for her to atrophy any further. All the scenarios she had meditated over, and all the paths she had envisioned for him could have never included what happened. He dreamed of becoming a teacher. He wanted to have a big farm and raise dogs. He wanted Eeman and Mona to go to college. He wanted to fix their house. He did not want to die.

How could he have thought of death when he had his whole life ahead of him? He knew his family depended on him, and for that, he needed to be strong. He also knew that it would take an extra effort to break out of the cycle his father was trapped in before him. He needed to bite his pain, gather his courage, and pull himself upward, and along with him the heavy package he was destined to pull.

The other two men who died that day were also locals. One of them was a young man of twenty, and the other was a father of two young children. Their families responded to my parents' invitation for dinner as part of the compensation that my father had concocted for them. Each family was to receive a respectful sum of money, which was enough to buy them a piece of land and build them a decent house. Aslan and I were to be present at dinner. I was desperate to see Mona, who had been avoiding me since the accident.

Mother was dressed in black. Without any makeup on, she looked even paler. As we all sat in the family room, Father went on with his apologetic, slow, and brittle tone about how distraught our family was and how unfortunate it was for Crescent to have to lay three of its finest men to rest. Mother was looking down at her hands in her lap as she rubbed at them, desperately trying to evade the eyes that were watching her.

I couldn't take my eyes off of Mona, but she refused to look at me. She kept her head low and arms crossed. She looked very pale. The pallor of dearth and privation. I was aching to hug her and tell her how much I loved Malec, how much his friendship meant to me. I wanted her to know that I was very angry with my family and deeply wounded by what had happened. Most of all, I wanted to hold her tight and never let go.

Aslan was there too. Although he managed to stay quiet, he showed no sign of compunction. He could not hide his contempt for these people. When our family gathered to plan what to say at dinner, he seemed very edgy.

"People of Crescent are ungrateful for all we've done for them, all the jobs we've created so that they can support their families. They're only concerned about their own interests. They're naïve and misinformed because in the long term, the project will be to everybody's benefit. They're open to bribery. I know they'll drop the subject if we give them more—and maybe they'll even forget their loss—but I say we shouldn't."

Two days later, I received her letter. A handwritten letter. The letter that made it to my heart only to break it. The letter I smelled and kissed and read for years to come. I could regurgitate it, even fifty years later. I folded it and put it in *The Miser*. I placed it on every nightstand. It became the light and my conscience, and I refused to divert from the path it set me on.


Rich people are powerful.

They make decisions to fatten their own pockets and anchor their own stance.

They can buy justice to support their clumsiest and most selfish decisions.

They don't care about us, the people they use in the process, the people who readily toil with their limbs and willingly sweat for their masters, the people whose boss is the son of their father's boss.

The people who, unbeknown to them, establish the reference point against which rich people measure themselves to get a sense of their own haughtiness.

They can never fathom our quandary.

The quandary of the helpless.

You are powerful, and I am powerless.

Please stop seeking me for I'd rather be without your pity.

# Chapter 17

"You'll know in due time," Mother answered.

The house had been tuned to a different buzz since the accident. Father had to take a sudden trip out of town. "It's an exigent trip," he told me. "I'll be back before you know it."

Aslan spent most of his time at the office, even after the project was put on hold. I could see him visiting the excavation site every chance he could, for it was not in him to be coerced into relinquishing his obsessions. I imagined him going through every file, every scrap of paper Father had in his drawers, taking advantage of his absence.

Mother, on the other hand, went on a hibernation spree. She withdrew to her room for the majority of the day and did not come out until Aslan came home. Although he barely spoke to her, she hovered around him silently, stealing furtive looks at him, and not calling it a night until he slammed his bedroom door shut for the day. She had several visitors during the day who were directed straight to her room, trailing suitcases and machines. She was not to be disturbed. She was suffering from back pain.

"A psychophysiological stress," she said. "I desperately need therapy to straighten my back."

The entire town stumbled too. The streets and fields were laden with stillness and boredom. A heavy drape of loneliness descended on me, enveloping and suffocating me. The sound of crickets with which my heart used to synchronize in jubilation became a nagging and melancholy rhythm of a heart beating without purpose. Mona's face would appear like a mirage before me, with her sweet smile and loving eyes, burning me with a fury of desire. She came to possess my mind and my heart. She took control of my days. I could not envision myself without her. She became my vision.

A recurring dream of us woke me up drenched in cold sweat, and thinking about it in full daylight gave me shivers. It always began with the two of us talking in our living room. Then, an earthquake would shake the house, collapsing the south-facing end of it, where we happened to be standing. Rocks and dust would engulf us. Miraculously, she and I would escape to the other side of the house, only to have that too fall on our heads. Every time, I woke up before the dream ended, and every single time, I lived the horror of being trapped in the face of my demise. I lived every moment of it as if it were real. I would jolt out of bed and pace around the room, trying to catch my breath.

*Damn you, Aslan. Damn you.*

I really could not stand Aslan around the house, especially after the accident. I was thrilled to learn that he was leaving. The news came as a surprise, considering he still had one more year of high school left. Apparently, my father had enrolled him in a two-year program at a boarding school of business. I didn't care in the slightest where my parents sent him—as long as he was out of sight.

"I hate school. I've told you that several times. School means nothing to me." He took the news sitting down in the living room after dinner. The house was quiet—the days when townsfolk used to crowd our living room in the evenings were gone. He talked while munching his apple. He always bit through an apple after dinner.

"We'll take it one school year at a time. Try it first and then decide to hate it," Father argued back.

Silence fell upon us for a few minutes. Mother and I did not dare look up. Aslan was holding the core of the apple up to his eyes. He looked at it for a moment, tilting his head to the left and then to the right, and finally flicked it at the open window, where it fell short of the sill. He looked at Father, and with a composed voice, said, "You're doing this to get rid of me. Did you not say I have good business mind? Why can't I just run one of our family businesses? I'm willing to take the one you pick for me. Even if it's overseas."

"It doesn't work that way. You need a college degree. It'll give you strength and credibility. Besides, this is an intensive two-year program at the best business school in the country. You're privileged to have been granted admission. And I made sure you'd get all the help you need to make it through. You don't need to worry about that."

"I still say you're doing it to get rid of me. You know what, Father? You'll regret it because you'll come to see that everything I pushed for was in this family's interest, especially your post as mayor."

"This has nothing to do with the accident. I'm doing it in your favor. You'll come back with fresh ideas. Fresh ideas are always good. Then we can pick up again."

"And in the meantime?"

"Nothing will change. Things will go on the way you've always known them to. Everything will be here when you come back."

That was how the conversation ended. No shouting. I was waiting for Aslan to do something crazy, to terrorize my parents and force them to change their minds, but he didn't. Mother was silent throughout the conversation, but I saw her lips moving the whole time. She was praying under her breath. The longer the conversation between Aslan and Father went, the more elaborate her list of votive offerings became.

The tension around the house for the next couple of days was extreme. Father was smart choosing to break the news to Aslan two days prior to his departure. Aslan barely had time to pack and get himself ready. As for me, I did a lot of thinking and reflecting. I spent the few remaining days of my summer reading under the oak tree, where Mona and I used to sit and discuss Molière. I was impatiently counting the days until school started. It would be the time we met again. I was not sure how she would look at me.

I did not dare think of Malec and the way he died. Too soon. Too young to be laid under the ground, sealed in a box. He left a hole in my heart. His death was my awakening to life's unfairness, the start of a monumental list of *whys* that cluttered my mind and lingered mockingly in bold font, unanswered and unrelenting.

"Why not me?" his mother cried in despair as his body sank into the ground.

One question in a sea of questions. Attempted answers are nothing more than expressions of the human determination to understand the ultimate meaning of life in the struggle for salvation and redemption. Answers are repeatedly contradicted and refuted as the world evolves. Even the sacred ones that have survived millennia, that claim to explain the inexplicable, challenge the diminutive logic. They make you doubt yourself. They make you deny your intuition. They make you surrender your determination. Yet most people cling to them. Vulnerability has its symptoms.

At the funeral, Mona's face looked agonized and wan. Her once lively eyes looked cataractous, clouded with desolation. They had lost their spark. She had hyper-aged. She had fast-forwarded years, skipping what was left of her childhood, and plunged right into life's misery.

Sometimes people are born to be in the fast lane, I suppose. And sometimes, certain stages have to be skipped altogether. People can wake up to realize that the control they have over the course of their simple lives is mere imagination. Nothing of importance remains. Dreams pile up in a nonsensical jumble, swept aside by harsh realities.

The accident did not only come to physically crumble bodies and mountains but also to chemically dissolve Malec's mother. Her ability to conceptualize became muddled. From the minute she woke up in the morning, she was on a mission. She boiled two eggs and put them in a paper bag. In it she also threw a piece of bread and a slice of cheese. And off she went "to visit Malec and give him some food." At first, her daughters tried to talk some sense into her, telling her that Malec was not hungry, that he no longer would be, but she didn't want anything to do with that foolish remark. Her son would soon come looking for food, so she had to take him some.

She would sit for hours at the burial site, talking to him, and then she would get up and go knocking on people's doors. All she wanted was to tell everybody that she had a son who went to work but had not come back ever since. She told everybody she was waiting for him and that they should remind him to go home in case they ran into him.

People felt sorry for her. In the beginning, they listened to her and paced with her, but this predicament had hit her like a flying ember. There was no eluding it. That much was obvious. And just like the ember strictly burns its point of contact, afflictions were strictly hers, highly localized to her and radiating just enough for their heat to be felt by her daughters. People who were spared did move on. They found salvage in forgetfulness and resilience. Doors no longer opened when she knocked. Kids ran away from her. They started calling her "the crazy woman," but she never understood why. Maybe she spoke too loud. Maybe she wasn't making sense. She got more confused and more desperate. She was confined to a slippery downward spiral.

On a couple of occasions, she made it into our courtyard when the gates were mistakenly left open. She swore at the house, shaking her fists at it. It was an outburst of anger venting the volcanic turmoil that had been smoldering inside her ever since the accident. Although my parents responded with cautious compunction, Aslan jeered at her with contempt written all over him. "Quite a melodramatic woman," he hissed.

Malec's mother turned around and trudged away, stammering plaintively, back hunched in defeat. She finally conceded that destitution was the category under which she was born to ever belong. And I stood there, appalled by his caustic remarks and frozen in sadness, not knowing what to say and whether anything would make a difference.

# Part 3

The world will not be destroyed by those who do evil, but by those who watch them without doing anything.

—Albert Einstein

# Chapter 18

Reflections

For whom am I writing this account of my life? In whose interest are the tribulations of a man who seemed so powerful? So invincible?

We are all born helpless, inexperienced. We go through youth learning to walk the walk of life, each on his or her unique path. We are encumbered, whether with a privilege or a disadvantage, yet we strive to learn. While most people maneuver within preestablished boundaries, only a few are adamant that learning is a personal and exploratory experience. A rebellion.

On the morning of your journey, turn your face to the light rising from the east, when the sun's rays will hit you strongest in the eyes. You may have to squint to be able to see what lies around, but you are naturally propelled by Earth's rotation. Let the warmth of the light seep into you and fill each of your pores. Let the light show you all ways of life. Let it cleanse you and reform you. Allow your mind to evaluate what you experience and guide you to your belief. And, although in the morning of your journey, your shadow, your pleasant walk, lies mockingly behind you, at the fall of the day, your shadow will only stretch longer ahead. You can open your eyes and make sense of your journey. You will have formulated your own wisdom. For wisdom is not a dictum, but a resolve, a manifestation of the mind. You will see the way, and the end of your walk will be a pleasurable and an easy one.

Should you turn your back to the light of your morning journey, you will stride with the tide and enjoy the site of your long shadow casting comfort around you. However, you will limit your experiences in life, at a time when you are most susceptible to stimulating and shaping your own thoughts. By the fall of the day, when your journey descends from its peak, when your realizations attempt to materialize, you will have missed out on a grand opportunity to feel and to perceive, to reason and to formulate. For what you have taken for granted early on lies long behind you. Your eyes will squint. You might try to grasp the truth of things, but the path ahead is running out. You will die with your eyes closed.

Philosophers and scientists alike boast of the human cognitive ability. It establishes our ingenuity. It is our asset to discovery and growth. Empowered by it, some feel entitled to rule the lives of others, and even rule the world. Their egocentricity and sense of imperiousness have clouded their basic mission in life. To seek the truth.

We are indeed limited when the answers lie within us, but we don't know how to retrieve them. We are blind when beauty lies around us, but we choose instead to chase it. We are hopeless when simple love, the transcendent of all bounds, is often shackled with presumption and prejudice.

I think I finally understand why I feel compelled to write these accounts. I am digging within to make sense of what lies beyond.

# Chapter 19

I woke up to another day, feeling heavy with apprehension. Like every morning for the past week, it took me a while to register where I was. Sleeping on my back, motionless, I was surrounded by white walls and humming machines. And, when reality finally set in, I sighed in despair. I came to hate the smell of hospitals ever since. The sun was already up. I couldn't tell what time it was. I couldn't turn my head. I closed my eyes, trying to dig deep inside. Trying to remember what happened. Still nothing. How could that be? What was in store for me? Everyone was painting a bright picture, but how could I miss the uncertainty in their eyes? The hesitation in their voices? The furtive looks they exchanged every time I asked them a question? I could still hear and see just as well as they did. What were they trying to hide?

And then it came. The pecking at the window. A small black bird came every morning, stood on the sill of the clerestory window, and started pecking at it. Every time the bird attempted to fly, it hit the glass panel and fell back onto the ledge. On and on it went. Relentless.

I liked the bird's determination, but the poor bird wasn't going to get anywhere with it. It would take it a while to realize that what lay ahead—what looked lush and promising—was nothing but an illusion, a mere reflection of reality, and not reality itself. All the bird needed to do was look in a different direction to be able to see the world with its infinite possibilities.

*What got me here?*

I closed my eyes and took a deep breath. It sure was the start of a different mission, a different path that I was forced to embark on. Incidents can transmute one's life and the whole package of dreams and hopes, plans and prospects that one has amassed throughout the journey.

Who decided on the timing of such a transformative event? Who was responsible for such a bad outcome? I was seventeen years old then, which would add up to more than six thousand days of my life. Was I on a countdown from the start? Was I all along, like the bird, on an illusionary journey? Could I have prevented what had happened by simply entertaining a different set of possibilities? Or was I like a point on a graph, whose function and trajectory are discontinuous and limited by the presence of holes and gaps that are unfathomable to all levels of reasoning, and undefined by any dimension? Where was the fairness of it all?

Where is the fairness of it all? Celestial retribution cannot ease my quandary, for I was nothing but a malleable entity, kneaded by the adults in my life. Nor can randomness explain it, for I believe that humans are not just physical entities pushed around unsystematically, but mind and soul on a purposeful and meaningful journey.

I felt lonely in that hospital room, although everybody had come to visit me at one point. Even Nana had made the trip. My maternal aunts and uncles all came to visit. I was told even Aslan came once, but not to the Spine Injury Center where I ended up. He had visited me while I was still in the trauma center, lying heavily sedated, but the more I thought about it, the less I believed he ever did. The last thing I remembered from the day of my accident was that we were having an argument, and then something happened, and I fell.

"Good morning, Mr. Jacob," said the nurse, stepping into my room and cutting through the viscous loneliness weighing down on me.

I liked her voice. It was gentle and sincere.

"Did you sleep well last night?"

And when I still did not answer, she put her face in my field of vision to flash a big smile at me. Her lipstick was too bright for my taste, but it looked good against her white skin. It cheered me up. She was beautiful.

"How are you today? Well, you sure look good. I see a smile and some color on your cheeks."

"My face is lying. It's just another day of incapacitation, confinement, worries, and confusion."

"Allow me, please," she interrupted. "You shouldn't worry. Your prognosis is good. And you shouldn't be confused, you just need to be optimistic and a little more patient, and we'll make sure you get out of here as soon as possible. One thing though," she added, still smiling, "I am going to miss you."

"The sooner you get me out of here, the sooner I'll come back to visit."

We both laughed.

"How much longer do I need to wear the neck collar?"

"Until all inflammation is gone and your spine is fully decompressed and stabilized. I think you're not too far from that at this point. The doctor will be updating you when he comes back to check on you later on today."

She was right. I was finally told that day that my neck no longer needed to be immobilized, but I had to be bedridden until all the inflammation in my lower body was gone. After that, surgery would be the choice for a better recovery. Although I was happy to be able to move my head and regain the sensation in my pelvis and legs, I was not completely relieved. I was anxious to get out of the hospital and back to my life.

"Incomplete!" my mother beamed as she entered my room. She cupped my face in her hands and showered me with kisses. Recently, it seemed that every time I looked at my mother, she looked thinner. "Do you know what that means?"

"Yes, Mother, I do. They just tested my lower body's motor and sensory functions. Luckily I was able to feel my legs all the way down to my ankles. I couldn't feel any pressure beyond my ankles though. Not even heat or cold."

"You'll get there, honey. You're young and strong. Your father and I will make sure of it. The best doctors and therapists will get you there. Don't worry."

"What happened, Mother? Tell me exactly how it all happened. Please."

For the past few days, she had been able to evade my gaze and my questions by stepping out of my field of vision, but not any longer. Although she tried. I followed her with an unremitting gaze. My relentless bird visitor might have inspired me. She approached my bed, her movements suddenly nervous and laborious, her face turning somber. She extended her hand to caress my hair. "You fell, honey. That's what happened," she said with a sorrowful tone. "A dark moment in your life. Thankfully it's all behind you now."

Last fall Aslan did end up going to boarding school. For the nine months he was away, we only got to visit him once. It was over New Year's Eve. We took him out to dinner to a fancy steak house, where he ate and ate, and did nothing else but give me nasty glances across the table. He didn't divulge any information about his program, regardless of the questions my parents showered him with. As a part of his school program, he was assigned to a summer practicum in market analysis at a business office in the city. That was to be only for the first part of the summer, however, which left him with a window of two weeks before he would head back to his second and last year of college. I couldn't comprehend why my parents were so eager to bring him home to visit us during those two weeks.

He looked subdued on the day he arrived home. He nodded in my direction and walked past me without any attempt at physical contact. My mother had to approach him herself. He stood at the door, suitcases still dangling from his hands, body stiff, while she embraced him. Father got a nod, and Nana was not even in his field of vision.

At dinner, he wore a scowl on his face. His eyes were steely, and his gaze was distant. When asked a question, his Adam's apple went up and down a few times before he uttered a word. He answered with a deep voice and a blank face. For one thing, he stopped humming at the dinner table. Whoever had coerced him to quit that irksome habit of his had done me the biggest favor.

After dinner, my parents and I went to the living room. For the past year, while Aslan was out of the picture, evenings became a time of bonding with my parents. Father and I would catch up on the latest news regarding the public library and the recreational center projects that he had allowed me to spearhead ever since Aslan left for college. I loved it when my parents and I indulged in various discussions about current affairs or just watched shows on television. We always had a visitor or two, but it was nothing like it used to be, when people would occupy every sofa and every chair. Nana must have loved the quieter evenings, for it meant she could retire earlier to her bedroom.

"Where's Aslan?" Father asked quietly, nudging me in the arm.

"I don't know. In his room most likely."

"Go call him. Tell him your father expects you in the living room at once."

I knocked on Aslan's door.

"What?" he replied with a despicable tone that made my scalp tingle.

"Father needs you in the living room."

"No thank you. I'm trying to get some rest."

"But he's expecting you at once."

And when he did not reply, I put my ear against his door and heard his shuffling steps. All of a sudden, the door flung wide open, and he jostled so violently against me that my whole body slammed against the wall of the hallway.

"Hey, slow down!" I shouted. "You haven't changed a bit."

"What, chump? Did it hurt?" he jeered as he dashed on.

I regretted ever missing his presence. And although Father's response to one of Mother's bouts of nostalgia was, "He's somebody else's problem now—we should appreciate the break," I couldn't help but feel the void my mother was feeling around the house.

He came to the living room and stood in the doorway, resting his weight against the doorjamb. He cleared his throat to announce his presence. "Good evening," he said with a deep voice, scanning the faces looking back at him, and nodding in their direction with an unfaltering smile.

"Good evening," everybody replied in unison.

An unmistakable tension swept across the bodies of those visiting us that evening.

"Aslan, you are in town! Are you here to stay?" one person asked, breaking the silence that had ensued.

"I have to leave for now. Good night everybody," said another as he stood up to leave.

At that point, the others also stood up to leave. They shook our hands and headed to the door.

"Have a good night," Father shouted after them as they stepped outside.

"Had I known my presence would push them to leave, I would've made my appearance earlier on," Aslan said as Father stepped back into the living room.

My parents exchanged furtive yet clearly worried looks, a confirmation of the inveterate fears that Aslan had managed to instill in them.

"Mother? What urged you to remodel the bedrooms? I kind of liked mine the way it was," he then said with a sour tone as he slouched heavily onto the couch.

Last April, Mother had decided to reconfigure our bedrooms, turning them into efficient quarters, each with its own bathroom, chimney, and study space. It took a good three months to bring my mother's vision to life, with all the furnishings that followed. I had welcomed the change.

"I thought you were going to be excited about your new room!" Mother responded with an ostensibly upbeat tone.

"Well, I hate it actually. I think you should've asked for my opinion first. It's truly an uncalled-for expense, to spend years fixing and enlarging this house. You know what, Mother? There's a much bigger world outside your world."

Right then, my mother's face responded with a metamorphic reaction to the turbulent emotions that had swiftly flared inside her. She received the comment with perplexity. Her face twitched, absorbing the shock as if Aslan had physically slapped her. Her right eyebrow arched up, creasing her forehead and twisting her nose. She froze there for a while, her mind racing, and her breath struggling. Her eyes then widened, and her eyebrows slanted inward. She looked offended. Surely his condescending words were meant to offend her. He could've disagreed without disrespecting her. And when tears welled in her eyes and seeped down her velvety complexion, I realized it was the first time I had ever seen my mother cry. She looked distraught and beat, but most of all, she looked betrayed.

I was mesmerized by my mother's reaction. I watched her with a swelling heart.

"You need to be respectful of your parents and this household," intervened Father with a sharp reprimanding tone. "Your ill-mannered and unpredictable behavior could cost you a lot, so I suggest you contain yourself and abide by what this family stands for. I never spoke to my parents that way in my whole life!"

Then the two of them got into a fierce contention, Aslan stubbornly justifying his point. Had my father bet on boarding school to change Aslan's character, he would have no doubt lost the bet. Aslan's moral fiber was imprinted in his genetic makeup and was readily triggered, totally erratic, and unpredictable. The year he had spent away in college had intensified his callousness. His words grew more pugnacious as he grew more confident.

That night, Aslan challenged my father to a game of chess. Mother, in an effort to ease the tension, decided to withdraw to her bedroom uncharacteristically early, underscoring her own vainness. She just got up and walked away, a zombie in a trance, mumbling a faint "good night" that I alone seemed to have heard.

I sat there watching the two men sinking into deep thought. They both took the game of chess very seriously. It was not an entertaining game that father and son played in the evening for the purpose of bonding. It was competition at its highest level. It was a son agog to step out of his father's shadow, thirsting for power and victory, and zealous to challenge and provoke. It was a father who was not yet ready to relinquish to his son, and whose stances and thoughts had never been disputed. Every iota of energy in their bodies was pooled into contriving their personal strategy, so their physical appearance was stripped down to sharp edges. Their looks intensified, their eyes bulged, their necks extended. And while they lost their color, I was lost in their rhetoric.

As they competed, their conversation oscillated between the chess game itself, and world history, business, and politics. My struggle with them both was over principle, whereas their arguments were always over dominance and power.

The next day, I couldn't even remember who said what for the most part. It wouldn't have mattered anyway because the conversation could've gone in either direction, and it still would've made sense:

"Has anyone challenged you to a game recently?"

"I have played a couple of times since you left."

"How do you usually devise your strategy?"

"Do you mean what I base it on?"

"Maybe."

"Well, I never underestimate my adversary. A small blister on the toe could lead to someone's demise, just as well as a bullet to the head."

"Yes, yes. I've heard the story of President Coolidge's son's death. So, you basically always fully charge, regardless of the nature of the opponent or the fight."

"I'm always vigilant, to say it correctly. A chessboard is like a battlefield, always changing, with infinite potential situations. You can never just advance head-on. Sometimes you have to step to the side or even take a backward step. Your strategy should be fluid because the environment can never be fully controlled."

"I disagree with your last statement. I think one can completely control the environment. A smart strategy can get you there."

"What do you have in mind?"

"Well, the key is to swiftly inflict a major and critical blow, then instill fear."

"It might work for a while, but it has shown through history to be ephemeral."

"It would be consistent as long as you are on the offense, and ready to devise counterplans of equally shocking magnitudes."

Father laughed at Aslan's comment, reclining his head backward.

"Put your ideology to work. You have yet to beat me in a game of chess."

"Maybe so, but I've held you in dynamic equality for hours before."

"Yes, I must admit your prophylactic approach has gotten better."

"I prefer to call it 'know your enemy.'"

"Have you been reading Sun Tzu's *The Art of War*?"

"What do you think I did last summer when I spent hours in your office? Do you still have that book?"

"I sure do. I read excerpts from it every day."

"Is that why you surrendered the excavation project?"

"I made a sound business decision."

At that moment, Nana Thabita walked into the living room carrying a tray with Aslan's apple and a grilled cheese sandwich. He had developed the habit of eating a second dinner while at college.

"Finally," muttered Aslan as he watched her setting the tray on the table next to him. Looking at Father, he said, "I really think you're going too far calling your decision sound. I describe it as a deficient rebound in the face of misfortune. You let a bunch of illiterates formulate your decision. It was totally incongruous with the image I held you in."

At that, Father lifted his hand off the pawn he was about to move and erected his body alarmingly. "You have a moral obligation to your father. I ask you to mind your choice of words."

Aslan had already moved on. "Business is less about ideology and more about financial supremacy. Just like politics are less about constitutionalism at the core and more about military supremacy, as well as population and resource control."

"I'm not in the business to control Crescent and its people."

"You either are in business all the time—or you never are."

"That's an extreme mentality."

"It guarantees sure success."

Father took a deep breath, squinted his eyes, and pondered for a few seconds.

"One of the main ideas of Sun Tzu's is to weaken your opponent by portraying yourself as weakened."

"Impressive. A tactical defense?"

"Maybe. Or maybe a tactical offense."

At that, Aslan's face lit up.

"What's next?"

"Not now, not here."

"Will you keep me in the loop?"

"You have to prove yourself worthy."

"What do you exactly mean by proving myself worthy?"

Father lifted his eyes off the chessboard and rested them on me. His face, unbeknownst to him, bore an intense and tormented expression.

Aslan, probably sensing an interruption in the conversation flow, lifted his eyes off the chessboard, looked at Father, and then looked at me. His head tilted to the side, and he pursed his lips. His eyes assumed a fiendish look. I truly believe that specific moment marked the beginning of Aslan's true malice against me personally. Father's pause to look at me framed me in the picture they were harmoniously painting, as they indulgently played the game, alternating brushes, stroke after stroke. I didn't know what Father had in mind for me at that instant, but his unconscious gesture had acknowledged my relevance to the conversation.

"A worthy leader is a balanced leader. How do you suppose your grandfather and I after him have managed to get this far?"

Aslan did not answer. He lifted his hands to his head and ruffled his thick hair as if to rid himself of some gnawing insect trapped in it.

Father said, "Your grandfather was able to conduct his world of power and money—and at the same time abide by the virtue of honor and humbleness."

There was still no reaction from Aslan, except for his face gradually heating up.

"It's excellent to be ambitious and determined, but you can't get too far with these attributes if you are forcible. You need to inspire people to work for you by being considerate and supportive. At least every now and then."

Aslan took a big bite out of his sandwich and chewed it slowly. He stood up, and with one swift move of his right hand, he toppled all the chess pieces. His face was the dark red color of an intense bruise, his eyes bloodshot. He reminded me of the time when he toppled the gifts my mother had received from our village neighbors with the same move of his hand.

"Keep one thing in mind, Father. I am the one. The only one. I refuse to be second best. I refuse to be second best. I refuse to be second best."

His words resonated as he moved across the room. I could see a blue vein throbbing above his right eyebrow.

Father, whom I expected to at least reprimand him, uttered not a single word. Instead, he sank into his chair, legs crossed with the top one pendulating to his resting heartbeat, his face not betraying the slightest disturbance.

In retrospect, it was the ultimate call for flight, but that night, I did not run away. I was not looking for a fight. I did not even scream. He was standing above me when my eyes popped open, and although I did not flinch, it felt like I had just run a marathon. My racing heartbeat repressed my ability to react to my predicament. His face had a faint distinctness in the dark, but his eyes were of an interesting clarity. They did all the talking. They told me I was not welcome in their realm of things. They even warned me not to obstruct their field of vision or even cast a shadow on its expanse.

It was not the only visit he paid me in the middle of the night that summer. Every single time he entered my room stealthily, by some magic, I woke up to see him bent over me, watching me with the same glaring eyes.

For the two weeks he was home, Aslan unleashed. He sought me around the house and was constantly provoking a fight. I tried to avoid him or flee at the least hint of his presence. I developed a heightened sense of awareness. However, even retreating to my bedroom and shutting the door did not save me from him. He was the danger lurking for me around every bend and every corner. My skin reacted with goose bumps to the sound of his voice. My airways seemed to constrict, and my sweat glands were thrown off balance every time I caught him staring at me.

"He's been acting weird," I told Father after the first night's incident.

"What do you mean by weird? Just stay out of his way. It's only two weeks—and then he's gone again."

But I knew it was not that simple.

# Chapter 20

"Good morning, Mr. Jacob. Are you ready for your session today?" beamed Mrs. White as she strode earnestly into the living room.

Mrs. White never wavered. She never missed a session and always arrived on time. She was true to her name, for she always dressed in white, from her shoes to the headband she neatly tied around her hair.

"How can someone be ready for a dose of excruciating pain?"

"It's said that pain puts you on the road for gain."

"So much pain just to get back to square one."

She laughed and gestured for me to follow her. "Nonetheless, it's still a big gain. And no, you won't be going back to square one. You'll be moving ahead. An instrumental leap ahead!"

I took a deep breath, and with the aid of my walker, I pulled myself up. I slowly unhinged my upper body as I tried to stand up.

"No more leaps for me. I'm learning to walk all over again, Mrs. White. I thought I had learned that some seventeen years ago."

"Yes, but just imagine all the things you have been anticipating for the past six months. You'll come back strong, not just physically, but mentally too."

"Thank you for enlivening my hopes."

"I have seen so many people with worse situations, Adel. Many of them were able to completely come around. The key is to not get discouraged and to keep believing in your capabilities."

"Well, I did go back to school. Yesterday was my first day."

"And how was it?"

"I loved it! I didn't know I could ever miss school."

"Will you be able to catch up academically?"

"Oh yes! My parents made sure of it. I have a tutor for every subject you can imagine. I'll still be able to graduate with my class this summer."

"Your friends and teachers must've missed you!"

I missed them even more. What I also missed was my old self who had long set on a pathway where the rise and the run were both favorable. I missed the child in me who no longer needed to be told he could not fly. Physical limitations had risen to a new and unforeseen level. There was an agonizing reminder that I could no longer stand up or sit down without thinking about it, that I couldn't just get in and out of bed every time I felt like it. I could no longer ride Marjana or run to meet my friends, stand up erect or walk without a limp, but the main reason why I had decided to go back to school was to spend more time with Mona.

For several months after Malec's horrifying death, Mona stopped going to school. That whole fall had crawled by with a monotonous rhythm that felt like draining inertia. It was also the fall when Aslan went away to boarding school. Time couldn't tick away my days any slower. There was no sense of urgency in anything I did. Mother, too, had slowed down with her projects. There were a few weeks when I didn't see any workers around the house, and on the days when Father was out of town, the house became eerily empty. Even weekends felt dreary, and I started waiting anxiously for school days, hoping Mona would show up again.

I had sent her many letters with Nana, but she did not reciprocate. I had knocked on their door several times only to hear Eeman begging me, from behind a closed door, to leave them alone. It was finally Mr. Joseph who came to my help. I had sought his help with the public library and recreational center projects. I made sure Father hired Mr. Joseph to the project's team as a consultant. Mr. Joseph's relentless efforts and countless visits to Mona's house had helped convince Mona to go back to school and Eeman to apply to a nearby community college.

It took Mona months to get back to her somewhat normal life. Gradually, she and I became inseparable again. I had her sit with me on every meeting regarding the building of the library and the recreational center, and I valued her opinion. Her mother's physical as well as mental health kept deteriorating, however, which made it unbearably miserable to be around their house, listening to her saying things that did not make sense half the time or crying in silence the other half. For the most part, Mona came to our house to do home-work. On good and warm days, we took our books to the oak tree in our backyard. It was under that oak tree where I had discovered my love for her the year before, and under the same tree where I kissed her for the first time.

She had just dropped her backpack on the ground and bent over it to retrieve her chemistry book when I slid mine off my shoulders and dropped it down next to hers. As I bent over to get my books, she happened to be standing back up, which made our heads bump against each other. She turned around, lifted the palm of her hand to my forehead, and pressed it hard—all the while apologizing and begging me not to hate her.

"I don't hate you," I kept saying. "I love you. I hope you know that. I'm truly, deeply, in love with you."

I cupped her face in my hands and touched her lips with mine. I kissed her. It wasn't a deeply indulging kiss, nor did it last too long. It was just long enough for her arms to tighten around my neck and mine to drop to her waist and pull her close to me. It was just long enough to feel her firm breasts and her subtle hips as her whole body sank into the grooves of mine. She then pulled herself back and tucked her hair behind her ear. Her face and neck had blushed to a radiant red.

Those days had undoubtedly etched the bright memories I would fall back on, time and time again, for the rest of my life. They lasted from the time Mona came back to school that fall until the end of that school year. And we drifted. We drifted into the woods; we walked trails no one had ever set foot on. We climbed trees. We rode Marjana and Godo across the river and into the thickets. We shouted, and the valley echoed. We sang, and the birds synchronized. Her skin had an aroma that awakened my senses. She filled me with a maddening desire, and she hollowed me of all other temptations.

Mona and I grew even closer after my fall. Mother liked her and became more appreciative of her lengthy visits. She brought life back to our house. She came to see me every day in the afternoon and take me on walks around our gardens. She filled me in on what was going on at school. We hugged, we kissed, and we talked about our dreams for the future. I promised to show her the world, and she promised to bring me happiness. Deep inside, however, I worried. I worried about the quality of my life, about my healing. Would I ever walk normally again—or would I have to live with a testing handicap for the rest of my life? And as high school graduation grew closer, I was not sure where our paths would lead us. Father wanted me to go to an overseas boarding school of business. Mother was arguing that four years was not a long time, that I would come back fresh and full of new ideas, that seeing the world would give me a good perspective on things, and that meeting new people would broaden my horizons.

"Here you go," said Mrs. White as she held open the door to the therapy room. "Let's see where we stand today."

My parents were adamant I continued therapy from home. They reconstructed one of the guest rooms on the main floor into a physical therapy room. They brought in all the necessary equipment. There was a treadmill, a stationary bike, a climbing machine, weight machines, a massage bed, and parallel bars running around the periphery of the room.

"Did you do your morning breathing exercise already?"

"I sure did. I also did the whole upper-body routine on my own yesterday," I told her as I lifted a dumbbell off the stand and demonstrated a couple of bicep curls.

"Let's focus on strengthening your back today. It'll build your posture and balance. Why don't you start with the parallel bars?"

"And, yes, I'll try not to lean on them." I smiled as I carefully let go of the walker and headed to the parallel bars.

"I like your attitude, Adel. By the way, I met your kitchen help the other day."

"Nana Thabita? I love her dearly."

"She asked me about your healing progress. She seemed sincerely concerned about your well-being."

"Did she talk about my fall?"

"No. She just wanted to make sure you'd be completely back to normal. She looked relieved when I told her that you've come a long way already."

"It was hard for her to see me fall," I said, regretting it instantly.

"Did she really see you fall? Where and how did you fall again?"

I took a deep breath, and without looking at her, I said, "I fell down the staircase that connects the kitchen balcony to the stables on the back side of the house. I had just finished breakfast and was about to go meet some friends. I guess I was rushing and just missed the first step, and I went toppling down."

I gave her the version of the story that my parents had been reciting every time they were asked about my fall. I had realized all along that Nana knew more than she was letting out. She, for one, had witnessed the accident firsthand, but she had remained faithful to my parents' version of the story. I must have lost consciousness when I hit the bottom of the staircase. Nana told me later that two of our gardeners heard her scream and came running to help. They carried me upstairs to the kitchen and laid me on the sofa.

Father had already left to the office that morning, and Mother was taking her morning shower. Neither of them got to see the accident firsthand, but they both seemed to know exactly how it had happened. Nana's expression would darken every time I approached her for answers. I could never forget the panic I saw on her blanched face when I opened my eyes that day. She was bent over me as I lay flat on my back, her hands cupping my head. "Don't move, my love," she said, tears streaming down her cheeks. "You're going to be fine."

"No need to go this fast, Adel. You should slow down and focus on every move," Mrs. White said.

I had unconsciously picked up my pace, feeling eager to get back on track with my life. I was waddling between the parallel bars, and my head was dropped, bending my upper body forward.

"As a matter of fact, just stop walking," she said as she approached me. "Hold the bars tight. Loosen your shoulders. Pull your head up straight. You wouldn't want to wear a cervical orthotic, would you?"

I shook my head.

"Now, take a deep breath."

I closed my eyes, trying to internalize my pain, and drew a deep breath.

"You're shaking. Are you all right?"

I thought I was. I thought if I were to trust Mother's explanations and overlook what I believed had happened that I could be all right—that a brighter story could erase a dark history. Apparently, I wasn't. Nightmares had haunted me ever since I was brought home. I would wake up in the middle of the night drenched and breathless. On a couple of occasions, I swore I could see him bent over me in the dark like he did that summer, a big, sly smile on his face. And I would scream, bringing both of my parents to my room.

"Adel, you need to clear your mind of all negative thoughts before you go to sleep, honey. You are torturing yourself," Mother told me once as she sat on the edge of my bed, wiping the sweat off my forehead.

"He pushed me, Mother."

"It's nothing but a bad dream."

"No, it's not a dream. He pushed me down those stairs. He did not care if I died. It's not a dream, Mother."

"He couldn't have pushed you, Adel. You just had a nightmare. Why don't you believe me so that you can move on and heal? You have a lot of healing to do, Adel."

"But he pushed me. It's all clear to me now. He pushed me down those stairs. How do you expect me to heal if you keep denying it?"

"Calm down now, Adel. We spoke to him, and he said he was playfully teasing you when you fell. Besides, he's far from home now."

It was pointless. I knew it. I closed my eyes and swallowed my tears. "You can go back to sleep. I'll be fine. Sorry I woke you up."

She kissed my head, whispered a good night, and shuffled out of my room.

I had given up on my parents a long time ago. I knew all along they would never concede that Aslan's behavior was dangerous. They had always interpreted the quarrels between the two of us as good-natured banter. Mona, on the other hand, listened to me and believed me. When I told her it was Aslan who pushed me, she did not even flinch.

"I'm not surprised," she said as she gently touched my face. "You told me you two were arguing. What was it about?"

I was not going to share what he had said that day with anyone, although I knew Nana Thabita had heard it all. His words were too wicked and ruthless. I thought it better to bury them deep, swallow them along with my bitter tears, rather than allow them to hurt Mona.

But my mind would not stop rewinding snapshots of an encounter that had left a more damaging impact on my heart and my soul.

"Have you had sex with her yet, chump?"

"What are you talking about?"

"I'm talking about Mona. Have you banged her yet? I can give you a hands-on lesson if you'd like to watch."

"Fuck off. You must be sick."

"I bet she's dying to have it. Do you think this girl is just waiting for you to wake up? Go see who is satisfying her lust because apparently you have yet to man up."

I got up to leave the kitchen once I noticed Nana Thabita's disturbed face, wanting so badly to spare her.

"Where are you heading? It's too early in the morning for that."

"Sex is all you have on your dirty mind. For your information, I'm busy with the public library project."

"Is that so?" he said as he followed me to the porch. "You really think Father will let you make any decisions?"

"I'm making decisions. And my decisions are helpful ones, unlike your destructive, evil ideas for the excavation project."

"Well, you won't be helpful for too long." He lifted his hand to my shoulder and pushed me backward.

I was facing him with my back to the staircase. I went rolling down a steep flight of fifty-two stone steps, banging my head and cracking my spine. Gravity and the force of his push had sent me all the way to the bottom.

It was too much to process, especially after the physical damage the fall had caused. I questioned my memory, and I believed explanations thrown at me, but my subconscious did not give up. Visions of a stark truth resurfaced when I was least prepared. I knew I had to leave, even if it meant leaving Crescent. I came to realize that my parents' plan for me to study abroad was, sadly, a smart choice.

What I did not know and could not have foreseen was that I would not come back to the Crescent I was leaving, that things would never be the same, and that I would never again see the dearest person to my heart.

Father called me to his home office a week before my departure. "I admire your love for Crescent, and I have no doubt that you'll remain on the path your grandfather had envisioned for this valley, but I also know that the world is changing. Urban development is irreversible. People are resorting to means that promise them immediate and more profitable growth."

He looked agitated and was nervously drumming his fingers against his desk.

"I'm giving you Crescent, Adel. I'd like you to preserve it as much as you can possibly fight for. Keep it closer to earth. Keep it a peaceful refuge from a world that's irreversibly heading toward madness and greed."

He stopped, got up, and walked to the window.

"Do you know what I regret the most?" he asked, turning his head to face me. "I regret ever considering that excavation project, and I'm trying my hardest to reverse the damage it did. I have a plan to replant that side of the mountain and build public gardens where the lands were eroded."

He walked up to the window and stood contemplating a view of Crescent that was undoubtedly imprinted in his mind down to every leaf and every twig.

"Keep it green, Adel. That's all I'm asking of you. And keep it simple. Make it a place where you can always come back to reflect and recollect. A place that reminds you of your roots and who you are. Love it, Adel, just the way your grandfather loved it."

My father's request had fermented a sense of responsibility in me ever since. It was a simple request. Loving Crescent was natural to me. No effort was required.

I thought that after graduating college, my journey would be an open book, with colorful illustrations of people and scenery I cherished, of promising beginnings, and foreseeable events that would lead to happy endings.

"What about Aslan?" I asked as I got up to leave.

"He'll be out of Crescent before you come back. His inheritance will depend on it."

# Part 4

There is a candle in your heart, ready to be kindled.
There is a void in your soul, ready to be filled.
You feel it, don't you?

—Jalaluddin Rumi

# Chapter 21

Reflections

Aslan was right. There was a bigger world outside my parents' world. In fact, that world was so big it made ours dispensable. Observing this world's myriad colors, and meeting people with a wide range of backgrounds and ethnicities, can have a humbling effect on one's ego. You are no longer a massive star whose rays vibrate in all possible directions, but an insignificant one in a sky of millions, all striving to shine. Maybe that was the reason why my father chose to remain in Crescent when he could have lived anywhere he wished. He was big in his hometown. He belonged to its people. He knew their fathers and grandfathers. It was his family tree.

He wanted me to preserve Crescent.

"Keep it close to earth," he had said. "Keep it a peaceful refuge."

And I vowed to carry out those wishes, but life had a different plan for me. Things don't stay the same. Things don't wait for you. You bend to avoid breaking, but when you are pushed beyond your breaking point, you are forced to uproot and call it a day. Then you are carried to a new soil, a land that could be better in everybody's objective opinion except yours. No land can measure up to where you came from. The water tastes different, and the air smells different. You adapt as the years go by since it is the only way to move on, but hidden deep inside, you carry your past.

Although humble in nature, and to some even prosaic, Crescent was the cradle of my dreams, the fount of my imagination, and the joy of my life. It was where I experienced pure and unconditional love. And although it was the beginning of things, it had coalesced, through my years abroad, to an old book of *The Miser*, shriveled and yellowed, pages curled in some spots and buckled in others as a testament to my tears. In it were folded her letters to me. Letters that would keep me on a mission for the rest of my life.

# Chapter 22

It was an expansive field of spring flowers, daisies with snow-white petals and yellow hearts, accentuated by emerald green leaves. The sun was majestically lighting up the earth in a sapphire-blue sky. It was a happy and glorious setting for a bright and precious day. I was running through that field, the aroma of spring filling my lungs, my legs swift and agile, my back no longer hurting. It felt liberating to run. I spotted her yards away, her back to me, her long white gown with tiered lace and tulle made her a swan floating on a cloud, feathers cascading in an avalanche of weightless snow. She looked beautiful. Innocent and pure, like the daisies. I was desperate to get to her, but the faster I ran, the wider the gap became between us. I called her name and begged her to wait for me. She did not seem to hear my cries, and instead, she rapidly slipped away until she disappeared.

"Sir, wake up," the hostess said as she tapped my shoulder. "I need you to pull your chair upright and buckle your seat belt, sir. We are facing some turbulence."

"All right," I said, fumbling for the seat belt as my seat began to shake.

I rubbed my face with the palms of my hands, struggling to open my eyes. It was a dream. Mona was in it, but I did not see her face. I wished I did. She looked so real. I was running in that dream. I closed my eyes and reclined my head against the back of my seat. My body ached. I rubbed at my knees.

*How long has it been since I could run? I miss running. I miss walking without a limp. I miss Mona and her smile.*

The hostess sat down and buckled herself up as the plane danced to angry air currents.

*Patience. I can be patient.*

For as long as I could remember, my mind would deploy long before my body could respond. It was horrible and soul-crippling to be physically crippled. No spontaneity in doing things. No sense of well-being.

I couldn't believe I was finally heading home. I knew the day would come eventually, but I was never sure when. My losses were monumental, overshadowing my gathered courage. Time did factor into the healing equation, and being distant contributed to my sporadic forgetfulness, but some wounds had been fossilized. My fall had left me with a handicap. And the worst of wounds had left a cleft in my soul.

I was always aware of the privileges granted to me and grateful for the freedoms that they entailed. I faithfully did what was expected of me. I graduated with a degree in economics and found myself financing and marketing several business ideas ranging from organic farming to medical research. Hunger for power was never an urge I needed to address or satisfy. Instead, it had always been a hunger for my father's face to be swept with a sense of pride when he heard of my entrepreneurial endeavors in a foreign land or for my mother's posture to erect when I told her of my accomplishments. The three visits they paid me during my twenty-five years abroad were fairly short and felt cold. In retrospect, I could sense a discord in their relationship as I delved deeper into conversations we had at the time of their visits. I had classified it then as edginess and age-related boredom.

Sitting in an airplane bound for home made my journey abroad suddenly feel tangential, like a footnote in a chapter of my life that most readers could just skip past without missing much. Twenty-five years ago, I left Crescent and my country, buoyed with hope and anticipation. I had not for one second entertained the idea of not going back after I graduated from college. Going home was my dream, but Mona's death came to taint that dream. I lost all interest in going back, and I came to accept my exodus as an inexorable fate.

For years, I lived away without being able to forget. The yearning of the immigrant manifested itself in trivial aspects of my daily life. The crisp breeze on a spring morning was a jolt of reality. The smell of certain foods or the face of a stranger would awaken some long-resting memories, without prior notice, leaving me engulfed by grief. I walked the streets at night. I sought distraction in theater, educational and spiritual seminars, and live music. I sought a robust business life. I worked long hours in the office, exploring new work ideas that fully engaged my time and my mind. However, deep inside, loneliness had festered.

"Yes, sir? You have your light on."

"Yes, I need some water please. How much longer until landing?"

"We still have two hours, sir."

Two hours is a long time when you are tallying seconds.

I hadn't been able to speak to Nana Thabita for two weeks.

"Her situation is worsening, Adel," Eeman told me when I called last. "Her heart is failing, and her lungs are congested. She's constantly gasping for breath. She hasn't left her bed for a week now. Her feet are swollen. She says it's painful to walk. I'm worried about her. All that's on her mind is you, Adel. She keeps telling me that her last wish is to see you before she's gone. That she has a lot to tell you."

"Here's your water, sir."

Water felt good. I always relied on water to clear my throat from the residual lump that seemed to swell every time I thought of home. So much had happened while I was gone, so many life-altering events. On several occasions, I contemplated going back, thinking my presence would bring solace, but it was not in my power to come to the rescue when I personally needed to be rescued. For twenty-five years, I endured, thinking my mind would at least forget—or maybe time would take its course—and my heart would stop yearning. Instead, the idea of never going back weighed on me like heavy penitence. Nana's deteriorating health was an eye-opener. And I came to realize that I could never just erase a chunk of my life and remain at peace with myself.

Eeman was the only person I could trust with issues regarding Nana Thabita. She had remained, through the years, my liaison with Crescent and its people. I trusted her and relied on her sound judgment with issues I could not physically be there to resolve. Her early life was trapped in a labyrinth of despair, but she knew she couldn't give up. She had to persevere because her mother could not be left alone. She had to take care of her. It was an unswerving promise. "Every time I felt discouraged," she wrote, "I told myself that I was not doing it for me—that I was doing it for my father, my brother, and my sister. That I needed to make my mother proud, even though I knew she wouldn't be able to grasp what it actually means that I am graduating from college. Her situation has worsened. Mentally she seems eons away, and her body is withering by the day."

Eeman went to the nearest college where she graduated with a degree in nursing, and she followed up, after her mother's passing, with a master of science in the same field. She took care of her mother until the last agonizing minute of her life. "I'm rebuilding our home," she wrote to me in another letter. "I can afford it now. Alas, my mother is no longer around to see it. She would've loved it. I'm keeping the two rooms we always had. I'm building around them. It'll still be tiny, mind you, but it would've made my father proud had he had the chance to live."

I wrote back asking her about the ancient cedar tree right outside the front door to their old house.

"That cedar tree is a *Cedrus libani*. A botanist friend of mine from college dated it to be at least two hundred years old. It's fascinating how such an ancient tree is evergreen, and its branches stay fairly leveled. It will always be here. It will live for hundreds more. It was why my father built our house in that particular lot. It gave him a sense of security when our house had no foundation to it. The cedar tree is here to stay."

I got up to stretch my body. My legs and back still hurt from sitting in the same position for so long. Although I ended up doing the surgery to help stabilize my lower spine, the pain had persisted. I accepted that pain as part of my life—just the way I came to accept that my brother was a psychopath. My parents had realized the problem on their hands, and instead of trying to fix it, they acceded to it with a veneer that cracked and chipped, too fragile to withstand the ponderous evilness lurking beneath.

I walked to the lavatory to splash some water on my face. I looked pale, and my eyes were heavy. I'd had a lot on my mind lately. I wasn't sure whether or not I should seek Aslan. I had a lot to tell him, things that had festered and gnawed at my spirit, turning me ill for days at a time. I had not seen him in person for more than twenty-five years. Making sure our paths wouldn't cross was a mutual effort. I saw pictures of him in magazines several times. He had put on a lot of weight, and his hair was turning gray. He married Susan, a girl he met in college, and they had two boys. I never received an invitation to his wedding.

When he called me five years ago on New Year's Day, his voice sounded just like Father's: deep and commanding authority.

"I have disturbing news for you," he said his voice orotund. "Our parents had a car accident last night. Neither one of them made it."

It took a while for me to register his words.

"What do you mean?"

"I mean they both perished," he said, and then he became distracted, talking to someone else about some files in some drawers.

Apparently, he was calling me from his office.

"Now," his voice sounding clear through the receiver, "I believe we should have closed caskets at the funeral, for neither one of them would have wished to be viewed in that state. It's up to you if you want to be present at the funeral, which is set for tomorrow afternoon, by the way, but to tell you the truth, you won't be able to make it on time anyways, so I really don't think you should stress over hurrying home."

I must have followed up with some mumbling. I couldn't remember what I said exactly.

"Listen, the situation is taken care of. An investigation into the cause of the accident is still ongoing. If you want more medical details, you can call the doctor. He can fill you in. I really have to leave now. I have an important meeting to attend. We'll be talking I'm guessing."

And that was how he dismissed the conversation, even colder than it had started.

My father was seventy-two, and my mother was sixty-eight. His health had been declining steadily as rheumatoid arthritis took control of his joints and his life. His impatience with his condition had stripped him of his mild disposition around the house and had turned him into a petulant and cantankerous person. Nothing would make him smile. He retired to his bedroom directly after dinner. He seldom went to his office and made a point to meet with his financial advisors no more than once a week. He became thin and struggled to keep his back straight. As for my mother, to whom my father was the pillar she never thought would crumble, reality hit her every morning from the moment she opened her eyes and realized her situation was not a dream, but a dreadful fact of life. Boredom and loneliness allowed depression to settle in. She responded to minor situations with nervousness and anxiety. She became irate at the most mundane provocation, which alienated her from family members and several of her friends. Consequently, the house was caught in a vortex of somberness.

Both my parents were in the back seat, I was told later. The weather in Crescent was particularly inclement that fall, and people mostly kept to their houses. Mother had looked forlorn for days, the house being empty and morose at a time when everything should have been festive and joyful. I heard that Aslan and his family had reluctantly promised to spend New Year's Eve with them in Crescent, but they had a last-minute change of plans and decided to go on a ski trip instead.

"I built this huge house in high hopes that one day I would see it buzzing with children and grandchildren. Where's everybody? Why is this house feeling so empty and cold?" she kept asking Nana Thabita as she sat in the family room, tears streaming down her face.

Father decided to get her out of the house to spend a couple of days with their friends in the city. I was told later that our driver had advised them against the trip. Snow and mudslides had made the serpentine roads out of Crescent dangerous to drive, but my father wouldn't hear any of it and had set his mind on going. The driver also perished in the accident.

"On the day of the funeral, massive clouds cleared to a beautiful blue sky. Hundreds of people showed up to pay their respects. Aslan's eulogy was short and to the point," Nana Thabita hastened to inform me as her blue-veined and knotted fingers fiddled with her handkerchief. "Life hasn't been the same since," she added, looking at me with tearing eyes.

As Eeman ushered me into the room where Nana Thabita was sleeping, I could feel my temples drumming to my heartbeat. She was reclining in bed. She was all dressed in white and covered with even whiter sheets, her back and head comfortably resting on a set of pillows. Her nose and mouth were covered with an oxygen mask, and intravenous tubes were inserted in her arm. Her eyes were unblinking and fixed absently on the door of her room as if waiting for someone to show up. She followed me with a languid gaze as I walked through the door and stepped close to her bed. Her face remained expressionless. I did not know what to make of it. My thoughts raced in all directions.

*Did she forget about me? Have I also drastically changed? Or is the expressionlessness of her face a reflection of a soul turned numb?*

"Nana, this is Adel. Adel is finally here. Adel is here to see you,

Nana," Eeman repeated, her voice crescendoing as she gently pulled the mask off of Nana's face and caressed her head.

Nana's face spread out in marvel, and her eyes welled with tears. Her bottom lip quivered as she tried to speak. She lifted her arm to touch me. "It's really you, isn't it? My angel. You finally came back."

"Oh, Nana, forgive me. Forgive me for all the time I wasted," I said as I bent down to hug her, tears already covering my face.

Hugging her did not feel the same as when I was a child. I was aghast at the way her body had atrophied. She must have sensed my hesitation.

"Twenty-five years, Adel. Twenty-five." She reached for my hand. "Not one day I did not think of you. You left a big void in this house—and in my heart."

I kissed the top of her head.

"I never forgot you, Nana. You listened to me when no one else did. You laughed to my jokes and sang to my tunes. Your wisdom guided me through my toughest times."

"Let's go sit by the window. It's a good day to get out of bed," she said as she struggled to prop herself up on her elbows.

Eeman and I helped her sit up and get out of bed. I took her right hand in mine and wrapped my left arm around her withered shoulders, trying to offset some of gravity's pull on her frail body. Nana had long lost all the fight in her. Her head was bent, and her back was hunched. She wore her loose and aged complexion respectfully. Every wrinkle was a strong credential in life's wisdom, every furrow a cry in the face of time.

We sat facing the window to the west side of Crescent. The sun was setting behind the mountains, adding a darker hue of orange to the halo around the peaks as they plunged deeper into the night.

"I was fourteen years old when your grandmother, may she rest in peace, took me into this house," she said. "I'm forever grateful to her. A venerable woman she was. I lived my childhood in abject poverty. My mother passed away giving birth to my brother, and my father did not seem embarrassed of baring his deficiency in parenthood, being openly alcoholic and abusive."

She stopped to catch her breath. I could feel the web of veins on the back of her hands as they nestled in mine. She was no longer the person I could lean my head against for comfort and warmth. She managed a smile.

"She was smart and watchful, your grandmother. She sensed my predicament and talked my father into letting me be her permanent help. She offered him a sum of money he could not refuse. 'One less mouth to feed,' my father mumbled as I packed the little I had and left home."

"That must've been an awful childhood, Nana, but why did you stick around all these years? Why didn't you marry? Didn't you want a family of your own?"

"Your father was born soon after I moved in. Oh, how I loved him. Your grandmother taught me how to take care of him. I followed her wishes exactly how she had set them out for me because I was eager to please her. She never entrusted him to anyone but me. I kept to his side like a shadow. Still, I was always scared of making a mistake. I didn't know whether I could take care of one of my own when my mother left me too young and all alone in this world. Believe me, I don't regret anything in life. I'm completely satisfied, especially having you too and being part of your life." She started weeping, her body rocking to her sobs.

"Please don't cry, Nana," Eeman said, wiping at her tears.

"You're so much like your grandmother. A grounding force so desperately needed to neutralize the currents that have swept through this family. High-voltage family if you ask me," she added, nodding her head.

A wave of convulsive coughs ran through her, shattering every iota of her being. As she tried to catch her breath, she interlocked her rheumy, sunken eyes with mine.

"No matter what Aslan might tell you, your parents loved you and worried about you until the last minute. He instigated terror in their hearts that made them feel helpless when it came to dealing with his behavior. It scared them to label him for what he was, and may very well still be, thinking that it'd become impossible to undo. They sent you away to protect you from him."

She stopped for a while, trying to catch her breath.

"You need to listen to me very carefully, Adel. Your father made many mistakes in life, some of which I could never forgive him for," she hastened to add with a hushed voice as she saw Eeman leave the room. "But your father was virtuous enough to understand that the family estate in Crescent must belong to you, and to you alone. Aslan might try to intimidate you into doing certain things or relinquishing your share of the estate. Don't cave in to him, and stay out of his way, for no one knows what his jealousy could lead him to this time. Take Crescent, Adel, and help it. It desperately needs you."

"What mistakes did Father commit that you could never forgive?"

"It's not for me to dig into his past. One thing I tell you for sure," she added as Eeman came back into the room with the medication tray, "is that Crescent is still abuzz with beauty. Don't go look too far for it's within your reach."

Her words left me confused. Was she referring to mistakes I did not know of? Besides, I had never, not for one second, thought of sharing Crescent with Aslan. His animus toward the village could never be forgotten. It was not a conjecture, but a deep conviction that making amends with him would be impossible. An erosive uneasiness toward him had been brewing inside me for years. I very much appreciated the fact that Father had so meticulously separated us in our inheritance. A genius dissection with a fine scalpel. Although I clearly knew that Aslan's assets were more valuable than mine, Crescent itself felt like a portion of my parents' heart.

"You need to rest, Nana. We'll talk some more tomorrow. Adel is here to stay. He won't leave you anymore," Eeman said, smiling sweetly as she looked at me with quizzical eyes.

"You're the winner, Adel, not him. He lives a miserable life. He's carried away by his blind passions. He's a slave to his own greed and love of subjugation. Nothing could ever make him happy," Nana added, her breathing turning into labored panting.

Eeman wrapped her arms around Nana and gestured for me to do the same. We helped her to her feet and guided her back to her bed. Eeman tucked her in, propping her head up on a set of pillows.

"Her heart is failing. Her lungs are literally drowning. I'll be by her side until the end. I'll make sure she won't suffer," Eeman whispered.

"Not only are you a great nurse, Eeman, and for that I'm so grateful, but also the loving daughter she could've never dreamed of having."

"I have you to thank for providing her with a good life."

"Say, Nana, how about we move you back upstairs tomorrow?" I asked as I kissed her good night.

"I haven't set foot upstairs for weeks, but now that you're back, I'd love to. You have no idea how much I miss it."

Ever since my parents' death, Nana had moved to the ground floor of the house.

"The main floor is eerily empty. I promise to keep it clean. It'll always be ready for you when you come back, but for now, I'll move downstairs. I hope you don't mind," she had told me five years ago over the phone. She was eighty-six years old then.

She struggled to fall asleep that night. While Eeman sat by her side waiting for the night nurse to arrive, I went upstairs to see the house again after all those years. I opened the mahogany entry door and stood for a while, thunderstruck by a vestige of familiar smells and old memories. The house felt big and cold. To my surprise, it had maintained its old magnificence and majesty. Everything stood as I remembered it. Not a single item had been moved or replaced. The same curtains hung flimsily from the ceiling. Furniture pieces, with cracked surfaces and frayed fabrics, must have gone unnoticed by Mother's keen eyes. Or had they?

The same portraits hung on the walls of the living rooms. A wedding portrait of my parents was centered on one wall, juxtaposed by a portrait of my grandparents on the one facing it. Their faces stood in testimony to their full, affluent past. A life as big as life itself grew to fill its universe, owning that universe, never for once entertaining it would all come to an end, coalescing into a fraction of a second captured by a camera lens, a somewhat faithful manifestation of the image and the ego residing inside.

What is a given manifestation other than a relative distortion of reality? Regardless of all attempts to calibrate and adjust, a residual variability is inherent to the heart of things. Unnoticeable to some, it stands frustrating for others.

I rubbed at my eyes several times. The vibrancy of colors and shapes was buried under the thick, hazy layer of the dust of time. One layer for every year I had been gone. Twenty-five layers deposited atop each other, compressing the image into a lifeless, two-dimensional frame.

I squinted my eyes and allowed my vision to carry me through the depths of cracks I alone could perceive. Stereoscopic images started jumping at me, one after the other, as I stood astounded. Here, Father sat with his left leg crossed over his right, his morning newspaper widespread at arm's length. Three feet of a newspaper stretch internalized in chunks. His life was big, and his imagination was even bigger.

"Come sit next to me Adel, and tell me about your plans for today," I heard him say as he temptingly patted the seat next to him with his right hand. "Why don't you visit me at the office this afternoon? I'll teach you a thing or two," he added with a smile.

"The boys are busy today. They have a full schedule of activities," interjected Mother with a sweet tone. She was sitting on the sofa across from him, surrounded by some townspeople, faces I did not recognize. She was busy with her needlework, softly smiling at the flabbergasted faces surrounding her, her eyes twinkling to their admiring praises. She stood up, extended her hand, and walked in my direction. "Come, Adel. Let me introduce you to these wonderful townspeople. She gestured with her hand as she approached me.

My heart started pounding. I wanted so much to feel her hand in mine, to be able to hug her, but the closer she got to me, the more phantasmal she turned, until she floated away like the cigar smoke out of my father's pursed lips.

I went from room to room, opening doors, shutters, and windows. The stillness was too much for me to bear in the light of my memories. The fresh air of the evening seeped in, filling the rooms with a familiar aroma. The light from the dying sun cast soft shadows on the walls, setting forth a perceptual depth and bringing things to life. Nana's kitchen looked smaller than the image printed in my mind. I had never seen the kitchen off duty. It still harbored the smell of coffee that used to brew for hours on a low and open fire. My father liked it dark and strong. He always filled his cup to the rim but sipped it intermittently, with each sip seemingly signaling the successful untangling of a thread from the ganglion of thoughts constantly straining his faculty.

That night, Eeman and I hardly got any sleep. We were carried away ruminating on the past. We stood on the "floating terrace," which was what Mother came to call the massive round balcony she designed for the main living room. It was off that terrace that Aslan had threatened to jump. Lamentably, my parents believed him. His defiant behavior was too challenging for them to mitigate but by a subordinate reaction.

I had forgotten how serene Crescent was. It was indeed where nature hummed its vociferously happy tunes, not humans and not their machines. The surrounding mountains were veiled in a light mist that lifted my spirit. Several houses stood in tiny silhouettes against the dark green slopes.

"It's only a matter of time before blocks of concrete swallow up the whole slope," Eeman said as she stepped onto the porch, as if she had read my thoughts.

"Do they belong to people from Crescent?"

"The majority no longer does." She sighed heavily. "Most of the agricultural parcels were neglected and sold. Some families have forgotten about farming, as if washing off their hands from the soil of their land would give them a sense of social and economic betterment. To others, the soil is no longer practical with their growing materialistic needs."

"Unfortunately, small-scale farming is an ideology of the past," I said.

"Well, the effective motivational force is no longer there."

"What do you suppose motivates Crescent's people today? I asked, struck by her response.

"People everywhere see an ambiguous future. They're feeling threatened by a constantly growing materialistic world. And to protect their families, they go with the tide. Also, they want to own a comfortable house, own a car, and be able to send their kids to school. Can you blame them?"

"Not at all. We need to do something about it though."

"Crescent needs a leader whose motivation lies solely in its interest. Someone who's armored with a deeper understanding of the world, a sharper vision into the future, and a shrewdness to secure the well-being of our people," she said, all in one breath.

I leaned my elbows on the ledge of the balcony and looked into the depth of the valley. "Where do you expect to find that person?"

She turned to face me. "Well, he's standing right here with me—on this very balcony. He's amazingly real because I can touch him." She tapped my arm and pinned me with a sweet and sincere smile.

A moment of silence encapsulated us. I could hear the heavy thumping of my heart, the fast rhythm of blood pumping into my ears, as flashbacks from a distant past unfolded like a camera roll. Eeman and I had not seen each other in twenty-five years. A lot could happen in twenty-five years, enough to alter geographies and eradicate species. Her eyes, however, had remained true to her identity: cautious yet amiable, reticent yet engaging. The former shyness that had revealed itself in her body language, as I knew it from our childhood, gave way to self-confidence and commanding presence.

"In case you didn't know, you're genuinely liked and respected." She turned to face the echoing valley. "People won't easily forget the good deeds you managed to carry out even when you were abroad, that you have never given up on them."

"I truly believe that Crescent should move on," I managed to say. "The Jacob family has done well taking care of it with my grandfather and father after him. What I contribute is only meek recompense to the self-realization I still cultivate from this fertile land. The new generation is smart and well learned. You told me that yourself in your letters. All we can do is call for open space and encourage organic living as much as possible. Besides, I'll always be around."

She looked at me with questioning eyes, and then she smiled. A cool breeze sent her hair dancing in the air before it fell gently on her face like a silken veil.

"Why can't it be you, Eeman? No one has loved Crescent more than you have," I said, inching closer to her as she pinned her hair behind her ears.

She took a deep breath, shook her head, and then turned her gaze away. "You see those tiny lights flickering in the distance?" She pointed to the lights emanating from the faraway houses. "Those lights, no matter how hard they try to shine, will never outshine the moon or the stars. They're limited. What you see is all the light they can ever dream to emit."

"Eeman," I said as I seized her cold hand, "you've been through a struggle in life, and still managed to come out triumphant. You're a smart and loving person, and these two attributes are the blueprint for true success in life."

"Triumph is relative," she answered, her eyes suddenly sinking deep.

"What is it that worries you?"

"Let's go inside. I'm suddenly feeling cold," she said as she turned around and headed back inside. "You must be hungry! Should we eat?"

I followed her inside. A few pots were spread on the dining table, still covered. She elegantly uncovered the casseroles, arranged two place settings, and poured water into the crystal glasses. The same china my mother used when I was a child. Her hands were moving nervously. When she was done setting the table, she looked at me and smiled. "I'm assuming you don't mind having dinner with the chef tonight."

"It's my pleasure, Eeman. Do you remember how you used to cook for us when we were young? I always loved your food."

"I hope you find it tastier now. A tad more elaborate maybe?"

She filled my plate with salad and uncovered a basket of freshly baked bread.

"Our public library has a whole section on culinary art. I must've tried a hundred recipes from different magazines," she added, smiling. "For the past five years, Nana Thabita and I have been cooking together on Saturdays. She let me pick the recipes. The more exotic they sounded, the more she would get excited. She was always young at heart. I'm going to miss her."

She wiped the corner of her eye with her napkin.

"You know, Eeman, when I left the country twenty-five years ago, I was devastated having to part from Mona and Nana Thabita. I carried them with me through every minute of the day. And what finally brought me back to Crescent was the debilitating thought that I would never see her again."

A somber mood fell upon us as we finished eating in silence, pushing down feelings of sorrow and anguish with every bite swallowed. I watched her every move.

"If I remember correctly, you loved peach pies," she broke the silence as she set her fork down. "I baked one, would you care for a piece?" She stood up, gathered a few dishes off the table, and headed to the kitchen.

I finished my soup and got up to help clear the table. I gathered a few plates and followed her into the kitchen. She was standing motionlessly at the sink, her slumped back to me. She had one hand on the counter supporting her weight, and the other rubbing at her forehead. On the counter next to her was a medicine bottle. Upon sensing my presence, she stood up straight. I noticed a tremor in her body.

"Are you all right, Eeman?"

She nodded and turned around to look at me, her face strikingly wan. "Yes, I'll be fine."

"What's wrong?"

"It's a weird pain. I don't know how to describe it."

We sat at the kitchen table, eating peach pie and drinking herbal tea. We continued to talk of the past, omitting all that was sad. I tried to cheer her up with different stories from our childhood, and she started to relax. I told her about my life abroad and the people I met. Her face lit up as I described foreign cities and their weather, people, and cultures.

She sighed. "That's a dream I have yet to fulfill."

"What is?"

"To travel the world."

She turned her head to look out the window. Neither of us spoke for a while. She kept her gaze fixed on the darkness outside while I sat motionless, conscious of her warm presence—and of the emotions she was stirring in me. I silently promised to help her fulfill her dream.

"Would you accompany me to the rec center tomorrow?" I asked. "I can't wait to see what it looks like."

She stood up and grabbed her purse. "Welcome back," she said as she hugged me. "Good night."

"Good night," I responded. "See you tomorrow."

# *Chapter 23*

The next day, I woke up at the break of dawn. I felt surprisingly rested after only a few hours of sleep. I pushed open the shutters. The view out the window, long imprinted in my mind, looked vastly different that morning. A shift in time is by itself a shift in perspective.

*Change is an inevitable theme of nature.*

On the kitchen table, I found a tray with a glass of fresh milk, a bowl of wild berries, and a handwritten note: "Good morning, friend. I'll be at the library."

Nana Thabita's situation had worsened overnight. I kissed her hand as she slept, the oxygen mask covering her exhausted face. I whispered to her my deep-felt gratitude for instilling so much love and wisdom in me. I told her how intricate her role was in my life and how she would permanently reside in my heart and mind as a symbol of pure and unconditional love.

Brokenhearted, I set on the winding brick road that led down to the village. It always felt long, but never too long for the legs of a young boy eager to play and discover. The air was crisp and dewy. The sun was slowly materializing from behind the peaks to the east, bursting through the clouds with its majestic rays of yellow and inundating the skies with hues of orange. Another opportunity. Another day.

From the top of the hill, I saw the houses and the trees as they stood gracefully, awaiting the sun's energy to awaken them and bathe them in its warmth. I could see the green mountains and the lush green valley nestled in between.

"Crescent, my home!" I said to myself.

From the top of that hill, the view was panoramic and dream-like. The effect of nature on me was surreal, and for that, I loved it. In Crescent's wilderness, I felt safe. In its disordered and untamable beauty, I saw an act of defiance.

As I set down the road, I was accompanied by the cheerful sounds of nature's awakening to yet another glorious day. The layer of dew glittered under the morning rays. Herds of cattle driven along the narrow trails looked like beads on a chain. Birds took to the sky, welcoming the new day with their happy singing. I felt the overwhelming power of rhythm, the universal ease of anticipation and expectancy, the driving force of continuity and hope.

Main Street was already filled with pedestrians. Some were running their morning errands, while others, dressed formally, were heading to their offices. Shop owners were hauling goods in and out of their shops, which lined both sides of the street. The sounds and smells emanating from them aroused my senses. What struck me was the unexpected number of cars driving by. Still, life was running peacefully, cheerfully, and lovingly. There was harmony among the people. It was apparent from the way they greeted and interacted with each other that they were one big family. I sighed in relief.

As I passed by the stone structure that had housed my father's mayoral office, I had to stop and reflect. It no longer was the jewel of the village. It stood overshadowed by numerous buildings surrounding it. I wondered what Father had thought of these changes. People passing by took notice of me standing on the sidewalk, engrossed by my surroundings. To the young, I was no doubt a stranger. Older people, however, stared unblinkingly at me, struggling to identify me. I had been gone for twenty-five years and had not come back once to visit. That could easily turn me into a stranger.

*My limp is a dead giveaway.*

I walked on. The people who finally recognized me spread out their faces in merriment. They approached me with warm greetings. Although I could only remember a few of them, they all wanted to invite me to their homes to meet with their extended families. Their attitude toward me surely withstood the twenty-five years I was gone. They collectively informed me of the affliction my parents' death had personally caused them. They were seriously concerned that the Jacobs estate—for all it had represented in their past and promised for their future—would shut its doors and crumble under the elements of time. The affection and respect I was shown would cloak me with humility for years to come.

"Kids I hardly knew back then are all grown up now, and the amazing thing is that they recognized me. They were telling me stories from my childhood that I don't even remember," I told Eeman when I met her in the lobby of the public library.

"It's your disposition that made every boy in Crescent like you. Your privileges posed no threat, so they harbored no envy or resentment toward you. I don't see why they wouldn't remember you when you're still the reason their children can afford to go to school—or college for that matter."

"It was only boys that liked me?" I asked her teasingly.

A light stroke of red instantly imbued her face. "Not at all. You, no doubt, were every girl's dream as well." She smiled sweetly.

Eeman's cheerfulness that morning was invigorating. Her steps were light and happy. She introduced me to her friends every time they stopped to greet her. Surprisingly, the library was already full of people that early Saturday morning.

"I cannot believe you finally came home. Now we need to work on keeping you from going back," she said as she poured two cups of coffee from an espresso machine.

"Believe me, I don't need much convincing."

"We have close to ten thousand books and periodicals, thanks to all the money you were willing to pour in. No one could have been happier than Mr. Joseph, may he rest in peace."

"Mona had tremendous love and respect for him. He was a good man. He masterminded this project. The library wouldn't have been here had it not been for him."

"I wouldn't have gone back to school had it not been for his support and faith in me."

After she gave me a quick tour of the library, we headed through an indoor walkway connecting it to the recreational center. Both were single-story stone buildings with multihued red tile roofs. The project was bigger than I imagined, yet the surrounding tall and shady oak and pine trees made it less intrusive on its green surroundings. She pushed open a set of double doors to the indoor ball courts.

"Like I told you in my letters, we're now hosting sports competitions, including swim meets. We also host musical performances in the lobby area. Kids of Crescent are showing good talent in both sports and music. I'm so proud of them."

We stood for a while watching the basketball team going through a number of drills, the squeaking of shoes echoing off the walls.

"Can I see the swimming pool," I finally asked.

"I wasn't sure you'd want to."

She stretched her stiffening neck and swallowed, as if to push down a bolus she had been trying to masticate for more than twenty years, and that had stubbornly lodged itself in her throat.

She led the way through another set of double doors. The smell of chlorine was overpowering, the air heavy and warm. The room was huge and brightly lit by massive skylights. In the far end, swimming drills were in full swing. She guided me to the edge of the pool where the water was calm. We stood looking down on it. It looked harmless. Limpid. We both knew, however, that it was far from being harmless. It could distort the image of a submerged body—and it could easily dissolve it down to its most basic chemistry. Why else would water be called the universal solvent? So supple, yet it always got to the very end of its path, eroding stone, bending light, and defying gravity. Its depths were shapeless and shameless. This water harbored a dark secret. It conducted Aslan's negativity and finished what his evilness had started.

"It was death by drowning. She could've survived the gun wound had she not fallen into the depths of this pool," Eeman whispered, her voice quivering. "He didn't even turn around at the sound of water splashing. He snatched the hunting rifle from my mother's shaking hands and headed out through those double doors, deaf to her howling."

A chill overtook me. My heart dropped, and I felt hollow.

"Eeman, I need you to tell me in—detail—how it all happened."

She looked at me with a sallow, worried face. "Let's get out of here."

She guided me out of the building and onto the street. She had her hands in her pockets and her head bent down as she walked in front of me, watching her own feet hit the ground. "You know our beginnings. You know how hard it was for our household with the loss of my father and then my young brother. Mona and I grew closer through our struggles. We were best friends. No thought she did not share with me. And although the road was rocky, we managed to go on. We helped each other focus on the road ahead. And then," she turned to look me in the eye, "then came your accident. Mona became depressed and would not stop worrying."

Eeman stopped talking and picked up her pace. I struggled to catch up with her, daggers of pain digging into my lower back.

"Then I left for college," I said. "Her letters to me seemed optimistic, but I knew she was not happy about our separation. I was miserable, but I tried to convey happiness in my letters."

Eeman slowed down, allowing me to catch up to her. "I see it clearly now, Adel. Your going away to college was the best decision your parents ever made. Just imagine what could've happened otherwise."

"My parents thought of Aslan as a provisional case. They thought time would take care of it for them. They came to realize, although too late, that his attacks were not just verbal, but physical too. Unfortunately, by the time they realized it, it was too late."

"Twice. They missed. Or three times I should say."

I looked at her, but her eyes were still fixed on the ground. The sun was inching its way up in the sky, and the streets of Crescent had somewhat calmed down after the morning rush. I started thinking of how a land so bountiful, so unsophisticated, and so simple could nurture so much evil. I knew Aslan was present when Mona's accident took place. I also suspected his evilness to have taken part in it, but no one I asked would implicate him in any shape or form.

"Eeman—"

"After you left, Mona became completely drawn to her inner thoughts and feelings. She fell into depression and self-reproach. She didn't talk much. She retreated to her mat early in the evening and buried her thoughts in her books for most of the night. She spent her days between school and the community center."

Eeman stopped walking. She reached for a high branch on a lemon tree and broke a twig that she kept breaking into smaller and smaller pieces.

"Then, one day, I saw a bruise on her arm, and when I asked her about it, she covered it nervously with her sleeve and did not answer."

I seized Eeman by the arm. "What are you talking about? Who did that to her?"

She took a deep breath. Her face turned pallid and her sunken eyes glistened with tears.

"Adel, I don't know if I'm doing the right thing here by talking about this after so many years. It really doesn't matter at this point. It won't do either one of us any good. No one could ever bring her back." She turned around and rushed ahead. "I need to go home. I need to lie down."

I followed her in silence, my mind lost in a surge of thoughts I did not know how to process. Her house looked beautiful with its artful stone entryway lined on both sides with shrubs of gardenia and hydrangea. The cedar tree that Mr. Ramsey used to park his wagon under was still there. So was the cowshed. She rushed inside and collapsed on the couch.

"Should I get you some water? Did you have something to eat this morning?" I asked worriedly. "You just lost your color."

"Just give me a couple of minutes. I'll be fine," she whispered as she rubbed the right side of her face.

I sat next to her on the sofa and waited. Her eyes were closed, her breathing methodical and light. I was captivated by her soft and radiant complexion as I let my eyes wander over her delicate face. A deep feeling of affection inched through my bloodstream. My heart fluttered.

Life is full of mysteries. Attempting to unravel them is grueling. What makes us is much older than us. Atoms are older than their elements, and the particles that make up the atom are even older than the atom itself. Older still are the intangible forces around us. Those forces pull on us, clustering us into an entity or separate us in time and space at an accelerating rate. Unfathomable is a scheme in which bangs and explosions lead to intricate designs of billions of galaxies and systems, stars and planets, dinosaurs and microorganisms.

She propped herself up on her elbows. "You spaced out. What's on your mind?"

"Just thinking. Are you feeling better?"

"I was fourteen in that picture," she said, standing up and walking to the other side of the room.

On the wall was a framed black-and-white childhood photo of Eeman, Mona, and Malec. Mona was the only one smiling to the camera, her eyes open and bright. She was so smart and full of life.

"Do you remember Mr. Ramsey, the peddler?" she asked.

"Of course I do. How could I forget?"

"Well, he arrived with a camera one day and started taking pictures of us. It's the only picture we ever had together."

"It's beautiful. It's natural and honest."

"Our meager and deprived past screams through it," she added with a smile.

She turned around and walked to the kitchen. On the counter was a collection of medication bottles. She checked her watch, opened one, and threw back her head. She then poured herself a cup of water and sat at the kitchen table.

"Had my parents had the means, and had their ambition not been blunted by the struggle to put food on the table, they could've been the kind of parents a child would hope for. Playful and mentally stimulating. Maybe I would've grown to listen to music and appreciate it more, and maybe Malec and Mona would've had longer and happier lives. Just maybe."

"My parents were never playful either, although they had all of life's privileges on their side. Yes, they took us on trips, and yes, they provided us with every luxury and commodity, but they never told jokes, laughed, or even whistled to a tune. It was Nana Thabita who made me believe in myself. Her reassuring and loving words erased my nagging doubts, and her praise fueled my self-esteem. She helped me survive Aslan's abuse and my parents' shortcomings."

She set her cup on the table and rested her head against the back of the chair. "Sadly, Malec and Mona did not survive that abuse," she muttered.

And then she told me the whole story. Uncensored. Abrasive and corrosive down to viscera and molecules. She told me about Aslan's lecherous gestures toward Mona. How Aslan would sneak up on Mona and take her by surprise. On several occasions, he groped her repeatedly. She tried to avoid him, but he was on a mission. A mission to torment her and destroy me along the way.

"I went to him one day and told him to stay away from Mona. I told him that life was not all about satisfying his pleasures and desires and that he needed to respect Mona's dignity and leave her alone." She stood up again and walked to the counter to refill her cup with water. "I even went to your father for help."

"What did he do about it?" I asked, eager to know how Father had reacted to Aslan's behavior, knowing too well that it would be disappointing.

She covered her face with her hands and started sobbing. "I was young and helpless and did not know what else to do or who else to go to. I had no way to take action against anyone."

*My father disappointing me yet again.*

I walked to her, seized her gently by the shoulders, and turned her to face me.

"Mona became very depressed and fell ill," she continued. "She would run a temperature for days at a time. And all along, my mother was watching. We didn't know she was listening in on our conversations and knew what was happening. We never thought she was capable of taking matters into her own hands."

I was all too familiar with that dark moment. I could clearly see his face and how it turned apoplectically red. I saw a savage capable of unconscionable acts. How his features became demonically distorted, and his eyes became those of the devil. And then he pushed me. I had no time to scream.

I shook the vision out of my head. Eeman was sobbing at that point. I wrapped my arms around her and pulled her closer. She rested her head on my shoulders and cried until my shirt was soaked from her tears. I kissed her head and caressed her silky black hair.

"I knew I couldn't continue had I kept looking back. I tried to forget. And let me tell you, Adel, it's blissful for me to be able to forget, but I had to learn to forgive and let go. And that took years of self-conditioning. It was not easy."

"I'm so sorry you had to go through so much hardship. My anger caused me to deny my past. I thought if I stayed overseas, I could get away from the bad memories and learn to move on."

"My mother was in a state of stupor. She didn't understand what went wrong. She kept repeating, 'Where is Mona? Why did she fall in the water? How come Aslan was still standing? I killed her, didn't I? How did I do that?' Surprisingly, her face would remain calm at times, though it would be impossible to say the situation did not upset her or even terrify her. At other times, she would scratch her hands until her skin peeled off. My mother dissolved from inside out."

Not only was Aslan a psychopath—he was a murderer. Unfortunately, his crimes were never attributed to his wrongdoing or to the shortcomings of my parents. Eeman gave me Mona's last unfinished letter to me:

Dear friend,

Whoever said that time makes you forget couldn't have been further from the truth. I miss you more by the minute. Being away from you has been horrible, and to think that there's one whole year left before you graduate is dreadfully frightening.

Forgive me if I'm being selfish. What you're doing abroad isn't easy and takes a lot of courage and perseverance. The last thing you need is for me to tie you down emotionally … but life in Crescent is no longer the same …

I'm confused about a lot of things, and I don't know whether things have really changed or whether it's just me. Is it because I see them differently now? Is it because I see their true color?

… …

Why did you have to leave? Why can't I touch your face and look into your sweet eyes? I haven't received a letter from you for the past two months.

...

Regarding Aslan: How can he remain sane when he's given anything he asks for? When no one ever says no to him. Nothing to him is impossible, and no one dares interfere.

I promise you to not give in to despair.

I will keep waiting.

The idea that Father or Aslan had intercepted some of my letters to her did not come as shocking. I folded her letter and placed it, with the others, carefully nestled in *The Miser*.

# Chapter 24

F or the next five years, Eeman was my healing muse, and for the rest of my life, she would remain my guiding spirit.

"The present is but a negligible window of time between the nagging past and the mysterious future. Our existence in the present can never be fully appreciated for, by the time we do realize it, it's already dusted down memory lane," she told me, "so learn to be happy in this fleeting moment."

We buried Nana Thabita in the family cemetery, next to my grandparents and parents. The only thing I regretted was that I never had the chance to learn about her past and those who were in her life, who she really was as a person, what her dreams and her worries were. She could have told me about my grandparents and their personalities, about my father as a child and adult. Certainly she could see through things better than I did before I left home.

I was glad, however, that she did not know of Eeman's illness. She did not have to see her wither like I did, day after day, treatment after exhausting treatment. The chronic pain in her gum was the tip of the iceberg, and the different drugs she was put on were hammer blows to its surface.

I was also glad to have been with Eeman since the beginning of the end. I accompanied her to the city in hopes of finding a cure for persistent mouth sores that were getting nastier and more painful. When the biopsy result indicated cancer, we followed recommended doctors and hospitals around the globe. She did not settle for standard options, but she was progressive in her approach and opened her mind to unconventional and holistic methods as well. And although a remission gave us a glimpse of hope, a menacing relapse came to doom the malignancy unburnable.

So, I made a decision. I proposed to Eeman. For days, I had pondered over Nana Thabita's advice to me the day before she died.

"Crescent is still full of beauty," she had said. "Don't go looking too far. It's within your reach."

"Will you marry me?" I asked Eeman one morning after a long hike on the trails of Crescent.

She looked at me with eyes bearing an expression I understood very well: happiness entrapped by reservation. She shrugged her shoulders as if to release a heavy burden. "It would be terrible to bind yourself to a sickness. It's known to be unwavering."

"My will is equally unwavering. Please don't deny me this happiness," I said as I cupped her face in my hands and touched my lips to hers.

## Part 5

A little while, a moment of rest upon the wind, and another woman shall bear me.

—Gibran Khalil Gibran

# Chapter 25

Reflections

The continuum of our lives advances imperceptibly, yet it leaves appreciable marks along the way. The trajectory for the most part seems ordinary, with no insurmountable obstacles.

No choice is ever spontaneous, though it might feel that way. Our choices are dictated by previous experiences, state of mind, and physical condition at the time of making a decision. Thereby, every step depends on all that precedes it—be it perceived as trivial or consequential—and every step is one of many that are possible at a particular time.

Though all paths cross, no two people take the exact same path, just as no two people look exactly the same. No one knows in advance what is waiting down the road. While the ultimate direction is one, every step we take dictates a set of possible future steps in that direction. And since the possibilities are endless, we are prone to face losses and gains, experience love and deception, rejoice with self-realization or suffer from fretfulness.

The overall journey can never be ascribed to a single step or a single decision, just as the sweeping force of a wind is not solely ascribed to that element alone, but collectively to other elements that help bring it about. The overall journey is the culminating result of all that lived and existed, from the present time extending to the infinite past.

On the infinite paths extending ahead, all human pursuits share a common denominator, which is ultimate happiness, attributed to

Aristotle's summum bonum. Eudaimonia. No matter how we add or simplify, without that denominator, all efforts and pursuits become undefined. On the other hand, as we nourish that happiness, both intellectually and morally, everything else becomes trivial, almost nonexistent.

# Chapter 26

"Is it the third Saturday of the month tomorrow?"

"Yes, Mr. J. It sure is. What's for the menu?"

"You know she likes salads and pastas. Be creative or have it specially catered. And like usual, fire up the chimneys and have the pianist put together a good list of tunes. Did you refresh her room?"

"We sure did. Do you know if she's staying for the night?"

"I hope so. Are the vases full of flowers?"

"Yes, Mr. J. White orchids this time. This florist sure is an artist. Her arrangements are breathtaking. If you let me take you around the house, you could see it for yourself."

"Maybe in the afternoon. I have to catch up on my writing."

"All right, then. Your desk is set up, and the outdoor heater is on. Ready?"

"Ready."

Reema pushed my wheelchair to the balcony where I had sat every morning for the past six months, snow or sunshine, and hammered at my keyboard. She wrapped my shoulders with a warm blanket and set a tray of fresh fruits and cereal on the table next to me.

"I'll keep checking on you," she said as she tuned the radio to my favorite station. "Buzz me if you need me."

"Thank you, Reema. I will. I'm not taking any visitors today," I reminded her.

"You haven't for a while, Mr. J."

"I promised her I would finish my memoir. Between my arthritic fingers and my failing memory, the task is becoming colossal."

For a whole month, with all its days and nights, hours and minutes, I patiently waited between her visits. I was so glad she stayed faithful to her scheduled trips.

"My work is very demanding, and writing my grants is a very stressful process," she told me two weeks ago, over the phone, when I asked if she would be spending the night in Mar Elias this time.

I did not want to sound like a desperate and selfish old man. I always tried to conceal my loneliness. As soon as her car pulled into the driveway, she honked a tune, ran into the house, and shouted my name.

She was a drug that remedied my ailment but raised a monstrous list of side effects. In her presence, I felt the ecstasy of happiness, the generosity and fairness of life. However, from the moment she hugged me goodbye, my heart would sink to the lows of many times passed. She was the reason I wrote my memoir.

"No one would be able to write it like you would. Complete and true," she had insisted.

She was always full of questions about her mother, our relationship, and our past. Some answers she accepted while others she revisited, confused and unconvinced. Did my answers ever fully satisfy her questions? Answers are always relative and subjective. Just like the truth, as we know it, answers stood tall until time came to modify them, but I couldn't remain silent. Silence meant betrayal.

"Did you want me to write my story from today's perspective?" I asked. "I think it would be closer to the truth, viewed in the light of a lifelong experience."

"No," she said. "I'd rather hear it the way it felt—at the time it was."

Miserable is the man who searches for the truth behind everything. As children, we are naïve to believe that people around us have the answers to our pestering list of whys. Yet we keep asking why. As adults, we learn not to bother anymore, succumbing impotently to the mystery of life and its living things. Is our cognitive mind a blessing or is it a curse? We analyze, and we foresee. We study theories and conduct experiments. We debate and manipulate. The list of whys does not get shorter, however. The more we unravel, the more there is to unravel.

Looking back on the course of my life, I couldn't help but look *through* it. My story is gripping. A book thick with loss and suffering, with love and compensation. I found it overpowering that each moment fell in its perfect place, like the tight and precise fit of a lock and its key, trapping me in their grip, chopping off protruding extremities, until I was trivialized, readily dissectible into individual discernable parts. Even then, understanding my life was nothing but an illusion. Individual parts put together could never account for all the factors of a lifetime or account for the mind and its different forms of consciousness.

Every person endures alone in a sense, dwelling in furrows and grooves deposited by his or her own fears and consternations, entombed beneath the buildup of unsparing social conformity. Consequently, one mostly lives within his or her own self, and own thoughts, which remain mostly unknown to any other person, regardless of how close that person may seem. And although the majority of life is spent within, the self remains a big challenge to the person. Self-understanding and conquering is a mission that could last several lifetimes. "The hardest victory is over self," Aristotle said.

"Let me see your fingers," she said as she took my hands between hers and caressed them. "Are you being able to type your notes?"

"These hands were once made of steel." I smiled, enjoying her affectionate touch.

"They still are." She kissed them. "Are you keeping to your medication and exercise regimens?"

"I am. Exercise was always excruciating—but not like the way it's become recently. Osteoarthritis is crippling me. It's preposterous how time sneaks on us so imperceptibly," I said, looking into her crystal clear brown eyes.

"Why not take a break from writing for a couple of weeks. I can come up and spend some time with you. I can take some time off work. And if you agree to it, I can do the writing and typing for you."

"I cannot stop the flow. Sometimes I don't sleep through the night stressing over a faded detail or a date. I need to iron this out. I need to settle my thoughts."

All my life, I tried to keep Aslan's face out of my mind. Memories of him were like a choker pulling tighter around my neck. Writing my memoir, however, made me look at my life as simply a series of events, one leading to the other, totally unanticipated. Testing events, with the guileful and the truthful, and the wide spectrum of personalities in between, strumming my life like strings on a guitar, sometimes with forceful strokes, and sometimes with soft brushes. The resulting tune of my life is a compilation of thoughts expressed, of more left unexpressed, and of yet many more thoughtless expressions.

"Looking back on your life, what do you regret the most?" she asked as her gentle fingers stroked what little hair I had left.

"I learned not to regret, my dear child. Age turns us into lumbering hosts, heaving with acquired immunity to the ever-growing list of misfortunes that life guilefully injects us with. That's why we become who we are. The only thing I would do differently, had I had a second chance at this life, is to live every moment to its utmost. Enjoy every moment by being in it."

"I do enjoy every moment I spend talking to you. I learn a lot from you." She hugged me.

"The truth is, Noura, my dearest angel, that the universe took my beloved from me twice. Every single time, it felt malicious and unfair, brutal and unbearable, but the truth is, dearest angel, that the universe placed you in my life. And I loved love all over again. I can look at you and enjoy you. Through your eyes I see my past and my future. I love you dearest child. I love you more than life."

"I love you too, Papa."

# Chapter 27

The rain had been pelting down on the windshield from the moment we left home, at times falling in heavy sheets, and at others gently drumming a soothing beat. Either way, nature's tune was nothing less than harmonious. Reyes had been driving for about an hour before Eeman's tension started to ease. I stole glances at her as we sat in the back seat of the car, her hand cradled in mine.

"Everything will be fine. You'll see," I assured her, completely aware of what was clouding her mind.

It was a mid-September day. The blustery wind that had bellowed through Crescent for a few days had capriciously waned with the dawning hours. It had rained all night, and the land felt soggy as we stepped out of the house that morning. Eeman had undergone a gingival biopsy the day before. Persistent ulcers on her gum compelled her periodontist to call for the procedure. I could decipher a lingering trace of grievous worry on her face.

My financial advisor had left me with a list of lots for sale down south, where a desperately needed medical hospital could serve several kilometers in radius and alleviate medical hassles for many neighboring towns. I asked Eeman to accompany me on the trip to help personally investigate the land, hoping it would lift her spirits. We had spoken at length about our future together. We had gone on a tour to different countries. I had the chance to introduce her to our chain of businesses overseas, only to become more adamant that back home was the most ideal place for us.

Reyes, whose father had devotedly worked our land in Crescent for years, accepted my offer as our full-time chauffeur. He was a well-respected and honorable man. We had been driving for two hours that day, and I started to worry about Eeman not being comfortable sitting in the car that long.

"I know of the best restaurant in the next town. It's about a kilometer east of the highway," Reyes said, looking at me through the rearview mirror, as if he had sensed my worry. "It's a family-owned restaurant, and the ingredients are organic and grown locally."

"Awesome," Eeman responded. "I can always go for some wholesome food."

Off the highway, the car zigzagged through meadows and circled along a natural river. We rolled down the windows and let the crisp air flow in. It had just stopped raining, and nature was in an extraordinary state, where juxtaposed colors of summer and fall intensified its marvel. Eeman stuck her head through the window and gazed in reverence at the rolling hills and meadows.

"Welcome to Mar Elias," Eeman read off a carved wood sign on the side of the road. "What a nice little town. We're stopping here, right, Reyes?" she asked cheerfully.

"Yes. In about a hundred meters."

The car rolled through a narrow street lined with shops and single-story country houses. Loads of firewood were stacked on the front porches in anticipation of the cold season. The few people who were walking on the streets stopped to watch the car pass by, nodding or waving in our direction. Reyes waved back in recognition.

"The nicest people you can meet," Reyes commented. "I once had a friend from this town. I used to visit him all the time. It's one big family here."

We parked the car right outside the Local Eatery. The heavy green wood door creaked as I pushed it open. The restaurant was quiet except for the sound of a fire crackling in an open wood chimney. The tables were made of tree trunks, and the stools of assembled logs were mounted by red cushions. It smelled of a medley of burning wood, fresh-baked bread, and a brewing stew. The owners were very welcoming, and after a brief introduction by Reyes, the table was covered with small plates of local inventions, spiced and cooked to perfection.

"I love this place," she said with a sweet smile that I hadn't seen for a while. She ate her bowl of stew and asked for a second.

"I think I love it too. You would never know this place existed by merely driving up the highway."

"That adds to its mysterious beauty," she exclaimed.

We kicked off our shoes and walked to the river, following the directions of the restaurant owner. The river bend was supposed to be a premier trout-fishing site, popular and targeted by fishermen from kilometers away. We walked along the river, our feet sinking in the fertile soil. The river was quiet, and the water was cold and crystal clear. Several trails cut through the terrain. We saw numerous campsites under the trees. Eeman's mood lightened, and hope ran through me again.

"Ah! The fresh smell of rain." She inhaled deeply, raised her head, and opened her arms wide.

We drove back to Mar Elias several times thereafter, ate at the Local Eatery, and walked the trails along the river, before a marvelous idea hit me. Looking back at it through the corrective lens of time, it became apparent that it was an attempt at clinging to hope for as long as I could, shielding my eyes from reality, and busying my mind with a lifetime purpose. I made a number of calls, met with the right people, and came up with an exciting plan.

Eeman was in the bedroom, recovering from a long day of procedures at the hospital. She was sitting in bed, knees up to her chin with her arms wrapped around them, her face veiled behind the rising steam from her teacup, her eyes looking out the window. "Hey," she said, without turning to look at me.

"Hi. Were you able to get some sleep?"

"You know I can never nap. The days are too beautiful."

I sat on the edge of her bed and caressed her long, shiny hair.

"What's on your mind?" I asked.

She sighed. "Mona has been gone for close to twenty-three years, and not one day has passed by without me thinking of her, of the sister she would've been had she lived. The things we could've done together. How she would've looked like. Twenty-three years—and my longing hasn't waned an iota."

She turned her gaze away from the window and rested it on me.

"I always hated how Mona and Malec were cheated by death," she added, her eyes glistening. "In my case, however, death is not cheating me. It's giving me a warning. A bold warning, but it's still a heads-up, I assume."

"Let's make the best of the life we have," I rushed saying, sensing a flicker of her indomitable spirit.

"I'm not supposed to be a part of your life. I'm not supposed to be sitting here right now. I can never change who I am, my past, or who my parents are."

"Please stop," I whispered, taking her in my arms and burying my face in her hair.

"Forgive me, Adel. Please forgive me," she said, pulling herself away. "I thought I could make you happy. Please go. Go live your life. There are a lot of brilliant and healthy women who would give anything to be part of your life. You deserve the best and nothing less. I'm afraid I might not be physically able to give it to you."

She stood up and walked to the window.

"I want no one but you. You're the reason I gave up the life I built abroad. You brought me back home. I'm not giving you up," I replied.

She sighed. "Twenty-five years is a long time."

"Time is relative. I'm here now. That's what matters."

"Many things have happened while you were gone."

"I want you to just remember the good ones," I said.

"I'm not the same. There are things that I take the blame for."

"You're not to be blamed for anything."

"I got pregnant when I was young. My baby came into the world eight months after Mona died."

She turned her head away from the window, and she looked at me with apologetic eyes.

"Is the child all right?" I asked.

She covered her face with her hands and started sobbing.

I walked to her and took her in my arms.

"I hope so. He was adopted by a good family. I was sure of that."

"Was adoption your decision?"

"Yes. It was the best option I had at the time."

"Have you seen your child ever since?" I asked.

"Not once. I believe it's better for him this way."

"How old would he be now?"

"Twenty-two."

Eeman had a child some twenty-two years ago, and I did not know. It must have been very difficult to put her son up for adoption and to live knowing that a piece of her is somewhere in the world, yet not part of her life.

"Those twenty-five years I was gone?"

"Yes?"

"We can make them up."

"Can we really?"

"Of course we can."

She took my promise to stand by her side until the end very seriously, and she was appreciative of it. Though inconceivable to me as I look back on it, we truly had the best time of our lives. Although her prognosis was not so grim in the beginning, we both knew, deep inside, that the clock would tick away our days—and we also knew there was no way to rewind that clock. We were aware of the only choice that was left, and that was to live it up. We emerged from hospital visits and carried on. We traveled the world. We went full blast with the hospital project.

"What do you say we settle in Mar Elias?" I finally said. "This way, we can be close to the hospital construction site. It'll be a good change of scenery for you and me."

"That's a great idea!" she said, suddenly feeling invigorated. "I love Mar Elias, and I love you. I'd follow you to the end of the world." She smiled and kissed me. "I feel so lucky—despite it all," she managed with a choked voice.

I wanted her out of Crescent, away from haunting memories. She picked a nice piece of land in Mar Elias, up the river. She spent weeks with the architects designing our future house and months helping me with the hospital project.

"I'm no architect, but I have a good idea of what I want the hospital to look like," she told me once. "I see the hospital in all white: white walls and white marble floors. Let the ceiling be high, windows oversized, and hallways wide."

"I like it already."

"Well, I worked at several hospitals, and do you know what I hated about every single one of them? The narrow and over-jammed hallways, the low ceilings, and the lack of windows. Let's make sure this one is more comfortable and less claustrophobic."

And so it was. The gigantic, state-of-the-art construction went at full speed. Eeman helped select the board of directors from doctors she had done work with, and most of them were renowned in their own fields. She also helped plan the residence hall, which housed permanent staffers. People who worked with her loved and respected her.

At the same time, we built our house. We moved in while it was still under construction. She did not mind the chaos and the disorder around us.

"This is fun. I don't mind it," she assured me.

While I was busy with all sorts of business engagements, she remained upbeat and active. She woke up early in the mornings and went off to manage her projects. On less hectic days, we met for lunch at the Local Eatery, ate their daily special, and sipped our tea over stories from the field.

There was so much to do that our days felt short. They mostly ended with us curled up in a hammock, listening to music and watching the stars. She had so much to tell me, but our conversations were never about her predicament. We reminisced about our past and dreamt of the future.

However, a splintering present holds no future. The truth is that most of the phenomena around us is unperceivable to our five senses. Something as small as a change in one's DNA could turn tables, wreck lives, and abolish hope. The wrong mutation, at the wrong time, in the wrong sequence of events, has a huge ripple effect, multiplying damage beyond any conceivable threshold.

Oral cancer drained her ardor and erased the pink from her face. And I saw her waste away, faster from the treatment than the ailment. Her breath smelled of medication. Her face became bruised and mutilated. Her eyes sank deep. And, as she shed her jaw, a centimeter at a time, she always found a way to whisper her words of gratitude.

"I'm the lucky one," I whispered back to her as we reclined in silence on the balcony, her head in my lap, our eyes fixed on the heavens for salvation, as I caressed a pain that would not succumb to numbness. "I am lucky to have won your heart."

# Chapter 28

I eventually came to realize that happiness was not meant for me. Every time my heart managed to regain a steady, healthy beat, some tragedy or another would hit me, leaving me confused and miserable. Every time I found my equanimity, the earth would move underneath me. Once again, I felt alone.

"Every time you fall into despair, just remember that life is a test—and that living it means rising to the challenge. Stay focused on the people who are depending on you in their daily lives. Think of the joy you manage to put in so many people's hearts and how you have made it your daily mission. This is true kindness. When you know you're committed to brightening a life. That should be the light of yours."

She did live up to her ideals. Everything around the house reminded me of her strong will. The fact that the house and the hospital were completed as she dealt with cancer was by itself a story of fight and hope. Her loss drove me into a déjà-vu depression that tied me to my bed for a week, weighed my body down with lethargy, and subjected my temples to a dull throbbing that never seemed to end. For days, I refused to let Reema crack open my windows for fresh air or slide open the heavy curtains to let sunshine in. I monitored the passing of time through the thin streaks of light percolating between the shutter panels as I drifted in and out of sleep. For days after she left, I sat in complete darkness, haunting thoughts glaring down on me. For days, I struggled to swallow my food. It tasted like nothing at all.

Since then, I kept to the custom of taking my morning coffee on the east balcony, contemplating the warming of the earth with the start of each day, just like she and I used to do, pretending she was with me. Although my evenings were no longer about listening to music and whispering in her ears, laughing to her jokes and wiping her tears, I vowed to continue our mission. Business and the hospital affairs still occupied most of my day. In the afternoons, I resorted to taking long hikes along the river. I would walk until the daggers of pain slicing through my back and legs suffused every interstice of my being. And in the evenings, I locked myself in my library, going through books like a kid would go through a bag of candy.

Eeman was buried in the family cemetery in Crescent. Hundreds of friends, colleagues, and neighbors came to pay their condolences. Even though Crescent's streets were narrow and challenging to crowds of that magnitude, her funeral was well planned. My business manager made sure to include me in all the details, but, for the most part, I weighed in absentmindedly. The last week Eeman spent at the hospital was dreadful. As she lied heavily sedated with an escalating dose of morphine, slipping in and out of consciousness, I paced the room, phasing between resignation and abject fury, confused and scared of what lied ahead. Never before had I felt so vulnerable.

Eeman was loved for the goodness that resided in her. In her enlarged photo I had on display at the funeral, she was wearing a simple blue cotton shirt, her hair floating in the air, her face brightened by the sun, and her smile wide and sincere. What one saw in that picture was truthfully all there was. She was a very practical person, sincere, free-spirited, and open-minded. She looked happy. People would stop by her photo and nod their heads as if to say, "Yes, that's exactly who she was."

Aslan did not come to the funeral. Nana had last seen him when my parents died. Since then, it seemed, he had not set foot in Crescent. The conglomerate company he had founded, Jacob Construction Enterprises, came to be very well respected. I had agreed to sign the proposal that his company submitted to build Mar Elias General Hospital for its competitive pricing and commitment to quality and efficiency. His people were able to complete the construction of the seventy thousand-square-foot structure in a record twenty months. The emergency room and delivery ward were in full swing eight months prior to the hospital's grand opening day.

I remember handing Eeman the ceremonial banquet agenda one evening, as we were about to get in bed. I watched her as she read it to herself. Aslan was to attend and give a speech.

"Oh!" she said with a puzzled look on her face. She handed the agenda back to me and headed to the bathroom.

"Voted for by the board of directors," I explained as I sat on the edge of the bed.

"Still, you can object to it," she responded as she walked back into the bedroom, patting her face dry with a towel.

"No need. Unless you see otherwise."

"I just never thought I'd ever again lay eyes on him in person."

"You need to be honest with me," I said, reaching for her hand. "We don't have to attend. There are plenty of other things we can do—just the two of us."

"No. Listen to me. Of course we need to attend. You, especially, need to attend. This hospital is your baby. Your dream come true. No one should take this day away from you." She sat next to me and kissed me. "Besides, we'll be together. Nothing could harm us."

I hugged her tightly to my chest, realizing how fragile and vulnerable we both were.

At the banquet, Aslan seemed respectable, his mien serious and his presence captivating. He walked tall, his neck overstretched. He had gained weight, which made his posture even more dominant. His hair had gray streaks in it. He wore it brushed tightly backward on the sides with a fuller top, adding an inch or two to his height. He was wearing an expensively tailored suit, dark blue with a subtle shine to the fabric, and accentuated it with a bright red tie. The sight of him overpowered each of my senses. When he entered the conference hall, the hustle and bustle around me fell flat. Pictures from the past rolled through my mind, the bitter taste of which became palpable in my mouth. I swallowed my surging saliva and took a deep breath.

"Are you all right?" Eeman whispered as she hooked her elbow around mine and guided me through the crowd.

"The sight of him."

"Breathe it out. And don't forget to smile. By the way, I love your smile."

"I love you."

"What do you think of the setup?" she asked.

"You did an awesome job, like usual. The color coordination and flower arrangements are perfect. Thank you, Eeman."

"Let's greet him."

The handshake was that of strangers, formal with a swift and cold grip. After all, we had not seen each other in more than twenty-seven years. Just as swift were the eye contact and the head nod. And then, thankfully, he was pushed aside by the staggering crowd. Government delegates, people of academia and medicine, people of biotechnology, people of the press, bankers, and manufacturers filled the conference hall. Reflecting back on that night, I could not place Eeman in that moment. I could not remember if she and Aslan had greeted or even acknowledged each other.

And then I spotted him. He was hovering around Aslan.

*How come I haven't noticed him yet?*

He was moving about jauntily, somewhat ostentatiously. He was shaking hands and patting backs. He was taller than Aslan and broader at the shoulders. His thick, black hair nicely crowned his young face.

*Did Aslan plan on introducing him to me?*

He looked so much like me when I was his age. As a matter of fact, he could have easily been mistaken for mine rather than Aslan's.

The double doors to the dining hall were swung open, and attendees were ushered to find their assigned seats.

Eeman was waving in my direction. She was about to take the podium to introduce the event. As I turned around to head to our assigned table, I felt a hand grabbing my shoulder from behind. And there he was. His face lit with a sincere smile.

"Hello, Mr. Jacob," he said. "I'm Adam. Your nephew."

It took me a split second to realize I could actually hug him. He had a pleasant disposition about him. His voice was full of energy. His smile was not cold and ill-natured, like that of his father, but sweet and from the heart.

"Adam! It's a pleasure to meet you, young man!"

"The pleasure is mine! Congratulations on the hospital," he said.

"Already up and running. Your company did an impressive job," I admitted.

"Well, our company strives to deliver the best-quality work without wavering from our founding values of commitment and integrity," he recited, affirming the sound mission of his company.

"Then maybe there'll be more projects in the future."

He flashed his sincere smile again.

"How old are you, Adam?" I asked him without knowing why I felt compelled to know his exact age.

"I'm twenty years old," he responded, still smiling.

"I'm glad we finally met. Enjoy the evening."

"Thank you," he replied bowing his head.

He turned around and walked away, struggling to loosen his tie.

Eeman walked up to the podium and gave a heartfelt introduction to the hospital project and the motive behind its inception. She elaborated on how it would benefit communities beyond the borders of Mar Elias. She ensured that the hospital, with its state-of-the-art technology in diagnostic and surgical equipment, as well as its top-of-the-line staff, would be available to all patients regardless of their financial or social status. Her genuine message received a standing ovation.

Cancer had already left its damaging imprint on her. She had lost weight and looked frail, but she believed in the hospital's mission, and it showed.

After I gave a brief introduction of the board members, the executive director of medical services, and several department heads, each had a short message to convey. And then Aslan took the podium as a distinguished guest speaker. For the first few minutes, I could not hear or understand what he was saying. I watched him absentmindedly. Images from our childhood collided in my field of vision, clouding my mind and his image at the podium. Loud applause would pull me back to reality here and there. I realized that he was actually still the same person I once knew. Eloquent. Haughty. Egomaniacal. The focus of his delivered message, however, was beyond the occasion at hand—beyond nonprofits and hospitals—but that did not surprise me. He unraveled projects as enormous as power plants and factories, hundreds of kilometers of pipelines and highways. He talked about commerce and manufacturers. He discussed propositions he would lobby for and urged government officials to sign into laws. When asked if he would ever run for government office, he shook his head and discredited the idea with a dismissive hand gesture and a smile. "I don't see that as worthwhile at the moment," he answered. "Our work is insightful. Our work is rigorous. And our work is creative. No, I sure would not give all that up."

Aslan was as provocative as he had always been—and as demagogic as he had distinctively planned to be.

After the speech, Aslan's face lost its zeal, and he assumed a look of boredom. It seemed that all the jabbing he took during his speech was premeditated upon, from the power jab to the status jab. *Has anyone ever challenged him or stood in his way?* Besides, he did not evince any intention to seek Eeman or me or even recognize our presence. I personally was happy our encounter ended as quickly as it did.

Hypocrisy, deceit, and greed were the foundations of Aslan's character and his protocol to success. He called on government officials for the divestiture of public land. He cut deals and crafted policies to turn "desolate, unused acres" into "useful grounds." Frenzies of rock excavation and highways erupted, connecting north with south and east with west. Towns were built, and others vanished. New jobs were created for the young, the strong, and those who were neither but simply willing to risk the little they had left. Others felt pushed to uproot or concede to demeaning jobs. Still, many deemed the work developmental. Huge fortunes were being made by the different industries involved. No attention was granted to grievances caused.

The most disconcerting of all was when I learned that Father had helped mobilize cash for Aslan's projects, cutting some of the deals himself. They were not all good deals. My father had contrived complex maneuvers to evade taxes and avoid paying penalties when things went wrong, all the while exonerating himself of any responsibility. I came to see my father as a man of contradiction and personal conflict. And the fact remained that Aslan had foraged and accumulated enormous fortunes that would make even my father's jaw drop.

All my life, I was conscious of my brother's destructive tendencies. I became obsessed with the urge to undo his harm. Philanthropy became my impetus to establish nonprofit organizations serving the needy and the environment.

# Chapter 29

On clear nights, the sky glimmered with hundreds of tiny stars. On clear, starry nights, the clouds unveiled majesty. Mystery. A lurking tempest. A glory, ablaze in its own glow. I felt trivial. Alone. Who was I in the realm of the skies? What did my life mean? I remembered Van Gogh's *Starry Night* replica hanging above my desk. Even Van Gogh himself thought it exaggerated in terms of composition, but how could someone exaggerate endlessness? My mind couldn't grasp endlessness. The mind is like a moth orbiting the light, drawn by its intense warmth. Round and round it goes until it merges with the light. The universal light.

I walked until I could walk no more. The stabbing pain in my lower back was a constant distraction, a grounding force. I had not seen my physical therapist in weeks. With the fall of every hour of the day, the sounds of nature would rise by decibels. How many times had I walked along this river? How many more times would I still walk it? I stood there watching Eeman kick her shoes off, laughing in anticipation. I watched her reach for my hand and pull me cautiously into the flowing water.

"Be careful where you set your foot," I heard her whisper. "These wet rocks are slippery."

Together we had witnessed this river in all its phases: from frozen and calm, to cold, raging, and gibbering, to seeping, soothing, and tuneful. A cycle. A comforting cycle. Predictability brings under-standing. A feeling of power. Just don't probe too deep. The core is molten lava. The surface, threatening geologic faults. The thought of her not coming back. A never-ending eclipse.

As I got closer to the house, I started hearing the commotion of the crowd. Tens of people were working the grounds of our gardens in preparation for the summer festival. I could not gather myself and offer my help this time around. Eeman and I had been overseeing the event for the past three years and had put our minds and souls into it. We took it from a local, small gathering of a few Mar Elias families at a clearing down by the river to a full-blown festival including families from surrounding villages and beyond. We offered the gardens that extended from our house all the way to the riverbank. A rolling meadow of fruit trees, lawns, and marvelous landscape. Eeman was no longer here to enjoy it. It broke my heart.

"Good evening, Mr. J." I heard from several directions as I stepped onto the grounds.

"Good evening," I responded, waving at the men and women hard at work.

As I attempted to walk straight to the main gate, Ramy hurried after me. "Mr. J., I have a few questions regarding the layout. Can you spare a moment?"

"Of course," I answered, my hand rubbing at my lower back.

"We built a stage for the talent show." He stopped to wipe the sweat forming on his forehead with the back of his sleeve. "What do you say we set it under the oak tree over there?"

"Sounds good, Ramy! Go ahead and do it."

"This way, we free the plum orchard area to set up the food tables."

"I trust your judgment. What's the count so far?"

"Just today alone, thirty-five more families signed up, which brings the total to close to a hundred and fifty families. We'll have to limit it to two hundred though, with the limited parking and camping space."

"Bigger than last year, eh?"

"Yes, sir, indeed."

"Great job, Ramy," I said, happy with the success of the event. "Good night. See you tomorrow."

"Take care, sir. We'll be turning the light projectors off in ten minutes. Sorry it took so long today. The guys are wrapping it up for the evening."

"No worries. Take your time," I responded, waving back at him.

Ramy was my business manager. He had a calm demeanor but the heart of a lion. He had married Louanne, his high school sweetheart, and they moved to the city together. They worked hard in search of a better life. She had worked as an elementary school teacher during the day and as a seamstress out of their one-bedroom apartment in the evening to support her husband through college. Four years later, Ramy graduated with a degree in business economics and started working full-time. Together they had a beautiful little girl who filled their house with joy. They named her Lily, but their joy was ephemeral. Louanne and Lily died in a car accident on Lily's fourth birthday. All alone in the city, Ramy felt empty and void of purpose. Two years ago, he sought me for a job. It was not long before I realized his potential and had him help me manage my business. His humble approach with others had decorated him with great social skills, and he soon proved to be reliable and honest.

On the day of the festival, Mar Elias woke to a bright and warm June morning. From my bedroom balcony, I could see the festival grounds. It was only six o'clock in the morning, yet the joyful buzz of dozens of employees and volunteers had already begun. Canopies were set up, tables were topped with colorful cloths, and miles of strand lights were wrapped around tree branches. Strands of paper lanterns zigzagged across the sky. Gas heaters were spread around. Although it was warm, by sundown, a cool breeze would rise through the branches, intensified by the river's mist. It made Eeman want to cuddle in a warm spot.

I spent most of the day in my office taking care of business issues that could not wait until Monday. On weekends, I usually oversaw issues of concern to Crescent. Since Eeman's passing, my visits to Crescent became few and far between. However, I managed to stay involved through the Crescent Foundation for Nonprofits.

"Mr. J., I am afraid it's Shatha on the home line again. She's been trying to reach you on your office phone. She's saying it is urgent. She needs to get through to you before tonight."

"I'll get the call, Reema. Thank you."

Shatha had been my physical therapist since Eeman and I moved to Mar Elias. Despite the fact that her hands had always worked magic on my back and legs, I made a decision to stop using her services. She seemed odd and disingenuous.

"I've been trying to reach you for a couple of days. With the summer festival being tonight, I assumed you'd be in town. I wanted to see if you'd like to have a session today. I can still accommodate you."

"Thank you for your concern, Shatha. Unfortunately, it won't be possible today."

"You haven't been back to the clinic for six months now. I was thinking that with all the standing and the walking you'll be doing tonight, it would be better—"

"I'll look at my schedule for next week and give your office a call," I said.

She fell silent for a moment.

"All right then. I'll be seeing you tonight."

"Goodbye."

I was not planning on attending the festival that year. It would be the first without Eeman. Besides, I could not reflect to the people what was not inside me. As I attended to pending work from my home office, I took breaks to walk outside and check on the progress of the event. A blinding headache eventually snuck up on me. By nightfall, I asked Reema to dim the lights around the house. I watched the festivities from my bedroom balcony, sipping on chamomile tea and hoping it would ease my tension and relieve my headache.

My mother used to get these horrible headaches and retreat to her room for a day or two. It seemed so long ago. There was one particular incident that was oddly etched in my memory.

**We're driving** home from a trip to the city on an uncharacteristically hot day. It's the seventeenth of April. For as long as I can remember, my mother has shied away from outdoor living on bright and sunny days, for fear of having sunlight touch her fair skin. On this April day, however, she claims she loves hot and sunny days because they brighten her mood. She rolls down her window and sticks her arm out, closing her eyes and letting the hot air blow through her hair.

Aslan and I are sitting in the back seat, and Father is driving.

"Can you please roll up the window? The heat is immense," Father says.

"I can't stand this heat," Aslan adds. "It actually makes me nauseous."

"All right. I'll roll it up." She immediately rolls up her window, and her mood takes a somber turn. "I think I know why all three of you hate the heat," she says, bundling me with Father and Aslan, even though I haven't uttered a word. She looks at Father. "You were born in the fall." She turns her head to look at us in the backseat. "And you two you were born in the winter. I'm the only one in this family who was born in the summer. And I love it."

"Since when you love summers, Mother?" asks Aslan.

"I was born in the winter, not fall," Father says.

"Well, November 20 is hardly winter," she argues. "Winter starts in December—so that puts you in the fall."

The argument continues for a while. Father argues that November never feels like fall, and that he doesn't care how people tend to look at the calendar.

Mother answers that if one is to follow the standard calendar of seasons, one has to stick to the specific dates of their periods.

Aslan defends Father's twisted opinion that November doesn't represent the fall and argues against Mother the whole way to Crescent. "You lose again, Mother. Just admit it."

**Mother spent** the following three days in her bedroom in complete darkness. Three disappointing days I had to conduct life normally around the house, all the while knowing that my mother was buried under her sheets, battling what I later realized was depression. Several times, I entered her room and watched her as she slept, trying to establish if she was breathing. If she was alive. And when she finally emerged from her room, she looked even thinner than before.

I stood up and leaned my elbows on the balcony rail, stretching my neck from side to side and rolling back my shoulders. The throbbing pain in my head had not subsided, but I couldn't let myself sink into my mother's abyss. I stepped into my room to retrieve a set of binoculars from my nightstand drawer and headed back out to the balcony. Looking at the crowd, I could recognize a good number of faces. It felt like I had always belonged in Mar Elias. Every year, however, new faces would surface, from new hospital staff members to neighboring villagers and even patients who had been released for the evening to attend the festival.

I remembered Eeman grabbing my elbow with both hands and walking me through the crowds, greeting everybody and spreading friendly smiles, going on her tiptoes to whisper comforting words in my ear. "I love it here." Her voice rang in my ears. I felt her lips kissing me on the cheek, filling my lungs with her smell.

"I love it here too," I heard myself saying out loud.

Long after she was gone, I found myself talking to her as if she were still with me. I covered my cheek with my hand, where she had just kissed me, and felt a tingling sensation race through my body. A sudden exaltation. What was I thinking? Her message to me had always been to carry on. I closed my eyes and took a deep breath. The music, the laughter, and the smell of food started to slowly arouse my senses. As my tension gradually settled, I felt the urge to step outside and sink my toes in the lush grass.

I walked outside and headed to the tables to get some food. The air was cool and misty. I filled up my plate, greeted the people around me, and sat on a chair under a heater. Most people had finished eating by then and were migrating away from the food tables. A group of young children was having a karaoke contest on stage, not too far from where I sat, filling the air with young and bubbly voices.

"Ladies and gentlemen, welcome to our annual summer festival," a voice bellowed through the speakers a few minutes later. "Midnight will strike in ten minutes. For those who wish to watch the midnight fireworks from up close, please head down to the river."

A roaring cheer rose in the air as everyone darted toward the river. I decided to stay warm by the heater and watch the fireworks from that very spot. As noise faded into the distance, the grounds started to look like a ballroom after a New Year's party. Empty chairs, quilts, and strewn personal items were spread out in all directions, distending the lining of a massive void that came back to hollow me.

A compelling yearning for wholesomeness, for something gone missing, emerged in me, heightening my senses. At the edge of the gardens, where the land sloped down leading to the river, rose a green phosphorescent haze. It was a reflection of the night-light projectors, the sparkles of fireworks, the mist in the air, and a lonely silhouette, in a white dress, resting her weight against the trunk of the weeping willow. Her image slowly came into focus as I squinted my eyes. She was not an ignis fatuus. She was real. She was facing the river. Oddly, however, her head did not lift up to watch the fireworks as they shot up to the sky. I did not see her face to read her expression. I did not hold her hand to know she was shaking. Something in her saddened me and aroused my curiosity. It was an intuitive awareness, indestructible and all-encompassing. One I could not analyze or systematically describe.

Who was this woman?

"Who are you?" I heard myself mumbling.

She seemed forlorn, scared, and out of place. I untied my shawl.

"Excuse me, miss," I approached a white-aproned young woman who was serving food at the table next to me. "Could you please give this to the lady standing under that tree over there? She looks cold."

I pointed to the weeping willow and handed her my shawl.

"Sure, no problem," she responded, grabbing the shawl from my hand.

I went back to my chair and sat down, watching from afar. The lady in the white dress took the shawl, nodded her head a couple of times, looked around her in both directions, and then wrapped it around her shoulders. I couldn't get my eyes off of her. She was mysterious—in a way I could not explain. She lifted the shawl to her face and held it there for a while. Was she smelling it?

"Do you happen to know who she is?" I asked the young woman as she was walking back toward the table.

"No, sir. I don't."

Once the fireworks show ended, people started heading back up from the riverbank. Those who had taken a dip in the river were running back with wet clothes to wrap themselves in blankets and claim a spot under a heater.

A young man with rolled-up sleeves and pants walked hurriedly toward the mystery woman, who was still standing under the willow tree, and said something to her.

She smiled at first, but as he playfully pulled on her arm, dragging her toward the riverbank, she shook her head and tried to free herself from his grip. She seemed frightened, but the young man was persistent and finally succeeded in leading her down the slope. And then she disappeared. I wanted to ask someone who she was, but no one I knew was nearby. I was wrapped with a sense of loss and felt an urge to follow her. My heart dropped, and tears started running down my cheeks. Hot, boiling tears that I could not explain. How could tears have a mind of their own? Covertly, I wiped my cheeks, then stood up and headed back to the gate, all the while looking in the direction where she had disappeared, hoping I would somehow catch a glimpse of her again.

"Sir," the white-aproned young woman called as she tried to catch up to me, "her name is Serene. My friend told me she works at the physical therapy center on Hamra Street."

"Thank you," I said. "Have a good night."

"Good night, sir."

# Chapter 30

A mysterious form of energy visited me that night. My eyes would not shut for a long time. It wasn't until the morning hours that the noise from the festival subsided. Noise did not usually bother me, and I used to welcome liveliness, but that night, I needed to synchronize with the strange waves of feelings that were channeling through me. I could only do it in total peace. I went down to the cellar, closed the door, and sat at the table, pouring myself a glass of whiskey. The waves running through me went in all directions, with crests and troughs crossing and overlapping, lifting me to my zenith only to drop me again. And for several interspersed split seconds that night, when the waves aligned out of phase, and the forces pulling on me underwent a total destruction, I entered a world of wonderment and veneration. Exultation and a complete surrender to something magical would halt my senses, and I would shudder.

**Noura, my** angel, I should tell you at this point that what I endured that night is worth reflecting upon. It was a moment that shed light on one of life's mysteries, but don't get your hopes up too much, because I still cannot find the right words to describe the thoughts that streamed through my mind that night. Since thoughts are the essence of any realization, I could only acknowledge their significance in awe. I spent hours writing and erasing words that would faithfully convey them to you, but for each one of us, a delicate balance of reason and emotion derives strong, personalized impressions from words. Consequently, words could be a limited mode of expression when a fine-spun definition is being sought. I can't seem to find mine.

Don't let this revelation discourage you, my angel, because I truly believe that each one of us can see the truth. Hints could come in any shape or form. And if you are in tune with nature and your creation, you get to rejoice. I guess I just want you to be grateful and take every experience in life, be it good or bad, as just that. An experience. A passing experience. A means to something new and unpredictable. Because life itself is volatile. Fly with it, my angel. And when you soar up high, look upon the skies and all that lies below, and say thank you.

"**Mr. J.,** wake up," Reema said as she softly tapped me on the shoulder. "You got us worried. I was looking all over the house for you."

"I had a hard time going to sleep last night," I said as I lifted my head and stretched my numb arms.

I had finally fallen asleep in the cellar, my head weighing on my arms on the table. The bottle of whiskey empty.

"Where would you like to eat your breakfast today?"

"No breakfast for me, thank you. I'm going to take a hot shower and try to go back to sleep."

It was Sunday, and the town was mainly recuperating from the festival of the night before. I slept all day and did not wake up until the early hours of the following morning. Had I accumulated a sleep debt over the last few months, the lengthy slumber I woke up from would have paid it in full. I sat up and stretched my arms. A slow and gradual descent of a dream came to me.

Aslan and I were arguing over something I could not remember. Oddly enough, the setting was not our house in Crescent, and the time was not our childhood. He looked exactly like I had last seen him when he came to the hospital's grand opening. We were here in Mar Elias, in the gardens of this very house, under the willow tree.

The argument grew extremely heated. I couldn't tell what it was all about. His voice was bellowing through the valley. Then, face knotted and nostrils flared, Aslan lifted his fist to punch me, but I was ready for him this time, and I dodged the punch. Being taller, I always had the advantage of size, but I never used it against him. In this dream, however, I did. I punched him in the face and knocked out his teeth. There was blood all over his face. Surprisingly, his expression was not one of pain but rather of shock. He turned around and walked away in resignation.

I sat processing the meaning of this dream. The fact remained that I grew up hungry to punch Aslan at the slightest provocation. His taunting behavior had caused so much incitement for violence, but I had always looked the other way. And since that hunger was never satisfied, it had turned into a recurring fantasy. Subconsciously, I wanted to see him hurt, bleeding, defeated. It was a deep-seated wrath, but why now? After all these years? And why in the gardens of my house in Mar Elias? Never before had he set foot on this property. Not until years later did I come to understand the true meaning of my dream.

Several years later, I accepted a request to meet with a senior executive from Jacob Construction Enterprises. The request came with a caption: "In an effort to establish possible future common interests." The meeting was scheduled for an afternoon at my home office in Mar Elias. To my surprise, it was Aslan who showed up, accompanied by Adam. Adam looked more mature since the last time I had seen him, and Aslan looked worn out. He had lost weight, and when he shook my hand, his grip had no strength to it. He stood in the vestibule of my house as he handed Reema his coat, looking up at the high ceiling with the skylight of beveled glass, and all around at the multicolored specs of light that reflected on the white walls and marble floors.

"You did a good job with this house," he said.

"It's all Eeman's making," I responded, ushering the two of them into the office.

"Anything to drink?" asked Reema.

"Just water will be fine," Aslan responded.

"I'll take water too," said Adam.

I walked up to my desk and turned around to claim my seat behind it. Aslan, with Adam trailing behind, was still by the door, hands in his pockets as he leisurely walked by the bookshelves. He was examining my book collection.

Reema poured three glasses of water and set a bowl of grapes on the coffee table before she exited the office and shut the door behind her.

Aslan walked up to the chair facing my desk, unbuttoned his blazer, and sat down. He crossed his legs and started rubbing at his knees. "I hope you know that the hospital project came at a loss for our company," he said. "Margins were low to start with. By the time the job was completed, we had taken a considerable hit."

"I must admit expectations were high," I said. "Your guys exceeded our expectations in every respect."

He stood up, buttoned his blazer, and walked to the window behind my desk. He stood facing the window for a while, hands digging in his pockets, his right foot pointing to the ground as it crossed over his left. "Nice view from your office window. Does it remind you of Crescent?"

"Crescent will always have its unique charm," I said.

He walked back to his seat and stood behind it, facing me. His fingers started brushing nervously over its upholstered back. "I finally took Adam for a visit last week." He circled around the chair and sat down again, spreading his arms wide and then locking his hands behind his neck.

"We had not visited since our parents' funeral."

"There have been two additional family funerals since then," I couldn't help but interject.

"Lovely place," interrupted Adam, looking at his father, who did not so much as flinch. It was the only thing Adam said during the meeting.

"I happen to agree with you," I responded. "Lovely indeed."

"I heard you let go of several lots," Aslan said, squinting his eyes.

"For charitable reasons," I responded.

"No doubt. No doubt." He nodded repeatedly, one corner of his mouth pulled back to the ear in a charitable, compromised smile.

His smirk, juxtaposed with his jaded eyes, underscored a sense of unease and weariness. I knew that something was physically wrong with him. He stood up for the second time and started pacing the length of the room. He stopped by the window again.

"Well," he continued gazing through the windowpane, his back to the room, "we're here to make you an offer for the, hmm," he cleared his throat, "whatever number of acres you have left of open space beyond the river. All of it." And then, turning to look me in the eye, he added, "you tell us how much you want for it."

Adam, a neophyte at deal-making body language, sat up straight, leaned forward, and stretched out his neck. He looked like a hatchling waiting to be fed. Nana Thabita's final words resounded in my ears: "Don't cave in to Aslan. Nothing could ever make him happy."

"Why would you want the land in Crescent?" I asked.

"The land has been in the family for close to a hundred years. It's ridiculous to see it disposed of unrepentantly. It'll be in good hands with Adam."

*Adam?*

He cleared his throat again, his face blank while that of his son remained artlessly blissful.

"The land is not—and shall never be—for sale," I said.

"Well, then, it would be right if it passed down to one of my sons after you since you have no heirs of your own. Adam has a solid head on his shoulders, and Najee, whom you never met, is equally shrewd and wise." At that, Aslan stood up and clapped his hands to announce the end of his visit.

Adam followed suit, adjusting his tie and buttoning his vest.

"Think it through," Aslan said, extending his hand.

"My mind is already made up," I answered. Antoine de Saint-Exupéry's words came to mind as I closed the door behind them: "Si tu diffères de moi, mon frère, loin de me léser, tu m'enrichis."

The motive of Aslan's visit did not surprise me. I knew all along that Crescent was a seedling, dormant in the back of his mind, and that at one point in time, it would sprout again, reigniting his desire for foraging and controlling whatever he could get his hands on. What did Adam know about Crescent other than it being a lovely place? Adam's emotional connection with Crescent was even weaker than his father's. Knowing very well that Aslan undermined no financial opportunity—and knowing that Adam was his father's lifetime apprentice in the world of money—I could only imagine what would happen to this chunk of Crescent had I agreed.

Eeman and I had discussed the land in Crescent time and time again. We had both agreed that open space was the best approach to maintaining the charm of the village. We had promised each other to work on turning the acres into protected land. However, with the hospital under construction in Mar Elias, and Eeman's deteriorating health, we were distracted. In light of Aslan and Adam's visit, the issue became a priority. I found it unfathomable that he never acknowledged my marriage to Eeman and that her passing was the type of news he would read in his morning paper and forget about by the time he flipped to the next page.

# Chapter 31

On the day of my appointment with Serene Doory, Ramy walked into my office to inform me of an emergency that needed my attention at one of our offices in the city. I had to miss my appointment. I was looking forward to getting back into my therapy routine, and I was even more excited to meet Ms. Doory.

"Would you like me to cancel today's appointments only? I believe it's safer to clear your schedule for tomorrow as well—in case you end up staying in the city," Ramy said.

"Just clear today. I'll take care of the physical therapy center myself. As for the next few days, we'll take care of them a day at a time. I'm still not sure how long I'll be gone."

"Will do."

"Before we get on the highway, I need to stop by the physical therapy center for a few minutes," I told Reyes as I eased myself onto the passenger seat.

It was not in my intention to meet with Serene Doory, especially for the first time, all dressed up in a suit and tie. I was nervous all morning thinking about our meeting.

"Are you all right, sir? Is it hot in here?" asked Ramy from the backseat of the car as I impatiently pulled on my tie. "It's dreadfully humid today."

"I'll be fine. I'm just not a fan of suits and ties."

As Reyes pulled the car into the parking lot, I removed my tie and threw it onto the backseat. "You can stop me by the main entry.

Please wait for me right there at the curb, no need to park the car. It won't take long."

I greeted the receptionist at the front desk. "Hello, Nadia. Long time, no see!"

"Hi, Mr. J. Long time indeed. How are you doing?"

"I'm doing well. Thank you. I have an appointment with Ms. Doory in half an hour, but I'm afraid I have to cancel. I'm on my way out of town."

"Would you like me to look up her next availability?"

"Not at this point. Thank you. I just want to have a word with her if possible to apologize for the cancellation. Ramy will be calling you to reschedule."

"Sounds good. Let me grab her for you. Nice to see you again, Mr. J." she said with a smile as she got up and left the lobby.

"Thank you, Nadia."

I stood facing the window overlooking the parking lot. The sun was blazing hot on that June day. The air outside was shimmering with distorted light. It looked thick with water droplets on their journey back to the clouds. Water had saturated the grounds through two generous seasons of rain that year. It must have been only a couple of minutes, but it felt like a long time.

Nadia offered me cold water, which I gladly accepted.

"Hello, Mr. J.," she greeted me with her silvery voice.

I did not hear her step into the lobby. I exhaled the lump of air in my throat, drew in a deep breath, and turned around to face her. She was all I had envisioned and more. It felt as if she were someone I was destined to meet—and that it was finally time.

"I'm Serene Doory," she said, extending her hand.

I could hear a slight tremble in her voice. I shook her hand. "Nice to finally meet you," I said.

All of the days that were displaced from my life, days that felt spiritually light and trivial, suddenly gained weight, and buoyed me up to where I could breathe again. It was one of those moments that make you stop and say, "So, this is it! So, that's why."

**Noura, my** angel, every time I look at your mother's photograph, my perception of her gets validated. All the inductions and deductions that spanned hours and days of my life proved to be real. I still see her as the most beautiful person I have ever known. She was mysterious, yet decipherable. Her eyes were timid, her smile nervous. She was imperfectly gorgeous.

**I stood** mesmerized by the energy channeling through me. She blinked unsteadily. Beads of sweat formed on her forehead and around her delicate nose.

"I'm unable to have the session today, Ms. Doory. I'm actually on my way out of town due to some pressing business issues. I just wanted to apologize in person for the cancellation," I said, smiling.

She looked deep in thought.

"I'll call back to reschedule," I pressed on to fill the silence.

"All right," she said. "No problem—and thank you for stopping by."

"And now, if you'll excuse me," I added and turned around to leave.

I could feel her watching me as I walked to the door. Outside, the air suddenly seemed lighter, crisper. A wave of happiness rose inside me. For a split second, I even thought of cancelling my trip to the city and walking back into the clinic. I looked up and saw the puffs of cumulus clouds hanging triumphantly in the stark blue sky.

"Tiny drops of water," I said to myself. "Until we meet again."

"Thank you," I told Reyes as he held the car door open for me, and I handed him my walking cane. "Off we go."

Reyes sat behind the wheel, looked at me with quizzical eyes, and then turned around to look at Ramy in the backseat.

"I mean it." I reached for my tie and hooked it around my neck. "Off we go."

"Good to see you smile again, sir."

*Off we go.* Thousands of thoughts bombard our minds every day of our lives. Some negative thoughts tend to spiral from a fault in our character, while others are memories that come back to haunt us at the slightest opportunity, sparked by a word, a gesture, or even a smell.

**"Off you** go," Father says. "All of you."

No one budges.

"I mean it. Off you go. Now!" Father's voice rises with each word.

Nana Thabita takes me in her arms and walks me back into the house, filing behind my mother, who has her hands covering her mouth to stifle her shock.

"What is it, Nana? Why did you scream? Why is Father upset? Are the cats all right?" I ask.

"No, darling. I'm afraid they're dead."

"All of them?"

"Yes, every single one of them."

**I reclined** my head against the back of my car seat and watched Mar Elias disappear through the window as Reyes merged onto the highway. I closed my eyes as images from the past came flooding back.

**I'm already** in bed for the night, and my eyes are halfway shut. I hear a faint scream that seems to be coming from our house. Soon after, I hear Aslan's bedroom door pull open, slamming against his bedroom wall. I get out of bed and follow him as he skips down the hallway and into the kitchen. He's ten years old. I'm nine. Father and Mother got there before us and are standing with Nana Thabita on the kitchen balcony. All three of them are gazing at something on the floor. Nila the cat is propped up in a seating position against the wall of the balcony, and the bodies of her kittens, all five of them, are arranged radially around her.

**Nana and** I loved Nila. Mother couldn't stand animals roaming around the house. I had heard her complain about them several times, but complaining was all she could do. My grandmother was a cat lover, and my father was brought up around them and would not hear her complaints. It got really bad when Nila gave birth to her five kittens. Nana had promised my mother to find a good home for them, but she was secretly dragging her feet so that I could enjoy them before they were sent away.

**"Just like** that," Aslan says, snapping his fingers, "and they're all gone."

**An entire** life is nothing but a fleeting moment. A snap of fingers. Opportunities, at times, never circle back, but that does not mean that one has to lose hope and stop persevering. Furthermore, when you are well into your forties, have been handicapped for most of your life, and have been challenged with not one, but several breaking points, you would surely have learned a lesson about hope and perseverance.

**"Ms. Doory** is on a two-week leave. Apparently, her father passed away just yesterday," Ramy said. "Do you want to see someone else at this point—or can you wait two weeks?"

"I can wait two weeks. Please send her a nice flower arrangement. Make them roses and carnations. All white. I need to add a condolence note."

Of the four hundred hospital beds that were at one point all white and empty, three hundred had just reached the occupancy mark. I was happy that the hospital was being put to good use and couldn't help but reflect on how proud Eeman would have been to see us changing the lives of so many patients. The hospital staff called for a celebration of this milestone achievement. The main-floor cafeteria was abuzz with cheerful employees who exuded youthfulness and enthusiasm. Their white coats imparted confidence and a strange sense of security. I walked around acknowledging and meeting everyone, for at that point, recent hires outnumbered the original staff.

That night, Serene walked into the dining hall wearing cropped jeans and a long-sleeved floral-print blouse. Coral peonies. Her hair was pulled back in a ponytail. Her face looked pale. She looked like she had lost weight since I met her at the physical therapy center two weeks ago. I did not anticipate seeing her that night. She was accompanying Sonia White, a radiologist and one of our original residents. From the minute I saw her, I felt a tingle spread under my skin. I couldn't help but keep my eyes on her as she and her friend circled around the cafeteria, shaking hands and exchanging greetings. She looked tense, and every now and then, she lifted her hand to tuck her hair behind her ear.

As the evening progressed, Sonia's animation started to carry Serene along, and her face started to gradually light up.

*She must be feeling terrible with the loss of her father.*

At one point, her eyes met mine, and we both froze. Every receptor in my body responded to a new stimulus, sending me sailing along unattempted pathways, my mind circling the globe, while my feet were firmly planted on the ground. I could no longer focus on the conversations around me. No one had ever made me feel this way before.

"Mr. J! Long time no see."

"Hello, Shatha. How are you?" I asked, feigning interest.

"I'm all right. We miss you at the center. It's been a while," she said with a shrug.

"Well, things are lightening up again. In fact, I'm due back at the center in a couple of days," I said as Serene passed behind her, acknowledging me with a shy nod.

Serene's proximity made my heart flutter. I followed her with my eyes, my mouth agape.

There are many different methods of communication. The most powerful of all is not imparted by words, and no words are absolutely representative of it. It is instead transmitted through body language. It is a silent and subtle language. Its effect is undeniable, however. An instantaneous race of the heart drumming in your ears. An immediate dagger of pain lacerating through your gut.

"So I see," Shatha responded as she turned her head to see what had caught my attention.

"Mr. J., my friend Serene and I would like to congratulate you on the success of the hospital," Sonia interjected as she stepped closer. "Oh! I'm sorry. I didn't mean to interrupt," she added, looking at Shatha.

"No problem at all," answered Shatha, and then walked away looking irritated.

"Anyways. Congratulations," Sonia said, looking at me again.

"I should thank you," I responded. "The success of the hospital is the result of the collective effort of all employees. We have the best and the most-qualified employees. The cream of the crop."

Serene was looking at me, her face serious.

"How do you like Mar Elias so far, Ms. Doory?" I asked, immersing myself in her radiance.

"It's hard not to fall in love with this town," she answered. "It's charming and peaceful."

"I'm glad you see it that way. I too fell in love with it a few years ago. As a matter of fact, my wife did too. We were on a road trip heading down south when we stumbled upon this hidden paradise. We happened to get off the highway looking for a place to eat."

"The Local Eatery?" exclaimed Sonia.

"An iconic place," I said. "Have you tried their food?"

"I have, actually. It's delicious," Sonia said. "I've been wanting to accompany Serene there."

"I'm sorry for the loss of your wife," she said.

"I'm also deeply sorry for the loss of your father."

She blushed. "Thank you for the flowers you sent me."

"A shy effort to alleviate your pain," I said, feeling the heat rise to my cheeks.

Her chin trembled. She held my gaze for a while. She then bit her lower lip nervously and looked around for her friend, but Sonia had already split away.

"What brought you to Mar Elias?" I carried on, for fear of her walking away.

"My friend Sonia recommended it. I'm glad she did."

"You can always work here at the hospital should the clinic become too small for you," I suggested, knowing the hospital and its staff would provide a better work environment.

"Thank you," she responded. "I'm already putting in a few hours a week here at the hospital. I really like this facility. A monumental edifice you built for this town. A brilliant idea and an inspiring gesture of charity."

"Thank you, Ms. Doory," I said, impressed with her praise.

How could I explain this extraordinary feeling that stirred in me ever since I laid eyes on her? How could I explain it when I was at least twenty years her senior?

When you are well-to-do, and you are single, you are bound to attract eager women who are more than willing to reshape their lives around yours. Life has it too where different growth stages are marked by different shades of one's character. What seemed at one point un-equivocally impossible becomes somewhat possible, and you go from having a clear answer to every question you reason through to having an ambiguous one to only a few.

"The sole foundation of this establishment is the moral aspect of it. I try to do what I see is right, that's all," I said as she looked at me.

She appeared engrossed in thought. "Moral relativism is not a mere theory one learns in a classroom. People defend and justify their behavior as being right all the time, but this is different. This is extraordinarily noble."

"I'm driven to be the best I can," I admitted. "When I see all the harm a person can cause, my ideology solidifies."

"Some see it as a burden … to constantly have to right people's wrongs."

"It becomes a way of life," I replied.

She smiled, and I smiled back. She turned her gaze away from mine. The crowd was fading toward the tables as dinner was being served. She looked back at me.

"Sonia saved me a seat at her table. It was a pleasure talking to you," she said. "Good night, Mr. J."

"The pleasure is all mine, Ms. Doory. I'll be seeing you soon."

As she turned around and walked away, I could not take my eyes off her.

**Cropped jeans.**

Coral peonies.

Time has its markers.

Time and time again, my mind went blank as I tried to write this memoir. Time and time again, I became frustrated with my failing memory, when whole chunks of my life seemed to have completely dissolved away. Certain images, however, became the authentication of a past unbeknown to anyone but me, and the lifelong validation I sought of my life.

Cropped jeans and coral peonies.

I am a child all over again.

**As the** hospital's director and his office personnel joined my table for dinner, I listened to their conversations, albeit distracted, on how to meet current and future challenges. They proposed incorporating information technology to improve the care quality of the hospital and expand its reach. At one point, I completely lost focus.

"What did you think of the new list, Mr. J.?"

"Pardon?" I answered upon hearing my name.

"Did you get a chance to review the seminar series program for next quarter?"

"I sure did. I'll be attending every single one of them," I promised.

Her presence was a distraction. My mind was completely absorbed by her slender image as she sat with her back to me, a few tables away. At one point, she turned around and saw me looking at her. She smiled.

I smiled back.

A sense of unworldly happiness seized me.

I was a child all over again.

She was running through empty fields as I tried to keep up with her, my eyes immersed in a field of coral peonies.

# *Chapter 32*

Days and nights, summers and winters, I witnessed the passing of time. Like a grain of sand, the waves of time washed over me, heedlessly raising my hopes, only to leave me insensibly at low ebb. Anticipation, the dream of a bright and happy tomorrow, was the dopamine in my veins. Happy moments, however, came to me in samples. Small portions. A sprinkle of water on desert sand. A mirage. A rainbow. An illusion.

"I cannot believe I'm witnessing a double rainbow!" Noura exclaimed as she pushed my wheelchair through the garden.

I had asked Reema to set up for breakfast under the willow tree. I knew how much Noura appreciated nature, having become a city dweller herself.

"This valley misses you. It's thanking you for spending the night," I told her, looking up to see her beautiful face perched above my head.

"I keep forgetting how serene this setting is. So therapeutic and salutary."

She parked my chair under the tree and pushed on the brake pedal.

"So true," I whispered as I tried to stand up, feeling invigorated by her presence.

I did not want to regret missing on the moment. I knew very well that I would replay its every second for many long days ahead. I walked up to the aging trunk of the willow and leaned my body against it.

"Have you been taking your breakfast here?"

"Under this willow tree is where I saw your mother for the first time. And under this same tree is where I saw her last."

"Amazing how nature stands as a powerful and silent witness to the passing of generations," she said as she slid her hand against the flaky and groovy bark.

"It took humans ages to conquer nature. And now that we understand it, we are struggling to preserve it," I opined.

She walked to the table. "I don't believe nature is conquerable for the mere fact that it is always changing."

I followed her to the table and sat down. She poured two cups of orange juice.

I said, "Heraclitus once said, 'The only thing that is constant is change.'"

"I think all we do is learn how to roll with nature just to stay on course," she added, dropping onto the chair across the table from me.

"It's in the human nature to keep probing and keep learning. The scientific research to which you and your colleagues are dedicating your lives will surely inch us to the truth."

"And with every truth comes its mutation. I'm afraid the truth is mutable, just like the genes I work on in the lab," she added, her voice suddenly assuming a seriousness so scalding to my heart.

"The truth never changes. It's our understanding of it that does. Chip off the dead bark until you get to the core."

She sipped orange juice from her cup, only to stand up again and walk back to the trunk of the willow tree. She ran her hand over its uneven surface as she circled around it. She looked so much like her mother. I had to look away to bottle up a sudden surge of nostalgia that was beginning to choke me.

"I know of a truth that never mutates," I said, steadying my voice. "True and pure love. The kind that is intercepted by the heart. Love that is shapeless and timeless, that is solely anchored in someone's intuitive self, that stands immune to the scrutiny and judgment of the mind. Love that doesn't answer to any question and exhausts all words of all languages."

She walked back to the table, wrapped her arms around my shoulders, and gently rested her chin on the top of my head. "You just reminded me of Antoine de Saint-Exupéry when he said, 'On ne voit bien qu'avec le cœur. L'essentiel est invisible pour les yeux.'"

"So true," I replied. "What you see with your heart is never an illusion. *Le Petit Prince* was the only book you kept in the drawer of your nightstand. You must have read it tens of times."

"As a matter of fact, I still do. I still read it before I go to sleep every single time I come to visit."

She kissed the top of my head. "Shoulders up. You're too young to stoop like this."

By that time, the gardens were immersed in sunlight. The green looked lush; the flowers were strikingly colorful. The stillness was so lively. There had been hundreds of beautiful mornings in my life. I regretted not seeing and hearing every single one of them.

I looked at her. She was spreading my toast with honey, her face illuminated with her usual smile. The gold in her hair was dancing to the morning breeze.

I said, "Tolstoy once said, 'Truth, like gold, is to be obtained not by its growth, but by washing away from it all that is not gold.'"

She lifted her head and gazed at the rainbow as it started to fade away.

On a summer afternoon, about six months after Serene's passing, and just as I was settling into my rocking chair on the west balcony, the heavy book *War and Peace* in my hand, I heard the doorbell ring. It was the second time I had taken a stab at the book. My father had given it to me on my trip away to college. "I hope this book captures you the way it captured me," he had said. *War and Peace* sparked a profound interest in Tolstoy's philosophy on life and claimed an accessible reference spot in my library. As I was not expecting any visitors, I didn't suppose it concerned me. It turned out to be Kameel, seeking me out for help.

I had met Kameel in person once before, at Serene's funeral. Although he was emaciated then, he looked much worse as he stood downstairs in the vestibule. My heart dropped when I first set eyes on him. His black suit was two sizes bigger than his frame. I knew he did not come with good news, and my premonition proved to be right. He said the doctor had told him he had six months to live. He said he wished I could be Noura's legal guardian, and that it was what Serene would have wanted. He said he had no doubt I would be the best person to take care of Noura's young life. He also said that Serene had told him everything during her last visit home and that he was very sorry for not being able to help her. "I'm torn between two lives. I don't know which one to live. I can't be in both. Nor can I just be in one," she had pleaded with Kameel.

Like the rainbow, Noura's parents vanished off the surface of the earth, within six months of each other.

"The mystery of rainbows," I said. "Not only is their presence an illusion but so is their absence."

She took a deep breath and drew her attention from the fainting rainbow back to me. "Interesting," she said. "How do you define existence then?"

"Existence is our setting as we speak. Anything beyond that is an illusion. Existence is you and me under the willow tree. Everything else is either in the past, subject to the frailty of memory, and is no longer existent, or is in the future, yet to materialize, and subject to all antecedents. Everything beyond the now is but an illusion."

"Existence to me is hope," she claimed, sitting up straight, a sweet smile drawn on her face. "What kept me going through my long years at boarding school was the thought that I would be spending my summer vacation with you."

"The same thought had equally sustained me. Hope made life possible for me too."

She took a deep breath. She was looking at me with bleary eyes.

"Your mother captivated my heart and my whole existence for the short time she was in my life. After her death, you embodied her memory and became the captivating force."

She wiped away a tear from the corner of her eye.

"Thinking of you instilled joy in my heart. Watching you grow up brought me back to when I was a child. You made me feel invigorated and energetic."

Silence fell upon us, each buried deep under our own thoughts and processes. Thoughts could weigh heavily, like tons of concrete on soft tissue. Not until I heard myself groaning did I realize I was actually crying. I turned my face away so Noura wouldn't see my tears.

A short while later, I felt her loving hand on my shoulder and her lips touching the top of my head. "Your hair feels like silk," she said as she caressed it.

"I'm an old man with scanty gray hair and wrinkled skin," I said.

"You're a man with silky hair and a blissful face." She crouched beside my chair, leveling her beautiful and youthful face with mine. "Your eyes have never lost their spark. Still a handsome man, and every gesture indicates a life of decorum, a life of achievements. You never cease to amaze me."

"I tried not to let her death eclipse the elemental purpose of my existence," I said. Tears, by then, were racing down my cheeks.

"It's all right, Papa," she said, wiping my tears with her fingers. "She's resting now. God knows the emotional turmoil she was born into."

"It'll still take years to forget—or maybe a lifetime. And maybe I'll never forget, not for many lifetimes, but I knew what I needed to do. I had done it before. I could only live on. So, I focused on the good memories until they became my reality. Only then did I know I would be fine."

**I know** she is resting, Noura, my sweet angel. And I also know she is in my memory to stay. Every single word she said, every gesture she made, every smile and touch, and every quiver in her voice are all in my memory to stay. How can I forget? Not as long as I still see you.

# Chapter 33

The last three months of Eeman's battle with cancer consumed our daily lives with a stern urgency and had a debilitating effect on both of us. As she waned under my watch, apprehension waxed in me at the thought of losing her. Scores of possible paths we had envisioned for our future suddenly collapsed at a vanishing point. Endurance. The uncertainty of how much fight I had left in me.

It took a good six months to disengage my thoughts from the thick fog of despondency. I fully understood that I was my own savior and that my mental and physical wellness was required for endurance. I started taking my physical therapy regimen seriously again. Serene became the healer. The soothing power of her voice was indubitable. The silky feeling of her hands rubbing at my aching back and numb legs stimulated my senses. My nerves fired up, and my blood thinned down. And although she left me feeling wholesome, rested, and rejuvenated, there were also times when she left me confused, restless, and weary.

My visits to the clinic became a priority. I started conducting most of my business meetings out of my offices at home and at the hospital, substantially reducing my travel time. I started delegating more tasks to Ramy. I had entertained the possibility of moving back to Crescent after Eeman's death, but my growing love for Mar Elias, and the sense of responsibility I had for growing the hospital while mandating its processes to be lean and environmentally safe, much outweighed that urge. Had I not wanted to pull Eeman away from her miserable past,

I would not have ended up in Mar Elias. By the same token, had I not come to Mar Elias, I would not have met Serene. Eeman, in a way, was the reason I met Serene. I wished the two of them had the chance to meet.

My body's range of motion increased. My nature hikes became less excruciating, and at night, I could lie in bed without the normal throbbing and shooting pain. Serene must have loved her job because she was excellent at it. I appreciated the fact that she was not like Shatha, always bold and probing. I could not attribute her reservation to lack of confidence, however, or to incompetence. She had a dignified bearing, and she was very knowledgeable.

At first, she seemed to evade my eye contact, blushing at the mere hello when I first entered the center. I saw every subtle movement of hers—even when I was not looking at her. It would take her a few minutes to relax and warm up her hands. Cold or hot, those hands were magical. Mysterious. From the moment her skin brushed against mine, I was in heaven.

As time passed by, she became much more than the stranger she really was. Although the feeling was undeniable on my side, I was starving for an explanation. The prospect of a personal relationship with her was illusory. I was probably her father's age, and she was married with a child. The ingredients were hard to mix, and the agendas were not aligned. The magnetism was irrefutable, however. Her tender eyes were on me every time mine squeezed shut in pain.

I was always more reserved than I ever admitted. Since Eeman died, I had not tried to rekindle my affection—or felt the urge to. With Serene, however, it felt easy to open up, and I slowly found myself divulging my most personal thoughts. It seemed that she did the same. It became apparent that her childhood was sorely worrisome.

She told me she was a late bloomer.

"At twenty-four months, I had not said a word yet. My mother told me I would respond to sound but refused to utter a single word. And when I finally said something it was the two-letter word 'no' that stuck with me for a while. I said no to everything. No to watching TV. No to food. No to taking baths. No to playing with friends. And mainly no to sleeping in my bed," she told me as she rubbed eucalyptus oil on my hands, massaging every pressure point while sending a tickle down my spine. "I hated to sleep alone in my room when I was a child."

"Who didn't? When you can feel safe and warm cradled in your mother's arms, why sleep alone?"

"True," she admitted, "but in my case, there were dreams. I had scary recurring dreams that messed up my childhood really bad."

"That's interesting. What kind of dreams?"

"It's a long story. I don't intend to burden you with it," she said.

I looked into her eyes and tried to unravel her thoughts.

"If it would put your mind at ease, I have an interesting story of my own," I said.

"Random scenes of random people I never met in my life."

"Did these scenes have anything in common? Could they perhaps be the result of some discomforting thoughts you carried to bed?"

"They could've very well been just that, but they were powerful enough to hamper everything else. No words to describe it. Pull your leg up please," she said.

She had me lie on my right side, lifting my top leg while she pushed down on it.

"Your legs are getting better," she said.

"Do you still experience these dreams?" I asked, not knowing why I had suspected she did.

She exhaled. Her hands relaxed, but her eyes became tense. "It's weird. I stopped seeing them for a while. I actually started enjoying a good night's sleep at one point, but there's a nagging apprehension in the back of my mind that keeps coming back."

I did not know what to tell her. I ached to know more, but I did not like to pry into her past. I wanted to help her, but I did not know how.

All my plans lined up between therapy visits. All of the normal and daily tasks I had busied myself with suddenly collapsed, becoming meaningless and boring. And as my visits to the center piled up, I learned more about Serene and her family. She told me stories from her past. The loss of her brother, her only sibling, was a recurring theme. I told her stories of the beautiful village I grew up in. She said she grew up in the city but often yearned for a life in the countryside. She said she loved Mar Elias for its rolling hills, its clean air, and the river that ran through it. She told me her best birthday gift ever was when her parents took her horseback riding for the first time. It was the first time she ever saw a real horse.

"I grew up around horses myself," I said.

"I can only imagine how wonderful a childhood that was." She was bent over me, going through the lumbar adjustment technique.

"She had a mahogany red coat that reflected a tinge of coral in direct sunlight. She was a gift to me on my sixteenth birthday. I loved taking her on the trails," I whispered dreamily. "I named her Marjana."

Her arms lost their pull.

"Is something wrong?" I asked as I propped myself up on my elbow.

"Not at all. It's a lovely name for a horse."

A palpable fluster swept over her. She rolled me on my back and helped me sit up. Her eyes were blinking. "I'll let you go for today," she said. "I'll have my assistant ice your back if you have a few minutes."

"I do. Thank you," I responded.

"See you next time."

She turned around and left the room. A strange feeling of desolation snuck up on me.

When I was little, Nana Thabita used to sneak into my bedroom at night and tell me a story as she caressed me to sleep. She must have improvised these stories since she couldn't read or write. Her mother had passed away when Nana was only a toddler, and her father had never shown any interest in good parenting. Impatiently, I would wait for her in bed until she finished her chores. Sometimes I had to wait for a very long time, trying not to let my eyelids surrender to the night. I don't remember how old I was when it had all started, but I know she stopped by the time I turned ten. "Tomorrow you'll be a big boy," she told me that night, her hands cupping my face. "You no longer need me to go to sleep. You have your imagination. Relax and let it soar."

I felt alone and desperate, like a baby bird on the edge of its nest, knowing it had to push out into the big empty sky to stay alive. What I did not know back then was that the same feeling would continue to revisit me. Do our fears and tribulations ever grow old? Aren't we supposed to grow tougher and more confident as we grow older?

"How could something as abstract as a thought, a dream, weigh us down, even paralyze us?" she asked on one of my visits to the therapy center.

I had expected her to jump into the pool with me as I went through my water conditioning. Instead, she coached me from the edge of the pool.

"I can't swim. It's embarrassing. I've always had a fear of water," she said.

"Fears can be overcome. Thoughts can heal too. It's the other side of the coin. I truly believe it," I assured her, remembering Eeman's words to me.

As her hands awakened my senses, I paid her back with soothing and reassuring words. I encouraged her to get into the shallow end of the pool. She agreed, her bottom lip twitching, her face blanching. She remained by the edge for the entire forty-five-minute session, guiding my movements with a trembling voice, her arm wrapped tightly around the ladder.

"You did it," I told her at the end of the session.

She hugged me, right there, by the ladder to the pool. Her body pressed against mine as her muscles shivered. "Thank you," she said repeatedly.

I felt the urge to protect her—to help her. Could that feeling be the fundamental truth behind the soulfulness she ignited in me? Only then did I understand it. My attraction toward her transcended my racing heartbeat and physical pleasure. I loved her with all my being.

We were two souls, each wrapped in its own dark, heavy cloak. Two people, each crippled by an empty feeling within, becoming substantially solid in each other's arms. Each filled the void of the other, and over a relatively short period of time, we became an intricate part of the other's life. Therapy sessions became a mutual necessity. A feeling I once had, but was stripped from, inundated my being. And I knew that life had more in store for me. Something new. Something different.

I started waking up every morning to that thought.

# Chapter 34

Because I had not seen her in three weeks, because I ached at the idea that something might have gone wrong with her personal life, and because she had not returned my calls, I decided to pay her a visit at her apartment. It was a Sunday morning, the seventeenth of November. The air had been gradually cooling down for the past month. I felt its cold bite as I stepped out of the house. I looked up and saw gray clouds moving stealthily to engorge the blue out of the sky and the warmth out of the autumn sun. I was so eager to get to her that I didn't bother going back inside to grab a sweater. My head felt light, and my heart was racing. I hadn't been sleeping well for the past three weeks.

Three weeks ago, Nadia called me from the physical therapy center to say that Serene had to take a leave of absence to tend to a pressing family matter, asking me if I wished to see Shatha in the meantime. I felt distressed about Serene's abrupt departure. The last time I saw her was two days before she left Mar Elias. She and her friends were having dinner at my house, and she never mentioned a leave of absence. The fact that she was gone without so much as a phone call deprived me of all hope. Not even her colleagues at the center expected her to be gone that long. What-if questions flooded my mind, the bleakest one of them being: What if she decided not to come back? I kept from calling her because I did not want to infringe on her privacy, but I finally decided to take my concern to Sonia.

"She came back last night," Sonia said. "I think she's planning on checking back at the clinic first thing on Monday."

"Is her family all right? Did she say why she had to leave?" I asked.

"She did not say much. We spoke briefly over the phone, but she did not sound well at all."

I could not wait until Monday.

I had never set foot in her apartment, although I must have passed by it at least twice a day. She had promised to host an engagement dinner in honor of Nader's proposal to Sonia, but she was concerned that her apartment was not big enough to host Sonia's long list of acquaintances. Sonia and Nader had met each other at the hospital when Nader joined the anesthetics department, a few months ago. Since then, the two of them had gotten along very well, and soon became inseparable. Serene was ecstatic at the prospect of the engagement, and she couldn't stop talking about it.

"They need my help planning the wedding," she said. "They both are so swamped with work. I need to figure out the venue and whatnot. I don't know if I can do it all by myself—or whether I should hire someone to help me."

"I'd love to help. Why don't you come over with your friends and have dinner at my house this weekend? We can figure it out then," I suggested casually. I had been mulling over a way to spend more time with her.

"I didn't mean to burden you, really," she said, looking at me with a puzzled face.

"I don't see it as a burden at all. I'd love to even offer my house for the engagement party."

She kept looking at me.

"Anything to lighten things up for you, that's all," I added on a closing note, hoping I didn't sound desperate.

"Mrs. Doory is here," Reema announced, knocking on my bedroom door.

"I'll be downstairs at once."

An intense feeling of excitement had overpowered me since my last session with her at the clinic. I felt full of energy. I decided to clear my agenda for that afternoon and took a long hike along the river. I came back and started pacing the house; carrying flower vases from mantel to table, only to return them to where they were; checking on the wine bottles I had picked out from the cellar for the occasion, and changing the selection altogether a couple of times; opening shutters, closing curtains, and fluffing up pillows. Things I had never touched before.

Reema must have sensed my anxiety. She gently sent me away when I intruded on her food preparations in the kitchen.

I had been ready for at least an hour when Reema knocked on my door. I grabbed my blazer, put it on, and limped down the staircase. She was not in the vestibule. I was heading to the living room when I heard her voice coming from behind me. My heart jumped.

"Hello there," she said.

I turned around, and there she was, walking up to me.

"I couldn't help it," she said apologetically, rubbing the palm of her hand over her stomach. "I smelled the food the minute I walked in. I had to steal a quick glance at the dining table."

Her smile was radiant. She was wearing a lightweight décolleté dress of the color goldenrod, delicately and beautifully embroidered with a green silk thread. It accentuated her dark green eyes, touching her olive skin like sunlight. She wore her hair down, parted on top in the middle, and pulled all together from the nape of her neck over her right shoulder. I was spellbound. She walked up to me and hugged me.

She smelled of citrus.

For a few heartbeats, nothing else existed. Nothing else mattered. I was on top of the world. Better yet, on top of all worlds. Dimensions disintegrated, dissolving the existence of all things, and highlighting their nothingness.

For those few heartbeats, my life reached an apogee. There was no way for me to have known it at the time. Only one natural course could follow such a climactic point. One that would take me on a slide, down a list of expectations. Everyday thereafter, I kept dreaming of a brighter tomorrow, trying to remain hopeful and renewed by clinging to positive thoughts that could slow my spiral descent, accepting all previous predicaments while fighting newly emerging ones. Until they became antecedents themselves.

Nothing and no one could deny me that moment. It is in my mind to stay. The mind does not succumb to spatial or temporal restrictions. Any experience ever lived, or ever wished to be lived, can be explored by the mind. At any time, in any place, and in any form. I could see her face in every face, hear her voice in every sound. She stood next to me wherever I went. Any experience can be lived and relived indefinitely. I don't even have to close my eyes. That is where freedom lies. In the freedom of the mind. Still, responsibility is a necessary restraint, for in the absolute sense of the freedom of the mind, there is a lurking delirium. Mental derangement does not necessarily come from a deficient mind—but from the failure to restrain it. Yet, all the geniuses who ever lived refused to restrain their mental freedom. While some of them were dubbed delirious, they advanced knowledge and inched us closer to the truth.

"You look beautiful," I said.

"Thank you. And you look very handsome. I love the color of your blazer," she added, eying it closely.

All at once, my mind took me back to the day when Eeman picked out a roll of fabric at the tailor's shop and exclaimed, "What a beautiful color for a blazer."

Serene turned around and headed to the living room. I walked behind her. Her dress undulated on her body like the smooth waves of a summer sea rolling to the gentle morning breeze. The light coming from the windows of the living room traced her body, from the top of her head down to her delicate ankles, with a subtle aura. She wore high heels.

"I would've never imagined a house as beautiful as yours, let alone one surrounded with private gardens, fruit orchards, and rolling hills of sage and rosemary," she said.

"Thank you. My late wife was very fond of this lot. This house is hers all the way."

"I love the openness, the high ceiling, the white walls, and the white stone floor." Her hands were pointing in all directions, her bare arms conducting in the air, her jubilant and silvery voice ringing music in my ears. "It's gorgeous. These huge windows must catch sunlight throughout the day," she added.

"They do," I said, staring at her. "I'll gladly show you around."

She walked to the far end of the living room where the Steinway stood. Its white lacquer contrasted strikingly with the spread arrangements of bright pink berry lilies and boronias. It stood, with the fallboard open, between two floor-to-ceiling windows on either side of the back wall.

"This is a beautiful piano! Do you play?" she asked while running her fingers gently over the keys.

"I did take a few lessons when I was a child. Never took it seriously, to my mother's disappointment. How about you?"

"No. I wish I did though. My parents tried with me also, but of course I wasn't receptive. How about your late wife?"

"No, she didn't, but she loved music. We used to have a pianist come over and play live music for us during different charity events and dinners. Things took a new turn ever since she passed away."

"That's wonderful work you do. Very few people sacrifice their lives to charity."

"It gives me joy, believe me."

She walked to the vase of lilies by the window, gently felt the flowers with her tender fingers, and then reached up to smell them. The pink petals of the flowers, the goldenrod of her dress, her bare arms, and the shy sunlight of fall sifting through the window to surround her with a gloriole, orchestrated an extraordinary moment. A picture-perfect moment. My eyes circled frantically around the room looking for a camera—as if by magic one would materialize on one of the tables or chairs.

She turned around and looked at me. She timidly tucked her hair behind her ear and smiled.

I could not move.

Her eyes caught sight of something behind me, and her smile slowly disappeared, her eyes growing more intense. "Is she in any of those framed pictures?"

"Pardon?"

"Your late wife," she continued, pointing in my direction. "Is she in any of those photos behind you?"

A collection of framed pictures was displayed on a curved, double-tiered console table in the far left corner of the living room.

"Yes." I walked to the console and picked up the picture of Eeman and me. We were standing in the shade of a huge blossoming cherry tree—before her face became mutilated by cancer.

Serene took it with both hands and examined it with a blank expression. "She was beautiful," she said after a long moment of silence, without taking her eyes off the frame.

As we stood facing each other, transfixed by the photo, the doorbell rang.

"It must be Sonia and Nader," I said, interrupting the silence.

She handed the frame back to me.

I set it back in its place. "I'll get the door."

"Hello, Mr. J!" exclaimed Sonia and Nader in unison as I opened the door.

I looked behind me, but I did not see Serene. "Hello! Please come in," I said.

"Serene's not here yet?" Sonia slid her scarf off her bare shoulders and laid it on a chair by the door.

"She's in the living room," I replied.

"I'm here," Serene said as she came hurrying. Her face, I noticed, was somewhat strained.

She hugged Sonia, who whispered something in her ear, and smiled timidly.

"Mr. J. was about to show me around the house," she said.

"Let's get our drinks first, and then I'll show you around," I suggested.

"Sorry we're late. I just never get off on time any more. I can no longer leave at the end of my shift. Too much work, and the staff is always falling short." Sonia looked at herself in the hallway mirror as she passed by it and ran her fingers briskly through her hair. She was wearing a beautiful sleeveless silk dress. Her long, spiral curls fell weightlessly down her back.

I said, "We're constantly hiring new staff. We've yet to catch up with the increasing demand. Quite an operation we have on our hands."

"Impressive to say the least," said Nader.

"We'll be launching a new plan next week. We're looking into expanding staff housing—and maybe even offering housing to part-timers to encourage them to sign up."

"Smart! That should attract quite a few applications," Sonia said.

"There are several options we're currently entertaining," I added. "We can discuss them later if you like."

"For sure," replied Nader.

I poured the champagne and handed glasses to Sonia and Nader.

Serene was standing outside our conversation circle. I replayed our conversation from earlier in my head, trying to figure out what could have caused her mood to change. "This is for you," I said, handing her the glass.

Her face was overtaken by a subtle flush that infiltrated through her neck and chest. "Thank you," she mumbled.

"Well, to Sonia and Nader. May it be a lifelong journey of accomplishments, love, and happiness." I raised my glass to toast the happy event.

As we walked through the house, Serene kept quiet and lagged behind us, touching dreamily everything her hand could reach.

Nader had his arm wrapped around Sonia's waist, and the two of them were stealing kisses when no one seemed to be watching, whispering happy words in each other's ears. I was not aware of how amusing Sonia could be and how much fun she was able to create around her. Undeniably, she cared a lot about Serene, and had her eyes on her the whole time, nudging her to catch her attention, trying to engage her in different conversations, but Serene remained withdrawn. A strong undertow was forcefully pulling on her. At the time, there was no way for me to know what it was.

And then she gasped. We all looked at her at first, but then turned around to see what had caught her attention.

"What a beautiful horse," she exclaimed as she approached a portrait of me on the wall. "Is this Marjana?"

The photo was taken before my debilitating accident. I was sixteen years old. It captured the right moment, from the right angle, which made Marjana and me look like we were flying in the air. Marjana looked like a bolt of fire with her red coat in full sunlight. Eeman had insisted on displaying the portrait. I had agreed to hang it on the wall of the hallway that led to the master bedroom, thinking it would be less ostentatious than having it displayed on the main floor.

"The colors are breathtaking!" added Sonia, her eyes wide open in admiration. She walked up to me and whispered, "Serene loves horses."

It took a few minutes for Serene to catch up to us in the dining room. Reema had already lit the candles and spread out the hors d'oeuvres on the dining table. She did a wonderful job with the menu. The food was thoughtfully prepared, and there were delectable vegetarian dishes for Serene and Nader.

"I never thought there were so many absolutely delicious vegetarian alternatives to meat dishes. For one thing, vegetarian people contribute to a healthier environment," Sonia said as we sat down to eat. "I'm almost there myself." Looking at Serene, she playfully asked, "Is Shatha still bothering you?"

"She hasn't been spending that much time around the clinic."

"Why? What's going on with her?"

"She got a good offer from the in-home care department, so she barely gets to spend time at the clinic."

"It's better for you this way, isn't it?" I asked.

"Much better," she said.

"Cheers to that," Sonia rejoiced.

We all drank to the news, and dinner was a joyful experience. Sonia lightened the mood with her jokes. She was savoring every dish, and Reema was happily sharing the ingredients, going over recipes with her.

Serene managed to put in a few words here and there. She did laugh and smile at times, but beneath her skin, somberness had settled. I could read it in her eyes.

Nader and Sonia were ecstatic at my proposition to offer the house for their engagement party. They had agreed on the first Sunday in January.

"That should give us enough time to plan for it. Two months. Don't you think?" asked Serene as she looked at me.

The smile on her face had a tinge of reservation. Nevertheless, my heart danced to that proposition. Both of us planning the engagement party. Her company was all I yearned for.

"Sure," I said. "It should be plenty of time."

"And," Sonia added teasingly, as she rested her hand on Nader's arm, "since summer solstice falls on a Sunday next year, we wanted it to be our wedding day!"

We all drank to the happy news. The apple pie and chocolate fondue were delightful. It was an evening I so much needed to lift the melancholy that had settled over the house ever since Eeman passed away.

We took our tea on the west balcony and stood looking beyond the rail into the night. It was not the lugubrious darkness that had visited me of late, but a peaceful one that trailed a promise of a bright tomorrow. Faint illumination radiating from dispersed garden lights punctuated the darkness and provided small windows into a night abuzz with life. Nature was hard at work condensing the moisture in the air and using its droplets in an orchestrated dance to the many sounds of nocturnal animals. Every season has its charming beauty. The tree leaves that had already yellowed or reddened, eager to finish their yearlong journey, were gracefully twirling from their branches to the ground, bringing an old cycle to its end, and at once starting a new one.

A tingling chill hung in the air. In the dim light of the balcony, I could see a slight shiver sweeping over Serene. I took off my blazer and placed it on her shoulders, cupping them in my hands.

She lifted her hand to her shoulder and placed it on mine. I, to this day, touch my hand the same way every time the thought of her crosses my mind. Such an agonizing feeling!

"Did you know that about fifteen kilometers south of Mar Elias, there's a large equestrian facility with boarding stables and a riding school? The trails are endless and mesmerizing. It's open year-round," I said to her as we stood looking into the night.

She turned around to face me. "That boy in one of the framed pictures in the living room?"

"Which picture?"

"The one with the young boy standing between two young girls. Are you related to him?"

"Yes. One of the girls in the picture is Eeman. The other two are her siblings."

She took a deep breath and then turned her face away from me. We stood there for a silent moment.

"Do they live around here?" she asked, her eyes focused on the night beyond the edge of the balcony. "Eeman's siblings?"

"I'm afraid they're both dead. Long time ago. Not too long after the picture was taken."

This time, a longer silence ensued.

I edged closer to her and tried to look her in the eye.

Her face was expressionless, belonging to a different world. One I could not read.

"Why do you ask?"

"Nothing important. The boy reminds me of the kid who delivers my morning paper."

"Alex?"

"I never asked him his name."

"His father is a fisherman. I see him when I go hiking along the river. Very nice family," I said.

Sonia and Nader were walking down the balcony. Their happy voices echoed into the night and lightened the mood.

"So, where's your mind carrying you?" I asked, resting my elbows next to hers on the rail.

"My mind?" she asked.

"What are you thinking about?"

"Life is mysterious."

"They say mystery evokes the imagination."

"Imaginations can be wild and sometimes scary. I can't allow myself to be overtaken by them," she answered.

I touched my hand to her cheek and gently turned her head to face mine. "What's scaring you, Serene?" I asked, not having the faintest idea about the many things that scare me in life.

"I have this inner fear and apprehension about the future," she said. "Or maybe the past. Nothing in my power to explain."

How could I have ever helped her understand the future when so much of my past was unfathomable to me? Even when I looked back at it with correcting spectacles many years later, I always saw it riddled with holes that opened up to eternity, to endless possible interpretations. Resignation to the power of the unknown is to many the road to inner peace. One just has to learn how to do it.

# *Chapter 35*

I had not seen her in three weeks. I had ached at the idea that something might have gone wrong with her personal life. Several thoughts crossed my mind, every one of them grim with anxiety and fear. Ever since she came to my house for dinner, her words and the anxious look on her face had hovered over me. I had an appointment to see her at the clinic, two days after our dinner together, but I was told she had left on an urgent trip back home.

It was a Sunday morning in November. The piercing cold seeped through my pores as soon as I stepped outside. I was so eager to get to her. So many times, I had drawn mental images of her apartment. I would envision her walking from room to room, her bare feet on the floor, her hair falling on her shoulders. Every time my imagination took me to her as I sat daydreaming in my bed, I tried to shake off the invasive thoughts. I could smell her citrus aroma every time I thought of her. I smelled it then, standing outside her apartment door.

She lived on the top floor of a three-story apartment building on Hamra Street. I took a deep breath and climbed the flight of stairs to her apartment. I got to her door and stopped to catch my breath and straighten my back. A sharp pain sliced through my right leg all the way up to my lower back. I clenched my teeth in agony and waited for my fired-up nerves to repolarize and the pain to subside. I ran my fingers through my hair to straighten it out and rang the doorbell.

*What will she think of me showing up at her doorstep unannounced?*

A few seconds later, I followed with a soft knock. The wait seemed too long. I stuck my ear to the door, and when I heard a shuffling noise, I followed up with another knock.

"Who is it?" she called from behind the door.

"Serene. It's me, Adel. Will you let me in?" I urged her with a low, nervous voice.

I heard her disengaging a double lock. She then stopped.

"Serene, please. I really need to talk to you."

She pulled the door open. She was wearing apple green pajamas. Her hair was disheveled, her face pale and eyes bleary. She looked gaunt and ready to drop.

"Good morning," I said, hoping not to sound dismayed.

"Hello. Come in. Please."

"I hope I didn't wake you."

"Not at all. I've been up for a while," she responded.

I stepped inside and closed the door. I wanted to hold her in my arms and keep her there forever. I wanted to tell her that I would never let anything scare her and that I would always be there for her.

She just stood by the door, a pained smile on her face, and my heart melted away.

I took her hand in mine, brought it to my lips and kissed it. "Are you all right? You look tired. Is your family all right?"

"My family's just fine, Adel. Thank you for asking."

It was the first time she ever called me Adel. I had never realized how sweet it could sound out of her lips.

"Have you had your coffee yet?" she asked, her voice low.

"No. I haven't."

"How about breakfast?"

"No, not yet."

"I usually take toast and honey with my morning coffee. Would you care for some?"

"If it's not too much trouble."

"Not at all, Adel. It's my pleasure," she added looking intently at me, and then turned around and walked to the kitchen.

It was the second time she called me Adel. There were a few times that followed. Did she know that she tenderly lulled my soul when she uttered my name?

I stood by the door, studying the details of her apartment. It was not what I had envisioned, except for the fact that it had only a few pieces of furniture. The lights in the hallway and the living room were on. I took a few steps into the living room and felt a cold whirl of wind above me. It made me shiver. I looked up and saw the ceiling fan turned on high. There were a sage green sofa facing the television set and a coffee table in the center of the room. A mirror hung on the wall that led to the bedroom in the back of the apartment. I envisioned her stopping to look at herself on her way to the kitchen. Under the mirror stood a console accent table with an empty vase. Besides that vase and a picture frame on the coffee table, there were no other decorative articles in the apartment. Next to the picture frame was a stack of two books and a magazine. The apartment lacked any outstanding or personal touch, but its simplicity was peaceful.

As I walked around the living room, I could hear her movements in the kitchen.

"Did you want the ceiling fan on?" I called out to her as I rubbed at my cold arms.

"No! Not anymore," she answered. "You can switch it off."

I turned off the fan and grabbed the cashmere scarf she had draped on the back of the sofa. It was the scarf I had sent to her when I first saw her standing under the willow tree. I wrapped it around my neck and shoulders and followed her into the kitchen. She was standing at the sink, her back to me.

"I need the ceiling fan on when I go to sleep." She was filling the coffee pot with water.

"Does it get hot in your apartment at night?"

"No, it's not that. Nights have been cold recently," she answered, shaking her head. With slow, robotic movements, she set the pot on the stove and grabbed the coffee canister from the overhead cabinet.

"It's a long story. I wouldn't want to bore you with it." She turned around to scoop coffee into the hot pot.

"I have all the time in the world," I told her as I grabbed a seat at the kitchen table.

She brought two mugs of coffee to the table and then went back to the counter to toast the bread. With slouched shoulders, she waited for the toaster. The kitchen window opened up to a beautiful backdrop of mountain peaks. Soon those peaks would turn white with snow. She had one arm wrapped around her stomach, and her other hand was patting the collar of her pajamas. She looked small and frail.

I could have been that arm that wrapped around her to protect her and that hand that caressed her temples, clearing her mind from all anxious thoughts.

She grabbed the toast and the jar of honey, brought them to the table, and sat across from me.

"Thank you," I said, interrupting the silence. "It finally feels like winter."

"It sure does. I'm sorry. You're cold, aren't you?" she asked, eyeing the shawl I had wrapped around myself.

"No worries. I'm fine now."

"It'll be snowing soon?"

"It sure will. Those hilltops you see through the window will be buried under feet of snow. You'll have a beautiful view from your kitchen on sunny days. The whole landscape will light up."

She slouched in her chair, smiling, and gazed at me with her sweet, dejected eyes. Without flinching, she pulled my heart out of my chest. "This is your shawl, isn't it?"

Before I could answer, we heard a knock on the door.

She glanced at the clock on the wall. "It must be Sunday's paper." She dashed out of the kitchen.

I heard her open the door and exchange a few words. Seconds later, she came back into the kitchen and set the paper on the table. She did not sit back down. She pinched the top of her nose with her fingers, her brows tightly furrowed, and squeezed her eyes shut. Her toast and coffee were still untouched.

"His name is Alex. I just asked him," she said, leaning with both hands on the table. "You know, I never really read the paper. It's a waste to keep getting it delivered."

"Why don't you cancel it then?" I asked, sipping my coffee.

"Something in Alex brings me comfort," she said. "I wait for him every morning. It's like I have to see him."

"Does he remind you of someone you know?"

She nodded nervously. Her eyes glistened with tears. Her chin trembled, and her mouth sank at the corners. She covered her face with her hands. "I'm sorry," she said.

My body froze. I was not expecting her to cry. Did my question upset her? My mind raced through endless sinewy mazes. I felt trapped. I felt my throat constrict and my chest hollow of oxygen. I could hear the repressed wailing of her suffering echo in my ears. She started to say something, but then changed her mind. "What brought you here today?" she finally asked as she walked to the sink and gazed through the window.

It was not a question I could answer. In fact, there were so many hairsplitting questions on my mind that morning. What compelled me to come to her house? What drove me insane, three weeks ago, when I learned she left Mar Elias? I did not know. What was it that made me feel as if I had known her all my life, from the minute I first saw her under the willow tree? What was that strange feeling that saturated my being and my mind with the thought of her? I could not understand. She consumed me from the minute I met her. Her pleasant voice and her soothing touch healed me from soul paralysis. Her smile awakened in me a forlorn feeling of desire and hope, her tears a pain more excruciating than the one constantly chewing at my back, like a metal chainsaw.

She turned around and walked in my direction. She tousled her hair frantically. "I must be losing my mind. I feel mangled beyond recognition. I don't know who I am anymore." She sat across from me and started rubbing at her knees. She stood up again and started pacing around the table.

I watched her as she circled around me.

"Well, not that I ever knew who I was. I've always had that problem. I never belonged anywhere. I was never the daughter of my parents. I could never be Kameel's wife or Noura's mother. God knows how much I wanted to be normal, just like any family member or acquaintance life threw my way. I always felt torn between two worlds, two lives, and two realities. How I've even made it this far beats me." Her arms were moving in all directions.

I instantly broke into a sweat. I was still sitting down, feeling more confused than she was, a tingling feeling rising within me. My mind felt like a long, narrow tube of effervescing bubbles, bumping and pushing against each other as each tried to rise to the top, bringing into the open scenes that did not make sense. I felt a painful twist in my stomach as my mind raced through these scenes that slowly became more and more vibrant. I unwrapped the shawl and laid it on the back of the chair. I stood up and walked up to her. My knees were trembling. I wanted to say something, but I knew that my voice would fail me. I did not trust my words to not make me sound delirious. I took her in my arms and pulled her to me.

She buried her face in my chest and cried.

I, too, was crying.

We stood in that kitchen, in each other's arms, for a long time. Her body sank into mine. Only then did I see what could not be seen and feel what could never be explained. I found myself in a world long gone. A world left meaningless to anyone else but me. I lost the concept of time and drifted beyond any tangible fiber. Years of my life coalesced to a dream. I was an immigrant who, after years of exile, was finally back with his loved ones, picking up from exactly where he had left them. Did he really ever leave? His foreign stay nothing but a vision, a dream. His reflection in the mirror the only photographic reminder of it. His body aches, wrinkled skin, and gray hair were the only testament to time passed.

We stood in that kitchen for what seemed like a short time. That time was the only one that existed, that mattered. For twenty-five years, in a foreign land, I searched for something I could not find because I did not know what I was searching for. I came back to my country looking for self-restoration, looking to heal the people around me, from that which was ailing me. Helping others and putting a smile on people's faces were the reasons I woke up every morning. The smile, however, was rarely mine. The happiness in my heart was riddled with shrapnel. A total eclipse came to test my resilience. Its evil cast its shadow over my life when, with hatred and envy, he pushed me down a flight of stairs. I was physically disabled. Then my parents pushed me out of his sight—and out of my life. I was alienated. Was I supposed to carry on as if nothing had happened?

Is an orphaned child in a conquered land supposed to lift his head and face his life, and the whole world, as if nothing is ailing him? How can he bury what is inside him? Doomed is he for burying inside that which crumbles mountains. Damned is he for letting his resentment surface.

In that kitchen, we stood for a brief moment. It was a converging moment. Although this moment seemed to be the most prevalent and tangible moment, to be everything that ever existed, it was unswervingly fleeting. A fraction of an infinitesimal period of time. The only moment where memory meets fantasy. Where pain is pain and joy is joy. The only moment of reality.

This moment was a turbulent sandbar created by clashing seas, but the arrow of time is partial and resolute. I didn't want this moment to end. My arms were desperately wrapped around her as I rooted myself in the sand shifting from under my feet. I could not remember how long we stood in the kitchen, but it was long enough for her body to relax in my arms. I could feel her breathing growing heavy.

"Oh! I'm sorry. I think I dozed off. I'm really sorry," she said as she pulled herself away. "I'm exhausted. I haven't slept well in a long time. I really need to sit down." She staggered to the living room and plopped herself on the sofa. She rolled her head back and closed her eyes.

I stood by the kitchen door, looking at her and not knowing what to say or what to do.

"Do you remember what I told you about my childhood? Do you remember when I told you I was afraid of water? Well, my worst nightmare has always been of me drowning. It's the worst feeling. To drown. To scream your lungs out for help, but no one hears you. You kick and reach, but you find nothing to support your feet. And you are conscious until the last drop of water tops off your lungs." Her head was still rolled back, her eyes closed. Her eyes were fidgeting to the rhythm of her restless mind.

"Well, that nightmare never leaves me. I had throat pain all the time growing up. I was always scared of running out of air. Scared that my throat would constrict and cut off my oxygen supply. I never played any sports for fear I'd run out of breath. My mother had to get me a doctor's note for school, every single year, to be excused from playing sports."

I walked to the sofa and sat next to her. I took her cold hand in mine. Her face was pale. Her breath was shallow. The wind had picked up outside, and an early autumn rain had begun to fall. I could hear its calming tap at the window.

"I'm sorry I wasn't there for you," I said.

She opened her eyes and smiled at me sweetly before closing them again. They were red and exhausted. "I'm cold," she whispered.

I got up, closed the window, and walked into her bedroom to find a blanket. The room was tidy, and her bed was made. There was an open suitcase on it still packed with her clothes. Was she planning to leave again—or did she not yet unpack? I grabbed the blanket that was draped at the foot of the bed, switched off the ceiling fan, and went back to the living room. I covered her with the blanket and sat next to her on the sofa.

"Thank you." She leaned toward me and rested her head in my lap.

I caressed her shiny hair. Her body started to relax.

"Is this for real?"

"What is?" I asked.

"You, here?"

"I am here."

She lifted her hand to my face and touched it. "I lived my whole life seeing dreams as reality and reality as a never-ending dream. Places, names, and faces I described. Scenarios I recited, of lives unbeknown to anyone but me."

"Serene," I whispered, "we have all our life to talk about it."

She took a long, deep breath and smiled. "Do we really?"

"Of course we do."

She sighed. "Nietzsche's book."

"What book?"

"On the table."

"What about it?"

She did not answer.

Hours went by with us on the sofa, her head in my lap as I caressed her hair.

Color started to gradually return to her face. Her heartbeat steadied to my touch, and her facial expression unwound. As I sat there, not daring to move for fear of waking her, she mumbled words I could barely decipher. She looked more beautiful than the first time I saw her. The threads of water tapping at the windows created a foggy film that encased the room in darkness and blanketed me with sorrow.

Certain heaviness engulfed my heart. Her anxiety was real, and the sadness it prompted in me was heavy.

I woke up to the sound of thunder, my neck stiff. I had fallen asleep on the sofa with her head in my lap and my fingers in her hair. It took me a while to untangle my foggy thoughts and realize where I was. The room looked dark. It was four o'clock in the afternoon. She was still in deep sleep, her face already looking more rested. I gently lifted her head from my lap and rested it on a pillow. I stood up and stretched my back. I adjusted the blanket on her and turned around to leave. On the coffee table, there were two books: Nietzsche's *Thus Spoke Zarathustra* and Freud's *The Interpretation of Dreams*. Under the books was a copy of the magazine that featured me on its cover: "A. J.—A Lifetime of Philanthropy." It was a two-year-old issue. *How did she get it?* I grabbed *Zarathustra* and headed to the door.

"Did you love her?" she asked as I was about to open the door.

I turned around and looked at her. She was still in the same position, eyes closed. "Pardon?"

"Did you really love Mona?"

I felt a sudden hollowness in my chest. My heart dropped so swiftly as if I had fallen from the roof of the house and my heart somehow landed before me. Did I hear her right? Did she say Mona? Or did she mean Eeman? I stood looking at her mystified.

"More than anything in the world," I confessed.

She smiled.

"Please don't leave without your scarf. It's cold outside," she said as she switched her sleep position to face the back of the sofa.

I grabbed the scarf, wrapped it around my neck, and left her apartment. The rain had stopped, but the air was so damp that it felt heavy to breathe. I had never realized how dreary a rainy day could feel. I straightened my back and cautiously stepped onto the flooded sidewalk.

Reyes approached with an open umbrella. "Good evening, sir."

"Good evening, Reyes," I said, trying not to sound and look as perturbed as I felt. "Take me home please."

**Noura, my** beautiful angel, the frame your mother had on her coffee table had a picture of you in it. It is the same frame I now keep on display on the piano. You were only two years old in that picture.

# Chapter 36

At first, the realization seeped stealthily through my veins, fluttering my heart, tingling my skin, and raising my hair. As I became more acquainted with her, this realization turned into a galvanizing impulse, so powerful it overleapt synapses, and the current gain left me awake for nights at a time, jittering to thoughts never previously entertained. Transforming thoughts that left me aware of how long the road to enlightenment was.

It was all about converging paths. And being a nonbeliever in random events, except when we fail to explain them, I started digging deep into my thoughts and my memory, trying to grasp the meaning of it all. It was definitely a mission left unaccomplished that came circling back for refinement. The interlude of time lying between converging points, though long in the standard concept of time, was just enough to bunker patience, widen horizons, and fuel awareness.

Two souls, separated for what seemed to be eons of metamorphosis and light-years of transcriptions and translations, were to spin and orbit, in agony, and collide like magnets. Clues had presented themselves to me. The feeling I had for her from the instant I saw her standing under the willow tree was all too powerful to be marginalized. I questioned my feelings. My intuition succumbed to reason when reason itself was heavily shackled by my own judgment and the opinions of the world around me. The answers to my entire list of hows and whys did not seem to make sense, nor could the questions themselves be encompassing. Yet, I fully understood those questions.

And the answer was one, final and ultimate. The embodiment of everything that boggled the minds of seekers for centuries. Once I accepted this intuition as a consequence of my cognitive ability, certain details became all too easy to accept. Life's moments, shelved for so long in a box labeled "The Unexplainable Trepidations of Life," finally aired out and unrolled in front of my eyes, showing me their true meaning.

When did she realize and apprehend Nietzsche's "Eternal Recurrence?" Had she read the works of Pythagoras or Plato or the many other philosophical and religious doctrines on the transmigration of the soul? The immortality of the soul?

Writing about my life, trying to remember details, and aligning those details with my perception of them at the time was not an easy task. I left her apartment on that rainy afternoon and went home to touch, yet again, everything her hands had touched when she came over to my house. Once again, I lifted the frame with the photo of Mona, Eeman, and Malec. Once again, I held it and looked at it for a long time, only to take it up to my room and set it on my nightstand.

I had kept Mona's letters to me in a shoebox, up high on a shelf in my closet, along with the copy of *The Miser* she had given me that summer in Crescent some fifty-five years ago. I had never discussed the existence of the box with Eeman for fear of bringing back burning memories. I had not touched it since I placed it in my closet in Mar Elias. I reached for it when I came back home from her apartment that evening, wiped the film of dust that had layered on its cover, and brought it to the edge of my bed where I sat looking at it, my hands shaking. I finally reached for the letters, read them several times, stopping every once in a while to splash my face with cold water and catch my breath.

I did not sleep that night. I rewound images, scenes, and dialogues in my head until I lost my grip on time and place. Events that happened at different times seemed to have interfered with one another. I felt overwhelmed. Faces superimposed on each other, and voices merged. Chunks of time and space were cut and pasted until new images emerged, different aspects of a multifaceted perception of reality, where each one became a reference point that solidified the existence of the other and simply collapsed under my probing gaze.

In the process of trying to decipher clues, there were moments when I felt weightless, floating with elation, a light-year closer to the light. Sadly, there were also moments when I felt overwhelmed by mourning and defeat. I couldn't help but remember Tolstoy's words: "If we admit that human life can be ruled by reason, then all possibility of life is destroyed." To that wisdom I add: If we admit that human life can be explained by reason, then all possibility of knowing is destroyed.

And nothing is left of a life to hang on to but what is left in memory. To you, I spill out my memory into words, dear Noura. Take them and build upon them.

Even in their simplest form, words are powerful. A simple yes or no could veer your path from east to west, filling you with hope or despair.

You told me once, Noura, my valiant angel, that existence to you means hope. Since then, I have not stopped ruminating on your words. They must have touched my innermost fiber. Your words liberated me. For years, you were hope's personification. Hope saved lives, and in its absence, many were taken. And so, Noura, I wish you hope.

# Chapter 37

I had so much to show her and so much to tell her. I needed to tell her about my twenty-five-year journey abroad. She needed to know about Eeman, the fine and exceptional person she turned out to be, and how she became an intricate part of my life. Eeman's story was heartbreaking, from every respect, yet she was always able to identify the few positives in her life and accentuate on them. Would Serene be able to do the same?

"I need to sort a few things out before I can resume with my life," Serene told me over the phone that Monday morning, the day after my visit to her apartment.

"Is there anything I can do to help you?" I asked.

"Not at this point. I need to figure out how to deal with my own situation in a sensible way. Do I accept the facts that are piling under my eyes? Or do I ignore them and shut the door on possible answers to my lifelong list of puzzling questions that has left me broken and out of touch with the world so that I can carry on again?"

"Either way, Serene, you must find a way to move on. Life is beautiful if you give it a chance. I can help you see its beauty." And when she did not respond, I added, "I have a lot to tell you."

"And there's even more that I'm dying to ask you, but I'm not sure at this point if it would help anyone. My life has been a mystery, a paradox. I'm here and yet not here. I don't know how to explain it to you. Besides, I have my daughter to worry about. She's the only one I need to focus on at this point in my life."

She paused again.

"Look," she continued with a trembling voice, "I have always experienced a foundering kind of panic, with different circumstances adding holes to my soul. I've been patching holes my whole life in fear of drowning, but there's one hole that keeps getting bigger. I don't know if I could ever patch it."

At that point, she went silent. I could imagine her curled up on the sofa, still wearing her apple green pajamas, the fan running on high.

"Eeman was so beautiful," she picked up with a breaking voice. "I cannot believe I missed her by four months."

"She was well taken care of until the end. I made sure of that. I was with her every moment of the five years we were together."

"I don't doubt that, Adel."

"Mona was always on her mind. It ached her deeply how Mona's and Malec's lives were cut short—and how no member of her family lived to see her graduate from college and become the independent and strong woman she was."

"Hold on one minute," she struggled to utter.

I heard her resting the receiver on the table and shuffling away from the phone. For the few minutes she was gone, I started doubting whether I was really having that conversation with her. It felt like a moment where reality and imagination merged, blurring the identity of each other beyond recognition.

"I'm back," she said.

I breathed again. "I want you to know that she and I ended up in Mar Elias because she loved this town. I would've gone to the moon to make her happy."

"She must've loved you."

"She saved me."

"Mar Elias is so much like Crescent. Crescent is beautiful too," she said.

It suddenly felt like my scalp was two sizes smaller than my head.

"Did you visit Crescent?"

"There's this little handbook that my mother gave me before I came to Mar Elias. In it, she had secretly compiled stories from my dreams as a child, with names of places and people. Scenarios and dialogues I had apparently regurgitated. She kept it all away from me. She said she did it to protect me. Unfortunately, I didn't believe her at first."

"Would you let me read it?"

"She gave it to me right before I left home to come to Mar Elias. I shoved it in my drawer, not knowing whether I should read it or not. I didn't touch it for months, but after I visited your house three weeks ago, and saw those photos you had on display, those faces that seemed so familiar, and the strange connection I had with you and your life, an irrepressible, uneasy feeling churned inside me. I thought it was high time I did. I left your house that evening and came home to rummage through my mother's writings. I desperately probed every note and every memory. The clues were all there."

"Would you let me read it?" I asked again.

"Did Mona drown?"

"Sadly, she did."

"Did someone throw rocks on Malec? Who would kill a child?"

I did not respond.

"And someone killed our dog? Does it sound right?"

*Our dog?*

"Malec's dog, yes," I answered.

"Who would do something like that? How could a beautiful little village like Crescent harbor so much evil?"

I did not answer. I did not know how.

"I went to Crescent last week," she said.

"You did?"

"I toured the village. The people were warm and welcoming. Your house is as beautiful as it is in my dreams. And our house looked like the most perfect little cottage. I couldn't get inside, but I sat under the cedar tree all night long."

I could hear her crying. Her voice sounded trapped in her throat.

"The mystical feeling I had that night still gives me the chills. You'd think I'd be terrified, in the night, all alone, in a place I had never set foot in. Well, at least not in this life." She laughed nervously. "Instead, I felt this inner peace I had never experienced before. Like a lost child reuniting with her mother."

She fell silent for a while.

"Life is complicated. I finally understand that much about it. I won't fight it anymore. I'll just try to live it. I'll rise up to its callings," she said.

"I can take you back to Crescent and let you inside the house. I'll give you the key, and you can keep it. I miss Crescent too. I can go back and live there too."

And then I stopped, realizing that what I was getting at was totally illogical, the idea of somehow sharing a future with her abutted upon the surging currents of our lives.

"Eeman remodeled the house. It's not what it really looked like back then, but the layout on the inside is still the same. I could've accompanied you. We can still do that. I can take you there and show you everything you want to see. Please say yes. I'll do anything for you."

"I'm afraid it's too late now," she said.

"It's never too late for anything in life, as long as you're willing to do it," I assured her.

"Certain things are irrevocable—even if they seem remediable," she said.

"Please don't give up on your fight. Listen, you don't have to do this alone. So many people around you will do anything to help you."

"Just once in the booklet did my mother write about Mona's mother. Were Mona and her mother not close? Did the mother die when Mona was little maybe?"

My heart raced at her question and jumped so high I could hear its pounding in my ears.

"No, actually, Mona passed before her mother."

"How awful. What a dreadful life for a mother to bury two of her children."

"The death of Malec wiped the spirit out of her life. And after Mona, she completely lost all faith in her existence. She gave up soon after."

"Is that how you see it? Is death the result of giving up on life?"

"I do actually."

"Did Malec give up on his life—a life so green at the time of his death?"

"Malec was living a life of struggle. I did not know, until much later when Eeman told me, that he was born prematurely. He was always thin as a twig, and he never developed well physically. The family's financial condition did not help. He had fallen ill a week before the accident. He was coughing blood, and he had lost the little weight he had on him. Eeman thought he had developed tuberculosis, but who could've known it at the time?"

"I could see the sadness on his face in that picture at your house."

"I'm sorry I'm telling you all this. Mona's life was not easy. She had too many worries on her mind. Her family was poor and helpless, but she was so smart. I learned a lot from her, and I loved every minute of my life when she was in it."

"Apparently, no matter how smart you are, people can still mess you up."

"What do you mean?" I asked.

"Well, the mayor and his son knew very well how to toy with people's lives." Her voice fell dead.

I could hear her silence through the hollowing depths of the receiver. I wasn't sure what to tell her. I wasn't sure how much she was able to remember and how much her mother had recorded of her dreams. I needed to spare her whatever agony I could.

"Are you still there, Adel?"

"Yes, I'm here."

"Were you there?"

"Was I where?"

"Were you around when all the abuse was taking place?" she asked, her voice sounding stern.

"No. I'm sorry. I wasn't. I didn't know until many years later when Eeman told me what had happened to Mona."

"How about what happened to Eeman herself? Did she ever share that story with you?"

I was sitting on my bedroom balcony that morning during my phone conversation with her. I did not know how a sky that seemed so clear and bright could, all of a sudden, close down on me with a roaring tempest. My body started jittering to an icy cold wind.

*Mayor and son. Eeman and Mona.*

Was that what Nana Thabita had hinted at before she passed away—when she said my father had made a mistake she could never forgive him for? Did she say *mistake?* Did she mean to say *crime?*

"What happened to Eeman?" I finally asked, scared to hear her response.

"I think she was abused by the mayor. If I'm to believe what my mother jotted down in that booklet," she responded.

I felt thunderstruck. Was there not a bottom to the well of suffering?

"Why? Why? Why?" I yelled. I turned around, entered my bedroom, and shut the balcony door behind me.

"She kept that away from you, didn't she? She wanted to spare you."

"She kept it all to herself until it festered into tumors that chewed on her from inside," I said as if I was talking to myself.

"Did the child make it?" she asked, now sobbing. "Did you get to meet the child?"

"No, I never did. Eeman put her son up for adoption right after birth. She made me believe it was totally her decision and that she was at peace with it. I don't know now if that was indeed the case," I said, completely dismayed.

"Your brother, do you still see him?"

"Our paths crossed once again a couple of years ago—but not as brothers."

"I wonder what your mother knew about your father."

"I wonder what else he kept away from her … and us. Especially from me."

"I need to go. The pain is intense and unbearable," she said.

"Do you not really think I know your pain? Do you not really think I feel it in my veins?" I implored, but she had hung up already.

Our conversation would replay in my mind until the end. She came back into my life to tell me what I did not know. What did it matter at that point? Eeman had made the decision to not tell me. She chose to keep it all to herself. I wonder how much my mother knew of my father's dealings—or maybe how much she cared to know. And Nana Thabita, didn't she basically raise my father since he was an infant? Wasn't it the reason she was hired into our family? And if she did raise him herself, didn't she know the person he turned out to be? Was it why she had kept to herself all those years and spoke only when it was required of her to do her daily chores? Why did she not tell me what she knew about my family before she died? Was she trying to protect me until the end? And Eeman's son, what happened to him? Did Eeman mother a half brother of mine?

How many more blows can an old wound handle? An old, unstageable wound, the depth of which was undetermined, had tunneled through my soul. How was I to worry about new scars when my old scars never healed? I left Crescent when I was eighteen years old. I thought I knew who my parents really were. Unfortunately, I do not believe I even came close.

# Chapter 38

She never got to see the snow on Mar Elias' mountain peaks. She never attended her friend's engagement dinner or live to see Sonia and Nader exchange their vows that summer solstice. She fought the pain for two additional days. I could not get her to talk to me after our phone conversation—no matter how hard I tried—but I got to see her one last time.

That Monday, the day of our last phone conversation, was one of the worst days of my life. The news about Eeman blinded me. I felt betrayed by the people who hid the truth from me—people I had loved and trusted. I spent the entire day in my home office with closed doors. I canceled all meetings and accepted no phone calls. At night, I drifted in and out of sleep. I would go out on the balcony and pace its length for a long time, talking to myself, only to go back into the room and throw myself on the bed.

From my balcony that night, I saw her shadow under the willow tree. It was close to midnight. At first, I thought it was just a vision. A slender, phantasmal silhouette swaying to the faint and flickering light of the garden post lamp, but then I saw her move. She was walking toward the slope that led down to the riverbank. Why was she heading to the river? I took my cane and hurried out after her. I walked through the garden and down the slope, but she was nowhere to be found. I called out her name several times, but I could only hear my voice echo. The night was soundless and icy cold. Shivering and confused, I turned around and walked home.

Sonia visited Serene on Tuesday, the day after our phone call. She stopped by her apartment on her way home from a long shift at the hospital. She had been trying to encourage her friend to get back to her life, but to no avail.

"I had not seen her for two days. I was shocked when I laid eyes on her," Sonia would confess later.

Serene had lost even more weight than when I saw her last, her back hunched like an old person. She was sitting on the edge of her bed, rocking back and forth, clenching her hands between her knees, her eyes fixed on the bedroom wall. She refused to eat no matter how hard Sonia tried. She would not take a bath to freshen up or change out of her pajamas.

When Sonia asked if she could call Kameel or her mother for her, Serene shook her head frantically. "All the dreams I told you about," Serene said, "I see them so clearly now. I finally know what they mean."

She reached for the handbook on the nightstand and handed it to Sonia. With a mournful smile, she turned to face the window, her eyes placidly gazing at the full moon.

Confused, Sonia took the book and started leafing through it. Serene's facial expression would mirror Sonia's thoughts, as she read on, horrified by the contents of the book.

"The idea frightened me," Sonia told me later. "It was that fear of defeat that claims you before you actually lose something. I think I might have sensed what was waiting for me, and I became furious at my own incapacitation. Oddly, fear gave way to anger. I can't tell you why I felt that way. Serene became terrified when she saw my facial expression. I rushed to the bathroom to splash my face with cold water. I sat on the edge of the bathtub with my hands cupped over my mouth. The last thing she needed was to hear me cry."

When Sonia came out of the bathroom, Serene was still sitting on the edge of the bed, frozen, gazing out the window as the moon bathed her in a mournful, ghostly light. Sonia sat next to her and brushed her hair slowly to help her relax. She stayed with her for at least two hours that evening.

"I sang songs from our childhood. I reminded her of the good times we shared throughout the years, the teachers we loved, and the plays we watched. I took her in my arms and rocked her to sleep. I didn't leave her apartment until her breathing became heavy, and I promised myself I'd check on her first thing in the morning," Sonia confided. "God knows I tried. I tried to bring her back to her life. I talked about Noura and how much she must be missing her mother. I told her that Nader and I were counting on her help for the wedding. I made her promise me she'd go to work in the morning, but nothing I said could stop the dark thoughts streaming through her mind. She kept comparing her life to Mona's. She told me that Mona's father and brother had passed away before Mona did and that she realized her death was imminent—with both her brother and father already gone."

I will never forget the sight of Sonia running frantically through the garden that Wednesday morning in November. I had just gotten into the car to head to the hospital for a meeting. She couldn't catch her breath, and she collapsed right there in the driveway. "Serene killed herself. I couldn't do anything to stop her," Sonia repeated on and on, like a turntable going awry with its stylus skipping back over the same grooves, unable to move on.

I was dumbfounded. Everything around me crumbled to the ground. The world no longer looked real. It was apocalyptic, moving in slow-motion. I was no longer associated with anything around me.

Was I wrong, all along, when I thought I could've saved her the first time had I never left Crescent?

Serene succumbed to the heavy burden of her struggle. She had a second chance at an unresolved experience. A chance to redeem. Retribution was not what Serene had ever sought in life. It was tranquility and peace of mind she was seeking, and she thought that only death could give it to her. She saw clues in life events. The death of her brother came to prepare her for her own. So, she decided to take an entire prescription of antidepressants.

One final letter I have from her. One final piece of paper was added to the collection I had kept in *The Miser* for years:

To you, Adel:
I'm tired of fighting this fight
I'm tired of reliving the nightmare
I'm tired of crying when I smile
I'm tired of lying to myself
I'm tired of lying to the world
I'm tired of being me
I think I'm giving up
Forgive me

# Chapter 39

Dear Noura:

When your father brought you to Mar Elias, I held you in my arms and pulled you close to my heart for a long time. I held onto you as if I were holding onto those I had lost. Your breath on my face was like oxygen, fueling the fire burning inside me, yet I breathed it all in. In your breath, I smelled her. In your voice, I heard her. In your eyes, I saw her. Those sweet eyes of yours were tinted with fear. That's when I realized that my mission was far from over. I had to take care of you. You were my responsibility. I had to live for you.

Your mother's life was edifying to me, and still is, even today, more than twenty-five years after her death. Experiences that don't result in growth and wisdom are wasted experiences. We live our lives so entrenched in mundane things that the universe, and our existence in it, become a mystery to us. Take time out of your busy life to ask yourself questions. Your mind knows more than you can ever imagine. Just ask it, and you shall receive the answer. An answer you are ready to grasp and are willing to embrace.

Four weeks later, you came back—this time for good. You had just turned three years old. Your father passed away a week later. You had celebrated your third birthday at the hospital, with both of your grandmothers and a few staff members. In the one photo I have from that occasion, you were sitting on the bed, next to your father, the cake held in front of you as you tried to blow out three tiny candles. Your father seemed heavily sedated, and not one person in the photo showed so much as a glimpse of a smile. I kept that photo away from you all these years because it reflected a terrible moment in your life. You know where to find it when you are ready to look at it—in the same box, up on the top shelf in my closet.

I hate to sound selfish, but I needed you desperately. In each other's presence, life became possible for both of us, promising and beautiful. Without you, I would not have known the true meaning of fatherhood. You brought joy into my house and filled it with life. Your toys were spread out in every room, and I asked Reema to let them be. Your piano teacher came twice a week. You loved the piano and filled the house with noise. The swimming pool was built so that you could learn how to swim. I sat with you through all your lessons. Your mother would've been so proud of you.

We went horseback riding through Mar Elias's trails. We would ride up along the river until you were ready to rest, and then we would sit on a rock, dip our feet in the water, and eat the sandwiches Reema had packed for us. You loved nature, and you were fascinated by birds.

"I want to fly, Papa. I want to fly like a bird," you would tell me, spreading out your arms and running around tree trunks and bushes.

You were so pleasant to be around as a child. I did not know you could cry until you were stung by a bee, one spring day. You were five years old. You were wearing a yellow dress and had your hair in pigtails. You looked like a bee yourself running around the rose garden with your friends. By the way, you made so many friends at Mar Elias Elementary School. Teachers loved you. Every boy and girl in school wanted to be your friend. They loved your house and your toys. You were caring and generous with them all. You shared some of your toys, and you gave away the rest. I encouraged the giver in you. Most of all, you and your friends loved the summer festival and the fireworks. You waited impatiently for them, year after year.

I took you to your mother's apartment regularly. At first, it was tough for me to be there, but you were with me. It soon became a cozy place where you and I would sit on the sofa and read a book. I would smell her lingering aroma from the minute I entered the apartment. And every time I asked you if you smelled it too, you would shake your head and start laughing. As the years passed, you stopped asking to go there, and I thought it was healthy for you to move on. Your childhood was happy, and the skies smiled down on you. You remain smart and pretty, and above all, you have a good mind and a kind heart.

It was hard to send you away to boarding school when you turned fourteen, but I wanted the best education for you. I also wanted you to meet new people and learn how to be independent. I knew you were strong and that you could handle it. I called you often and visited with you every weekend in the beginning. I knew you were happy, and that was all I needed to know. We always went on trips during holidays and summer vacations. The photo albums stand witness. You loved visiting home, and I would send Reyes to bring you over for the weekend when your school allowed it. You told me all your secrets, and I loved it. You told me about your first love in high school. I was fully aware how precious those moments could be to you, and I knew very well how much those moments had meant to me, in my childhood and beyond. I listened to you and guided you. Life is full of disappointments, and I was glad I was there for you when you needed me.

I am leaving you with all I have and all I built. I trust you will continue giving and helping. The world is in need of someone like you, a compassionate and smart young woman who is dedicating her life to cancer research to help heal those from what ailed one of the closest people to her heart. It is much easier in life to take smaller and simpler steps, but unless you reach for high grounds, you won't get there.

Also, I must have told you this before, but I need to stress it again. I am forever grateful to you for asking me to write my memoir. I always thought my past had a crippling effect over me, but disgorging its events and dates in the form of words on paper helped me put everything in perspective.

Souls are trapped in their own manifestations, limited to their own physical expressions. And life is a struggle. A struggle to un-shackle. A struggle for freedom. A struggle for elation. I would not be honest if I told you it was easy to live. You will inevitably hit dead-ends in your life, but when that happens, remember that alternate paths lie around you in every direction. Just don't lose hope, and you will soon embark on a brighter path. Have faith in that. Just know your purpose in life and love life fully, the way I love you. And just like Rumi said, "If you find me not within you, you will never find me. For I have been with you, from the beginning of me."

# Chapter 40

So much of life is left unspoken
From that day on
And until the end of this journey
So much will lie forgotten
Until
A dry leaf under my foot
A drop of water on my nose
A cry of desperation in the night
And the memory is bright
But the feeling is mercurial under my thumb
An outburst of inexplicable happiness
Commensurate with it
An unsettling fear
Don't things start with their end drawing near?
When did it all start?
When does it all end?
Interpolations raised to extrapolations
Land of impossible realizations
A chase of a shadow
A flight from pain
The madness of it all
The travesty
Consciousness in a body
Are we each a particle?

Or do we all comprise a wave
Flowing with a rhythm
Interfering directly with one another?
Besetting questions
Are the shadowy furrows of the brain
The cradle of the mind?
Or is my chemistry an illusion?
How come I feel the pain?
My night is long
Why can't I get out of bed?
My day longer
Why can't I go to sleep?
Were decisions ever my own?
When my start was a cell and my end
A grain of sand in the wind?
So much lies around the bend
Pleading fervently for redemption
Until it is all lived again

# Epilogue: Thoughts Left Unspoken

The winding road to town feels narrower than usual on my last trip back to Crescent. Nature lies heavily dormant under a thick layer of dazzling snow. The yellow sun is shimmering like gold on the hilltops. I remember how empty I felt every time I came back to visit. For years, I have been avoiding Crescent on snowy days like this one. They reminded me of my parents. On this last visit, it is no day to be sad.

Reyes helps me out of the car. Earth, saturated by rain, is left to freeze at the whims of the frosty, unforgiving wind. Like earth, every interstice in my body is suffused, and pain has left me heavy and lumbering under the urgency of passing time. Even my favorite book, *War and Peace*, which I carried around with me from room to room, quoting from it like it were my bible, feels heavy. I hand it to Reyes and limp my way to the house.

My childhood home stands in an overpowering silence—a silence I have recently learned to enjoy and cultivate. It was in silence when my imagination soared the highest and probed the deepest. It was in silence when nagging questions were answered. Like my father, I was born in Crescent, and, like my father, I will die in Crescent.

As I step inside the house, I feel the peace. From my journey, I arrive back to where it all started. I know my death is drawing near. I can sense it with all my being. Death used to scare me. Every single time it took someone I know, it was cruel and unreasonable, but not this time. This time it feels liberating. I welcome it. There is no way to continue without it. Nothing matters anymore. Nothing else can torment me, and nothing worldly can excite me. Since life is a test of endurance in the face of two extremes, the good and the bad, what is left of a life when both no longer have any effect on me?

I understand it fully, the inevitable course of a life. Nothing can be done to stop it or hinder it, rewind it or hasten it. So, I will run with it until the end. Its irrevocable end.

As the last stretch of my life ticks away, the hands of my watch skip over each other, eager to wipe away what is left. I lie in my child-hood bed, feeling grand. The whole universe inside my body. My perception of all things is limitless. I can feel it all, touch it all, and take it all in, indefinitely, without lifting a finger.

Pictures of my life roll out of the intertwined lines, like a black-and-white film, as I gaze at the cracking ceiling. My body feels heavy. I can't move. The pictures are so vivid that I can touch the people in them. I feel them breathing on my face. The longer I gaze in one spot, the more sonorous the scenes become. They manifest themselves randomly, in no specific order or time, sometimes blended together, and other times standing alone. What will happen to these images after my death? Will they travel with me? Will they be stored somewhere in the realm of this huge universe, where perhaps I can recapture them all?

My mother is charmingly dressed. She's sitting on the sofa in the corner of the family room, surrounded by people I don't recognize. Her shoulders are square, but her head is slightly slouched. She smiles at times, and at others, she looks withdrawn. She's trying to remove her wedding band, but the band is stuck on her finger. The closer I get to her, the more bewildered she becomes. She looks scrawny down to the bone. Her face is gaunt, and her eyes are sunken. She starts swaying her head reproachfully from side to side. She's mumbling the same sentence over and over again.

I can hear her taut voice, but I can't make out the words.

She looks at me and reaches out to touch me.

I want to take her hand in mine, but the more I walk in her direction, the quicker she slips away. I pick up my speed, but I'm suddenly hit by a gust of wind that blows open every window and door in the house. My mother's ornaments come tumbling down from every shelf of every display cabinet. Then comes thunder. I rush to the balcony and step right outside. I'm baffled to see the balcony extending all the way to the mountain that will forever be disfigured by Aslan's disastrous project. Village people are pressing closer together, pushing each other, stampeding toward what looks like a puff of dust rising from the valley. The scene is disturbing. My body's shivering.

My eyes pop open. My hands are covering my ears. I draw in a deep breath. I'm back in my childhood bedroom. My arms and legs are no longer under my command. My eyelids feel very heavy. Something is deeply tormenting me. My recollection of the collapse never dwindled with time; instead, it became more vivid and more disturbing.

Everybody's shouting in distress. They are angry. At what? Their hands are waving furiously. At whom?

As I shuffle through the crowd, people elbowing me, a hand grabs my shoulder from behind and pulls me backward. I turn around and see my father. "Get back—get back for your own safety," he shouts, then disappears into the crowd.

I run back toward the house. The landscape is so thick I need to cut my way through. Shrubs and vines intertwined in mazes tighten around my neck. I'm suffocating. Is this how it all looked when my grandfather discovered this valley? The few houses I pass look old and grayish. Where did the lush, green landscape go?

I pass by Mona's house. I stop and look through the dim windowpane, but I can't see anything. The house is empty and dark. Suddenly, I hear a shriek of pain from inside. A shiver of horror. I turn ice cold. Where did my blood drain?

I push open the door and enter the house. My hands are wet. Is that water? I lift my hands to my face and smell them. Why is blood smeared on the door?

The shrieks lead me to Mona's mother. She is crouched in the far corner, hugging a blanket to her chest and weeping desperately.

I kneel down beside her and put my hand on her shoulder. "What's wrong?" I ask. "Where are Mona and Malec? Where's Eeman?"

She mutters something, but all I can hear are her sobs.

Aslan comes running up to me and starts pushing me backward. "Go back, you have nothing to do here. Go back now!"

I run up the driveway to the house, and when I approach the main gate, a man is standing high on the wall. *Is that my father? Where's his face? It sure sounds like him.*

People are jumping up the wall and trying to reach his feet as he shouts with all his might, "People of Crescent, compensations will be made in full."

The people are getting angrier.

Nana Thabita's standing on the other side of the gate. She's desperately gesturing for me to go through it. "Why?" she mouths. "Why would you let go of her again?"

I run back to the house. Mother is still sitting where I left her. She's crying. I still cannot make out her words. I run to my room and shut the door. My heart's pounding. I sit on my bed with my eyes closed, trying to catch my breath.

I open my eyes again. I'm sleeping on my back. Someone's holding my hand. A gentle and loving feeling. Where am I? What year is it? Time and space are so distorted that sounds lag behind scenes, and scenes lag behind sounds. Good moments jumble with bad ones. I blink my eyes.

In the stillness of the room, I feel her close to me. I gather all the strength left in me so that I can see her face form out of those lines in the ceiling. She looks down on me compassionately, her eyes forgiving. I'm finally ready to go. Nothing scares me anymore. Nothing can destroy the look she's leaving me with. But where will our hearts beat again? A cool breeze rising from the valley carries me on its wings. The windowpane rattles as I glide through it. Did my mother forget to fix the window?